LIFETIME

Liza Marklund

CORGI BOOKS

TRANSWORLD PUBLISHERS
61–63 Uxbridge Road, London W5 5SA
A Random House Group Company
www.transworldbooks.co.uk

LIFETIME
A CORGI BOOK: 9780552161954

First publication in Great Britain
Corgi edition published 2013

A CIP catalogue record for this book
is available from the British Library.

Addresses for Random House Group Ltd companies outside the UK
can be found at: www.randomhouse.co.uk
The Random House Group Ltd Reg. No. 954009

The Random House Group Limited supports the Forest Stewardship
Council® (FSC®), the leading international forest-certification organisation.
Our books carrying the FSC label are printed on FSC®-certified paper.
FSC is the only forest-certification scheme supported by the leading
environmental organisations, including Greenpeace. Our paper procurement
policy can be found at www.randomhouse.co.uk/environment

Typeset in Sabon by
Kestrel Data, Exeter, Devon.
Printed and bound by
CPI Group (UK) Ltd, Croydon, CR0 4YY.

2 4 6 8 10 9 7 5 3 1

LIFETIME

Part 1
JUNE

Thursday, 3 June

1

The call went out at 03.21. It was sent to all patrol cars in the centre of Stockholm, and was short and to the point: 'Control to all units, report of shots fired on Bondegatan.'

No more details. No house number, no information about casualties or who had made the call.

Even so, Nina's stomach clenched.

Bondegatan's a long street: there must be a thousand people living there.

As Andersson, in the passenger seat, reached for the radio she grabbed it, pressing the transmit button on its left-hand side while steering with the other hand.

'1617 here,' she answered. 'We're one block away. Have you got a house number?'

Andersson let out a theatrical sigh and looked demonstratively out of the car window. Nina glanced at him as they rolled towards Bondegatan. *Okay, sulk if you want to.*

'Control to 1617,' the operator said. 'You're the closest unit. Is that you, Hoffman, over?'

The number of the patrol car was linked to the number on her police badge. Before each shift started you fed the car's registration and your badge number into the Central Operations Planning System, handily abbreviated to COPS, so that the operator in the communication centre always knew who was in which vehicle.

'Affirmative,' she said. 'Turning into Bondegatan now.'

'How does it look, over?'

She stopped the car and looked up at the heavy stone buildings on either side of the street. The dawn light hadn't reached between them yet, and she squinted as she tried to make out shapes in the gloom. There were lights on in one top-floor flat on the right-hand side, but otherwise everything was dark. It was evidently a street-cleaning night, no parking allowed, which made it look particularly empty and abandoned. One rusty Peugeot stood alone, a parking ticket on its windscreen. 'No activity, as far as I can tell. What number was it, over?'

The operator gave her the address and she went completely cold: *That's Julia's place. That's where Julia and David live.*

'Take a look, 1617. Approach with caution.'

She wound down all the car's windows to make it easier to hear any sounds from the street, put the car into gear, turned off the headlights and drove slowly down the familiar street, no flashing lights, no siren. Andersson had perked up and was leaning forward intently.

'Do you reckon it's anything, then?' he asked.

I hope to God it isn't.

She stopped outside the flat and switched off the engine, then leaned forward to peer up at the grey cement façade. There was a light on in a second-floor window.

'We'll have to assume the situation is dangerous,' she

said tersely, and grabbed the radio again. '1617 here, we're in position, and it looks like there are people awake in the building. Should we wait for 9070, over?' That was the operational command vehicle.

'9070 is still in Djursholm,' the operator said.

'Are there any other cars in the area? Or the armed-response unit, over?' she asked.

'We're switching frequency,' the operator said. 'All concerned, switching to zero six.'

Silence spread through the car. Nina's bulletproof vest was rubbing the base of her spine. Andersson shuffled restlessly in his seat and peered up at the building. 'This could easily be a false alarm,' he said.

Dear God, please let it be a false alarm.

The radio crackled.

'Okay, has everyone switched? 1617, come in?'

She pressed the transmit button again, her mouth dry. 'Zero six, we're here, over.'

The others responded, two patrols from the city centre and one from the county force.

'The armed-response unit isn't available,' the operator said. '9070 is on its way. Hoffman, you're in charge until the command unit gets there. We need a considered response. Hold some units back. We'll form a ring around the location, get cars in place. All units to approach in silence.'

At that moment a patrol car swung into Bondegatan from the other direction. It stopped a block away, the headlights going out as the engine was switched off.

Nina opened the car door and stepped out, her footsteps echoing in the street. She pressed her ear-piece into her left ear as she opened the boot. 'Shield and baton,' she whispered to Andersson, as she tuned in to frequency zero six on the handheld radio.

At the next block she saw two policemen get out of their car. '1980, is that you over there?' she said quietly, into the microphone on her right shoulder.

'Affirmative,' an officer replied, raising his hand.

'You're coming in with us,' she said.

She ordered the other patrols to take up positions at opposite corners of a square, to ensure they had all lines of sight covered, one at the corner of Skånegatan and Södermannagatan, the other on Östgötagatan.

Andersson was rummaging around among the bandages, fire extinguishers, shovels, flares, lamps, anti-septic gel, cordon tape, warning triangles, paperwork and other clutter that was stuffed into the boot.

'1617 to Control,' she said. 'Do you have a name for the person who called in, over?'

A short silence.

'Erlandsson, Gunnar, second floor.'

She noted a light in a kitchen on the second floor. 'He's still up. We're going in.'

The other officers came over, introducing themselves as Sundström and Landén. She nodded curtly and tapped in the entry-code on the keypad beside the door to the apartments. None of the others reacted to the fact that she knew it. She stepped through the door, turning down the volume on the radio to barely audible. Her colleagues filed in silently behind her. Andersson, the last to enter, wedged the door open so that they could retreat to the street quickly if need be.

The stairwell was dark, deserted. The only source of light came from the lift, seeping through the oblong glass window in the metal door.

'Is there a courtyard?' Landén muttered.

'Behind the lift,' Nina whispered. 'The door on the right leads to the cellar.'

14

Landén and Sundström each checked a door; both were locked.

'Open the lift door,' she said to Andersson.

He wedged it wide so no one would be able to use it, then stopped by the stairs and awaited her order.

She could feel panic thudding at the back of her head, and calmed herself with words from the police rulebook: *Make an initial evaluation of the position. Secure the stairwell. Speak to the man who made the call and find out where the suspected shooting occurred.*

'Okay, let's take a look,' she said, and headed quickly up the stairs, floor by floor. Andersson followed her, keeping one flight below her.

The stairwell was gloomy. Her movements were making her clothes rustle in the silence. There was a smell of cleaning fluid. Behind the closed doors she could sense the presence of other people without hearing voices – a bed creaking, a tap running.

There's nothing here, no danger, everything's fine.

Finally, slightly out of breath, she reached the flats on the top floor. It was different from the others, with a marble floor and specially designed security doors. She knew that the housing association had renovated the attic space as luxury apartments in the late 1980s, just in time for the crash in property prices. The flats had stood empty for several years, almost bankrupting the association. Today, of course, they were ridiculously expensive, but she remembered Julia telling her that David was still angry about the previous committee's poor judgement.

Andersson came up behind her, panting heavily. 'Looks like a false alarm.'

Nina sensed his disappointment as he wiped his forehead. 'Let's hear what the man who called in has to say,' she replied, and went back downstairs.

Sundström and Landén were waiting on the second floor, beside a door marked 'Erlandsson, G. & A.'.

Nina stepped up to the door and knocked quietly.

No response.

Andersson shifted his feet impatiently behind her.

She knocked again, considerably louder.

A man in a blue and white striped towelling dressing-gown appeared at the crack behind a heavy safety chain.

'Gunnar Erlandsson? Police,' Nina said, holding up her badge. 'You called about some suspicious noises? Can we come in?'

The man closed the door, fumbled with the chain, then opened it again.

'Come in,' he whispered. 'Would you like some coffee? And there's some of my wife's Swiss roll, with homemade rhubarb jam. She's dozing at the moment – she has trouble getting to sleep and took a pill . . .'

Nina stepped into the hall. The layout of the flat was exactly like David and Julia's, but this one was considerably tidier. 'Please, don't go to any trouble for us,' she said.

She noted that Gunnar Erlandsson had been addressing Landén, the largest of the men. Now he was glancing uncertainly from one to another.

'Gunnar,' Nina said, taking his upper arm, 'can we sit down and go through what you heard?'

The man stiffened. 'Of course,' he said. 'Yes, of course.'

He led them into a pedantically neat living room with brown leather sofas and a thick rug on the floor. Out of habit he settled into an armchair facing the television, and Nina sat on the coffee-table in front of him. 'Tell me what happened, Gunnar.'

16

He swallowed, his eyes still flitting between the officers.

'I woke up,' he said. 'A noise woke me up, a bang. It sounded like a shot.'

'What made you think it was a shot?'

'I was lying in bed, and at first I wasn't sure if I was dreaming, but then I heard it again.' He pulled out a pair of glasses and started polishing them nervously.

'Do you hunt?' Nina asked.

Gunnar Erlandsson stared at her in horror. 'Good grief, no,' he said. 'Murdering innocent animals? That's barbaric.'

'If you're not familiar with firearms,' Nina said, 'what made you think you heard a shot? Could it have been a car backfiring, or some other sudden noise out in the street?'

He blinked several times and looked up at Landén. 'It didn't come from outside,' he said, pointing at the ceiling. 'It came from the Lindholms'. I'd swear that's where it came from.'

Nina felt the room lurch and stood up quickly, clenching her teeth to stop herself screaming. 'Thank you,' she said. 'We'll be back later to take a formal statement.'

The man said something else about coffee, but she went out into the stairwell and up the stairs to the floor above, two steps at a time, to David and Julia's door.

She gestured to Sundström and Landén that they should cover the stairs in both directions, and that Andersson should approach the door with her. They took up position on either side of the door, leaving any line of fire clear.

Nina tested the door. Locked. She knew it closed automatically if it wasn't held open. She fumbled for the ASP baton in her belt, then opened it with a light flick of the wrist. She pushed it gently through the letterbox and peered in cautiously.

The light was on in the hall. The air from the flat smelt of newspaper print. She could see the morning paper on the mat. She laid the baton horizontally so that it held the letterbox open. Then she pulled out her pistol and made sure there was a bullet in the chamber, then gestured to the others to be on the alert. She nodded towards the doorbell: she was about to make their presence known.

Pointing her weapon at the floor, she pressed the button and heard the bell ring inside the flat. 'Police!' she called. 'Open up!'

She listened intently for any sound from the letterbox. No response.

'Julia!' she called, quieter now. 'Julia, it's me, Nina. Open up. David?'

Her vest was tight across her chest, making it hard to breathe. She could feel the sweat breaking out on her forehead.

'Is that . . . Lindholm?' Andersson said. 'Officer David Lindholm? You know his wife?'

Nina holstered her gun, pulled out her personal mobile from the inside pocket of her jacket and dialled the familiar number.

Andersson took a step closer to her. 'Listen,' he said, standing far too close to her. She resisted the impulse to back away. 'If you have a personal connection to anyone in there, you shouldn't . . .'

She stared blankly at him as the phone started to ring on the other side of the door, a long, lonely sound.

Andersson took a step back. The ringing stopped abruptly and the answer-machine clicked in. Nina ended the call and dialled another number. A cheerful tune struck up just inside the door. Julia's mobile must be on the hall floor, probably in her handbag.

She's at home, Nina thought. She never goes out without her bag.

'Julia,' she said, as the mobile's voicemail clicked in. 'Julia, are you there?'

The silence echoed. Nina took several steps back, pressed the transmitter on her radio and spoke quietly into it. '1617 here. We've spoken to the informant, who heard what he thought were shots, probably from the flat above. We've made our presence known but there's been no response from inside the flat. What do you advise, over?'

There was a short pause before the answer reached her earpiece.

'The armed-response unit is still unavailable. Your call. Over and out.'

She let go of the radio.

'Okay,' she said quietly, looking at Andersson and the other two officers on the stairs. 'We'll force the door. Have we got a crowbar in 1617?'

'We've got one in our vehicle,' Landén said. Nina nodded towards the stairs and he hurried off.

Andersson began, 'Do you think it's appropriate for you to be leading the operation if—'

'What's the alternative?' Nina cut him off, more harshly than she intended. 'Handing over command to you?'

Andersson gulped. 'Wasn't there something funny about Julia Lindholm?' he said. 'Wasn't she involved in some scandal?'

Ignoring him, Nina took out her mobile and called Julia's number once more. Still no response.

Landén returned with the equipment in his arms:

a length of metal almost a metre long, basically a reinforced crowbar. 'Can we really do this?' he said breathlessly, as he passed it to her.

'Any delay could just make things worse,' Nina said.

Paragraph twenty-one of police legislation: *The police have the right to gain entry to a property, room or other location if there is reason to believe that someone inside may have died, be unconscious or otherwise incapable of summoning assistance . . .*

She passed the crowbar to Andersson and clicked off the safety catch of her pistol, nodding to the others to take up their positions.

As Andersson inserted the end of the crowbar beside the door-frame, she put her foot down close to the door so that it wouldn't fly open and injure him, in the event that someone inside tried to force their way out.

After three carefully judged attempts, the door gave way and the lock broke. The air that streamed out into the stairwell carried with it the faint smell of cooking.

Nina listened intently for any sound in the flat. She shut her eyes and concentrated. Then she jerked her head quickly to the left, taking a first glance at the hall: empty. Another glance, this time towards the kitchen: empty. A third, towards the bedroom: empty.

'I'm going in,' she said, pressing her back against the door frame, and turning towards Andersson. 'Cover me. Police!' she called again.

No response.

Her body tense, she slid round the door frame, kicking the newspaper aside and stepping silently into the hall. The lamp hanging from the ceiling was swaying slightly, presumably from the draught. Julia's bag was indeed lying on the floor to the left of the door. Alexander's jacket was next to it. David and Julia's coats were hanging from hooks on the rack to the right.

She stared straight ahead, towards the kitchen, hearing Andersson's breathing behind her.

'Check the nursery,' she said, gesturing with her gun towards the first open door on the left, without taking her eyes from the kitchen.

Her colleague slid in – Nina could hear the fabric of his trousers rustling.

'Nursery clear,' he said, a few seconds later.

'Check the wardrobes,' Nina said. 'Close the door behind you when you're done.' She took a few steps forward and took a quick look in the kitchen. The table was bare, but there were plates with the remains of spaghetti bolognese on the worktop.

The draught was coming from the bedroom: one of the windows must be open. The curtains were drawn, making the room completely dark. She stared into the shadows for a few moments, detecting no movement. But there was a smell, something sharp and unfamiliar.

She reached out a hand and switched on the light.

David was lying on his back across the bed, naked. Where his genitals should have been there was a bloody mass of entrails and skin. 'Police,' she said, forcing herself to act as if he were still alive. 'You have a weapon aimed at you. Show your hands.'

Thundering silence in response, and she noticed that she had tunnel vision. The curtains were moving. There was a half-full glass of water on the bedside table on Julia's side of the bed. The duvet was in a heap on the floor. On top of it lay a weapon identical to hers, a Sig Sauer 225.

Nina felt mechanically for her radio.

'1617 to Control. We have one casualty at the scene,

21

unclear if he's still alive. Looks like gunshot wounds to the head and groin, over.'

As she waited for a reply she went to the bed, looked down at the body and realized the man was dead. His right eye was closed, as if he were still asleep. In place of the left there was a gaping hole into his skull. The blood wasn't flowing so his heart had stopped beating. His bowels had opened, leaving a sludge of acrid excrement on the mattress.

'Where's the ambulance?' she asked, over the radio. 'Didn't they get the same alarm as us, over?'

'I'm sending an ambulance and Forensics,' Control said in her ear. 'Is there anyone else in the flat, over?'

Andersson appeared in the doorway, glancing at the body.

'You're needed out here,' he said, pointing towards the bathroom door.

Nina put her gun into its holster and hurried out into the hall, opened the bathroom door and held her breath.

Julia was lying on the floor next to the bath. Her hair was a pale halo round her head, spread in a mess of vomit. She was in her underwear and a large T-shirt, her knees pulled up to her chin, in a foetal position. She was lying on one hand; the other was clamped in a fist.

'Julia,' Nina said gently, leaning over her. She brushed the hair away from her face and saw that her eyes were wide open. Her face was covered with pale-red splatters of blood. A string of saliva hung from the corner of her mouth to the floor.

Oh, God, she's dead and I didn't save her.

Julia jerked and gasped, then retched.

'Julia,' Nina said, loudly and clearly. 'Julia, are you hurt?'

She gave several dry retches, then slumped back on to the floor.

'Julia,' Nina said, putting a hand on her friend's shoulder. 'Julia, it's me. What happened? Are you hurt?' She pulled her into a sitting position, leaning her against the bath.

'1617,' Control repeated in her ear. 'I say again, are there other casualties in the flat, over?'

Julia closed her eyes and let her head fall back against the enamel. Nina checked the pulse in her neck. It was racing. 'Affirmative, two casualties, one presumed dead, over.'

She let go of the radio.

'Andersson!' she called. 'Search the flat, every inch. There should be a four-year-old child here somewhere.'

Julia moved her lips, and Nina wiped the vomit from her chin. 'What did you say?' she whispered. 'Julia, are you trying to say something?' She checked that there was no sign of a weapon in the bathroom.

'How much do we want to cordon off?' Andersson asked from the hall.

'The stairwell,' Nina said. 'Forensics are on their way, and people from the crime unit. Start questioning the neighbours. Take Erlandsson first, then the others on this floor. And find out if whoever delivers the papers saw anything – he must only just have been. Have you searched all the rooms?'

'Yes. Even checked the oven.'

'No sign of the boy anywhere?'

Andersson hesitated in the doorway.

'Is there something you don't understand?' Nina asked.

Her colleague shifted his weight from one foot to the other. 'I think it's bloody inappropriate, you being part of this investigation,' he said, 'considering—'

23

'Well, I'm here and I've got it,' she said curtly. 'Get the cordon sorted.'

'Okay, okay,' Andersson said, and lumbered off.

Julia's lips were moving, but she wasn't making any sound. Nina was supporting her head with her left hand.

'The ambulance is on its way,' Nina said, as she examined her with her free hand, following the outline of her body under the T-shirt, tracing her skin. No wounds – not even a scratch. No weapon.

In the distance she could hear the sound of sirens and was gripped again by panic. 'Julia,' she said loudly, slapping her cheek. 'Julia, what happened? Tell me!'

The woman's eyes flickered and cleared for a moment. 'Alexander,' she whispered.

Nina leaned down close to her face. 'What about Alexander?' she asked.

'She took him,' Julia gasped. 'The other woman, she took Alexander.' Then she fainted.

2

As Julia Lindholm was being carried out on a stretcher from the flat she shared with her husband on Södermalm, Annika Bengtzon was sitting in a taxi on her way into the centre of Stockholm. The sun was rising over the horizon as the car passed the city limits at Roslagstull, colouring the rooftops a blazing red. The contrast with the black, empty streets hurt her eyes.

The driver kept glancing at her in the rear-view mirror, but she pretended not to notice.

'Do you know how the fire started?' he asked.

'I told you, I don't want to talk,' she said, staring at the buildings flashing past.

Her house had just burned down. Someone had thrown three incendiary grenades through the windows, the first at the foot of the stairs, then one into each of the children's rooms. She'd managed to get her son and daughter out through the window of her own bedroom at the back of the house, and now she was clutching them tightly as they sat at either side of her in the back seat. The three smelt of smoke, and her cornflower-blue top bore soot stains.

I bring death and misery with me. Everyone I love dies.

Stop it, she thought sternly, biting the inside of her cheek. I made it. We're alive. Just focus.

'I never usually drive anyone on credit,' the driver said sullenly, pulling up at a red light.

Annika closed her eyes. Six months ago she had discovered that Thomas, her husband, had been having an affair with a female colleague, an icy little blonde called Sophia Grenborg. Annika had put a stop to it, but she had never told Thomas she knew about it.

Yesterday he had found out that she did. *You've been lying and pretending and fooling me for months*, he had yelled, *and it's the same with everything you do. You decide what the world looks like, and anyone who doesn't agree with you is a fool.*

'That's not true,' she whispered, aware that she was about to burst into tears.

She wanted us to meet again. I'm on my way there now.

She opened her eyes wide to stop the tears overflowing. The stone façades of the buildings flickered and shone.

If you go now, you can never come back.

He had stared at her with his new, strange, narrow gaze, his dead eyes.

Okay.

She had watched him cross the parquet floor, pick up his briefcase, open the front door and go out into the grey mist. The door had closed behind him and he hadn't looked back.

He had left her, and someone had thrown three grenades into the house. Someone had tried to kill her and the children and he hadn't been there to save her. She'd had to cope alone. She knew perfectly well who'd thrown the bombs: the neighbour on the other side of the rear hedge, the one who'd driven across her lawn

26

and destroyed her flowerbeds, the one who'd done all he could to get rid of her. Wilhelm Hopkins, chairman of the villa-owners' association.

She held the children tighter.

I'm going to get you back for this, you bastard.

She'd tried calling Thomas, but his mobile was switched off. He didn't want to be reached – didn't want to be disturbed – and she knew what he was doing. She hadn't left a message, just breathed into his new, free life, then ended the call. It served him right.

'What number did you say it was?' The taxi-driver turned into Artillerigatan.

Annika stroked the children's hair to wake them. 'We're here,' she whispered, as the taxi pulled up. 'We're at Anne's. Come on, darlings . . .'

She opened the door and the night chill swept into the car. Ellen curled into a little ball. Kalle whimpered in his sleep.

'I want your mobile as security,' the man said.

Annika shepherded the children out of the car, turned and dropped her phone on to the back seat. 'I've turned it off, so you can forget about making any calls,' she said, slamming the door.

Anne Snapphane turned her head to gaze cautiously at the man lying on the pillow beside her, at the dark, gelled hair sticking out over his forehead, his quivering nostrils. He was falling asleep.

It was a long time since she'd slept next to anyone.

How pretty he is, and how young. Scarcely more than a boy.

I wonder if he thinks I'm too fat, she wondered, checking to see if her mascara had run. It had, but not much. Too fat, she thought. Or too old.

27

For her the most exciting bit had been the taste of strong lager in his mouth. She felt rather ashamed of this. It was six months since she had touched alcohol. Was that all? It felt like an eternity.

She rolled on to her side and studied the profile of the young man beside her.

This could be the start of something new, something fresh, fun and good. It would look great in the little boxes of basic information the papers published when they interviewed her: *Family: daughter, five, and boyfriend, twenty-three.*

She reached out a hand to touch his hair. 'Robin,' she whispered, almost soundlessly, moving her fingers just above his face. 'Tell me you care about me.'

The angry buzz of the doorbell startled him awake, and he looked about in confusion. Anne jerked her hand back as if she'd burned herself.

'What the fuck?' he said, staring at her as if he'd never seen her before.

She pulled the sheet under her chin and tried to smile. 'It's just the doorbell,' she said. 'I won't bother to answer it.'

He sat up. His hair product had left a stain on the pillowcase.

'Is it your old man?' he asked anxiously. 'You said you were on your own.'

'It isn't a man,' Anne said, and got up, still holding the sheet, trying in vain to wrap it around herself as she stumbled out to the hall.

The bell rang again.

'All right, for fuck's sake,' Anne said, irritated. She'd been without a man for so long and now . . . Shit. She fumbled with the lock and swallowed something that might have been a sob.

Annika was standing outside with Kalle and Ellen.

'What do you want?' Anne said hoarsely.

Annika sighed, as if she hadn't the energy to explain why they were there.

'Do you know what time it is?' Anne said.

'Can we stay? Our house has burned down.'

Anne glanced at the children. Burned down? Behind her she heard Robin flush the toilet. 'This isn't a good time,' she said, hoisting the sheet further up her chest.

Kalle started to cry, which started Ellen off as well. Anne felt the chill from the stairwell around her feet. 'Can you be quiet?' she said. 'It's the middle of the night, after all.'

Annika was staring at her with moist eyes.

Christ! Don't tell me she's going to start too.

'We haven't anywhere to go.'

Robin coughed from the bedroom. *Please, don't let him go!*

'Annika,' she said, 'that's hardly my fault, is it?'

Annika drew a breath as if she were about to speak, but nothing came out.

Anne tried to smile. 'I hope you understand.' She could hear Robin moving in the bedroom. 'I'm not on my own right now, and you've no idea how much this means to me.'

Annika's eyes narrowed. 'How selfish can you get?'

Anne blinked.

'I didn't manage to get any money out of the house,' Annika said, 'so I can't even pay the taxi. Perhaps you think we should sleep in the street.'

Anne gasped. She was angry now. 'Time for me to pay you back,' she said. 'Is that it?'

Annika's voice rose. 'Is it really too much for me to expect some help, just this once?'

29

He's getting dressed, he's going to leave.

She knew it: he was going to leave her now, and to get him to stay a bit longer she went out into the stairwell and closed the door behind her.

'After all the times I've had to listen to you!' Anne said, trying to restrain herself. 'Year in, year out, I've had to put up with your constant whining, everything going wrong, your boring husband and your awful job. I'll tell you one thing, *I'm* not the one letting anyone down!' She could feel her legs beginning to tremble.

'You can't be serious?'

'All the energy I've wasted on you,' Anne said unsteadily, 'I could have spent it on myself. Then I'd have been the one who made it. I'd have been offered a presenter's job and made shedloads of money.'

'Presenter's job?' Annika was clearly confused.

'Don't think I've forgotten how bloody arrogant you were when you were offered that job – *I* should have got it! It was me who put in all those years at that shitty company.'

'What on earth are you talking about?'

'You see? It didn't mean anything to you! Nothing I've achieved has ever been good enough.'

Annika was crying, tears running down her cheeks. She'd always been such a baby.

'I realize that it's completely irrelevant to you, but now I've *finally* got a chance that could lead somewhere. Do you begrudge me that?'

There was a brief silence. Then Annika blew her nose. 'I won't bother you again, ever,' she said. She took the children's hands and turned back towards the staircase.

'Good,' Anne said. She went back into her hall,

then leaned out again. 'Book yourself into a hotel!' she shouted at Annika's back. 'You've got enough money, after all.'

Robin was standing behind her as she closed the door. He had pulled on his jeans and top and was doing up one of his trainers.

'Where are you off to?' she said, trying to smile.

'Got to get home,' he said. 'Early start in the morning.'

Anne fought an impulse to pull the sheet tighter around her. Instead she let it fall to the floor, reaching out her arms to him.

He tied the other lace.

'But,' Anne said, stiffening, 'I thought you were unemployed.'

He glanced up at her breasts. 'I've got a band rehearsal,' he said, the lie obvious.

Anne picked up the sheet and wrapped it around her. 'I like you,' she said.

He paused a fraction too long. 'And I like you too,' he said.

Just don't say, It isn't you, it's me.

'Call me?' she asked.

He swallowed, then kissed her quickly on the ear. 'Course,' he said, then went out, shutting the door behind him.

The doctor stepped into A&E, his white coat flapping behind him. Nina was surprised by how young he was, younger than her. He glanced at her as he walked over to the stretcher where Julia was lying. 'Do we know what happened?' he asked, shining a little pocket torch into one of Julia's eyes.

'She was found in her flat,' Nina said. 'There'd been a murder – her husband had been shot on the bed.'

'Has she talked to you?' the doctor said, moving the torch to the other eye.

Nina suppressed an urge to unbutton her bulletproof vest. 'Not much. At first I thought she was dead.'

'Her pupils are reacting normally,' he declared, switching the torch off. 'Do we have ID?' He reached for a computer tablet.

'Julia Maria Lindholm, thirty-one years old. Maiden name Hansen.'

The young man made some notes and put the tablet down. He hung a stethoscope round his neck and Nina waited quietly while he took Julia's blood pressure.

'Slightly high, but stable,' he said.

Then he picked up a pair of scissors and cut off Julia's T-shirt. 'Were there any traces of blood where the patient was found?'

'Apart from the splatters on her face, I didn't see any,' Nina said. 'I don't think she's physically injured.'

'No entry or exit wounds? No cuts?'

Nina shook her head.

'She could have been hit by a blunt instrument that hasn't left any visible trace,' the doctor said, as he moved his hands over her body.

Julia didn't react.

He felt her neck. 'No stiffness, pupils normal, she isn't concussed.' He raised her legs. 'No fractures to the hips.' Then he took her hand and stroked it. 'Julia,' he said, 'I'm going to check your level of consciousness. I want to see if you react to pain.'

He squeezed her ribcage. Julia's face contorted and she screamed.

'It's okay,' the doctor said, and noted something on his tablet. 'I need to do an ECG, and then I'll leave you in peace.' He fastened some electrodes to Julia's chest, then wrapped her in a thick blanket. 'Do you want to sit with her?' he asked Nina.

Nina nodded.

'Hold her hand and talk to her.'

Nina sat on the edge of the stretcher and took Julia's hand, which was damp and cold. 'What's wrong with her?' *Just don't let her die! Tell me she's not going to die!*

'She's in a state of psychological shock,' the doctor said. 'They sometimes get like this, mute and paralysed. They stop eating and drinking. You can look them in the eye but they don't know you're there.'

He glanced up at Nina, then quickly away. 'It's not dangerous,' he said. 'It'll pass.'

It'll pass? Will everything get back to normal?

Nina stared at Julia's white face, her pale eyelashes, her hair. The blood on her face had dried and darkened. Fragments of their last meeting were rolling through Nina's mind, like short film sequences.

I can't bear it any longer, Nina. I've got to do something about this.

Just tell me, what's happened?

Julia had looked desperate, chapped red marks on her cheeks. They were still visible under the blood. How long ago was that? Three weeks? Four?

'Julia,' she said quietly. 'It's me, Nina. You're in hospital. Everything's going to be all right.'

Really? Do you believe that?

Nina looked at the doctor, who was sitting by the end of the stretcher, filling in a form. 'What happens now?' she asked.

'I'm sending her for a CAT scan,' he said, 'just to rule out any injury to the brain. We'll give her a sedative and she can go up to the psychiatric ward. With a bit of luck,

33

she'll get a course of therapy.' He stood up. 'You know her personally?'

Nina nodded.

'She's going to need a great deal of support over the coming months,' he said, then went out into the corridor.

The door closed slowly with a sucking sound. In the silence every sound seemed much louder: the rumbling fan, Julia's breathing, the bleep of the ECG machine. Steps hurrying past in the corridor, a phone ringing, a child crying.

The sterile room was cramped and cool, windowless, harsh light coming from flickering tubes in the ceiling. Nina freed her hand from Julia's and stood up. Julia's eyelashes fluttered. 'Julia,' Nina said quietly, leaning over her friend. 'Hello, it's me. Look at me . . .'

Julia gave a little sigh.

'Listen,' Nina said. 'Look up, look at me. I want to talk to you.'

No response.

Anger rose in Nina, like vomit. 'You're just giving up,' she said. 'Typical. You just lie back and leave everyone else to clear up your mess.'

Julia didn't move.

'What do you imagine I can do?' Nina said, taking a step closer to the stretcher. 'I can't help you now! Why didn't you tell me? Then at least I'd have had a chance—'

Her radio crackled.

'1617 from 9070, over.'

Her boss trying to locate her.

She turned away from Julia and stared into a cupboard full of bandages, as she pulled out the microphone and pressed the transmit button.

'1617 here. I'm with Julia Lindholm at Södermalm Hospital. She's just been examined in A&E, over.'

34

'You can't just sit there waiting,' he declared. 'We need your report as soon as possible. I'm sending Andersson with the car. He can stay until I've found someone else to guard her. Over and out.'

Fear clutched at her throat.

Someone to guard her.

Of course, Julia was a suspect.

The prime suspect in the murder of a policeman.

She left the room without looking at Julia again.

BREAKING NEWS
DAVID LINDHOLM MURDERED

Updated 3 June, 05.24 a.m.

Police Superintendent David Lindholm, 42, is reported to have been found murdered in his home on Södermalm.

Lindholm is Sweden's best known and most respected detective, not least for his role as an expert commentator on Criminal.

He was also personally responsible for several of the most remarkable police operations of recent decades, helping to solve the most brutal and complex cases in Swedish criminal history.

David Lindholm had an affluent upbringing in Djursholm on the outskirts of Stockholm. In spite of his background, he chose to enter the police force. After several years in the tough environment of the rapid-response unit of Norrmalm Police, he was promoted to detective.

He became familiar to the Swedish public as the straight-talking and fair-minded police superintendent in the television programme *Criminal*, but it was his handling of the hostage crisis at the Cowslip Nursery School in Malmö five years ago that made him a legendary figure in the force.

An armed man had barricaded himself in the toddlers' room and was threatening to kill the children one by one. David Lindholm established contact with the man, and after two hours of negotiation, he was able to walk out to a waiting patrol car with the disarmed gunman.

Evening Post photographer Bertil Strand won Picture of the Year in the category Best News Image in Classic Photography for the story.

While questioning an American who had been sentenced to life imprisonment two years ago, David Lindholm gained information on the robbery of a security van in Botkyrka. Five men were arrested and the majority of the missing cash, 13 million kronor, was recovered.

(updates ongoing)

3

Andersson roared up outside A&E, skidding to a stop and leaving marks on the tarmac. Nina opened the driver's door. 'Julia Lindholm has been examined,' she said. 'Stay here and keep an eye on her until you're relieved. It shouldn't be long.'

Andersson swung his feet to the ground. 'So what's wrong with our killer, then?' he said. 'Period pains?'

Nina clenched her fists. 'I'm heading back to write my report,' she said, getting into the patrol car.

'Have you heard the preliminary evaluation of the cause of death?' he said to her back. 'First she put a bullet in his brainstem, then blew off his cock.'

Nina shut the door and let the car roll down towards Ringvägen. It was daylight now, and the traffic was already building up. She glanced at her watch, twenty-five to six. Her shift ended at six, but it would probably be seven or eight o'clock before she had finished her report and filled in all the paperwork . . .

How can I be thinking about forms to fill in? What sort of person am I?

She took a deep breath that ended up as a sob. Her hands were shaking on the wheel.

Right on to Hornsgatan. Change gear. Pull away.

Then came the thought that had been lurking at the back of her mind since she'd walked into the flat: *Must ring Holger and Viola.*

She had to talk to Julia's parents. The only question was how much she could tell them. Nothing of what she'd seen at the crime-scene because they were not involved in the case . . . but this was about something else. *Decency, possibly just basic morality.*

She'd practically grown up with Julia and her parents. They had probably saved her from the life that her two siblings had ended up with. She had spent many long weeks out on the farm every summer while her mother had worked shifts in the chicken factory at Valla. During term-time she would often go home with Julia and have tea at the big gate-legged table in the farmhouse kitchen. She could still remember the taste of the oxtail soup and sandwiches, the faint smell of farmyard that always hung around Holger. Then, when her mother's shift ended, she would take the bus home to Ekeby . . .

Nina shook herself.

I was lucky, having Julia.

Some drunken teenagers in school-graduation caps were staggering about on the pavement to her left, arm in arm, three boys and a girl. The girl could hardly stand, and the boys were more or less dragging her along.

Watch out, little one. Don't let them take advantage of you . . .

One of the boys caught sight of her and made an obscene gesture. She switched on the blue lights and siren. The effect on the youngsters was instantaneous. They ran off like antelopes, the girl as well.

She pulled up and parked outside the station. The silence that followed was so great that it echoed. She sat there for several minutes, listening to it.

Then she sighed, undid her seatbelt and picked up Andersson's hamburger wrapper, with her own Diet Coke can, to throw into the car-park bin.

Pettersson, the station head, was on the phone when she went in, and waved at her to sit down opposite him.

'At five?' he said, into the phone. 'Isn't that a bit late? A lot of our officers . . . Yeah, that's true enough . . . Yes, you're right. Okay, seventeen hundred it is, then . . .'

He put the receiver down. 'What a terrible business,' he said, rubbing his bald head. 'What's happening to this society?'

He sounds like Inspector Wallander, Nina thought.

'We're going to have a minute's silence for David Lindholm,' Pettersson went on. 'At five o'clock the evening shift will have turned up but the day shift won't have left, which means that most people will be able to take part. Every police district in the country is joining in. Lindholm was known and respected everywhere, and after all those years lecturing at the Police Academy he's got friends throughout the force, new recruits and older officers alike . . .'

'Just don't tell the media,' Nina said.

Pettersson looked surprised, then irritated. 'Of course we're going to inform the media. Apparently radio news want to do a live broadcast.'

'If you were planning to rob a local shop, and found out that all police activity throughout Sweden would stop for a minute from seventeen hundred, when would you choose to do it? Anyway, how do you broadcast a minute's silence? Won't it be a bit . . . bleak?'

Her boss stared blankly at her for a few seconds, then leaned back, making the Ikea chair creak. 'Okay, let's get down to business,' he said.

Nina took out her notebook. She ran through all the facts in a monotonous tone, the call at 03.21, suspected shots heard on Bondegatan. Because the command unit and rapid-response squad were both out in Djursholm, Hoffman in 1617 had been in command of the operation. The informant, a Gunnar Erlandsson, a resident of the building in question, reported that he had been woken by what he thought were shots in the flat above. When there was no response from the apartment in question, patrol 1617, with patrol 1980, had gained entry under paragraph 21 of police regulations, suspecting that any delay could exacerbate the situation. In the flat they found two people, David and Julia Lindholm. David Lindholm was lying on the bed, shot twice, in the head and torso. Julia Lindholm was found in the bathroom in a state of severe shock. She had been taken to Södermalm Hospital for treatment.

Nina closed her notebook and looked up at Pettersson.

He was shaking his head again. 'Who would have thought it would end like this?'

'There's one more thing,' Nina said, looking down at her closed notebook. 'Julia said something odd before she fainted.'

'What?'

'She mentioned her son, Alexander. She said: "She took him. The other woman, she took Alexander."'

Pettersson raised his eyebrows. ' "The other woman"? What the hell did she mean by that? Was there anyone else in the flat?'

Nina felt stupid. 'No,' she said.

'Were there any signs of a break-in or struggle?'

Nina thought for a moment. 'Off the top of my head, I don't think so, but Forensics will—'

'And the door was locked?'

41

'It closes automatically if you don't wedge it open.'

The station head let out a deep sigh. 'Bloody hell, poor David. Looks like she was crazier than anyone imagined.'

'Alexander is missing, though,' Nina said. 'He wasn't in the flat. His room was empty.'

Her boss stuck some chewing tobacco into his mouth. 'And?' he said. 'Where is he?'

'Don't know.'

'Has he been reported missing?'

'Not yet.'

'Do we know if anything's happened to him?'

'No,' Nina said. 'It's just that . . . we searched the flat and couldn't find him.'

'Obviously the information about the other woman and the missing boy will have to go in your report. Just choose your words carefully.'

She could feel her cheeks starting to burn. 'What do you mean by that?'

Pettersson looked at her intently for a few seconds, then stood up and stretched his back. 'You weren't supposed to be on patrol last night, were you?' he said. 'Weren't you meant to be off?'

'I was doing an extra shift,' Nina said. 'I go back on my normal rota at sixteen hundred hours.'

He sighed. 'The papers have already started calling,' he said. 'Don't talk to them. All comments go through the press office. No leaks to that woman on the *Evening Post* . . .'

Nina got up and walked away down the corridor, past the staffroom and into a small office. She sat down, switched on the computer and went into the database for reporting incidents. Systematically, she set about clicking and filling in the relevant information in the correct boxes, time of call, personnel involved, address of crime scene, injured party, deceased, suspect . . .

Suspect?

She would be listed as the author of this report. It would be attached to the case of David Lindholm's murder for ever, would probably be examined and investigated at the Police Academy in fifty years' time, and she would be named as the person behind it. She was the one who had to record all these preliminary details; she had to formulate the case.

Suspect: Julia Lindholm.

She pushed away the keyboard and went out into the corridor, taking a few aimless steps to the right, then turning and going left instead.

I need something, she thought. Coffee? Then she wouldn't sleep. A sandwich from the machine? The very idea made her feel queasy. She went over to the confectionary vending machine instead. All that was left were bags of sour sweets. She found a ten-kronor coin in her pocket and bought the last but one packet. Then she went back to the station head's office and knocked on the door frame.

Pettersson looked up from his screen.

'Sorry,' she said, 'but who should I put as the injured party? The murder victim, or his family?'

'The murder victim,' Pettersson said, and went back to his screen.

'Even though he's dead?'

'Even though he's dead.'

Nina lingered in the doorway. 'There's one more thing,' she said. 'Alexander.'

Pettersson sighed.

'He ought to have been in the flat,' Nina said. 'I think we should . . .'

Her boss continued to stare at his screen. 'If Mummy did shoot Daddy, then it's probably a good thing the kid wasn't around to see it,' he said, and Nina realized the conversation was over.

She turned to leave.

'Hoffman,' he called after her.

She stopped and looked back over her shoulder.

'Do you need a debriefing?' he asked, and his tone revealed that he thought it would be the most ridiculous thing she could ask for in a *tragic case* like this.

'No, thanks,' she said, and went back to the little office, opened the bag of sweets and gasped as she put the first into her mouth. They really were sour.

Instead of clicking in the box for *suspect*, she picked up a form for recording instances where paragraph 21 of police legislation had been applied. It was easier to fill in than Julia's name.

In the end she had completed several forms, including one that detailed her interview with Erlandsson on the second floor.

She stared at the screen.

Clicked on *suspect*.

Quickly typed *Julia Lindholm*.

She closed the program, then hurried out of the room before her thoughts caught up with her.

4

'Mummy, I'm hungry. Do they have peanut butter here?'

Annika opened her eyes and found herself staring at a white curtain. She had no idea where she was. Her head felt like a lump of rock, and there was a big black hole in her chest.

'And chocolate and jam?'

The hotel. Reception. The room. Reality.

She rolled over. Her children were sitting next to each other in their pyjamas, bright-eyed, hair a mess.

'Did our peanut butter burn up in the fire?' Kalle asked.

'And Poppy,' Ellen said, her lip starting to quiver. 'Poppy and Leo and Russ burned up in the fire too . . .'

Oh, God, what do I say? How can I answer that?'

Groggily, she fumbled her way out of the sheets and pulled the children towards her without a word, held them in her arms and rocked them while the hole in her chest grew. 'They've probably got some chocolate,' she said, in a thick voice. 'And jam. I'm not sure about peanut butter.'

'My new bike,' Kalle said. 'Did that burn up as well?'

*The computer. All the emails stored in it. My phone-
book and diary. Our wedding presents. The pram.
Kalle's first shoes.*

She stroked his hair. 'We've got insurance, so we can
get them back again.'

'Poppy too?' Ellen asked.

'And we can rebuild the house,' Annika said.

'I don't want to live in that house,' Kalle said. 'I want
to go home and to my proper pre-school.'

She shut her eyes and the world lurched.

The family had been living in the villa on Vinterviksvägen in Djursholm for just a month when it had
gone up in flames. Their old flat on Kungsholmen had
been sold to a gay couple who had already moved in and
ripped out the kitchen.

'Let's go and have breakfast,' she said, forcing her legs
over the side of the bed. 'We'll put some clothes on first.'

Ellen looked at her reproachfully. 'But, Mummy,' she
said, 'they burned up in the fire too.'

By the time Annika had got back to the street after Anne
had refused to let them in, the taxi had driven off with
her mobile. She couldn't call for another and they didn't
have anything else to barter with, so she had no choice
but to pick the children up and start walking. She had a
vague idea that there was a hotel in the neighbourhood
and spent three-quarters of an hour walking in circles
before she found it. She was on the point of collapse
when she stumbled into Reception. The receptionist
looked scared when Annika explained why they were
there. They were given a room on the second floor.

Now she let the door of the hotel room swing shut
behind them, took the children's hands and got into the
lift.

The restaurant was a minimalist, ambitious affair: a floor-to-ceiling window, and bookcases, with steel and cherry-wood furniture. The clock behind the counter said it was a quarter past nine. She had slept for about four hours.

The breakfast buffet had been stripped bare, and the room was half empty. The businessmen had gone to their important meetings, leaving just one middle-aged couple and three Japanese tourists to stare at her and the children, at her torn jeans and soot-stained designer top, at Kalle in his silky Batman pyjamas and Ellen in her flannel ones with the butterfly print.

Sorry if we're disturbing your lovely breakfast with our unbrushed teeth and bare feet.

She clenched her jaw, filled a teacup with coffee, then helped herself to a yogurt and three slices of gravad lax. The yogurt was the only thing she managed to swallow, but she took the salmon because it was included in the price, 2,125 kronor for a 'twin standard room' that resembled a lift-shaft.

I can't do this on my own. I need help.

'That's impossible,' Berit Hamrin said. 'You sound completely normal.'

'The alternative is just lying down and dying, and if I was going to do that I might as well have stayed in the house,' Annika said, checking that the bathroom door was closed.

She had found the Cartoon Network on the hotel television, and had put the children back to bed, each with a little box of sugared cereal in place of sweets. Then she had shut herself into the bathroom, where there was another phone, and called her colleague in the newsroom.

'And you didn't manage to take anything with you? I read about the fire on the agency feed, but I had no idea it was your house. Bloody hell!'

Annika slumped on to the toilet seat and propped her head on her hand.

'According to the news agency, the house was completely gutted,' Berit added. 'Hasn't anyone from the paper called to ask what happened?'

'Don't know,' Annika said. 'I left my mobile as a deposit with Stockholm Taxis. I don't think anyone's been in touch, though. No one died, after all.'

Berit was silent. A chill crept up Annika's neck.

'So, what do you need help with first?' Berit asked eventually.

'The children have only got their pyjamas and I couldn't bring any money with me.'

'What size are they?' Berit wondered, clicking a ball-point pen.

'110 and 128.'

'Shoes?'

Annika's throat tightened and she was finding it hard to breathe.

Don't start crying, not now.

'Ellen's a twenty-six, Kalle's thirty-one.'

'Stay where you are. I'll be there in an hour or so.'

She remained seated on the toilet, staring at the towel rail, feeling the hole in her chest throb and ache. But she couldn't lose herself in the fog of self-pity and hopelessness that beckoned – she had the children to think of.

Your life is gone, a voice whispered, but she knew that wasn't true: in the bedroom Scooby-Doo was howling that he was scared of ghosts.

You've got nothing left!

48

'Of course I bloody have,' she said aloud.

Home was important, the place you belonged, but it didn't necessarily have to consist of four walls. It could just as easily be people, or projects, or ambitions.

You've got nothing that means anything.

Was that true?

She didn't actually have much less today than she'd had yesterday.

The children had no clothes, and her computer had gone up in flames, but pretty much everything else was still there.

Apart from Thomas.

And Anne. Her best friend.

She got up and looked in the mirror.

Only the children left. Me and the children. Everything else has been stripped away.

She had lost.

Shouldn't it feel worse than this?

The editor-in-chief of the *Evening Post*, Anders Schyman, had surrendered his privileged corner office in the name of cutbacks, and installed himself in a cubbyhole behind the comments desk, something he regretted more with each passing day. The only advantage of the reorganization was that he was in direct contact with the newsroom: he could sit in his office and watch the work in progress.

Even though it was only eleven o'clock in the morning, the level of activity out there would have been unthinkable just a few years back. Nowadays the website was updated round the clock, apart from a few hours of downtime around four in the morning, and not just with text, but video content, radio, adverts. The ever-earlier print deadlines for the paper meant that the entire production process had been brought forward so that now everything was done during the day, which was new. Tradition dictated that the evening papers were put together at night, preferably by a gang of hard-drinking, weather-bitten editors with red eyes and nicotine-stained fingers. Today there were hardly any such relics left on the paper. They had either adapted to the new age, kicked the booze and polished their shoes, or been cleared out with a redundancy package and an early pension.

Anders Schyman let out a deep sigh.

Over the years the feeling that something was slipping from his grasp had grown stronger and stronger until eventually he had worked out what it was: the very point of what they were doing, the fundamentals of journalism.

Nowadays it was so important to keep the website updated that occasionally everyone forgot that they actually had to have something to say.

He remembered the critical slogan their rivals had levelled at the *Evening Post* in the old days when the paper had sold more copies in Sweden than any other: 'Biggest, but never first. Most, but never best.' Now everything was done much faster, at the cost of truth and analysis.

But it isn't all crap, he forced himself to think. Today's paper was another bloody good edition, with Annika Bengtzon's inside story on the Nobel killer, Berit Hamrin's incisive articles about terrorism, and Patrik Nilsson's interview with a docu-soap star speaking about her eating disorder.

The problem was that all this was already old. Even though the paper had scarcely reached the news-stands, it was reporting yesterday's news because David Lindholm had been found dead in his bed and his wife was suspected of murder.

There was an endless torrent of praise for the dead police officer on the Internet. He had had an unparalleled insight into human nature, and an astonishing ability to communicate. As an interviewer he was unbeatable; he was the most loyal friend ever.

How do I handle this? Anders Schyman wondered. He was no longer used to wrestling with ethical dilemmas. His mind, which should have been dominated by basic journalistic principles, such as news evaluation, checking sources and reflecting upon whether or not to identify people by name, had little time for anything but financial analysis and sales figures.

He looked out over the newsroom.

First I need an awareness of the situation, he thought, standing up decisively and striding out of his office. 'What are we doing with the murdered supercop?' he asked Spike, head of news, who had his feet on his desk and was eating an orange.

'Front page, newsbill, seven, eight and the centrefold,' Spike replied.

'And the news that his wife is a suspect?' Schyman asked, sitting down on the desk, demonstratively close to the man's feet. Spike took the hint and dropped them to the floor.

'You mean what point size are we making the headline?' he asked, tossing the orange peel into the recycling bin.

'If we name David Lindholm as the murder victim, then say his wife is a suspect, we're identifying her as the murderer,' the editor-in-chief said.

'And?'

'She hasn't even been taken in for questioning,' Schyman said.

'Just a matter of time.' Spike was staring at his computer screen. 'Besides, it's everywhere already. Our rivals and the oh-so-refined morning rag have already got character assassinations up on the net.'

Okay, Schyman thought, so much for taking the ethical initiative.

Berit Hamrin came over to the desk, handbag swinging from her shoulder and her coat over one arm.

'Bloody good articles in today's paper,' Schyman said, trying to look encouraging. 'Has there been any response?'

Berit nodded towards Spike's screen. 'Julia Lindholm,' she said. 'Have we taken a conscious decision to identify her as the murderer on the Internet?'

'"We", meaning the collected journalists of Sweden?' Spike said.

'As far as I know, only the other evening paper and one of the morning papers are running the story that Lindholm's wife is a suspect,' Schyman said.

'We don't have to give her name,' Spike said.

Berit moved closer to Schyman. 'The very fact that we're publishing David Lindholm's name, how he was shot on his bed and that his wife is a suspect means that we don't have to give her name. Anyone who knows Julia will clock that she's the person we're referring to.'

'We have to be able to cover sensational murder cases,' Spike said indignantly.

'I wouldn't exactly describe what we've got on our website right now as "coverage",' Berit said. 'It's called "gossip". So far the police haven't confirmed anything, so all we're publishing is rumour.'

Schyman noticed that the journalists around the main newsdesk were raising their heads to listen. Was this good or bad? Were ethical discussions at the newsdesk healthy or did they made him look weak? He decided it was probably the latter. 'We'll continue this discussion in my office,' he said firmly, ushering them towards his cubbyhole with his hand.

Berit responded by pulling on her coat. 'I'm heading out to meet a source,' she said. She disappeared down the stairs leading to the garage.

Schyman realized that he was still holding out his hand towards his office. He let it fall to his thigh. 'So we've already put what we've got about his wife being under suspicion on the website?' he said to Spike. 'Who took that decision?'

Spike's face bore an expression of wounded innocence. 'How should I know?'

How indeed? The printed paper and the online edition had different editors.

Schyman turned on his heel and went back to his office.

What am I actually doing here?

5

Berit was carrying eight large bags. 'I tried not to get too caught up in gender stereotypes,' she said, as she squeezed into the room and dropped the bags on the floor. 'Hello, Kalle, hi, Ellen.'

The children glanced at her, then went back to the television. Annika switched it off.

'Look, Kalle,' she said. 'Aren't these great jeans?'

'Those are for Ellen,' Berit said, sitting on the bed-side table and unbuttoning her coat. 'Underwear's in that bag, and that one's got some bits and pieces, soap, toothbrushes and so on . . .'

The children got dressed of their own accord, silent and serious. Annika helped Ellen brush her teeth and caught sight of her own eyes in the mirror. The pupils were enlarged, almost covering the irises, as if the hole in her chest was visible in her eyes.

'How much do I owe you?' she asked Berit.

Berit stood up, pulled an envelope out of her handbag and handed it to her. 'I went past a cashpoint and got some money out. You can pay me back later.'

The envelope contained ten thousand kronor in five-hundred notes.

'Thanks,' Annika said quietly.

Berit looked around the cramped room. 'Shall we go out for a bit?'

The four walked silently through Reception and out into the street, crossing the road towards Humlegården. The clouds were hanging thick and grey in the sky; the wind was gusty and cold. Annika pulled her new cardigan more tightly round her. 'How can I possibly thank you?'

'If my house burns down, I'll be in touch,' Berit said, turning up her collar against the wind. 'You have to make a start by phoning the insurance company. They'll cover any costs you have to pay for staying somewhere until your house is rebuilt.'

They reached the park. The children were a bit hesitant in their new trainers, Kalle's green, Ellen's blue.

Annika forced herself to smile at them. 'You run ahead,' she said. 'Berit and I will wait here.'

They raced off towards the playground.

'Where's Thomas?' Berit asked quietly.

Annika gulped. 'I don't know. We . . . we had a fight. He wasn't at home when it happened. I don't know where he is. His mobile's switched off.'

'So he doesn't know?'

Annika shook her head.

'You have to try to get hold of him.'

'I know.'

Berit looked at her thoughtfully. 'Is there anything you want to talk about?'

Annika sat down on a bench. 'Not right now,' she said.

Berit sat beside her and looked at the children, who had taken possession of the playground. 'They'll get over it,' she said. 'But you have to hold yourself together.'

They sat for a while without talking, watching the children play on the slide. Ellen was laughing.

'By the way, have you heard about David Lindholm, that police superintendent?' Berit said. 'He was shot this morning.'

'What – the one on television?' Annika said, waving to Ellen. 'Married to Julia Lindholm?'

'Do you know them?' Berit said, sounding surprised.

'I spent a night in a patrol car with Julia. Do you remember that series of articles about women exposed to danger in the course of their work?'

Berit shook her head and pulled a bag out of her pocket. 'They're allowed sweets, aren't they?' she asked Annika. 'Kalle, Ellen!' She waved the bag and the children came running.

'How many can we have?' Ellen asked, panting.

'You can't even count,' Kalle said scornfully.

They each took a handful, Ellen picking out the pink ones, and Kalle the green.

'I was actually doing a profile of Julia's colleague,' Annika said, as she watched the children walk away. 'Nina Hoffman. It was the night we stumbled across that triple murder on Södermalm, if you remember?'

Berit took a handful of sweets and offered the bag to Annika, who declined. 'The axe murders? Hands chopped off and all that?'

Annika gulped.

'Bloody hell, yes,' Berit said. 'Sjölander and I covered the court case.'

Annika shivered and crossed her legs. She had been heavily pregnant with Ellen that spring, and at the *Evening Post* pregnant reporters were treated as if they were suffering from severe senile dementia: in a friendly, firm and utterly undemanding way. Eventually she had nagged her way into a fairly relaxed job, a series of workplace reports about women doing what were usually dangerous jobs for men. On the night of 9 March five years ago she had gone on patrol with two female police officers on Södermalm. It was a cold night, quiet, and she had had plenty of time to talk to the two officers. They had been close friends since they were children, had attended Police Academy together and now worked at the same police station. One of them, Julia, revealed that she was pregnant as well. No one at work knew about it yet; she was only in the fourteenth week, and she felt violently sick all the time.

Just before midnight they'd had a call about a disturbance in a flat on Sankt Paulsgatan, at the Götgatan end. It was a routine call: a neighbour had phoned in to complain about fighting and shouting from the flat downstairs. Annika asked if she could come along, and they let her, as long as she agreed to stay in the background.

They went up the stairs to the second floor, which was where they found the mutilated woman. She had crawled out into the stairwell and was still alive when the police patrol turned up. Her right hand was missing and blood was pumping out of the severed veins, running over the stone floor and down the stairs, splashing the walls whenever she moved her arm. Julia had thrown up in a window alcove and Nina had forced Annika back down to the street with astonishing force and efficiency.

'I didn't see much, but I can still remember the smell in the stairwell,' Annika said. 'Sweet, and sort of . . . heavy.'

'There were two men in the flat,' Berit said. 'They'd both been mutilated as well.'

Annika changed her mind and reached for a sweet. 'They solved the case pretty quickly.'

'Filip Andersson,' Berit said. 'A financial expert. He denied it but was still found guilty. He's in Kumla Prison. Life.'

Berit tipped the last of the sweets into her hand and dropped the empty bag into the rubbish bin beside the bench.

'Crazy,' Annika said, 'leaving your fingerprints all over the place if you've just chopped up three people.'

'Well, the criminal element of the population doesn't usually register as being particularly smart,' Berit said, standing up to help Ellen, who had fallen over and scraped her hand.

Annika didn't move. Her body felt as heavy as cement, and the wind was pulling at her hair, but she couldn't be bothered to brush it away from her face.

'The last I heard before I left the newsroom was that they think Julia killed her husband,' Berit said, as she sat down again.

'Really? She seemed so timid . . .'

'Looks like their son's missing too.'

'Oh, she had a boy, then.'

They sat in silence again, watching the children, who had evidently found something interesting beneath a large oak on the other side of the playground.

'Have you got anywhere to go?' Berit asked eventually.

Annika didn't answer.

'Your mum?' Berit suggested. 'Thomas's parents?'

She shrugged.

'Do you want to come out to Roslagen with me? Thord is in Dalsland this weekend, fly-fishing with his brother. You can have the guest cottage, if you like. It's standing there doing nothing.'

A couple of years ago Berit and her husband Thord had sold their house in Täby and moved out to some stables between Rimbo and Edsbro. Annika had been out there a couple of times – in the summer it was idyllic, with the lake and horses in the paddock.

'That would be great.'

'I have to go back to the newsroom and finish my follow-up piece on the terrorist articles, but I should be finished by eight at the latest. I'll pick up your mobile, then collect you from the hotel, if that sounds okay?'

'Thank you so much.'

Nina stopped in the doorway, uncertain.

There was an unusual number of uniforms in the small staffroom. They were standing in small groups with their backs to her, their heads close together. The hum of their voices sounded like air-conditioning, low and constant.

This is what grief sounds like, she thought, not knowing where the idea had come from.

It was a quarter to two, and her shift didn't start until four, but at first she hadn't been able to sleep, hadn't *wanted* to sleep. When she'd eventually drifted off, her dreams had been so confused and unsettling that they'd woken her. Rather than try to sleep again, she'd got up.

She pushed her way in behind Pettersson, who was blocking the door, and made her way to the coffee-machine, squeezing sideways between people, muttering apologies and stepping over helmets, boots and jackets.

The further into the room she got, the quieter it seemed.

By the time she reached the coffee-machine there was complete silence around her. She turned.

Everyone was staring at her, their faces closed. She got

the feeling that they were all leaning back, away from her. 'Is there anything you'd like to know?' she asked.

No one spoke.

She turned away from the coffee-machine, put her hands behind her back and looked directly at her colleagues. 'Is there anything you want to know that isn't obvious from the report?'

They seemed uncomfortable, and some of the officers standing closest to her looked away.

'How come you were first on the scene?' someone shouted, from the back of the room.

Nina craned her neck to see who it was. 'Why was I first on the scene?' she called, loud and clear. 'And why would anyone wonder about that?'

Christer Bure stepped forward, one of David's former colleagues from his days in uniform with the Norrmalm force. His face was dark from lack of sleep and grief. 'I just think it's bloody odd,' he said, stopping half a metre away from her, 'that you're the one who storms into the flat where David was shot, and that you whisked away his crazy fucking wife and hid her in hospital. How do you explain that?'

Nina suppressed an impulse to back away from him. She wouldn't get far anyway – the coffee-machine was in the way. He was glaring at her with such undisguised derision and ill-will that she had to take a deep breath before she spoke.

'The answer is perfectly simple,' she said. 'Andersson and I were sitting in 1617, and we were closest. Anything else you'd like to know?'

Christer Bure moved another step closer to her and clenched his fists. There was a ripple around him, as if several other men were following his example.

'His crazy wife,' he said. 'Why did she do it?'

Am I really supposed to put up with this?

'Julia Lindholm is the prime suspect for David's murder,' Nina said, her voice trembling. 'I presume that the investigation will uncover the murderer's motivation, whether it was Julia or someone else who—'

'Of course it was her, for fuck's sake!' Christer Bure shouted, his forehead deep red. 'Why the fuck are you still pretending?'

A few drops of saliva hit Nina's face. She turned and forced her way towards the door. She could feel tears burning at the back of her eyes and had no intention of giving him the satisfaction of seeing her break down in front of the entire station.

'The press conference is starting!' someone yelled, above the noise that had suddenly erupted. The introduction to Swedish TV news flickered across the screen in front of Nina and everyone fell silent. On the television, someone in a Hawaiian shirt settled behind a desk on the rostrum of the large conference room at Police Headquarters on Kungsholmen. Two men and a woman sat down beside him. Nina recognized the police press officer and the head of the National Crime Unit. She had never seen the woman before. A storm of flashbulbs broke over their clenched features, and the press officer said something into the microphone.

'Turn the volume up!' someone shouted.

'. . . by the murder of Police Superintendent David Lindholm,' the press officer was saying. 'I will hand you over to the head of the preliminary investigation, Prosecutor Angela Nilsson.'

The woman leaned towards the microphone. She had a blonde bob and was wearing a bright red suit. 'I have today remanded one individual in custody,' she said, 'on serious suspicion of having murdered David

61

Lindholm.' Her voice was cool, with a faintly upper-class accent.

On serious suspicion: the higher level of suspicion.

'An application for the formal arrest of this individual will be presented to the magistrates' court by Sunday at the latest,' she went on, without changing her tone. 'I would like to point out that, as head of the preliminary investigation, I am keeping an open mind as far as this case is concerned, and that we are not focusing on just one scenario, even though we have made a breakthrough at such an early stage.'

She leaned back to indicate that she had finished.

'Well,' the press officer said, clearing his throat, 'I will now hand you to the detective inspector leading the case for the National Crime Unit.'

A large police officer with his cap still on moved to stand in front of Nina; she stepped to one side to see.

'David Lindholm was found shot in his home early this morning,' the man in the brightly coloured shirt said. 'One person who was found alive at the crime scene was taken to hospital, and has today been remanded on grounds of reasonable suspicion. We have secured some forensic evidence, but there is still one large question mark hanging over our investigation.'

A blown-up picture of a small child appeared behind the people on the rostrum.

'This is Alexander Lindholm,' the detective said, 'David Lindholm's four-year-old son. He has been reported missing this morning. The boy lives in the apartment that is also the crime scene, but he wasn't there when officers arrived. We are keen to receive any information about Alexander and where he might be now.'

There was feverish activity in the press conference as

the photographers started taking pictures of the image on the wall.

The press officer adjusted his microphone and spoke quickly to calm the press corps. 'The boy's picture will be distributed to all media,' he said.

'Murders of police officers are extremely rare in Sweden,' the head of the National Crime Unit said slowly, and a heavy silence fell, both at the press conference and in the staffroom of Södermalm police station. 'David Lindholm is the first such victim since the murders in Malexander in the late 1990s, and we should be very grateful that we are spared such occurrences more often.'

He took off his glasses and rubbed his eyes. When he spoke again it was with greater focus and solemnity. 'When one of our fellow officers is killed,' he said, 'we don't just lose a person, but also a friend. Part of our social structure has been attacked, part of our democratic foundations.'

He nodded thoughtfully, and Nina saw several of her colleagues nod with him.

'David was also . . . special,' he said, lowering his voice. 'He was a role-model for people far beyond the police force, an inspiration to all.' Now the head of National Crime was almost quavering. 'I myself had the honour of watching David at work, and could appreciate the impact of his dealings with serious criminals, those with drug addictions and lifetime sentences, how he made people like that feel hope again, and believe in the future . . .'

Suddenly Nina didn't want to hear any more. She pushed past two officers and hurried out towards the changing room.

6

Thomas steered his heavy jeep through the streets of the suburban idyll as an early summer breeze rushed in through his window, ruffling his hair and tugging at his clothes. Sophia's smooth thighs were still burning on his skin; her scent was still in his stubble.

He felt alive.

He had spent the past twenty-four hours in her big double bed. She had called in sick: for Sophia, some things were more important than her career. They had had breakfast and lunch between the sheets.

Was it really only a day since he had been out here? Only one day, one night since he had lived here, among the birches? He saw lawns flash past, unfamiliar, as if they belonged to another world.

All those years with Annika already felt like a long, dusty trek through a desert, a drawn-out ceasefire with regular skirmishes and protracted negotiations.

How did I put up with it? Why didn't I leave her before?

The children, of course. He had done his duty.

He cruised through the cars parked outside the local supermarket, waving at a neighbour he thought he recognized.

Practically the first thing that had happened in his relationship with Annika was her pregnancy with Kalle so he hadn't really had much choice. He could either try to live with the mother of his child, or be one of those absent fathers whose child ends up disadvantaged and ostracized. But now it was over. He would never again have to put up with her contrary outbursts. He would just gather up a few clothes, pick up his computer and record collection, and on Monday he'd get hold of a shit-hot divorce lawyer. Sophia had good contacts: she didn't have to sit down with the *Yellow Pages* as Annika did whenever she needed a professional.

No two women could be less alike. Sophia was everything Annika despised, mainly because she could never be like her: educated, feminine and well mannered.

And Sophia enjoyed sex, unlike frigid Annika.

Wow, that was mean. Was he allowed to be so unkind?

He turned right, into the area where they lived, his eyes roaming over the pale-green trees and white fences. Houses loomed up on either side of the road, patrician villas and big brick palaces in the national romantic style, with ornate verandas, pools and summerhouses.

She'll have to buy me out of the house, and it won't come cheap.

He was prepared to fight, he really was, because the house was just as much his as it was hers. They'd had no pre-nuptial agreement, so half of it was his.

Sophia had been born into money: her penthouse suite was owned by her family.

He saw the turning to Vinterviksvägen ahead of him and his pulse quickened. This was likely to be unpleasant.

Sophia had asked if he wanted her to come along, had said she would be happy to support him. He had been firm: he had got himself into this mess so it was his job to sort it out.

She had thought him very responsible.

I'll sort it out. I can do it.

He turned into the road with a heavy sigh.

I don't want to fight. I've just come to get a few things . . .

At first he couldn't work out what was wrong with the scene that greeted him, what it was that didn't make sense. Then it hit him, like a punch in the face, before he identified the smell of smoke and ash, before he worked out what he was looking at.

He stopped the car in the road, leaning over the wheel and staring through the windscreen.

His home was a smoking ruin. The whole building had collapsed. The remains were blackened and warped. Charred roof-tiles lay scattered over the grass. Annika's car stood on the drive, a blackened wreck.

He turned off the engine and listened to the sound of his own panicked breathing.

What the hell have you done, you fucking witch? What have you done with the children?

He opened the door and got out on to the road, as the car alarm shrieked to tell him he had left the key in the ignition. The noise followed him as he made his way unsteadily towards the police tape and stared helplessly at the crumbling walls.

Oh, God, where are the children?

His throat constricted and he heard himself whimper.

Oh no, oh no, oh no!

He sank to his knees, hardly noticing the damp seeping through his trousers. All his things, all his clothes, the football from the tournament he'd played in over in the States, his student graduation cap, the guitar from Sunset

Boulevard, his reference library and vinyl records . . .

'Terrible, isn't it?'

He looked up. Ebba Romanova, their closest neigh-bour, was standing beside him. He hadn't recognized her immediately. She usually had a dog with her. She held out a hand. He took it and stood up, brushing some wet ash from his trousers. 'Do you know what happened?' he asked, wiping his eyes.

Ebba Romanova shook her head. 'It was like this when I got home.'

'Do you know where the children are?' he asked, and his voice broke.

'I'm sure they're fine,' she said. 'They haven't found any . . .' She trailed off. 'And when it comes down to it, it's just possessions,' she went on, staring out over the ruins. 'The only thing that really matters is life itself.'

Rage rose in Thomas. 'Easy for you to say.'

She didn't answer, and before Thomas could think of anything to say she had turned and started to walk unsteadily towards her gate, sobbing.

Thomas was left standing on the road, confused and lost.

What do I do?

He fished out his mobile and checked the display: no messages, no missed calls.

That told you, eh? Well, it serves me right!

He might have had his phone switched off last night, but only so she wouldn't phone and scream and cry. She could have left a message. She could have told him his house had burned down.

Is that too much to ask?

He raised the phone to call her and tell her a few home truths, but realized he didn't know her mobile number. He had to look it up, dialled it and was met by the automated voice message. She didn't even have a personal one.

He turned his back on the ruins and went to his car.

At the station, work had slowly got going again, but the four o'clock handover had passed without any great enthusiasm. Nina was told to go out with Andersson again, and couldn't think of a reason not to. None of the other young men was much better.

Now they were sitting in the staffroom, talking. No one was going to head out before the minute's silence at five. Nina walked silently down the corridor, glanced quickly over her shoulder, then snuck into an empty interview room. She listened at the door and heard Andersson's deep voice rolling along the walls.

How am I supposed to handle this?

She went over to the telephone, picked up the receiver and listened to the dialling tone. Then she dialled the ten-digit number and waited.

Eventually someone answered with a muffled cough.

'Hello. It's me, Nina.' She could hear someone breathing heavily and sniffing at the other end. 'Holger? Is that you?'

'Yes,' Julia's father said.

Nina checked that the door was properly closed, then sat down at the empty desk. 'How are you?' she asked quietly. 'How's Viola?'

'Desperate,' the man said. 'Utterly desperate. We're . . .' He fell silent.

'I know,' Nina said, when he didn't go on. 'Have you heard anything about Alexander?'

'Not a thing.'

Silence again.

'Holger,' Nina said, 'I want you to listen very carefully

to what I say. I'm about to tell you something I'm not supposed to, not you or anyone else. You mustn't tell anyone what I tell you, apart from Viola. I was the one who took the call. I was the first into the flat. I found Julia on the bathroom floor. I looked after her and went with her up to the hospital. She wasn't hurt. Holger. Do you hear me? She wasn't physically hurt at all. She was in deep shock, not really there, but there's nothing wrong with her. Julia's going to be fine. She'll soon be back to normal. Holger, do you understand what I'm saying?'

'Did you . . . ? What were you doing in Julia's flat?'

'I was on duty, doing an extra shift. I was the closest patrol when the call came in, so I responded. I thought that was the best thing to do.'

'And Alexander wasn't there?'

'No. Alexander definitely wasn't in the flat when I got there.'

'But . . . where is he, then?'

She could feel the tears rising. 'I don't know,' she whispered, then cleared her throat. 'Are you getting any help? Have you got anyone to talk to?'

'Such as who?'

He might well ask. He and Viola weren't regarded as relatives of a murder victim, but of a murderer: there would be no crisis team ready to help them with their grief. 'I'm working Saturday and Sunday,' Nina said, 'but I can come down to see you on Monday, if you like.'

'You're always welcome here,' Holger said.

'I don't want to intrude,' Nina said.

'You never do. We'd like it if you could come and see us.'

There was another silence.

'Nina,' the man finally said, 'did she shoot him? Was it Julia who shot him?'

She took a deep breath. 'I don't know,' she said, 'but it looks like it. The prosecutor has remanded her in custody.'

Julia's father took several deep breaths. 'Do you know why?'

Nina hesitated: she didn't want to lie. 'Not exactly,' she said, 'but I think they'd been having problems recently. Julia hasn't really told me much. She hadn't mentioned anything to you?'

'Nothing to indicate that things were seriously wrong. About a year ago she said she thought it was a shame that David didn't seem to like Björkbacken, but nothing else . . .'

She could hear noise out in the corridor, then Andersson's voice. 'I have to go,' she said quickly. 'Call me whenever you like on my mobile, Holger.'

The electronic bleeping was forcing its way into Annika's head. She resisted the urge to put her fingers in her ears. She had used some of Berit's money to buy the children a new Game Boy each. They were sitting at the head of the bed, staring intently at the small screens. Ellen was playing Disney Princess, and Kalle was playing a Super Mario golf game, to the accompaniment of much bleeping, pinging and popping.

She couldn't see any further ahead than a couple of minutes at a time. In some peculiar way this calmed her. Now I'm going to buy a new handbag. Now we're going to eat hotdogs. Now I'm going to make a phone call . . .

At that moment the phone beside her rang and she jumped. She went into the bathroom and picked up the receiver there.

It was Detective Inspector Q, Annika's contact in the police force.

'How the hell did you know I was here?'

'I spoke to Berit. It's about the fire in your house. Forensics have just got back, and they've got a preliminary cause. The level of destruction and the explosive way that the fire spread suggest that the fire broke out in several places simultaneously, and probably on more than one floor, which in turn suggests that it was started deliberately.'

'But that's exactly what I told you!' Annika said. 'I saw him, I know who started it.'

'Who?'

'Hopkins. The neighbour. He was standing in the bushes spying on us after we got out.'

'I think you're wrong, and you should think very carefully before pointing the finger at anyone. Arson is a serious offence, one of the worst in the book. It can carry a life sentence.'

'It would serve him right,' Annika said.

'And insurance fraud is also serious,' Q said. 'We investigate that sort of case very thoroughly.'

Annika snorted. 'Don't try that one,' she said. 'I know exactly what happened. Anyway, haven't you got anything else to worry about but the fire in my house? The Nobel killer, for instance? Or David Lindholm's murder? By the way, have you found the boy yet?'

There was a noise at the other end of the line, someone entering the detective's office and voices in the background. The receiver was put down. Now she could hear rustling and clattering.

'I'll be in touch,' Q said, then hung up without waiting for an answer.

She was left with the phone in her hand, listening to the sounds of the computer games in the bedroom.

Suddenly she was overwhelmed by a desperate longing for Thomas.

71

You never gave me a chance. Why didn't you say something?

She wants to see me again. I'm on my way there now.

He'd walked across the parquet floor, picked up his briefcase, opened the front door and looked out at the grey gloom. He'd stepped outside, closed the door behind him and hadn't looked back, not once.

'Mummy,' Kalle said from the bedroom. 'There's something wrong with Mario. He won't hit the ball.'

She pressed the palms of her hands to her eyes for a few seconds, breathing through her mouth. 'Coming!' she said, standing up.

She ran some water in the basin and rubbed her face hard for a few seconds.

Kalle opened the door. 'I can't press "hit",' he said, holding out the Game Boy.

She dried herself on a flannel and sank on to the edge of the bath. She took the computer from him and pressed various buttons, then realized what had happened. 'You must have pressed "pause",' she said, showing him the command to start the game again.

'No, I didn't!'

'You probably didn't mean to,' Annika said. 'You must have done it by mistake.'

'No, I didn't!' Kalle's eyes were full of tears as he snatched the game from her.

For a moment Annika's eyes flashed black, and she lifted her hand to slap him. She stopped herself with a gasp.

Oh, God, I mustn't fall apart. What would we do if I did?

'Well, at least Mario can hit the ball now,' she said breathlessly.

Friday, 4 June

7

The door of Detective Inspector Q's office was ajar. Nina hesitated, not sure if she should press the button beside the three little lights on the wall, labelled Busy, Wait or Come In, or if she should just knock.

Before she had made up her mind, the door opened abruptly and the detective was standing in front of her, hair all over the place, his loud shirt only half tucked into his jeans.

'What the hell?' he said. 'What are you doing? Eavesdropping?' He held out his hand. 'Nina Hoffman, I presume?'

She looked him in the eye. 'Yes, that's right. And you're Q.'

'Come in, for God's sake. My secretary isn't here to-day, so I'll have to get the coffee myself. How do you take it?'

Nina stared at him. What was he on about? 'Thanks, I'm okay,' she said, stepping into the office.

It was on the third floor of Police Headquarters on Kungsholmen, so impersonal that it bordered on spartan. There weren't even any curtains. A dead pot-plant stood abandoned in the window, perhaps part of the furnishings when he had moved in.

She stood there for a minute or so while he went to the coffee-machine further down the corridor.

'Don't worry, the chair isn't booby-trapped,' he said, pointing at it when he came back with a steaming plastic mug in his hand.

Nina sat down on the worn old chair, feeling extremely uncomfortable.

She had heard about Detective Inspector Q, even if he wasn't anywhere near as well known as David Lindholm. And, unlike David, he wasn't universally liked either. There were a lot of officers who thought his weird clothes were a bit affected, and then there was his passion for cheesy pop music. There were also stubborn rumours that he was gay.

Q settled down on the other side of the desk. 'That was a bit of a bloody coincidence, wasn't it?' he said, blowing on his coffee.

'What?' Nina wondered.

'That you just happened to be first on the scene of that particular crime.'

'Is this an interrogation?' Nina asked, tilting her chin.

He threw out his arms. 'Absolutely not!' he said. 'Call it a conversation between fellow officers, if you like. I'm just curious to hear what you think about the things that don't have their own little box on the official report.'

He really was extremely odd, Nina thought, considering he was such a senior officer. 'What do you want to know?' she asked.

'How did you react when you got the call?'

Bondegatan's a long street – there must be a thousand people living on it.

'I didn't,' she said. 'Why would I have thought anything in particular?'

The man on the other side of the desk toyed with his

mug of coffee, and looked at her in silence for a whole minute. Nina felt her tongue swell in her mouth. She had an almost unbearable urge to lick her lips.

'Do you know what?' Q said eventually, his voice now tired and muted. 'I think you're lying. I think you know much more than you've reported so far, because you want to protect your best friend. But, believe me, you won't help her by keeping quiet. If I'm to stand any chance of sorting out this mess, I need to know what happened.'

Nina made an effort to keep her back straight, and nodded. Yes, she could see that.

'I knew David Lindholm,' Q said. 'Better than most people. Let's just say that I'm not an unqualified supporter of the current claims that he was a great hero.'

Nina was astonished. 'What do you mean?'

'We trained together. Why David joined up is one of life's great mysteries. He wasn't remotely interested in police work, just wanted to carry on with his extreme sports and chase women.'

'That's just part of being young,' she said.

'He could be violent as well, at times, went in far too hard. Had you noticed that?'

'I never worked with him. He'd left active fieldwork behind long before Julia and I got to know him.'

Q sighed and leaned forward over the desk. 'Yes, well, right now there's something considerably more important than David Lindholm's character and the question of Julia's guilt, and that's their son. Have you any idea where Alexander might be?'

Nina tucked a strand of hair behind one ear. 'Julia's parents live in Södermanland, on a farm just outside Katrineholm. They look after Alexander sometimes, but he's not there. I spoke to them yesterday.'

'It was Julia's parents who reported him missing,' Q said.

Nina sat completely still. 'David's father died years ago, and his mother lives in an old people's home. I haven't spoken to her but he's unlikely to be there. Julia didn't have much to do with her neighbours or the other mums at nursery, but I suppose he could have been spending the night with one of them.'

'The boy hasn't been to nursery for the past week. No one's seen him since last Friday, neither the staff nor the other parents.'

This is worse than everything else. How did it get to this?

'So what . . . do you think's happened?'

'Was the Lindholms' marriage in trouble?'

Nina looked down at her lap. 'I suppose you could say that,' she said.

'Enough trouble for Julia to be on the point of leaving him? For her to have prepared her departure somehow?'

'I don't know,' Nina said.

Q fixed his eyes on hers. 'Could she have hidden the boy somewhere?' he asked. 'Could he be alive, locked up somewhere?'

Could Julia have done that? Could she have locked Alexander away somewhere, then gone home and shot David?

'It's now thirty hours since the murder,' Q said. 'Time's running out. If the boy doesn't have access to water, we need to find him within twenty-four hours, forty-eight at the most. I hope you appreciate just how serious a situation this is.'

A draught from the door made her shiver. 'Julia's got a summer cottage,' she said. 'Out in the woods near Katrineholm. She rents it from her parents' neighbours.

They don't spend much time there. David thinks it's too basic, but Julia's very fond of it.' She realized she'd used the present tense when she'd referred to David.

Q was making notes.

'She rents it? That'll be why we haven't found any trace of it in the property register. Where is it?'

'In the woods outside Floda, halfway towards Granhed,' Nina said. She took a sheet of paper and drew a shaky map showing the way to Julia's cottage. 'It's called Björkbacken,' she said, 'but there's no sign. You can't see the house from the road, and the post gets delivered to a box in Floda, but there's an old milestone beside the track, an iron sign saying how far it is to Floda Church. You can't miss it.'

She pushed the sheet over the desk and the detective picked it up.

'How often does she go out there?'

Nina thought. 'I don't know,' she said. 'We haven't seen much of each other over the past few years . . .'

'Why not?'

Nina hesitated. 'David,' she said. 'We . . . we didn't really get on.'

'Because?'

She looked at the dead plant, remembering the first time she and Julia had met David.

He'd come to give a lecture at the Police Academy, dressed in jeans and a white T-shirt, big cowboy boots on his feet. His hair was short and spiked, and he'd had several days' stubble.

She recalled their teacher's breathless enthusiasm.

We should really have been looking at crime prevention today, with a particular focus on racism, but now that we've got the opportunity to hear David Lindholm instead, obviously we're delighted . . .

Several of the other teachers had turned up in the lecture room, which was highly unusual.

David had sat down on the table at the front of the room, one boot dangling, the other firmly on the floor. He leaned forward with one elbow on his thigh. The impression was at once nonchalant and authoritative.

Julia's whisper had been like a warm breeze in her ear.

Just look at him! He's even better-looking in real life than he is on television . . .

The lecture had been fascinating, one of the best of the whole course. David talked about the art of negotiating with criminals in extreme situations, when hostages were involved, for instance. He described situations and events that made everyone gawp, shifting easily between seriousness and banter. His smile was radiant and white, and he'd noticed Julia straight away. Nina had seen him turn towards her when he made a joke, and once he even winked at her. Julia had blushed.

Afterwards several of the teachers and students flocked round him, but when Nina and Julia were getting ready to leave he excused himself and came over to them.

There is a future for Sweden, he said. *With you two in the force the bad guys will be queuing up to get arrested . . .*

He was pretending to talk to both of them, but he was looking at Julia.

Julia smiled her wonderful smile and her eyes sparkled.

Nina could still remember the prick of jealousy. Now she said to Q, 'I think David felt I was too close to Julia. Some men find that sort of thing difficult.'

Q looked at her intently for several seconds. 'You reported that Julia mentioned another woman in the flat.'

'Yes, that's right. There was nothing to indicate that

that had been the case, but obviously I made a note of what she said.'

'Do you think she was telling the truth?'

Nina said nothing for a few moments. 'I don't know. It's probably up to Forensics to see if there's any evidence of an intruder . . .'

'There were a lot of different fingerprints in the flat,' Q said. 'It must have been a while since it was last cleaned properly. You didn't see any signs of a break-in, no indication that the door had been forced?'

'No.'

'Forensics have found traces of blood on the floor of the hall. Did you notice anything there?'

'No. But I saw a gun on the bedroom floor, at the end of the bed.'

'That was Julia's.'

Nina said nothing.

'Could this other woman have got in by any other way?' Q asked. 'Through an open window?'

The breeze from the bedroom, a window open slightly. Curtains drawn, a room in complete darkness. Shadows but no movement. Only the smell, sharp and unfamiliar.

'The bedroom window was probably open,' she said. 'I didn't check, but there was a draught from in there.'

'Which way does the bedroom face?'

'Towards Bondegatan.'

'Is it possible to get in or out that way?'

'The flat's on the third floor, and the façade of the building is plastered. In theory it would probably be possible, using a rope, but you'd have to attach it some-how, either up on the roof or somewhere inside the flat.'

Q sighed. 'And you're quite sure of the information about the other woman?'

Nina stiffened. 'What do you mean?'

'There's no way you could have misunderstood it?'

What were they really thinking? And what lay behind this peculiar conversation?

'Do you think I fabricated it in order to help my friend?'

'I don't think anything. But I would appreciate your help in trying to work out what happened.'

Q leaned forward in his chair and held her gaze. 'It's like this. Julia isn't talking to us. We're extremely keen to get her to communicate. I was wondering if you could pay her an informal visit to hear what she's got to say.'

Aha. So this is where we've been heading.

Nina folded her arms. 'You want me to spy on my best friend? Is that what you're suggesting?'

'Call it whatever you want,' the detective said calmly. 'I'm offering you the chance to see Julia and find out how she is. If you think it fitting, you could always ask about the other woman, and about what happened in the flat yesterday morning.'

'So I'm supposed to conduct some sort of interrogation without there being any sort of defence lawyer present?' Nina said. 'That's completely unethical!'

'Maybe,' Q said, looking at his watch. 'She's in Kronoberg Prison, as of now, more or less. I could get you permission to go in, if you think it would help, I mean.'

'So she's been discharged from hospital? Already?'

'I saw her last night,' the detective said. 'She was as fit as a fiddle.'

'But she was completely out of it yesterday morning.'

'She wasn't particularly talkative, but that's hardly unusual. She's behaving like people normally do in custody.' The detective inspector wrote something on a sheet of paper and stood up. 'There's nothing wrong with Julia,' he said. 'I think she'd appreciate a visit from you. These are my telephone numbers. Call me when you've made up your mind.'

Nina took the piece of paper and stood up too. 'Just one question,' she said. 'How come you're in charge of this case?'

'I work here, and I had nothing better to do,' Q said.

'But police officers suspected of any crime are supposed to be investigated by the police authority,' Nina said. 'Why isn't that happening with Julia?'

The detective held the door open for her.

'Julia Lindholm resigned from the force on the fifteenth of May,' he said. 'The senior prosecutor with the police authority has decided that she should be treated as an ordinary mortal. She can hardly be investigated by her former colleagues on Södermalm, which is why the case has come to us at National Crime rather than to the local district.'

Nina stared at him. 'That's not possible.'

'I can assure you that I take the rivalry between the district police authorities and the National Crime squad very seriously, but in this case we had no option.'

'She can't have resigned. She would have talked to me first.'

'My secretary is off today, as I said earlier, so I'm the one who gets to sit and file their nails. So, if you don't mind . . .'

He nudged her out of the bare room and left her standing in the corridor.

Annika was leaning against the door frame with a mug of coffee in her hand, watching the children chasing Berit's dog around the large lawn in front of the house.

Kalle was quicker, of course, but Ellen was keeping up fairly well on her little legs. She had a good stride . . . Maybe she'd turn out to be a sprinter.

The view from the porch of Berit's guest cottage was wonderful. Up to the right lay the main house, two storeys, a terrace, ornate woodwork. To the left the meadow sloped down towards the lake and the beach, where the neighbour's horses usually went to shit in the summer. Straight ahead, on the far side of the paddocks, lay the forest.

Maybe this is the way to live, close to nature.

But she knew she'd get cabin-fever within a week.

'Mum, I caught him!'

Kalle had managed to get his arm round the neck of Berit's good-natured old Labrador. They were rolling around on the grass together, and Annika could see that her boy's new clothes were going to have permanent grass-stains. 'Don't be too rough!' she called. 'And the dog's a she!'

Berit was coming towards her, a mug in one hand and Annika's mobile in the other. 'Did you sleep well?'

Annika tried to smile. 'Sort of. Funny dreams.'

Berit sat down on the steps. 'About the fire?'

'About . . .' Annika stopped herself. She hadn't told Berit that Thomas had been unfaithful. She had been tormented by macabre nightmares about Sophia Grenborg for months now; afterwards she woke up breathless and in a cold sweat.

'There's something wrong with Thord's old charger,' Berit said, 'so I'm not sure how full the battery is.' She put the phone down on the porch.

Annika sat next to her and looked out over the meadow. 'You've got a lovely place here,' she said.

Berit screwed up her eyes against the reflection of the

sun on the lake. 'This was the last chance for me and Thord,' she said. 'We grabbed it, and it worked out.'

Annika followed her gaze towards the water. 'How so?'

Berit glanced at Annika with a little smile. 'I had an affair,' she said, and Annika gasped.

Berit? An affair?

'I got very fond of another man,' Berit went on, 'but of course it was just an illusion. I fell in love with love itself. It was a great feeling – that sparkle again, being head over heels . . .' She laughed, slightly embarrassed. 'Of course it didn't last. When I saw him in the cold light of day, he was just another bloke. There was no reason to throw away everything I had with Thord just for a bit of decent sex.'

Annika was staring down into her mug, unable to think of anything to say.

Berit? An affair? Decent sex? But she was fifty-two years old!

'I know what you're thinking,' Berit said, 'and I can assure you of one thing: it felt exactly the same as it did when I was eighteen. In some ways I'm glad it happened, but I'll never do it again.'

Without being conscious of what she was doing, Annika put the mug down, wrapped her arms round her friend's neck and started to cry. She wept silently, Berit holding her, for several minutes. 'He's got someone else,' she whispered, wiping her nose with the back of her hand. 'I keep dreaming of killing her. He left me for her, and then the house burned down.'

Berit sighed and stroked her back. 'And you still haven't spoken to him?'

Annika shook her head and dried her cheeks on the sleeve of her cardigan.

'You have to get through this,' Berit said. 'There's no way round it.'

'I know.'

'There's a phone in the office. The children can stay here if you need to go out for a while.'

Berit stood up, brushed the dirt from her behind and headed for the house again, mug in hand. Annika watched her go, trying to see her with different eyes, a man's eyes. She was fairly tall and thin, with broad shoulders and cropped hair. She was wearing a loose top that swung out at her hips. She didn't dress like that for work. She usually wore a jacket and dark trousers, perhaps with a bit of expensive but discreet jewellery. It had never even occurred to her that Berit might be capable of having an affair. That her serious, well-educated colleague was a sexual being. It was actually a bit uncomfortable, a bit like realizing that your mum and dad must have had sex once upon a time.

Then she was struck by the most obvious thought of all: who had she had the affair with?

Someone at the paper?

It was almost bound to be.

Or one of her sources? Berit met a lot of different people to get information. She had said the farm was the last chance for her and Thord, and when had they bought it? A couple of years ago? Annika had been working at the paper then. Maybe it had happened longer ago, when she had been on maternity leave, so perhaps it wasn't strange that she'd never noticed anything.

As long as it wasn't Spike!

Please, don't let it be Spike!

Somehow the idea of Berit having an affair was strangely heartening. Annika felt like calling her colleague back and asking her all about it.

It was possible to carry on. Everything wasn't finished just because things had been a bit difficult.

Her eyes fell on the mobile phone. She must remember to buy a charger next time she was in the city.

Suddenly anxiety overcame her and she took several shallow breaths to keep it at bay.

Got to get through this. There's no way round it.

She went back into the cottage, picked up the phone and rang Thomas's mobile.

One ring: she could hear the children racing around outside.

Two rings: the sunlight on the water caught her eyes.

Three rings . . .

'Hello, this is Thomas . . .'

'Hello,' she managed.

Her heart was thudding so hard that she could hardly hear his reply.

'Where the hell have you been?'

She was shaking, and had to hold the receiver with both hands. 'I've . . . The house has burned down.'

'Really? You didn't think it was worth telling me before now?'

'It was yesterday morning—'

'Why haven't you called? Why didn't you tell me? How the hell do you think I felt, driving out there and seeing the house like that, in ruins? Have you any idea what sort of shock it was?'

'Yes, sorry—'

'And how the hell did the fire start? I mean, the whole house is a wreck! What on earth did you do?'

'I didn't do anything. I just—'

He cleared his throat loudly. 'How are the kids?'

'Fine. They're playing. Do you want to see them?'

He put the phone down and was gone for a long

87

while. 'Now isn't a good time,' he said when he came back. 'What do the insurance company say?'

He doesn't want to see the children! He doesn't care about Ellen and Kalle!

Her tears overflowed and ran down her cheeks. 'I haven't sorted that out yet,' she whispered. 'I suppose I'll do it next week.'

'Fuck,' he said. 'How long does it take to get the money?'

'Don't know . . .'

'I need to get this sorted as soon as possible,' Thomas said, sounding as if he really meant it.

'I'm so sorry,' Annika said.

'Not half as sorry as I am,' Thomas said, and ended the call.

She put the receiver down carefully and let a wave of self-pity course through her. She wiped her cheeks with her fingertips, gazing out through the window at the sunlight and the children playing.

Why isn't this enough for me? Why isn't life ever enough?

She went out on to the porch again and sat down, still watching the children.

Where was she going to go with them?

Their nursery and pre-school were in Djursholm, but the thought of taking them back there made her feel ill.

No more suburbs, never again.

The countryside was fine, but she was happiest in the city.

Maybe they could go back to Kungsholmen. Things had been good there. If they were lucky, their places at nursery and pre-school would still be available: they didn't usually take new children until the start of term. Maybe she should phone and find out.

She picked up her mobile and switched it on. Thord's old charger had managed to squeeze a bit of power into the battery. She dialled the manager's number and got a message telling her that the nursery was closed for a training day.

She wrapped her arms round her shins.

Was she wrong about this? Would it be better to make a fresh start? Move to a new part of the city, maybe even a different town? Go home to Katrineholm?

Her mobile buzzed: it had connected properly to the network and the messages were tumbling in. Annika looked at the screen. There weren't that many. Five voicemails and three ordinary texts.

The voicemails were, in order, from Spike, Schyman, Spike, Thomas and Thomas. The texts were all from Thomas, their tone progressively angry.

Spike wanted her to go in and write about David Lindholm, Schyman wanted the same thing, then Spike wondered if she could write an eye-witness account of her house burning down. Finally her husband had called, with the fury he had shown in the text messages.

This was actually fairly symptomatic of her life, she realized. This was what happened whenever she was hit by some catastrophe. These were the people who got in touch. Two of her bosses, wondering if she could do some work, and an angry man who thought she didn't fuck him often enough.

She went back into the house and called Schyman.

'How are you?' the editor-in-chief asked. 'You're still in one piece?'

She sat down. 'I'm okay. Berit came to get me last night. I'm at her place in the country now.'

'We've been trying to call you but couldn't get through.'

'I know, but now I've got my mobile going again. Was it anything in particular?'

'First of all it was this business with Julia Lindholm. You know her, don't you?'

'Well, I spent a night in a patrol car with her five years ago.'

'They're keen to publish the story,' Schyman said. 'But I understand the situation you're in. Did you have time to rescue anything from the house?'

'The children.'

He coughed awkwardly.

'Bloody hell,' he said. 'It's hard to imagine. Do you need some time off?'

'Yes,' she said. 'I've got a lot to sort out.'

'Do you think you could write up the story about Julia Lindholm? "My Night With the Cop-killer?" You could do that from home.'

'I don't have a computer.' She didn't have a home either, but she didn't mention that.

'You can pick up a new laptop here at the newsroom, I'll sign a requisition slip at once. When can you get in to pick it up?'

She looked at her watch. 'This afternoon,' she said. 'And if I'm going to write about Julia Lindholm, I ought to talk to the other officer who was with us, Nina Hoffman. She was the one I was actually profiling.'

'Okay, I'm counting on you.'

8

She left the children in Berit's care, playing on the lawn, and went off to the bus-stop. She took out her mobile and checked the contact list. She tried 'N' for Nina, then 'H' for Hoffman, and finally found a number under 'Police Nina H'.

She pressed dial, and waited as the phone rang.

'Hoffman.'

She swallowed. 'Nina Hoffman? My name's Annika Bengtzon, I'm a journalist on the *Evening Post*. We met five years ago – I spent a night with you and Julia?'

'Yes, I remember.'

'Is this a bad time?'

'What's it about?'

She looked out over the fields and meadows around her, at the clouds slowly drifting north towards the horizon, at red-painted wooden houses, the old glass in their windows flashing. 'You can probably guess,' she said. 'My editors want an update on what we did that evening, what Julia said and did, what I made of it all. I've said I'll do it, but I wanted to talk to you first.'

'We have a press spokesman who looks after all communication with the media.'

'I know that,' Annika said, and heard her irritation.

'But I wanted to check with you before I write anything about Julia because I got the impression you were quite close.'

Nina Hoffman said nothing for a few moments. Then: 'What are you thinking of writing?'

'Julia said quite a lot about David. And now our idle chat has suddenly become very interesting. Have you got time to meet me?' Annika could see the dust of the approaching bus at the brow of the hill. 'I'm not planning on dishing any dirt,' she said. 'That's not why I'm calling. In fact, it's rather the opposite.'

'I believe you,' Nina Hoffman said.

They agreed to meet at a pizza restaurant close to where Nina Hoffman lived on Södermalm an hour and a half later.

The bus drove up and stopped. Annika clambered aboard and held out Berit's last five-hundred-kronor note as payment.

'Haven't you got anything smaller?' the driver said.

Annika shook her head.

'I can't change a note that big. You'll have to take the next bus.'

'You'll have to throw me off,' she said, picking up the note and walking towards the back.

The driver sighed, then put the bus in gear and pulled away.

She sat right by the window, and watched the landscape flash past. Everything was different shades of green. The speed of the bus blurred the edges and turned the world into an abstract painting.

Annika shut her eyes and leaned her head back.

Thomas walked briskly into the government offices at Rosenbad with his back straight. Without looking left or right, he slid past a group of citizens queuing at the security desk in the white hallway, and prayed that his pass would still work.

Officially his secondment had ended on Monday, and his pass hadn't been renewed, which had come as an unexpected and unpleasant surprise. So far in his career he had been recruited from one job to the next without having to produce a lengthy CV or tortured application. It would be a blow if that were to change now, when he had finally managed to get a research post with the government.

Yesterday the head of his section in the Ministry of Justice, Per Cramne, had asked him to look in, and Thomas had been careful not to sound too keen. He had said he had a meeting in the morning, which was true, even if it was with Sophia.

If he was in luck his entry code would still work, and he could avoid the humiliation of having to wait in the queue of visitors. He held his breath and pressed in the digits. There was a whirring sound and the green light came on.

He pulled open the heavy steel door and stepped into the corridors of power. He could feel the eyes of the people in the queue on the back of his neck: *Who's that? What does he do? It must be someone important.*

Naturally, he went over to stand by the lift on the right – the one on the left was a goods lift that stopped at every floor. Waiting for the one on the left was an elementary mistake. He got out on the fourth floor and walked straight to the head of section's office.

'Good to see you,' Cramne said, shaking his hand as if they hadn't met for several months. In fact they had had dinner together at Thomas and Annika's house in Djursholm as recently as Monday.

'Awful business about the house,' his boss went on, gesturing to a chair. 'Are you going to rebuild it?'

Nice and calm, Thomas thought. Just relax and wait for what he's got to say. 'Yes, I suppose so,' he said, sitting down and leaning back.

'Well, the bugging proposal's going through smoothly,' Per Cramne said. 'Everyone's very happy with the research you did for us.'

Thomas swallowed and held up his hands as if to stop the praise. 'It was really just a continuation of my work for the Association of County Councils.'

Cramne was leafing through some files in a cabinet to the right of the desk. 'Now we've got to take care of the follow-up work,' he said. 'The government will be appointing a parliamentary inquiry which will go through all the clauses and suggest changes.'

'A proper inquiry?' Thomas wondered. 'Or to bury the proposal?'

The problem with inquiries was that they were set up both to get something done and to prevent something you *didn't* want done.

The assistant under-secretary opened another drawer and carried on leafing through it.

'You haven't read the memo? I thought it went out while you were still here.'

Thomas fought an impulse to cross his legs and arms in a sort of basic defence posture. 'No,' he said. 'What are the conditions?'

Cramne slammed a drawer and sat down. 'The directives are simple,' he said. 'Any proposed reforms mustn't drive up the cost of criminal custody. We need an economist in the group to analyse the consequences of any proposals, and it's going to require a fair bit of political dexterity. One of our aims is to abolish life sentences, and some of our critics are already screaming that this is going to be bloody expensive. I'm absolutely convinced that they're wrong.' He smiled and leaned back in his chair. The back hit the wall. 'This is where you come in,' he said.

'As an economist?' Thomas said, his heart sinking.

He hadn't reckoned on this. He'd hoped for some sort of position within the department. Being an economist for the Justice Ministry didn't sound much, scarcely better than caretaker.

'We need an expert on the committee,' Cramne said, with a nod.

'To provide economic analysis?'

'Exactly. We're extending your appointment until the inquiry is complete, and that could take a couple of years.'

Thomas could feel the blood rushing to his head. A couple of years! His immediate reaction had been wrong. This was brilliant! It meant he'd be guaranteed employment protection, would have first chance at any permanent post, and he'd get to stay in the department. A government official! That's what he'd be.

He had to show how sharp he was, right from the start. 'Abolishing lifetime sentencing,' he said, 'why should that be expensive? Shouldn't it make things cheaper?'

'Any change has cost implications. Today a lifetime prisoner serves on average thirteen, fourteen years because they get out after serving two-thirds of their sentence. If you get rid of the lifetime sentence, the new maximum term would be something like twenty-five years.'

'Really?' Thomas said.

'Which would obviously place a severe strain on the

prison service. But we can deal with that later. We have to start by going through what the direct consequences would be today, then look at how they would change over time, and how the range of sentencing is being applied.' He leaned forward and lowered his voice. 'Up to now, the government hasn't increased any sentences, apart from some adjustment to the Sexual Offences Act, so in my opinion it's high time they did.'

He leaned back, his chair hitting the wall again.

Thomas lifted one foot on to his knee and rubbed at a spot on his shoe to avoid having to look up and reveal that he was blushing. 'So I'd do cost analysis of possible legislative proposals?' he said. 'And then carry on as usual?'

'You'll keep your office, and work as you've been doing up to now. I've already discussed this with Halenius, the under-secretary of state, and he's given it the okay. Welcome to the team!'

Per Cramne held out his hand again and Thomas took it with a grin. 'Thanks, boss,' he said.

'This business of statistics,' Cramne said, 'it's like herding cats.' He got to his feet and gestured towards the door with one hand.

Thomas got up clumsily and found that his legs were unsteady. 'When do I start?' he asked.

Cramne raised his eyebrows. 'Well, what the hell?' he said. 'There's no point hanging about, is there? Get hold of someone at the National Council for Crime Prevention and ask them to put together an analysis of current sentences so we've got something to get our teeth into.'

Thomas headed off towards his old office. It was only on the fourth, far below the real centres of power on six and seven. It was also cramped and dark and looked out on Fredsgatan, but at least it was in Rosenbad.

He stopped in the doorway and gazed silently at the furnishings, took a deep breath and shut his eyes. He'd had so much sex that his crotch ached, he was living in a huge apartment on Östermalm, and he worked for the government.

Fuck me, it doesn't get better than this, he thought, stepping into the room and hanging his jacket on the back of the chair.

The bus braked sharply, throwing Annika forward so that she banged her head on the seat in front. Confused, she rubbed the bridge of her nose. The bus had stopped at a red light just in front of Eastern Station.

She jumped out, caught the Underground at Tekniska Högskolan and checked her watch. If everything went according to plan, she'd have time to go to the bank before she met Nina Hoffman. She got off at Slussen and headed along Götgatan until she came to a branch of her bank. She had to wait twenty minutes before she got to see a cashier. 'I've got a problem,' Annika said, putting the form she had filled in on the counter. 'My house has burned down. I haven't got an ID card, or any bank cards, because I didn't manage to get anything out of the house. That's why I need to withdraw money like this. I hope that's okay.'

The cashier looked at her from behind thick glasses with a neutral expression. 'Obviously I can't hand any money over to someone if the person in question can't identify themselves.'

Annika nodded emphatically. 'Yes,' she said, 'I understand that. But I don't have any identification documents because they all went up in the fire. I haven't got any money either, which is why I need to withdraw some now.'

The woman behind the counter was starting to look as if Annika smelt. 'That's out of the question,' she said.

'I know my account number,' Annika said. 'And I know exactly how much I've got in my current account. I've got a phone account too and I know all the codes.' She held up her mobile and smiled.

'Sorry,' the cashier said. 'I'll have to ask you to step aside.'

White-hot fury flashed up instantly. 'Listen,' Annika said, leaning towards the cashier. 'Whose money is it, yours or mine?'

The cashier raised her eyebrows and pressed to call the next customer in the queue. A man stood up and walked over to Annika, stopping demonstratively close to her.

'I have almost three million kronor in various accounts in your damn bank,' Annika said, far too loudly. 'I want to withdraw every single *öre* and close every account.'

The woman looked at her with unconcealed loathing. 'You have to be able to give proof of your identity before you can close an account,' she said, turning to the man who was muscling past Annika now.

'But it's my money!' she shouted. She turned and walked quickly towards the door. From the corners of her eyes she could see the other customers staring at her with a mixture of fear and distaste. Close to tears, she tore the door open and started running down Folkungagatan towards Danvikstull.

I've got to calm down, otherwise everyone will think I've robbed the bank.

She slowed and forced herself into a normal walking speed.

Five minutes later she reached the pizzeria.

It took her a few moments to recognize Nina Hoffman.

The police officer was sitting in a corner at the back of the restaurant, studying the menu intently. Out of uniform she looked like any other young Södermalm woman, jeans and jumper, her light brown hair loose.

'Hello,' Annika said breathlessly, holding out her hand. 'I'm sorry I'm a bit late, I was trying to get some money out of my bank account, but I haven't got any ID at the moment.' She realized she was about to burst into tears again, and took a deep breath. 'Sorry. It's very good of you to see me at such short notice.' She sat down at the table. 'My house has burned down and I didn't manage to get anything out with me.'

There was a flicker in the police officer's eyes. 'In Djursholm? That was your house?'

Annika nodded.

Nina Hoffman looked at her carefully for a few seconds, then picked up the menu. 'Do you eat pizza?'

'Absolutely.'

They each ordered mineral water and a *calzone*.

'It's a while since we last met,' Annika said, when the waitress had disappeared into the kitchen with their order.

Nina Hoffman nodded. 'Down at the station,' she said, 'just before your article was published. You brought me a printout to look through.'

'It was the day that that financial consultant was locked up,' Annika said. 'Filip Andersson. I remember everyone being relieved that those terrible axe-murders could be sorted out so quickly.'

'I've hardly ever felt such unanimous loathing within the force for one individual criminal,' Nina said.

'Rich, cowardly and sadistic,' Annika said. 'Not a combination that's ever going to win any popularity contests. He's in Kumla Prison, isn't he?'

Nina Hoffman raised her chin. 'What exactly do you want from me?'

'I don't know how much you remember, but Julia talked a fair bit about David that night. David didn't want her to work in the force while she was pregnant. He didn't like the fact that she'd had her hair cut. He didn't like the fact that her pregnancy was starting to show. He hoped it would be a boy. He called three times just to find out where we were. I got a hint of control-freakery.'

Nina looked at her coldly. 'How come you remember it so well?'

'David was already a television celebrity, even then. And I'm allergic to control-freakery, it brings me out in a rash. How was their marriage, really?'

Nina folded her arms. 'Don't you think that's a very personal question?'

'You don't kill your husband without a very good reason.'

The pizzas arrived and they started to eat in silence.

Annika paused halfway through, put her knife and fork down and leaned back. 'Eating a whole *calzone*'s like putting a big rock in your stomach,' she said.

Nina carried on with hers.

This isn't going well.

'How have things been for you since we last met?' Annika asked. 'Do you still work at the Katarina station?'

Nina shook her head and wiped her mouth with the napkin. 'No,' she said, glancing up quickly, then looking down again. 'I got promoted. I've been an inspector for the past year or so.'

Annika studied her. Nina Hoffman was a smart woman who played according to the rules.

100

I'll have to try a different approach.

'It's always a sensitive matter, writing about tragedies within relationships like this,' she said. 'While there's a lot of public interest, everyone in the media has to consider all the people involved. David was one of the best-known police officers in Sweden. I don't know if you saw the press conference yesterday when they announced that Alexander was missing, but the head of National Crime said straight out that David's murder was an attack on the structure of society as a whole, an attack on democratic principles.'

Now Nina's expression had changed.

'He seemed personally affected in a way I haven't seen before,' Annika went on. 'The head of National Crime usually looks fairly wooden. If I've understood it correctly, his reaction is shared by a lot of police officers. The entire Swedish police force seems to have taken David's murder personally. That makes our job in the media even more difficult.'

Nina put down her knife and fork and leaned forward. 'How do you mean?'

Annika chose her words carefully. 'We're always walking a tightrope when we write about ongoing criminal investigations,' she said slowly. 'We want to publish as much information as possible for our readers, but at the same time we have to take into account the work of the police. They have the same conflict of interest, only reversed. You want to work undisturbed and as effectively as possible, but at the same time you wouldn't get anywhere if you didn't communicate with the public, which usually happens via the media. Do you know what I mean?'

Nina Hoffman was looking hard at her. 'To be honest, no, I don't,' she said.

Annika pushed her plate aside. 'We need to know what happened with this murder, and we need an open dialogue about what we can and should publish. That requires trust and loyalty from both sides. If we can establish that, maybe we have a chance of succeeding, you and us alike.'

Nina blinked several times.

'We always know much more than we publish,' Annika went on. 'I mean, I was there when you and Julia walked right into the axe murders, but I didn't write anything about it in the paper the next day. And I let you approve the way I described your work in the profile I did of you. That's how I work, and that's what I mean about us taking responsibility on both sides . . .'

It was entirely true that Annika hadn't written anything about the axe murders the following day. She had promised Nina that she wouldn't. Instead she had given all the details to Sjölander, who got a scoop and a front page for nothing.

'What do you want to know about Julia?' Nina asked.

'Did she do it?'

'The investigation has only just started,' Nina replied.

'Are there any other suspects?'

Nina sat silent.

'This must put you in an extremely odd situation,' Annika said. 'Professionally as well, I mean. You can't be part of the investigation, I understand that, but at the same time—'

'I'm involved whether I like it or not,' Nina Hoffman interrupted. 'I responded to the call first. My colleague and I were the first officers inside the flat.'

Annika jerked. 'It must be hard for you,' she said, 'trying to remain objective.'

A couple near them burst into simultaneous laughter.

Another couple stood up, chairs scraping. Annika moved her cutlery.

'Objective?'

Annika waited until the couple near them had gone out. 'Not having a preconceived idea of culpability.'

'David was shot in his sleep,' Nina said. 'We found a gun by the bed. We've already linked it to the culprit.'

'With fingerprints? That was quick.'

'It was easier than that. It was Julia's service revolver.'

Annika had to stifle a gasp. 'How do they know? Don't they all look alike?'

'Most officers have a Sig Sauer 225. But each gun has a serial number that links it to a particular individual.'

'Can I publish that?'

'Absolutely not.'

Silence rose up between them. Groups of people around them were getting up and leaving.

'What do the police think about Alexander? Is he still alive?' Annika asked, when the silence had become too oppressive. 'Is there any point in asking the public to help look for him?'

Nina Hoffman looked at her sternly for several long seconds. 'We don't know if Alexander's alive,' she said. 'For the time being we're assuming he is. It's extremely important that the public keep their eyes open.'

'If he's dead, what might have happened to him?'

'He hasn't been at nursery all week. Julia rang to say he was ill. The last person to see him was the downstairs neighbour, Erlandsson. He looked out through the spyhole in his door and saw Julia going out with the child on Tuesday morning. They had a flowery fabric bag with them.'

'And I can't write about that either?'

They reverted again to silence. The waitress took their

103

plates away. Neither of them wanted coffee, just the bill. Annika paid with Berit's money as Nina gathered her things.

'Julia resigned a couple of weeks ago,' Nina Hoffman said, standing up. She was tall – a head taller than Annika.

'She did?' Annika said. 'Why?'

'I can come with you to the bank if you like,' Nina said. 'They usually only need someone to confirm your identity.'

Annika stopped mid-step. 'Could you? That would be great.'

They left the restaurant and walked towards the branch on Götgatan. The queue of lunchtime customers was gone. Annika filled in a new withdrawal form and went straight up to the cashier with the thick glasses. 'Hello,' Annika said. 'It's me again. I want to withdraw my money now.'

Nina Hoffman put her driving licence and police badge alongside the form. 'I can vouch that the person in question is the person she claims to be,' she said firmly.

The cashier's mouth pursed and she nodded curtly. She counted out twenty-five thousand kronor in thousand-kronor notes and held them out to Annika with a little flick of the wrist.

'Can I have them in an envelope, please?' Annika said.

The cashier gave a little cough.

'As soon as I've opened an account with another bank I'll come back and close everything I've got here,' Annika said.

When they emerged on to the street she let out a deep breath. 'Thank you,' she said, holding out her hand. 'Imagine, that it could suddenly be so easy . . .'

'The police badge usually helps,' Nina Hoffman said, and smiled slightly for the first time.

'Have you still got my mobile number?' Annika asked.

They parted and went in different directions, Nina towards Danvikstull, Annika to the Underground station at Slussen.

9

Schyman was sitting at his desk, staring helplessly at the report from the management board, dated the previous day.

Sixty employees had to go.

He stood up and did the short circuit of his tiny cubbyhole, one step in each direction.

He sat down again and tugged at his hair.

If he protested, there would be only one outcome: he would have to take his things and leave. There was no other option – he had learned that during his years in the warm embrace of the Family, the proprietors. Anyone could run the paper. He was under no illusion that he was indispensable. The question was, what journalistic ambitions might any new management harbour? Would they turn the *Evening Post* into a gutter-press rag with naked girls on page three? Cut out anything political, investigative or analytical and focus exclusively on gossip and celebrities?

Or would they simply close it down?

The *Evening Post* wasn't one of the Family's most warmly regarded publications, to put it mildly. If it weren't for the fact that the paper brought money into the business, it would have been dead and buried long ago.

It had been made clear to him when he accepted the position of editor-in-chief and legally responsible publisher some years before that he had to run it at a profit, and Anders Schyman had never let them down – but lose *sixty employees*?

He would, of course, have to discuss the matter with the new managing director, a lad who had graduated from business school a few years ago and had got the job at the *Evening Post* because his friend's dad was on the board. So far he hadn't made too many waves (much to everyone's relief).

Anders Schyman put the report down on his desk.

That wasn't such a bad idea, damn it.

Perhaps it was time for the lad to take some responsibility and do something in return for his million-kronor salary. On the other hand, someone so inexperienced couldn't judge which measures needed to be taken, or which employees could be let go, so it would obviously have to be himself who identified the priorities and the dead wood. If Schyman sent the young man into battle and the cutbacks worked, then the new guy would be the one who got all the credit. And he would be left looking weak and ignorant.

And that would never do.

So what would be the points of conflict?

The unions, of course, would make a terrible fuss.

The newspaper had approximately five hundred employees, half of them on the editorial side, which meant they were members of the Swedish Journalists' Association. (Those who weren't already members would join up the moment the proposed cutbacks were announced. There was nothing better for promoting solidarity than a serious threat to people's wallets.)

The other two hundred and fifty were in the Salaried

107

Employees' Union (advertising, marketing, administration), and a couple of dozen poor sods were still working in graphics.

What could be cut?

Not advertising – that was out of the question. They would have to accelerate out of the crisis, and advertising was the only way to rake in profits. The analysts and distribution people couldn't be touched either. Technical support had already been pared to the bone.

Which left editorial staff and admin.

Anders Schyman sighed. He wondered if he could be bothered to go and get a plastic mug of coffee from the machine. He closed his eyes, imagined the bitter taste and decided against it.

The other way of raising profit was to increase the number of copies sold, which placed serious demands on the journalists' competence. Which in turn meant that every cutback on editorial staff needed to be done with surgical precision.

Which brought him back to the union, and likely conflict.

He needed to keep and fire people according to their abilities, but the union was guaranteed to trot out the old maxim 'last in, first out'.

If they got their way, everyone who had been recruited recently would be thrown out, leaving just the old hacks, and that was impossible if the paper was going to survive. The new website people were essential, or the entire online investment would collapse. But he also needed to retain the experience and competence of the older employees, the ones who still knew who and what the Chancellor of Justice was, for instance.

He let out a loud groan.

The Salaried Employees' Union and the Journalists'

Association were relatively weak and flexible unions. They seldom rode into battle. Schyman could still remember his astonishment when the Journalists' Association had unilaterally suggested that trainee reporters should be forced to accept other types of work (dishwashing, cleaning, the Volvo production line) as soon as they became unemployed, a suggestion so controversial that not even the government or business community had considered it.

He scratched his beard.

The local branch of the union had its annual general meeting on Monday. They would be choosing a new chair – the current incumbent was going on study leave from August. The post was much sought-after because the holder spent all their time on union matters, and therefore played no part in the editorial work of the paper. It also meant power, because you became part of the management group and took part in some sections of committee meetings as the staff representative.

Just let it be someone with a brain, Schyman thought, and made up his mind to go and get that cup of coffee after all.

Annika thought people were looking at her rather oddly as she walked through the newsroom with her newly purchased bag over her shoulder. Naturally, her colleagues loved gossip, it went with the job, and she realized that her burned-down house must have been yesterday's hot topic.

She hoisted the bag higher on her shoulder and quickened her pace. First she had to get the requisition note to pick up the new laptop from Technical Support, then try to track down her old notes and put together a piece about Julia Lindholm.

But before any of that she needed coffee.

She dropped her bag and her new jacket at the long desk shared by the day-shift reporters and went off to the machine.

She found Anders Schyman staring short-sightedly at all the options. 'Strong with sugar but no milk. How do you get that?' he asked. Annika swiftly pressed a few buttons.

'The laptop,' she said. 'Can I get it now?'

'The requisition's ready and waiting on my desk,' he said. 'Is there anything else you need?'

She paused. 'If I could borrow one of the paper's cars for the weekend . . .'

'That'll probably be okay,' Anders Schyman said, and started to walk towards his office. 'By the way, do you know what the CJ is?'

'The Chancellor of Justice?' Annika said. 'A dinosaur. Why?'

He stopped. 'A dinosaur?'

'Or some other prehistoric relic,' Annika said. 'It's completely absurd that a post like that is still bestowed for life because that was what happened in the 1700s. Everyone in Sweden has the right to change their lawyer, apart from the government. It's completely ridiculous.'

'Can't the CJ be dismissed?' Schyman said.

'Nope.'

'Follow me, and I'll give you the requisition note.'

She trudged after him to his office. The room wasn't actually that small, but Schyman was so expansive that it shrank when he went in. 'Here you are,' he said, handing her the sheet of paper. 'Have they found whoever set fire to your house yet?'

She shook her head and swallowed.

Hopkins, the miserable old bastard. May he burn in Hell.

Schyman hunted through a desk drawer and pulled out another requisition request, which he signed with a scribble. 'You can have the car for a week,' he said. 'If Tore makes a fuss, refer him to me.'

She put the piece of paper into her bag and went to see the caretaker. She could feel people's eyes on her as she crossed the newsroom.

She had to wait for five minutes as Tore concluded an important telephone conversation about racing tips. 'You can have this one,' he said, putting a battered laptop on the counter when she had explained why she was there.

'Does it work?'

Tore looked affronted. 'Of course it bloody works. I checked it over.'

'Hmm,' Annika said, switching it on.

The programs loaded. Explorer logged in automatically to the paper's wireless network. MS Word turned out to be full of Sjölander's old articles.

She sighed quietly. 'Great,' she said. 'And a car as well, please . . .' She handed over the requisition note with Schyman's signature.

Tore looked sceptically at the sheet of paper. 'And what do you need a Volvo V70 for?'

'I'm thinking of robbing a bank, and I need a discreet getaway car,' Annika said.

'Sounds fun,' Tore said, handing her the keys. 'It's got a full tank. Make sure it's full when it comes back.'

She went back to the newsroom and set up the laptop on the reporters' desk. She began by reading everything she could find about the police murder from the main news agency and in the *Evening Post*'s internal files.

111

'Annika,' Spike said, putting his hand on her shoulder. 'How do you feel about writing a true story? "How I Escaped the Flames"?'

She looked up. A troop of people had gathered around her.

'Is it true they know who started the fire?' wondered crime reporter Patrik Nilsson, currently the only reporter on the paper with that title apart from Berit.

'I need you to fill in a report about the loss of your old laptop as soon as possible,' said Eva-Britt Qvist, the editorial secretary, who had been promoted to paper-shuffler in Admin. She looked almost happy for the first time ever.

Even the girl with the piercings, who ran the commercial radio station with all the adverts, had left her nest in Annika's old office and come out to stare. 'I mean, like, what the fuck?' she said. 'Like, poor you.'

'Okay,' Annika said, rolling her chair back to the edge of the table. 'I'm fine, everything's fine. Thanks for your concern, but I'm kind of busy . . .'

Nobody moved.

'Must be really fucking awful for you,' said the girl with the piercings.

'Go and get on with your work,' Spike said, rather loudly, and they began to move away, muttering in disappointment.

'I want the loss report by Monday at the latest, otherwise you'll be liable for it,' Eva-Britt Qvist said, over her shoulder.

Spike turned back to Annika. 'We haven't put anything in the paper, but if you feel like writing an eyewitness account, we've got a gap on eleven.'

Annika cleared her throat. 'Thanks, but no thanks,' she said. 'Schyman's asked me to write about Julia Lindholm.'

'That's great,' Spike said. '"Exclusive: Cop-killer's Secret History".'

'Mm,' Annika said. 'She hasn't been found guilty yet, of course.'

'That's just a technicality,' Spike said, and went back to his desk.

She left the news pages and logged into her personal email archive. Slowly she began to click open notes and documents from several years before. Some were so old that she had almost forgotten them.

All of a sudden it hit her: *This is all I've got left. Everything else went up in flames. What a relief that I thought to keep my archive on the Internet . . .*

She pushed her hair from her face and carried on clicking. It had to be here somewhere. Finally she found the document, and glanced through the single page.

Nina Hoffman and Julia Lindholm had grown up in the Södermanland countryside, had been in the same class since their third year at school, and were both good at athletics, one or the other winning the regional championships over several consecutive years. They had joined the youth wing of the Social Democratic Party in Katrineholm when they were fifteen, and had studied social sciences at Duveholm School, just as Annika had done. If they had been just a year or two older, maybe she would have remembered them, but four years made a big difference at that age. After high school, Nina had travelled in Asia for six months while Julia had worked as a teaching assistant at Stenhammar Middle School in Flen. When Nina had returned to Sweden they had applied to the Police Academy, and had been accepted at once. By the time Annika had spent a night with them, they had served about five years as neighbourhood police officers in the Katarina district of Stockholm.

113

Both girls had agreed that they were fed up with the macho atmosphere in the police station. You could never show any sign of weakness, because then you were finished.

Pretty much like the Evening Post.

Annika logged out of her archive and began reading the articles about David Lindholm in the *Evening Post* and elsewhere. The obituaries were uncritical in their praise and admiration, precisely as the situation demanded. She made a note of a couple of officers who had commented on the dead man: Christer Bure of Södermalm Police, and Professor Lagerbäck at the Police Academy. They described David Lindholm in terms that suggested he was Christ reincarnated.

She looked through the great work the officer had done for society. Naturally, there was the famous hostage drama in Malmö, with the pictures of David and the hostage-taker emerging from the nursery arm in arm. Then there was the security van: he had single-handedly cleared up a major robbery in which two guards were shot and wounded, and reclaimed the stolen money.

This wasn't the whole picture of David Lindholm, she knew. The hero who had solved these spectacular crimes had been murdered in his bed, shot by his wife.

There's another truth. She must have had a reason.

She closed the battered laptop and went over to Patrik Nilsson. His nose was almost pressed to his screen, and he was reading intently.

'Have you ever thought about glasses?' Annika asked, as she sat down on Berit's seat.

'National Crime have been searching a farm in Södermanland, trying to find the boy,' Patrik said, still concentrating on the screen. 'There are signs that he may have spent time at the location during the past week.'

'I hope you're not thinking of writing that,' Annika said.

Now he looked at her in surprise. 'Of course I am,' he said.

'"May have spent time at the location" is police-speak,' Annika said. 'Anyone normal would say "may have been there". What makes them think that?'

Patrik read on. 'They've found evidence to support the idea,' he said. 'Doesn't say what. I'll have to check my source.'

'Something that suggests a child has been there,' Annika said slowly. 'The floor covered with Disney comics? Half-eaten lollies in the bin? A plastic bath on the kitchen table full of lukewarm water, bubbles and rubber ducks?'

Patrik was chewing a biro. 'Or footprints of exactly the right size in the sandpit,' he said.

'I'm guessing the bin,' Annika said. 'If anyone ever throws anything in a bin, you can tell pretty much exactly when they were there.'

'How do you mean?' Patrik said.

'Date stamps,' Annika said. 'Every family with children buys and drinks milk. All milk cartons have a best-before date.'

'But the bins are always being emptied,' her colleague said.

'Not that often,' Annika said. 'Katrineholm Council does fortnightly collections. Or you can request collections only during the summer, although the bin-men are so nice they usually empty them anyway.'

Patrik raised an eyebrow.

'I used to be a local reporter for the *Katrineholm*

Courier,' Annika said. 'I've written thousands of articles about rubbish collections from the farms between Floda and Granhed.'

Her colleague leaned back in his chair and folded his arms. 'How do you know where the cop-killer's summer place is?'

'Nina told me,' Annika said, getting up. 'I don't know exactly which house it is, but I have a rough idea. It's outside Floda, on a road called Stöttastenvägen.'

'There's nothing in the property register.'

'Yes, there is, just not under her name. I think she rented it. Have the police released anything about the murder weapon?'

Patrik shook his head, eyes on the screen again.

'Anything about when Alexander was last seen alive?' Annika asked.

'What do you mean?'

'Has anything got out about David? Have you heard any gossip about him?'

'What are you after?' Patrik asked suspiciously.

'Have we done all the usual checks on him? Money, businesses, property, cars, TV licence, tax?'

'No, but—'

'You never know,' Annika said. 'It might give us an idea of what he was like without his halo, some kind of lead or explanation for what made his wife flip out like that . . .'

'You won't find that sort of thing in the archive,' Patrik said, and returned to the screen.

Suddenly something clicked inside Annika's head.

'The Personnel Committee of the National Police Board,' she said. 'Has anyone checked there?'

Patrik pulled a face.

'To see if there were any complaints about him?'

'As if they'd be public!' he scoffed.

'You can check everything they do,' Annika said. 'You just have to go in, ask the clerk and they give you the information.'

'They always hush up that sort of thing,' Patrik said.

Annika opened up her laptop, then did a search for 'Lindholm, David, Stockholm' on the National Registry. She made a note of his date of birth and ID number, then slung her bag over her shoulder and walked out.

The entrance to the National Police Board was via the main doors of Police Headquarters on Polhemsgatan, the part of the complex that had been built in the 1970s, its façade covered with brown panelling. The taxi dropped her off beside a cluttered motorcycle park. She zigzagged her way towards the doors and went into Reception.

'I need to check some information with the personnel office,' she said, without introducing herself or showing any ID: she was there to look at public documents in her capacity as an interested citizen.

'Have you made an appointment?' the receptionist asked, a young man with a heavy fringe and thick-framed glasses.

Annika shifted her weight to the other foot. 'I don't need one,' she said. 'I'd like to check possible complaints.'

The receptionist sighed and picked up the phone. He turned away and muttered something into the receiver. 'He's coming,' he said, then went back to his Sudoku.

Annika looked out through the doors and up towards the park.

'How can I help you?'

An older, bearded man in a cardigan was blinking amiably at her. Annika was at a loss for words, then remembered why she was there. 'I'd like to know if a

117

particular police officer has ever been prosecuted for criminal activity,' she said.

'Is there reason to believe that he or she might have been?'

'Isn't there always?' she said.

'This way,' the man said. He led her through a glass door and into a lift, then pressed the button for the eleventh floor. 'You've got the ID number of the person in question?' the man asked, and Annika nodded.

The lift came to a halt with a little sigh, and Annika's stomach lurched. She followed the man through the police complex, along winding corridors, until finally they reached a cramped little room with a contrastingly stunning view of the park.

She held out her notepad with David's date of birth and ID number and the man typed the details into the computer.

'Do you hold all the records of police officers who have been charged with offences?' she asked, as the hard disk chewed its way through its files.

'Not all of them,' the clerk said. 'Only from 1987 onwards. The older records are kept by the County Administrative Board.' He looked up at her. 'Which of the reports did you want to look at?'

Which of the reports?

Her heart skipped a beat. 'There's more than one?'

The man peered at the screen. 'Two.'

'Both.'

'I need to check that they're not confidential. Could you come back on Monday?'

Annika leaned across the man's desk to squint at his screen. It was angled in such a way that she couldn't see anything. 'Couldn't you check now?' she asked. 'Please?'

118

The man looked more closely at the screen. 'Interesting cases,' he said. 'They were a long while ago, but the subject has, of course, become very interesting now, through no fault of his own.' He smiled and glanced over his shoulder. 'Our lawyer is here today, and the files are in the archive. I'll fetch them and see if we can't get them checked at once.'

He disappeared back into the labyrinth of corridors.

Annika resisted the urge to go round his desk and sneak a look at the screen. Instead she went to stand by the window, looking out over Kronoberg Park. Their old flat was on Hantverkargatan, just two blocks from here. Once she had passed this building every day with Kalle and Ellen, in rain and sun and snow. She had struggled up the slopes to take the children to the playground by the fire station and always ended up on a hard park bench surrounded by café-latte mothers trying loudly to outdo each other with their tales of troublesome building work and trips to France.

She let her thoughts wander. If she was honest, she hadn't been particularly happy in the city either, but at least the neighbours had never tried to burn her house down.

'That didn't take too long.' The clerk had reappeared and was unbuttoning his cardigan. 'There's nothing confidential in these reports. Here you are.' He handed them to her.

She glanced through the main points and felt a surge of adrenalin. 'Thanks very much indeed!' she said, and hurried off towards the lifts.

Pp. 6–7

Evening Post – Stockholm Edition

Saturday, 5 June

POLICE SEARCH FOR ALEXANDER

- Search expanded
- Army called in
- Forest searched last night

By Patrik Nilsson

Evening Post (Södermanland). Efforts to find the missing four-year-old, Alexander Lindholm, are getting increasingly desperate.

'We're close to a breakthrough,' a police source said.

It's now a matter of hours rather than days.

The missing little boy has to be found on Saturday, or hope of finding him alive will start to fade.

In the middle of idyllic countryside, near a cottage called Björkbacken in the depths of the Södermanland forests, an intensive search is currently under way to locate Alexander. The trees whisper quietly, and only the cries of the search teams disturb the peace.

The police have confirmed that the boy has been here, close to the summer cottage used by Julia Lindholm, who is currently in custody, within the past few days.

'This is probably based upon material gathered from bins,' a well-placed source has told the *Evening Post*. 'Milk cartons are always a valuable source of information in this sort of search, because all families with young children buy milk. Using the sell-by and best-before dates on the packaging, the police will have been able to confirm that the child was at this location. The bins are emptied fortnightly in the

120

forests around Katrineholm, which will have made the work of the police easier.'

The police are also believed to have found small footprints in the mud outside the house, which means that a child has been at the cottage since the last downpour on Tuesday.

Officers in Södermanland have expanded the search to the surrounding district. A helicopter equipped with a heat-seeking camera joined the search yesterday.

'That will only work if the boy is still alive,' a source in the investigation said. 'If he's dead, his body would be the same temperature as the surroundings.'

Do you believe he is still alive?

'The fact that we're using an infra-red camera indicates that we believe he is alive, and simply missing.'

As of today, Saturday, the military will also be joining the search. Conscripts from the P4 Skaraborg Regiment in Skövde will be taking part.

There have been indications from the National Crime Unit that the evidence implicating Julia Lindholm is mounting. It is believed that she will be formally charged shortly. The hearing could take place this weekend, or on Monday at the latest.

Police analysis suggests that they are close to a break-through in the case.

'Naturally, we are still hoping to find the boy alive.'

Any information regarding the disappearance of four-year-old Alexander Lindholm should be given to the National Crime Unit in Stockholm, or your nearest police station.

Saturday, 5 June

10

Nina was walking through the long glass corridor that constituted the official entrance to Police Headquarters on Kungsholmen. Even though she had been working for Stockholm Police for almost a decade, she had hardly ever used this entrance. The glass walls and the sloping glass roof made her feel both enclosed and exposed, and oddly guilty.

She quickened her pace.

The man in Reception made her wait almost a whole minute before deigning to notice her. She was dressed in plain clothes and realized he had taken her for an ordinary troublesome member of the public. 'I'm here to see Julia Lindholm,' she said, holding out her police badge.

The man's eyes narrowed and his mouth set hard. There may have been 301 people in custody, but he knew exactly who Julia was. 'Lindholm's in isolation,' he said. 'There's no question of her receiving any visitors.'

Nina raised her chin slightly and made sure her gaze was firm when she replied: 'Obviously this isn't an ordinary visit, it's an informal interview. I was assuming it had been sanctioned.'

He looked at her sceptically, took her police badge and disappeared into an office.

She waited at the counter for ten long minutes.

I'm going. I can't be bothered with this. Julia, I can't help you . . .

'Nina Hoffman?' A female guard had appeared at the door that led further into the complex. 'I must ask you to put all items like outdoor clothing and your mobile phone in a locker before I can let you enter the prison. This way.'

Nina put her pashmina, jacket and handbag in a locker to the left of Reception. She was given a badge that had to be visible at all times while she was in the prison, then was let through the gates.

She followed the guard down a corridor that ended in a lobby in front of some lifts, painted a gaudy blue. 'Aren't we going to one of the visitors' rooms?'

'My orders are to take you to Julia Lindholm's cell in the women's section,' the guard said, rattling a ring of keys at the end of a long chain.

Nina didn't reply. She had never been inside Kronoberg Prison before.

They got into the lift and the guard pressed a button. There was a short pause before the machinery began to work, and Nina glanced up at one of the cameras.

'The lifts are kept under surveillance,' the guard said. 'All movement through the building, up or down, is controlled remotely.'

They stopped at the third floor. Nina made to leave the lift but the guard held her back. 'This is where police jurisdiction ends,' she said. 'We need further authorization before we can go up into the actual prison.'

A few seconds later the lift juddered into action again.

They got out on the sixth floor and went through three locked doors before reaching one of the secure units.

'If you wait here for a moment, the food trolley can get past,' the guard said.

Nina looked down a long corridor, its grey linoleum running the length of the building and ending at a barred window. The sunlight outside and the neon tubes on the ceiling cast reflections on the floor. Green metal doors lined the walls, each with a small sign giving information about the cell's occupant, restrictions, case number. Each door had a hatch so that the staff could look in, and substantial locks. She heard someone cough behind the nearest.

'Are you full?' Nina asked.

'Are you kidding?' the guard said.

Two men lumbered past them with a trolley full of trays.

The guard walked to the end of the corridor and unlocked one of the green doors with her jangling keys. 'Julia Lindholm,' she said. 'You've got a visitor.'

Nina took a deep breath before walking into the cell. Her mouth had dried. The walls closed in on her.

This isn't remotely humane! How can they treat you like this?

Julia was sitting on a desk that was fixed to the wall, looking out of the small window at the sky. She was wearing regulation green and grey prison clothing, clutching her knees and rocking back and forth. Her toes were moving frenetically inside thick socks. Her hair was tied in a blonde knot on top of her head. She didn't seem to notice that someone had come into the cell.

'Julia,' Nina said quietly, so as not to startle her. 'Julia, it's me.'

The cell door closed behind Nina. There was no handle on the inside.

At first Julia didn't react, just carried on staring out of the window.

Nina looked around the cell. The pine desk was connected to a bed that was also fixed to the wall. The wood was yellow from old varnish and covered with cigarette burns. There was a chair, two small shelves and a metal washbasin. The room smelt of stale smoke.

'Julia,' she repeated, taking two steps to the desk and carefully putting a hand on her friend's shoulder. 'Julia, how are you?'

Julia turned to Nina and her face lit up in a smile. 'Nina,' she said, wrapping her arms round Nina's neck, hugging her as she rocked. 'How sweet of you to visit me! What are you doing here?'

Nina disentangled herself and looked at her intently. Julia's eyes were bloodshot and the rash on her cheeks was worse, but she seemed alert. 'I wanted to see how you are,' Nina said. 'How are you feeling?'

Julia shrugged and jumped down from the desk. She went over to the door and felt it with the palms of her hands.

'What are you doing?'

Julia went back to the desk, sat down, then stood up again and went to sit on the bed.

'Julia,' Nina said. 'I heard you resigned. Why?'

Julia looked up at her in surprise, then started biting one of her thumbnails. 'I need to buy washing-up liquid,' she said. 'I've run out of powder. I've got those little cubes, but they never dissolve properly . . .'

Nina's throat tightened.

'How are you feeling?' she asked again. 'Is there anything I can help you with?'

Julia got up and went to the door again, running her hands aimlessly over the green metal. 'Nina,' she said, sounding suddenly scared. 'Do you really think we ought to apply to the Police Academy? Wouldn't it be better to go into social work?'

Something's seriously wrong here.

'What are you talking about?'

Julia got up from the bed and stamped her feet impatiently, her gaze meandering out of the window to dart restlessly over the brown wall on the far side of the inner courtyard. 'David hasn't come home yet,' she said. 'He was supposed to pick up Alexander on the way, and the nursery's been closed for several hours now.' She looked at Nina hopefully. 'Has he called you?'

Nina opened her mouth but couldn't reply. Tears choked her. Eventually she controlled herself. 'Come and sit down with me,' she said, taking Julia's hand. 'Come on, we'll just have a little talk . . .'

She sat Julia in front of her on the bunk and put her hands on Julia's cheeks, looking her in the eyes. 'Julia,' she whispered, 'where's Alexander?'

Confusion flickered in Julia's eyes for several long moments.

'Don't you remember what happened to David?' Nina said. 'In your bedroom? Do you remember the shot?'

Julia's eyes darkened. She seemed to be looking at something just above Nina's head. She gasped and her face contorted. 'Get her out of here,' she whispered.

'Who?'

'The other one. She's evil.'

Nina turned and looked at the wall. A previous prisoner had carved her initials into it. 'Do you mean the other woman? The one who took Alexander?'

Julia's body jerked and she struggled to free herself, her forearm hitting Nina's nose. Without a word she staggered to the door and banged on it, first with her

129

fists, and then with her head. A whimpering sound was coming from deep in her throat.

Oh, no, what have I done?

With two long strides Nina was at the door, taking a firm grip on Julia from behind to calm her down, but her embrace had the opposite effect. Julia started screaming, an angry howl that was only muffled when she tried to bite Nina.

'Julia, I'm going to lay you on the bunk, on your side,' Nina said, twisting her friend's arms up behind her back, then pushing her down with her head on the pillow.

The hatch opened and the female guard looked into the cell.

'She needs a tranquillizer,' Nina said.

Julia was crying hysterically, her whole body shaking. Nina kept a firm grip of her, trying to calm her with the weight and warmth of her body.

A moment later, the guard called, 'The medics are on their way.'

Slowly the convulsions ebbed and Julia lay still. The screams turned into a wailing sob. Eventually she fell silent, panting for breath. 'It was my fault,' she whispered. 'It was my fault.'

Nina called Detective Inspector Q the moment she emerged into the glass corridor outside Reception. 'You can't keep her locked up like that, not in a prison cell,' she said abruptly, when he answered. 'She's verging on psychotic and needs proper psychiatric care.'

'What makes you think that?'

'She's seeing things – obviously suffering from delusions.' Nina was walking quickly towards the exit, eager to escape the unpleasant glass tunnel.

'So our informal interviewer's been transformed into a psychiatric expert? Did you get anything out of her?'

Nina pushed the door open and stepped out into the gale on the street. 'She talked incoherently about irrelevant things – said she'd forgotten to buy washing-up liquid, that she wasn't sure about applying to the Police Academy. She seemed confused about time and space, and isn't aware of what's happened. She asked where David had gone with Alexander.'

'Did she mention the other woman?'

'She said she was evil and asked me to get rid of her. I think Julia should be sent for paragraph-seven investigation – immediately.'

'So she didn't say anything about whether or not she was guilty?'

Nina breathed in and out twice. 'Maybe I haven't made myself clear. Julia was so confused that she didn't know where she was. When I tried to ask about the murder she became extremely agitated. A medic had to come and give her a tranquillizer. She's sleeping now.'

Detective Inspector Q sighed loudly. 'Well, I suppose it's progress,' he said. 'She hasn't spoken to us at all.'

'Nothing?'

'Not a sound.'

Nina stopped and looked up at the façade of Police Headquarters, trying to imagine the caged walkways on the roof where the prisoners got their fresh air for an hour each day.

'So you were aware of how disturbed she is,' she said, 'but you didn't tell me before you asked me to question her?'

'Hey, now,' Q said, 'she was just refusing to talk. That's hardly unusual.'

'If you want to have anything like a sensible interview

131

with Julia, she has to get some sort of treatment first,' Nina said. 'I don't know the details, but people experience traumatic events every day and get psychiatric treatment.'

'In an ideal world,' Q said. 'That's going to be difficult in this case.'

She started walking towards the Underground. 'Why wouldn't the health service have the resources to deal with this case?'

'I'm not talking about the health service, but whether there's any desire to do it. Let me put it like this: there's a certain resistance in the force to treating David's murderer with kid gloves.'

Nina stopped mid-stride. 'Kid gloves?'

'If everything goes according to plan, Julia will be charged on Monday. Naturally, that's just a formality, but I'd like you to be there. It's possible there'll be questions about her arrest that the court will need to clear up.'

Two teenage boys walked past Nina, giggling, but she didn't bother to lower her voice: 'Let's get one thing absolutely clear,' she said. 'I did this for Julia's sake, not yours. I've no intention of getting involved.'

'Right now, this is about finding the boy.'

She rocked back and forth on the balls of her feet. 'You haven't got an easy job,' she said. 'Either you keep our colleagues happy or you solve these crimes. Good luck.'

She ended the call and went down into the Underground station on shaky legs.

Only when she was standing on the escalator did she realize what she'd said.

Crimes, plural.

I'm assuming that you killed Alexander as well.

She hurried towards the platform.

The children were parked in Berit's living room, watching a Moomin cartoon on television. Annika put the breakfast things in the dishwasher, wiped the kitchen table and worktop, then took the copies of the misconduct reports against David Lindholm from her bag. She sat down beside the drop-leaf table and let her eyes wander out of the window towards the lake.

People treated each other so atrociously. Was there any hope for humanity, with so much evil everywhere?

She could hear Little My shouting something at Moominmamma and put her hands over her ears.

Berit had gone shopping for dinner ages ago.

Why do I get so upset at being on my own? Why am I so restless?

She grabbed the photocopies from the Police Board's personnel committee and read through the reports again.

The first case concerned a young man called Tony Berglund. The complaint had been made by a doctor in A&E at Södermalm Hospital. The file describing the man's injuries was three pages long and extremely detailed. In the doctor's opinion, the injuries had been inflicted during a prolonged and vicious attack, leaving him with four fractures and extensive internal bleeding. The victim had said in the ambulance that 'a cop' had kicked him. In A&E he had described the policeman as well built, blond, with a prominent brow.

The description fitted David Lindholm very well.

Every time he was questioned, Tony Berglund stuck to exactly the same version of events on Luntmakargatan. He and two friends had been on their way to see a girl over on Frejgatan, up by St Stefan's Church, when five youths wearing caps had jumped them at the corner of

133

Rehnsgatan. Mostly it was just shouting and pushing, there hadn't been any real violence. After a while, the rapid-response team of the Norrmalm Police had arrived, tyres screeching, from the direction of Norra Real School. Four cops had leaped out, and the big blond one had led the charge.

'Are you Tony?' he had asked, and when Tony said, 'What the fuck's it got to do with you?' the attack had begun. Tony Berglund couldn't say how long it had gone on: he had lost consciousness when his cheekbone was fractured, and he hadn't woken up until he was in the ambulance. The description of the police officer had been made in writing because Tony's jaw was immobile. The crumpled note was among the documentation.

The lad had changed his story during the trial.

Most peculiar.

David himself had claimed that by the time the police arrived a fight was already in progress, and that they had probably saved Tony Berglund's life with their rapid intervention. The two friends who had been with Tony had been chased off by a couple of other officers, and were unable to support any of his statement. The other officers on the unit had corroborated David's version of events.

Further information revealed that Tony Berglund had a criminal background. Foster-homes, remand school, probation for minor drugs charges.

Annika sighed. *Poor sod.*

She put Tony Berglund's case notes down and moved on to the second report.

A man named Timmo Koivisto (*Was his name really Timmo? Apparently so*) had been on his way to a minor amphetamine deal in Ropsten. He had gone for a piss in Central Station, but when he was in the Gents the door had been yanked open and a large, blond man in a police uniform had come in. At first Timmo had thought it was someone dressed up as a policeman, then the man had grabbed him by the ears and asked, 'Are you Timmo?' He had got scared and tried to twist free but the man had started banging his head against the tiles on the toilet wall, and he couldn't remember anything after that.

The ambulance had been called by David Lindholm, who said he had found a seriously injured man lying unconscious in the toilet, and that he had probably saved his life with his rapid intervention.

Timmo Koivisto stuck to his story right until the case went to court, when he had suddenly changed his mind.

Timmo Koivisto's background details revealed him to be one of society's more unfortunate children, with a similar history to Tony Berglund. Three short prison sentences for drug-dealing.

He's guilty. He did it. He beat these small-time crooks to within an inch of their lives, but why? On whose orders?

Annika got up and went over to Berit's electric coffee-machine. She could never work out how these things operated. At home she had always had a French cafetière, the sort where you poured in coffee and boiling water, then pressed down a filter and it was all done. Here you had to pour water into various containers, and fit paper filters into other bits, measure out the coffee and wait for what seemed like hours.

Instead she went to see the children in the living room. 'Hello,' she said. 'Is *Moomin* good?'

Ellen leaned to one side. 'Mummy, you're in the way.'

Annika went back into the kitchen. She ran her fingers

135

over the reports. Made a feeble attempt with the coffee-machine and gave up.

She wondered about getting her computer out, but didn't want to take over Berit's kitchen table with her stuff. Instead she called Directory Enquiries and asked for a Tony Berglund's number.

'Do you have the address?'

No, she didn't, of course.

'I've got sixty-three results in Stockholm and the northern district.'

'What about Timmo Koivisto?'

'In Norrtälje? The Vårtuna Home? He's the only one I've got in the whole country. It's a mobile number. Do you want me to connect you?'

Annika said yes and the call went straight to voicemail. The man had a strong Finnish accent, and explained in a rather long-winded way that this was Timmo and he'd call back as soon as he had time. He wished the peace of the Lord to everyone, and said that the love and forgiveness of Christ applied to everyone, no matter where on earth they were.

Then came the bleep and Annika hesitated.

'Er,' she said, 'yes, I'm calling from the *Evening Post*. My name's Annika Bengtzon. I was wondering if this was the Timmo Koivisto who had a rather unpleasant . . . encounter eighteen years ago with a police officer. His name is, or was, David Lindholm. If you *are* that Timmo, and *if* you feel like talking about what happened so long ago, please give me a call.' She gave her mobile number, then hung up.

She got up and looked out towards the road. Still no sign of Berit.

She went back to the kitchen table, picked up her mobile again and called Nina Hoffman.

She answered after four rings.

'Is this a bad time?' Annika asked.

'What do you want?' She sounded tired and sad.

'I've had a few thoughts about David,' Annika said. 'I understand that he was accused of physical abuse, and I know it was a long time ago, and that he was never found guilty, but I was wondering if you knew anything more about those cases.'

There was silence but for faint traffic noise, so she knew the line hadn't gone dead.

'How did you find that out?' Nina said eventually.

So she knows.

'Why do you ask? Is it strange that I should know about the complaints?'

More silence.

'I don't want to discuss this on the phone.'

Annika glanced towards the living room. She'd just have to take the children with her. 'I can come to the pizza place,' she said.

'No. Too many of my colleagues go there. Do you know where Nytorgsgatan is? There's a café on the corner with Bondegatan.'

11

Berit came into the kitchen and put three large bags from the ICA supermarket on the draining-board. 'It's going to rain this afternoon,' she said. 'The clouds are practically sitting on the tops of the trees.'

'Did you know that David Lindholm was accused of physical abuse?' Annika said. 'Not just once, but twice?'

Berit leaned against the worktop and thought for a moment. 'No. Was he found guilty?'

Annika stood up to help her empty the bags. 'Of course not. The first incident was twenty years ago, when he was with the rapid-response unit in Norrmalm. He worked with a Christer Bure, who seems to have been one of his big buddies.'

She opened the fridge and put in the milk, with a packet of chicken drumsticks.

'According to the prosecution, David Lindholm kicked and broke the cheekbone of a young lad who was arrested during a street brawl. The lad changed his mind in court and said he'd only made the complaint against David to cause trouble for the police, and that one of the gang they were fighting must have kicked him, he just didn't see which one.'

'That could well be true,' Berit said.

'Of course,' Annika said. 'In the other case, David was said to have attacked a drug dealer in a toilet at Central Station, banging his head against the wall so hard that he ended up with serious concussion. He was left with permanent injuries, including double vision and impaired hearing in his left ear.'

'Which could have been the result of serious drug use?'

'Sure. The weird thing is that the same thing happened as before: the lad changed his mind when the case got to court. Said another junkie beat him up, and that he tried to blame David to cause trouble for the police.'

'What did David say?'

'Exactly what the victims ended up saying in court: that they were attacked by other criminals and blamed the police to damage the force.'

'So David was cleared?'

'The cases were dropped. Even if he'd been found guilty he'd have been allowed to keep his job. The personnel committee had already decided that.'

Berit nodded thoughtfully. 'He was evidently a controversial but popular officer right from the start,' she said. 'How long ago was the most recent complaint?'

'Eighteen years ago.'

'So he'd kept his nose clean since then?'

Annika was folding up the bags. 'Well, he was never charged. Where do you keep these?'

Berit pointed at the bottom kitchen drawer. 'Have you seen the papers? We're running your piece on Julia on page twelve. It's very good.' She handed both tabloids to Annika, who sat down at the kitchen table with them in front of her. Both the *Evening Post* and the competition had exactly the same picture and headline on the front page: 'WHERE IS 4-YEAR-OLD ALEXANDER?'

The photograph showed a small boy, smiling uncertainly at the camera. The classic marbled background indicated that it had been taken at nursery. So that was how he had turned out, the little boy who was born six months after Ellen. He had untidy blond hair, finely chiselled features, and was almost girlishly pretty. A shirt-collar could just be seen at the bottom of the picture, presumably a gesture in honour of the occasion. The picture unsettled her. He looked so defenceless, so vulnerable, and the headline seemed to imply that he was already dead.

What if Ellen or Kalle was missing?

She shuddered and opened the paper. Berit put on her reading glasses and sat down next to her.

They read in silence for a while. *Moomin* had been replaced by *Pingu*, and the jaunty theme tune found its way into the kitchen. The wind whistled through a gap under one window.

'I don't understand this,' Berit said. 'Where could the boy have got to? If the mother hasn't hidden him, she must have killed him, but when could she have done that?'

Annika opened the other evening paper and turned to pages six and seven, which always carried the heaviest news. Both pages were covered with a photograph, stretching across ten columns, of a forest clearing with a little red cottage in the middle, white eaves and a water-pump at the front. It was an atmospheric picture, the light filtering through the treetops on to the white shutters beside the windows, and the blue and white tape of the police cordon.

'POLICE SEARCH FOR ALEXANDER, 4,' Annika read. 'They've got exactly the same angle as us,' she said.

Berit sighed. 'I still don't see how it all fits together. If the mother took him to their summer cottage and killed him there, did she go straight home afterwards? Or did she wait a day or two? And didn't the father think it was odd that she came home without the boy?'

'Maybe she lied about where he was,' Annika suggested, 'said he was staying with a friend, or with Grandma and Grandpa.'

Berit read on for a while. 'But why go to such trouble hiding him? She wasn't remotely bothered about trying to hide the murder of her husband.'

'Maybe she's sent him away,' Annika said, 'abroad, to distant relatives or something.'

Berit shook her head. 'What sort of mother would do something like this?'

'Or what sort of person?' Annika said.

'Maybe something went wrong when she shot the father,' Berit reasoned. 'Maybe she'd planned to kill him and hide his body as well. Is that your phone ringing?'

Annika sat up straight and listened. Yes, it was her mobile. She ran to the dresser by the door and looked warily at the screen as the ringing continued.

'Aren't you going to answer it?' Berit asked, turning a page of the paper.

Annika put the phone down on the dresser where it bounced and vibrated against the wood. 'It's Anne Snapphane. I have absolutely no desire to talk to her.'

'Oh,' Berit said. 'I thought you were friends.'

'So did I,' Annika said. The telephone fell silent, only to start jumping and ringing again a moment later. Annika groaned and picked it up again. 'Jesus,' she said. 'It's my mother. I have to take this.' She went outside and stood on Berit's porch.

'Annika?' her mother said, in an agitated voice. 'Annika, is that you?'

141

She sank on to a step, letting the wind tug at her clothes. 'Yes, Mum. How are you?'

'Has your house *burned down*?'

Annika shut her eyes and put a hand over them. 'Yes, Mum, our house has burned down. There's nothing left.'

'Buy why haven't you called and *said* something? Well? I found out in the shop, from someone I work with – what on earth were you thinking?'

Annika sighed quietly. 'Well . . .' she said.

'Do I really have to hear news like that as gossip? *About my own child?* Do you have any idea how that made me look?'

Annika couldn't suppress a laugh. 'So *I*'m supposed to feel sorry for *you*?'

'Don't be so nasty,' her mother said. 'Can't you see how insulting it is to have that sort of thing thrown in your face? As if I don't know what's happening to my own child?'

'Well, you don't, do you?'

'I still think—'

'Now that you've got me on the phone, you can ask me how we are,' Annika said, and got to her feet. 'You can also ask what really happened. Maybe you'd even like to volunteer to help somehow, with a place to stay, or by looking after the children, money maybe . . .'

Now it was her mother's turn to laugh. 'You want money from me when I might have to take early retirement on grounds of illness? Social Security are looking into it. I have to go to the Mälar Valley Hospital once a week nowadays, but I don't suppose that's important to someone living in Stockholm.'

'Goodbye, Mum.' She ended the call, and in the silence that followed she could hear her heart racing.

Berit came out on to the porch with a mug in each hand. 'Coffee?'

Annika took it gratefully. 'Can you trade in your parents?' she asked.

Berit smiled. 'Don't be so hard on her. She's doing her best.'

Annika sat down on the step again. 'She only ever thinks of herself. It doesn't matter what happens to me, she's always the interesting one.'

'She's a small person with a narrow frame of reference,' Berit said. 'She hasn't the capacity to see you for who you are, and isn't even aware of it.'

Tears welled in Annika's eyes. 'Why can't I have a mum like everyone else's, someone who supports and helps me, someone who cares?'

Berit sat down beside her. 'Not everyone has a mum like that,' she said. 'A lot of people have no mum at all. I think you have to realize that you can't change her. She's never going to be the sort of mum you'd like. You just have to accept her the way she is, just like she's going to have to accept you.'

They sat in silence for a while, looking out towards the forest. The wind had got up, and the firs were swaying. Annika looked at her watch. 'Is it okay if the children stay here with you while I head into the city for a bit? I'm meeting Nina Hoffman again.'

Berit nodded. 'I can't stop thinking about this business of the missing boy,' she said. 'The whole story really is very peculiar.'

'Anyone can go mad,' Annika said. 'When everything's going to Hell, human beings are capable of absolutely anything.'

Berit looked at her thoughtfully. 'I don't agree,' she said. 'Not everyone could kill their child. There has to be something missing for someone to do that, some sort of internal barrier that just isn't there.'

Annika looked at the shimmering grey water of the lake. 'I'm not so sure about that,' she said.

A moment later it started to rain.

Nina Hoffman was waiting for her at a messy table in the café on Nytorgsgatan. She didn't notice that Annika had arrived because she was sitting with her back to the door, staring blankly out of the misted-up window. Her hair was tied up in a ponytail and she was wearing a grey padded jacket. The light fell across her profile, giving nothing away. She was resting her chin on one hand and seemed to be miles away.

Annika went round the table. 'Hello,' she said.

Nina stood up and they shook hands.

Annika went over to the counter. 'One coffee, black.'

She returned to the table. The café was starting to fill with lunchtime diners. Their wet jackets exuded the smell of damp wool.

'There was something you were wondering about?' Nina said. 'Something about the allegations against David?'

No small-talk, then.

Annika lifted her bag on to her lap and hunted through it, finding a bag of sweets and the folder of documents from the National Police Board's personnel committee. 'So you know what David was accused of?' she said, putting the sweets back in the bag.

Nina Hoffman's eyes flashed. 'How did you find out?'

Annika put her hands on the tabletop. 'I checked at the NPB,' she said. 'Why do you sound so surprised?'

Nina looked out of the window again. 'I didn't know...'

She was silent for a long while. Annika waited. A

144

woman with a pushchair forced her way past them to the next table, but Nina didn't react. Eventually she turned towards Annika, pulled in her chair and leaned towards her. She had dark circles under her eyes.

'I've never told anyone this,' she said, 'because I don't really know what it means. Can I trust you?'

'I won't write anything without your consent, you know that. You're my source, and your identity is protected under the constitution.'

'I got a bit confused when you called me because I thought those old complaints had been buried and forgotten.'

'How did *you* find out about them?'

Nina adjusted her ponytail. 'Julia showed me. The last time we met before the murder. She'd come across them in David's archive down in the cellar.'

Annika suppressed the instinct to reach for her pen and start taking notes. *I'll just have to try to remember.* 'Why did she show them to you?'

Nina hesitated again. 'I've always tried to support Julia, and it hasn't always been easy. But when it really mattered, she knew she could come to me. I thought she was on the verge of leaving him. She never said as much, but I just got the feeling . . .'

She moved even closer to the table and lowered her voice still further. 'Did you see any police on your way in here?'

Annika looked carefully at her. 'Should I have done?'

'I chose this place because none of my colleagues usually come here. David often treated Julia very badly, and the rest of the force are no better. The way they're treating her now is appalling. Regardless of what she may or may not have done, they've decided she's guilty. She's never going to get a fair trial.'

The espresso machine behind the counter hissed and whined, and Nina waited until it had stopped. 'You were right about him being a control freak. Julia always had to watch herself when David was listening. She could never be really honest then.'

'Did he hit her?' Annika asked.

Nina shook her head. 'Never. He wasn't that stupid. But he threatened her, even when I could hear. Said he'd make her life hell if she didn't go home at once, things like that. He could be very sweet and loving one minute, hugging and kissing her even in front of other people. The next minute he'd say such cruel, hurtful things that she was practically in tears. He would frighten her, then regret it and ask her forgiveness. Julia isn't a strong person. She could never stand up to anything like that. And it got even worse when she found out that he had been repeatedly unfaithful . . .'

The juicer started up noisily, and Annika shifted, irritated, when the woman with the pushchair wanted to take her child to the toilet. 'Repeatedly?' she said.

Nina waited until the mother had struggled past.

'I don't really know how to explain in a way you'll understand,' she said eventually. 'David was a notorious womanizer before he met Julia. They still talk about his escapades in the station – well, it's mainly Christer Bure and his crew who keep the stories alive. Mostly because it shows how popular they themselves were, once upon a time. But when Julia came into the picture all that stopped. At least, the public boasting about his conquests did, and the lads weren't particularly pleased about that.'

'They'd lost their iconic shagger,' Annika said.

'Outwardly, at any rate, but only for a while. He must have been having affairs the whole time, but Julia didn't

146

grasp it until several years later. One of the women called her at home and told her that *she* was the one he really loved, that Julia should understand that and set him free. That was just after Alexander was born.'

'Jesus,' Annika said.

'She found a letter to David containing an ultrasound picture of a foetus. "I've killed our daughter. Her name was Maja. Now it's your turn," it said in the accompanying letter. I thought that would shake her out of it.'

'What did she do?'

'I presume she tried to talk to David, but I don't know for sure. It wasn't so easy keeping in touch with her. David's career was always pretty unconventional. Sometimes he was posted abroad. Once they lived outside Málaga for six months.'

'Málaga?'

'In the south of Spain. The house was in Estepona, just east of Gibraltar. I went down to visit them. Julia looked like a ghost. She said she was fine, but I'm sure she was lying.'

A gang of teenage boys tumbled into the café, jostling and shouting. The café-latte mothers frowned.

'When Alexander arrived things got really bad,' Nina went on, ignoring the teenagers. 'He was born prematurely and Julia got post-natal depression, and it was like she never quite shook it off. When she came back to work she couldn't handle anything happening to children, abuse, traffic accidents, anything that hurt them. She was signed off sick with nervous exhaustion more than two years ago. She hasn't worked at all this past year.'

Annika tried furiously to structure the information she'd been given.

He'd tormented Julia until she'd become ill.

147

He was a notorious womanizer.

And where do the allegations of misconduct come into the picture?

'If I could just rewind a bit,' Annika said. 'Can you tell me a bit more about Julia? What happened to her when she met David?'

Nina cleared her throat. 'There was a small gang of us girls who stuck together after we'd graduated from the Police Academy, but Julia pulled away. She changed how she dressed, stopped wearing jeans. We were active in the Social Democratic Youth Movement, but suddenly she started voting for the Moderates. We had a discussion about it that ended with her in tears. To begin with it was just little things like that . . .'

Annika waited in silence. 'And it got worse after Alexander was born?' she asked, when Nina didn't go on.

'I knew something was wrong, but I didn't understand just how badly wrong until the last few weeks before the murder. David was incredibly jealous – I once heard him call her a whore and a slut. He must have locked her in the flat at least seven times. It was like she stopped counting. Once she was shut up for something like a week. Another time he threw her out into the stairwell without any clothes on. She got so cold she had to go to hospital. At A&E she said she'd got lost in the countryside.'

'And you heard about all this quite late?'

'Julia's been terribly fragile the past couple of years. She was taken in for psychiatric treatment on one occasion. She hasn't been in touch with me much, but I went to see her when I knew David was working or away travelling. It was on one of those visits that I found she was locked in. It was only then that I understood just how bad things were for her.'

'Why didn't she report him?'

Nina actually smiled slightly. 'You make it sound so simple. I wanted her to, of course, and offered to support her all the way. Maybe that was why she started going through his old files and found the allegations: she was getting ready to leave.'

'And what about the affairs? Did they ever stop?'

'No, quite the opposite. It got worse and worse. David evidently thought they were becoming a nuisance towards the end. He'd asked Julia to forgive him, said he was sorry, but he *would* say that sort of thing . . .'

'And what do you think about the allegations of abuse? Did he do it?'

Nina snorted. 'Well, what do you think?'

'It's strange that two insignificant small-time criminals had exactly the same thing happen to them with exactly the same result.'

Nina studied her in silence, so Annika went on: 'They were very badly beaten, and every time they were questioned they said David had done it, and they stuck to their stories right up to the trial, when they suddenly went into reverse. Their stories are also identical on several points – for instance, when David spoke to them and asked their names.'

Nina looked at the misted-up window. 'That struck me as well,' she said quietly. 'The chances of them both inventing the same lie strike me as fairly slim.'

Then she looked at Annika. 'You're not going to write about any of this, are you?'

Annika gazed at her weary face. 'Why did you tell me if you didn't want it to get out?'

'As far as I'm concerned, you can put it all over the front page, but it has to be Julia's decision. I don't know if she'd want it to come out, everything she had to put up with.' Nina got up and wrestled with her dark-green raincoat. 'You can use the information if you can get it confirmed elsewhere. But I'd still like you to tell me first.'

'Of course,' Annika said.

Nina Hoffman left the café without saying goodbye, and without looking back.

Annika was left sitting there with her cold coffee.

Nina hadn't liked David Lindholm. That much was crystal clear. If what she had said was true, then that was completely understandable. It must be awful to watch your best friend get drawn into a destructive relationship and be unable to do anything about it.

It must be terrible to have to sit on all that knowledge, then read acres of coverage on what a hero he was.

Annika gathered her things and went out to the car – she had parked it illegally on Bondegatan, but she hadn't got a ticket. Which was something.

She'd just started the engine when her mobile rang. She sighed, hesitated, then fished it out of her bag. She checked the display: it wasn't a number she recognized. She took the call anyway.

'Annika Bengtzon? It's Timmo. You tried to call me.'

Timmo? The man who was beaten up.

'Hello,' she said. 'Thanks for calling back. Would you like to meet up with me for a chat?'

'About David Lindholm? I'd be happy to. I owe that man everything.'

Sunday, 6 June

12

Nina let the patrol car roll slowly across the Djurgård Bridge. Andersson was sitting beside her, staring sullenly through the passenger window, his gaze sweeping over the crowd of drenched civilians on their way to the open-air museum at Skansen to celebrate National Day.

'None of these people really give a shit about Sweden,' he said. 'They're only going to try to get on telly and stare at the Royal Family.'

Nina clenched her teeth. *Patience, patience.*

The rain had been tipping down when she had gone to work, and had carried on all the way through her shift. Sometimes it had been raining so hard that she had had no visibility at all. The wind forced her to keep a firm grip on the steering-wheel.

He won't survive weather like this. If he's been outside since Thursday, he must be dead now.

Nina braked at the junction with Långa gatan. An elderly woman on a bike had been hit by a car; she was sitting on the edge of the pavement holding her left ankle. The driver was in his car, looking simultaneously embarrassed and annoyed. She opened the door but paused before she got out. 'I wasn't planning to get soaked on my own,' she said. 'You talk to the driver and I'll take the old dear.'

'God, I could do without a fucking awful day like this,' Andersson said, and climbed out into the torrential rain.

He had been in a dreadful mood ever since the handover meeting at six thirty that morning. There had been only six of them plus a senior officer; everyone else had been called in for Special Police Operations, as always on National Day, or the anniversary of the death of Charles XII and other loaded dates.

'So how did this happen, then?' Nina asked, as she squatted beside the woman, who was wearing a poncho with a hood made of some sort of waterproof material, but the rain had got through anyway and she was soaked to the skin. She was crying.

'My foot hurts,' she said, pointing at her ankle.

It was at such an odd angle that Nina knew it was broken. 'We need to get you to hospital at once,' she said. 'That foot needs to be plastered, and we can't have you sitting here like this. You'll catch a chill.'

She radioed Control and asked for an ambulance to the junction of Djurgårdsvägen and Långa gatan.

'He was driving like a maniac,' the woman said, pointing to the man in the car. 'I was cycling along, nice and safely, and he comes up and hits me from behind. I mean, it's not on, is it?'

Nina put her hand on the woman's arm and smiled at her. 'Don't worry,' she said. 'We'll get to the bottom of what happened. The main thing now is to get you to a doctor.'

Andersson came over to her, holding in his hand the breathalyzer that the motorist had just blown into.

'Looks like someone started celebrating National Day at lunchtime,' he said.

'We'll take him in for a proper test,' Nina said, as she saw the ambulance emerging through the rain.

Once the woman was being looked after by the paramedics, Andersson put the suspected drunk-driver on the right side of the car's back seat, then slid his seat so that his prisoner had no room for manoeuvre.

'The old bag was weaving all over the road,' the driver said. 'It was impossible not to hit her.'

I wonder if they've found him.

During the handover meeting that morning, when they were told who was going out and in which cars, they had gone through new missing-person reports as well as ongoing cases. *The search for David's boy was due to start again at six o'clock this morning, but they're holding off to see if the rain eases . . .*

'If I were you,' Andersson said, 'I'd keep seriously fucking quiet until I'd got hold of a good lawyer.'

Nina glanced at her watch. Their shift ended in an hour and they hadn't managed to get back to the station all day.

It took a long while to drive to Torkel Knutssonsgatan on Södermalm. Nina went straight into the garage, then took the drunk-driver to the duty officer, where he was made to blow twice more into a breathalyzer, with the same result: 0.8 parts per thousand.

'That's not too bad,' the driver said, relieved.

'You could have killed someone,' Nina said. 'That woman's foot may never be right again. You may well have ruined her life.'

The man glowered at her.

'I'll go and write the report,' she told the officer, Pelle Sisulu, leaving the drunk to his fate.

Nina felt exhausted, even though it had been a relatively calm shift. She had been close to tears most of the day. It would be good to have a few days off now.

She quickly filed the report and logged out.

On her way to the changing room she stopped at the duty officer's room. The drunk was gone.

Pelle Sisulu was in his forties, and had worked at the station for as long as she could remember. 'Anything special to report?' he wondered.

Nina shuffled her feet. 'No, not really, RTAs, a couple of slight injuries, and this drunk-driver . . . Has anything happened in the search? For Alexander, I mean.' She had been on the point of saying 'Julia's son'.

Sisulu raised his head.

He must have been the first black police officer in Sweden.

'They've called off the search for today,' he said. 'Visibility's too poor. The helicopter never got up.' He went back to his computer screen.

'But what about the ground search?' she said. 'Surely they could have carried on with that.'

'Evidently some of the local officers from out in the bush are poking about in the mud,' he said, 'but we haven't got anyone there.'

'That's probably the village squad from Valla,' she said.

He looked at her questioningly.

'Julia comes from round there. Her dad's chair of the local business association.'

'I'd be surprised if they found anything.'

Nina walked to the rear of the station, which was deserted. The corridor to the changing room was dark and gloomy. The ventilation system hummed quietly, stirring up dust from the grey linoleum floor, and she

156

could smell rubbish from the recycling facility next door.

She unbuttoned her jacket and bulletproof vest, and let out a deep sigh. She could still remember the first time she had been here, how nervous and tense she had felt. During the fourth term of their course she and Julia had done their practical experience here, known as 'integrated study orientation in the workplace'. Julia had been joyful.

Just think, this is it for us, our careers. We're going to have a chance to make a difference . . .

That had been almost ten years ago.

Nina opened the door on the left at the far end of the corridor with her security pass and went into the women's cramped changing room, making her way through the maze of blue lockers until she came to her own. She dropped her bag on the floor with a thud. Her arms felt heavy as she shrugged off her jacket, took off the belt containing her holster and handcuffs, the extra ammunition and baton, then her bulletproof vest, boots and uniform trousers. She glanced at the clothes: they were muddy, splattered with vomit and snot from one of the accident victims. They needed washing. She sighed.

Oh, well, she had three days to do it.

She opened her bag and inspected her helmet, shin-pads, cap, scarf, protective gloves, map and extra set of clothes.

She showered and washed her hair, then dried herself until her skin glowed, and put on her jeans and a grey sweatshirt. She closed her locker and made a brief attempt to brush her hair, then went to the armoury and locked up her Sig Sauer in the correct place. She should really have done that first. She stood for a moment, looking at the rows of weapons.

I don't know, Nina, oh, God, I don't know. I'm sure I put my pistol in alongside David's.

She was heading for the main entrance, with the sense that she was about to be released from captivity, when her mobile rang.

'Nina? It's Holger.' Julia's father.

She stopped abruptly. 'Have you found him?'

'No, but I'd like to talk to you. Nina, is there any chance you could come down?'

She could hear the rain lashing in the background: he must be standing outside somewhere. 'Of course,' she said, her heart racing. 'I've got a few days off now, so I could get the train first thing tomorrow morning.'

'I'd rather you came straight away, Nina. We've found something.'

She put her hand out to the brick wall. 'What?' she said. 'What have you found?'

Someone said something in the background, she couldn't make out what.

'Holger?' she said. 'Where are you? Who else is there? What have you found?'

Julia's father came back on the line. 'There's four of us, and we're standing on the marsh at Sågkärret. Do you know where that is?'

'No,' Nina said.

'Three hundred metres south-east from Björkbacken, you turn off towards Nytorp then take the first left. The road leads straight here. We'll be waiting for you.'

'Holger,' Nina said, 'can't you tell me what you've found?'

There was a whistling sound on the line from the squalls of rain. Julia's father's voice sounded hollow when he replied. 'We'll talk when you get here,' he said.

158

'We don't want to make a fuss in case we're wrong. It would be best if you took the decision.'

'And it's not Alexander?' she asked.

'No.'

'But you have to call the police,' Nina said.

'That's what I'm doing, isn't it?' Holger said. 'We won't go anywhere. Drive carefully.' He ended the call.

She stood still, her pulse racing.

She started to run towards the garage – she knew exactly where the keys to the closest car were kept.

Then she stopped.

I'm crazy. I can't just steal a patrol car.

She stood in the corridor.

Where can I get hold of a car, any car?

She rushed back into the station, to the duty officer's room. 'Pelle,' she panted, 'have you got a car?'

He looked at her in astonishment.

'What?'

'That's your blue Merc in the garage, isn't it? Can I borrow it? I'll be back before the end of your shift.'

'I don't suppose there's any point in asking what you want it for?' he said, fishing the keys out from his trouser pocket.

Nina swallowed. 'I'll tell you later,' she said. 'At least, I hope I will.'

He got up and walked round the desk, holding out the keys. 'It's almost worth it,' he said, 'just to see you in civilian clothes with wet hair.' He dropped them into her palm. 'My shift ends at twenty-two hundred,' he said. 'If you're not here, you can pay for my taxi home.'

She closed her fingers round the keys, turned on her heel and hurried towards the garage.

*

Annika had just passed Norrtälje, and was following the E18 towards Spillersboda when the rain started. She hadn't had the nerve to ask Berit to babysit again today so Kalle and Ellen were sitting in the back playing with their Game Boys, bribed temporarily with a packet of sweets each. She wasn't sure how sensible it was, taking them to a home for young drug addicts.

The Vårtuna Home was supposed to be on the outskirts of the town. She turned up the speed of the windscreen wipers and peered out, searching for the right turning. When she reached a more built-up area, she turned off towards Klemensboda.

She was seriously regretting setting off at all. She had had a terrible night, full of nightmares, and had woken up in tears twice. She was absolutely exhausted.

What she really needed was to lie on the sofa in Berit's living room and watch a Sunday movie with the children. Instead she was on her way through driving rain to meet a born-again drug dealer who was going to sing David Lindholm's praises.

I don't need to do this. I'm going home.

She was considering turning round and driving back, when she realized that the Vårtuna Home was right in front of her.

'Why are we here?' Kalle said, as she parked between an old Volvo and a misshapen birch tree.

She let out a deep sigh. 'I'm so sorry I had to bring you with me,' she said. 'I'll be as quick as I can.'

She had read about the place on the Internet. It was actually an old campsite and youth hostel that had been bought by a Free Church organization and turned into a care home. Several buildings were scattered across the slope towards the sea. To the left there was a large building that Annika assumed was the main house. Ahead of

160

her she saw small cabins with little porches that were probably where the clients lived, unless they were called patients.

'I want to go home,' Ellen said.

'I know, but we can't go just yet,' Annika said, far too sternly and loudly. 'I promised I'd talk to a man, and now we're here. Come on!'

She got out of the car quickly, holding an old copy of the *Evening Post* over her head, yanked open the rear doors and pulled the children out, then ran towards the main building with them.

They were all soaked by the time they reached the porch. The door had swollen in the damp and they had to push it, and when it finally opened they tumbled into an old cafeteria. Annika helped the children to get up and they stamped their feet, instantly making a puddle of water round her trainers.

'We're very wet,' Ellen said, blinking as the rain from her fringe dripped into her eyes.

There were seven people in the large room. Kalle huddled closer to her and took hold of her sleeve.

'Hello,' Annika said, raising one hand in a little wave.

Four young men had been playing poker at a table by the window. They were staring hard at them, and the dealer had frozen in the middle of what he was doing.

The room was simply furnished, rib-backed chairs and kitchen tables with laminated tops. The floor was yellow linoleum, and the walls had layers of different-coloured paint.

She pushed the hair off her face.

Immediately ahead there was a counter with cakes and a hotplate for a pot of coffee. Behind it stood a middle-aged man, and behind him, two more young men.

'Are they junkies?' Kalle whispered.

'Yes,' Annika whispered back. 'They all are.'

'Are they dangerous?'

'No, I don't think so. They're better now.'

The middle-aged man came towards them. 'What terrible weather,' he said. 'Welcome! I'm Timmo.' His Finnish accent was sharp and pronounced. His shoulders were slightly hunched and he had a bald head with a ring of pale blond hair.

Annika tried to smile. 'It's good of you to see us at such short notice.'

'Not at all,' he said. 'It's nice to have visitors. This is the dining room, where we have our meals and group activities. Shall we go into the office?

'This place was bought by the association almost four years ago now,' Timmo Koivisto said, squeezing along a narrow corridor lined with crates of soft drinks and big sacks of jasmine rice. 'Reoffending rates among our lads are very low . . . This way.'

He held open the door for Annika, gesturing them through.

The children trod on her heels as they went in.

'Mum,' Kalle said, tugging at her arm, 'I left my Game Boy in the car. Will the junkies take it?'

'You can never be too sure,' Timmo Koivisto said, leaning towards Kalle. 'Never leave valuables in the car, because opportunity makes the thief.'

The boy was on the point of tears.

'There are no thieves about today,' Annika said quickly. 'It's raining far too hard. Thieves don't like getting wet.'

Timmo Koivisto nodded. 'That's actually true,' he said. 'Crime figures go down when the weather's bad. In harsh winters there are hardly any opportunistic rapes, because sex-offenders don't like getting cold backsides.'

Dear God, what have I brought the children to?

She forced herself to smile. 'Maybe we could get down to business. I don't want to take up any more of your time than I have to.'

'Oh,' Timmo Koivisto said politely. 'We've got all afternoon ahead of us.'

There was only one spare chair in the room. Annika sat down and lifted one child on to each knee. Timmo sat on the other side of the desk.

'There's one thing I must ask you,' he said. 'You can't write anything that reveals the identity of any of our clients. They weren't very happy when I told them someone from the *Evening Post* was coming. But I think it's really great that you want to write about what we do.'

Annika could feel her desperation rising as the flow of blood to her legs was slowly cut off. 'I'm sorry,' she said, 'but I think you might have misunderstood me. I'm sure what you do here is extremely interesting, but I was wondering if you could tell me anything about David Lindholm? I'm writing an article about him.'

Timmo Koivisto raised one hand. 'I know,' he said. 'I just wanted to explain that the Vårtuna Home is the most important thing in my life. Serving the Lord and helping my fellow unfortunates gives my life meaning, and it was David Lindholm who set me on the right path.'

Annika moved the children so that they were standing beside her, then took out her pen and notebook from her bag and leaned over to write. 'I didn't know David was religious?' she said.

'Well,' he said, 'I wouldn't know about that. I didn't actually know David Lindholm, but after my encounter with him I came to a new awareness. I had a choice, and I chose Christ.'

She wrote *chose Christ* in her notebook, feeling the rainwater running down her spine.

Should I ask the children to wait outside? They shouldn't be hearing this. But can I trust those young men out there?

'So it was after the attack in the Central Station that you decided to . . . change track?'

Timmo Koivisto nodded. 'I was a sinner,' he said. 'I had let down a lot of people around me, my mother most of all, I think. The mothers of this world never get enough recognition. I was only a small-time dealer, selling drugs to other small-time dealers to fund my own habit. It was my fault other young people became drug-users, but my income still wasn't enough to keep me going. I started cheating, diluting the smack with icing sugar, but they found out and gave me a warning I'll never forget.' He turned his head to show the hearing-aid in his left ear. 'And I see double,' he said. 'My eyes don't refract the light properly. I have special glasses, but they make me dizzy.'

Why ever did I bring them? I'm a terrible mother! If Thomas finds out about this, he'll take them away from me.

'Why did he do it? Why did David beat you up like that?'

The look in Timmo Koivisto's eyes was calm and clear. 'They wanted to show me that I could never get away. Wherever I went, they would find me. If even the police did their bidding, there was nowhere to run.'

'And who were "they"?' Annika asked. 'The drugs Mafia?'

'That's one way of describing them.'

'Mummy,' Kalle said, 'I need a wee.'

Timmo Koivisto reacted at once. 'I can take him.'

164

Annika flew to her feet. 'No!' she said. 'There's no need. I'll take him.'

They went out of the office, Ellen too, and walked a few metres to the right.

'Can you wait here until I've finished talking to the man?' she whispered, once they had entered the small toilet.

'But I want to stay with you, Mummy,' Ellen said.

'I'll be back soon,' she said, closing the door and hurrying into the office.

'So, you were saying that David Lindholm did errands for some drug syndicate? Why?' She sank on to the chair.

'I don't know, but I wasn't the only one he went for.'

'Tony Berglund,' Annika said.

Timmo Koivisto nodded again. 'Among others. There were more who never reported it. I've met Tony. Things didn't turn out too well for him. The last I heard, he was homeless, selling the *Big Issue* at Medborgarplatsen.'

'And why did he attack Tony?'

'The same reason he attacked me.'

'Yet you're still grateful to him?' Annika said. 'You say he saved your life?'

Timmo Koivisto smiled. 'It's true. I woke up in hospital and found myself in the Valley of Death. David Lindholm had shown me the only way out, and I took it.'

'Why did you retract everything during the trial?'

'Surely you can work that out for yourself.'

She could hear Kalle crying in the corridor. Annika stood up. 'I'm really sorry,' she said, 'but I think I'm going to have to go now.'

The man stood up. 'Mind you, there's one thing I must admit.'

'What's that?' Annika asked, from the doorway.

'I'm very pleased he's dead.'

The storm had turned the road ahead of her into a muddy ditch. Nina stopped the car and peered into the darkness between the fir trees.

Pelle Sisulu's car was a two-seater soft-top with a ground clearance of about five centimetres. Stones sticking out of the mud scratched the entire underside of the chassis.

She paused, wondering how much further it could be. A couple of hundred metres? A kilometre? It had almost stopped raining, and the wind had eased. Should she park and walk?

She looked up at the steel-grey sky.

The marsh of Sågkärret was right in front of her. She had taken the motorway to Åkers styckebruk, then gone across country until she'd got to the junction at Sköldinge. She had then followed the Stöttasten road until she reached the turning to Nytorp, then taken the first left, and here she was.

She put the car into first gear and accelerated cautiously. The wheels slid a little in the wet, then found their grip. She had never driven such a responsive car: it held the road like a limpet.

They had to be here somewhere!

She had hardly finished the thought before the wall of trees opened up to reveal a large clearing in the forest. A watery expanse was visible between the reeds and moss, and some stunted birches struggling against the wind on a small island further out.

She put the car into neutral, pulled on the handbrake and peered into the growing darkness.

Is this it?

Then, to the left of the island with the birches, not far away at all, really, she saw a small group of men.

One waved to her, and she could tell by his hat that it was Holger. She switched the engine off, opened the door and got out. Her foot sank straight into the boggy ground and she gasped as the water soaked through her trainer to her skin. The wind was buffeting her from behind.

Holger was holding his hat on with his right hand and slowly making his way towards her. Nina clung to the car door as she waited for him to reach her. His eyes were red when he finally stopped beside her, and it was hard to work out if that was the result of the weather or something else.

'Thanks for coming,' he said, and in spite of the chasm in his voice she recognized her Holger, with all his strength and stability.

She took a step towards him and gave him a hug, holding him tight for a whole minute. 'I'm so sorry,' she whispered.

Holger nodded. 'So are we,' he said. 'Haven't you got any better shoes than those?'

Nina looked down at her Nikes and shook her head.

'Hold on to me,' he said, stretching out his arm.

Together they set off across the marsh. Sometimes the ground held their weight, but occasionally Nina sank into the mud to her ankles. Holger was much better off in his heavy hunting boots. The wind was pushing them from behind, making them take long strides. The rain picked up and started lashing them again, and soon Nina could feel the damp soaking through her denim jacket and gathering at the small of her back. The birch trees out on the island were twisting in the wind.

They soon reached the other men, Kaj from the neighbouring farm and two more she didn't know. She held out her hand in greeting, and noted that it was frozen while theirs were dry and warm. Their eyes were wide, and no one said anything.

She realized that they were now standing on firmer ground, rock and hard-packed earth underfoot, a small island similar to the one further out with the birch trees.

'Here,' Holger said, pointing to a rod sticking out of the water close to them. 'When Kaj pulled the pole this floated up.' He pointed to a bundle at the edge of the solid ground.

Nina took a few steps over to it, then bent to look at it.

Cloth. Muddy, but not torn.

She felt the ground with her hand until she found a stick. She carefully prodded the bundle to see how stable it was.

It doesn't split, so it hasn't been in the water long. But what is it?

She didn't want to touch the cloth, even though it could hardly hold any vital evidence. Instead she grabbed another stick and poked the fabric. It fell into two pieces. She stretched out the smaller of them.

It was a little shirt.

A child's shirt.

She bent down close to the cloth and scraped the edge with a nail.

No, not a shirt, the fabric was too thick, it was . . .

'Flannel,' Holger said.

Pyjamas.

She smoothed out the other piece.

A little pair of trousers.

A pair of flannel pyjama trousers.

She pulled one sleeve of the shirt over her wrist, not caring about possible evidence, and wiped the mud away to see the pattern and colour of the fabric.

Pale, with blue and green balloons.

'Blue and green?' Holger wondered.

Nina nodded.

'Do you recognize it?' he asked.

'Not off the top of my head,' she said.

'What about that, then?' Holger said, pointing to a tree-root close to the pole.

Nina straightened and stepped closer to it.

It was about twenty centimetres long, muddy and twisted, with odd pieces sticking out of it. She poked it with her stick and was surprised at how soft it was.

'We, too, thought it was just a piece of wood,' Kaj said.

Nina let go of the stick and picked the object up with both hands, wiping the end on her sleeve.

A pale blue eye looked up at her.

She wiped the other side.

Another eye.

She scraped the mud off and a pair of ears and a nose appeared.

'Is it him?' Holger asked.

Nina nodded. 'Yes, it's his teddy,' she said.

'You're sure?' Holger pressed.

She turned the bear over and inspected one of its paws. The seam along the leg had been repaired with dark blue cotton, although now that it was wet it looked black. 'Yes,' she said. 'I mended it.'

'Viola bought Alexander a pair of flannel pyjamas last Christmas,' Holger said. 'I don't know if these are the ones. But you're sure about the teddy bear?'

Nina felt water running down her face.

It's only rain, it's only rain.

'Yes,' she said. 'It's Alexander's. He never went any-where without Bamse.'

The four men around her bowed their heads.

Monday, 7 June

13

The office was on the thirteenth floor, with a view of the Skanstull bridge and the whole of what had once been the industrial quarter of Hammarby. The furniture was grey, the walls white, the floors polished. The chairs in the corridor were black leather, designed to be uncomfortable.

Annika felt constricted and sweaty in her knitted cardigan, and her jeans were muddy from crossing Berit's lawn. She pulled her feet under the chair and looked at the time.

Thomas ought to have been here by now.

The claims assessor was talking on the phone behind the closed door in front of her; she could hear him chuckling.

For him this is just another day in the office. For me it's Hell.

She'd slept badly again. The visit to the care home was still burning inside her. She hoped desperately that the children wouldn't tell Thomas she had dragged them out there.

The office door opened. 'Mrs Samuelsson? Please come in.'

The insurance man held out his hand, smiling broadly and disingenuously.

'Bengtzon,' Annika said, standing up and taking his hand. 'It's my husband who's called Samuelsson.'

The lift pinged behind them, the door slid open and Thomas stepped out. Annika turned towards him and her heart lurched. *God, how lovely he looks!*

His briefcase was swinging from one large hand, his hair had tumbled across his forehead and he must have bought a new suit at the weekend, because she had never taken the one he was wearing to the dry-cleaner's.

'Sorry I'm late,' he said, shaking the claims assessor's hand a little breathlessly.

He glanced at Annika, and she turned away hastily.

'My name's Zachrisson,' the man said, and his smile was slightly more genuine now. 'If you'd both like to come in . . .'

Annika picked up her bag and went into the office, noting that the whole of the exterior wall was glass. The clouds pressed against the panes and water was visible far below. She could feel Thomas's presence behind her, his tall, sinewy body in the new suit and ironed shirt, and he smelt *different*: he smelt of *her*. She was struck by an urge to run straight through the glass and fly, fly, fly away across the Hammarby Canal and off into the sky.

'This is, of course, a completely alien situation for most people,' Zachrisson said, trying to smile in a calming manner. 'I appreciate that it's a shocking experience, seeing your home burn down, with all the memories and . . .'

Annika was staring into the middle distance, into the greyness above the man's head. She heard him running on, going through the same speech he must have made to hundreds of other clients over the years, about how sympathetic the company was, how they would offer almost unlimited help. And she could feel Thomas sitting beside her, and she realized that she wouldn't ever be able to live with him on Vinterviksvägen again, not there, not in that part of town.

'Does the house have to be rebuilt?' she asked abruptly.

The insurance man lost his train of thought and his smile faded. 'Er, no,' he said. 'Your insurance covers reconstruction and contents, but if you choose not to restore the house to its original condition, there are other alternatives.'

'Hang on a minute,' Thomas said, leaning towards him. 'Can we start at the beginning? What would be the usual course of events in a case like ours?' He cast an annoyed glance at Annika.

Zachrisson fingered some documents on his desk and adjusted his glasses. 'What usually happens is that the house is rebuilt as it was. Plans are drawn up, planning permission sought, and reconstruction is put in place. Usually this is done as soon as possible, and in most cases begins at once.'

'And if that's not what we want?' Annika said, refusing to look at Thomas.

The official thought for a moment. 'In that case we would evaluate the house as it was, then as it is now, burned down, in other words. Because it can still be sold, of course, in spite of that. The plot itself has value. The clients would get the difference paid into their account. They would also be recompensed for the loss of contents – furniture, clothes, television, DVDs, and so on.'

'I think that sounds like a reasonable option,' Annika said.

'I don't know that I agree,' Thomas said, looking furious. 'Even if we don't want to live there, there's probably much more to be gained from selling a newly built property than a smoking ruin.'

Zachrisson raised both hands as if to stop them.

'There is a problem,' he said, 'which we must take into account before we can discuss any form of payment. No insurance company would pay out damages to anyone under suspicion of arson on their own home.'

The silence that fell in the room ran right through Annika's body. Suddenly she could hear the hum of the air-conditioning and the noise of the traffic below on Götgatan. She glanced at Thomas and saw that he had frozen, leaning forward with his mouth half open. The claims assessor's mouth also hung open, as if he were surprised that he had actually said those words.

'What?' Thomas said. 'What are you saying?'

Zachrisson loosened his tie. Sweat had broken out on his brow.

'As we understand it,' he said, 'there's an ongoing police investigation into your case. There are suspicions of arson.'

'It was definitely arson,' Annika said, 'but neither of us started the fire.'

The claims assessor leaned back, as if he were worried about coming into contact with something infectious. 'We can't make any payment until the police investigation into the circumstances of the fire is complete,' he said. 'Even if the preliminary enquiries don't lead to a full investigation, we still wouldn't make a payment. We carry out our own investigation as well.'

Annika looked at the bespectacled man on the other side of the smart desk, and felt as she had when she had faced the cashier in the bank a few days before. 'But that's ridiculous!' she said, and could hear that her voice was too loud and too shrill and too emotional. 'Someone tried to kill us, and now you're insinuating that we started the fire ourselves. *Ourselves! Would we really have tried to kill our own children?*'

'We have to take everything into account,' Zachrisson said. 'We can't pay out any money to arsonists.'

Annika stood up so quickly that the leather chair almost toppled over behind her. 'Take everything into account?' she said. 'For whose benefit? Your shareholders? What about us, the people paying for your fucking office's view all these years? And now you're accusing us of *arson*?'

Thomas stood up as well and grabbed her hard by the arm. 'I must apologize for the behaviour of my . . . wife,' he said, and dragged her out of the room.

'Ow,' Annika said, following him like a helpless doll, her bag slapping against her legs.

They got into the corridor and then the lift. Thomas pressed to go down to the lobby and didn't let go of her arm until the metal door had closed. Annika was breathing fast and her heart was racing. 'Sorry,' she said. 'I didn't mean to blow up.'

Thomas was leaning against the wall of the lift. His hair had fallen forward and he was staring at the floor. She wanted to brush his hair aside, stroke his cheek, kiss him and tell him she loved him. 'Sorry,' she whispered again.

The lift stopped with a little shudder and the doors slid open. Thomas took a better grip of his briefcase and walked quickly towards the main entrance. Annika followed him, running to keep up, her eyes on the back of his head. 'Wait,' she said. 'Wait a minute, we have to talk.'

They emerged into the grey haze, the noise of the traffic hitting them at the same time as the exhaust fumes.

'Thomas,' she said, 'don't you want to see the children? What are we going to do about them?'

He stopped, turned and stared at her with his new

eyes, swollen and predatory. 'What the hell are you playing at?'

She held out her hand to stroke his cheek but he pulled back. He looked as though he felt like spitting on her.

'Thomas,' she said, and the world around her dissolved and all sound vanished. The hand that had tried to caress him landed on her own chest.

'You're completely out of control,' he said, taking a step back.

She went and stood right next to him, wanting to reach out and touch his hair. 'I'll do anything,' she said, suddenly aware that she was crying.

'Where are the children now?'

Her hands started to shake uncontrollably: the sign of an imminent panic attack. *Nice and calm . . . There's nothing to be afraid of, nothing to be afraid of . . .*

'They're with Thord. He offered to look after them while I—'

'*Thord?* Who the hell's he? I'm going to get them right away.'

She let his fury wash over her. What was he saying? What was it he wanted?

He's angry and upset and he wants to cause trouble.

The world came back, with its driving rain and traffic noise.

'No, you're not,' she said, noticing that her pulse had slowed.

He turned away and began to walk towards Götgatan, then turned back and stopped in front of her, eyes blazing. 'My children aren't going to be looked after by someone like you,' he said. 'I'm going to apply for sole custody of them.'

She looked into his eyes and saw nothing she recognized. 'You won't manage,' she said. 'You never have.'

178

'Well, at least they won't have to live with some fuck-ing *arsonist*!' He screamed the last word.

So this was what they had come to. She was suddenly completely calm.

Okay, if it's like that.

Grief spread through her.

'I'll see a lawyer today,' Thomas said. 'I want to get divorced as soon as possible, and the kids are mine.'

She gasped, her whole body tense and ready for flight. Thomas's face was hovering above her, his jaw clenched so tight that his cheekbones turned white.

'I think we should have them alternate weeks for the time being,' she managed to say, looking at him through her tears. 'You can pick them up on Friday.'

He turned to go, marching determinedly towards Götgatan, leaning forward, his shoulders hunched against the wind.

I'm not dying. I'm not dying. It just feels like it.

Nina came into the station with a nagging anxiety. She had called Pelle Sisulu during the evening to explain that she wouldn't be back with the car before he finished, but he had already reached the end of his shift and gone home.

She headed towards his room but stopped a metre or so from the door.

Christer Bure was in there, talking to the duty officer about a case involving a dead body. There was a question mark over the death certificate and the seizure of prescription medication from the scene.

Nina hesitated. Should she go away and come back later?

'Don't worry about telling the next-of-kin about the death,' she heard Pelle Sisulu say. 'I'll take care of that.'

Christer Bure walked out of his room, glanced quickly at her and his eyes narrowed.

Nina adjusted her hair and walked up to the door. Her boss was standing with his back to the door, putting a file on top of a bookcase. His back almost blocked the window.

She knocked on the door frame and he looked over his shoulder. 'Ah,' he said, turning back to his desk. 'It's you.'

'I really can't thank you enough for the loan,' she said, feeling oddly embarrassed. 'I know you had to get a taxi home and of course I'll pay for it.'

'That was a joke,' he said, tucking in his shirt again. 'Was everything okay with the car?'

'Absolutely,' she said, 'but it's very muddy, and I didn't dare take it through a car-wash because of the soft top, but I'm happy to drive it to the garage and wash it by hand if you like.'

'Thanks,' he said, sitting down. 'That would be great.' He gestured at her uniform. 'Aren't you supposed to have today off?'

'Yes,' Nina said, 'but I have to go to the remand hearing.'

'Is Julia being officially remanded today?' he asked.

Like he didn't know.

'Three o'clock,' Nina said.

He stood up and came round his desk to her. 'There's something I've been wondering about,' he said quietly. 'I understand that you were on the scene when the Katrineholm police picked up the evidence of the Lindholm boy. How did that come about?'

She didn't answer.

He sighed. 'I'm not trying to catch you out,' he said. 'Let me say that I'm impressed by your contacts. I don't suppose you happened to be at Sågträsket by accident.'

Nina sat down on a chair by the wall. 'Sågkärret,' she said. 'Julia's dad called. He and the other men in the village had been searching the marshland around Björkbacken all day. It was the neighbouring farmer who found the things. Holger wanted to make sure that they could really have been Alexander's before he made a fuss.'

'And how come he thought you'd be able to judge that better than him?'

'He's colour-blind,' she said. 'He thought he recognized Alexander's pyjamas, but he wasn't sure about the teddy bear. Its name is Bamse Lindholm. Holger didn't want to frighten his wife if they weren't Alexander's things, and by phoning me he was actually phoning the police as well, so . . .' She fell silent, worried that she was babbling.

'And what did his wife say? She made the formal identification?'

Nina nodded. 'She bought the pyjamas from H&M last Christmas, slightly too big but she'd thought he'd grow into them . . .'

'You've no theory about how they might have ended up in the lake?'

Nina thought for a moment, seeing the scene in front of her. 'It's not a lake, more of a marsh. Before all this rain it was probably possible to walk there without getting your feet wet.'

'How far from a public road?'

'There's a forest track that goes all the way to the marsh.'

'So someone could have driven a vehicle to the edge, dumped the body and then left the scene. Any tyre tracks?'

Nina looked at him. 'No body was found,' she said. 'Just a pair of pyjamas and a teddy bear.'

'Did you happen to see any journalists there?'

Nina frowned. 'Yes,' she said, 'the local reporter from Flen, Oscarsson. He lives in Granhed and heard about the discovery on police radio. If I've done something wrong, if I've broken any rules, I'd like you to tell me.'

'You did exactly the right thing,' he said. 'You made the initial decision that the find was interesting and encouraged the finder to contact the local police authorities.' He paused. 'And I appreciate that this wasn't just an ordinary police matter for you.'

She folded her arms and leaned back. 'How do you mean?' she asked.

The station commander smiled slightly and turned towards the window so that Nina could only see his face in profile. 'I still remember the day you and Julia turned up here for the first time. I've seen lots of girls on practical experience, and I can't claim to remember them all, but I remember you two.'

Nina was unsure if she should feel flattered or insulted.

He glanced quickly in her direction. 'So keen,' he said, 'big eyes, long hair . . .' He looked down at his hands, then stood up.

Nina followed suit. 'So, you won't be reporting me for doing something stupid?'

He shook his head. 'Why would I do that?' he said, then added in English: '"Go and sin no more."'

He sat down behind his desk as Nina headed out of the door towards the main entrance.

14

Anders Schyman was staring at the front page of the *Evening Post*. It was dominated by a grainy picture of a marsh with the photograph of the Lindholm boy in the top right-hand corner.

'ALEXANDER'S GRAVE' was the uncompromising headline.

No question mark.

Is this all right? Isn't this just unpleasant speculation?

From the teaser on the front page it was clear that the boy's pyjamas and teddy bear had been found pushed down into marshy ground close to the main suspect's summer cottage.

'Now it's just a matter of time before we find the boy,' a source said.

The last line reported that Alexander's mother was due to be remanded in custody that afternoon.

The editor-in-chief ran his fingers through his hair.

No, this isn't all right. We're going to get hell for it.

He let out a deep sigh.

Through the glass wall he could see the members of the Journalists' Association moving towards the long table shared by the day-shift reporters for their annual general meeting. Their body language suggested that nothing of any great importance was on the agenda.

Their rival evening paper had missed the story about the findings in the marsh: they hadn't mentioned it at all in their first edition, and had had text but no picture in their late Stockholm edition, so he could be pleased . . .

The intercom buzzed. 'Anders, there's a call for you.' The receptionist's voice sounded even more adenoidal than usual.

'Well, put it through!'

'It's the press officer from Stockholm Police.'

Oh, no . . .

Schyman closed his eyes, then picked up the receiver. 'Yes,' he said abruptly.

'I'm not trying to find out your sources,' the press officer said, in his characteristically weary voice, 'and I have no ethical opinion on your wild speculations about crime and guilt. But I would like to let you know that you're publishing confidential material from the preliminary investigation.'

'I can't agree with you,' Schyman said. 'We've done nothing but go about our usual journalistic business, as we always do.'

'That's bullshit and you know it,' the press officer said. 'But I don't want to argue with you, just clarify some of the circumstances surrounding our mutual interests.'

'Really?'

'The police and I personally have long been keen on developing an open and honest relationship with the media, a sort of mutual loyalty and respect for each other's specific working conditions.'

Schyman groaned inwardly. *He doesn't half make a meal of things*. 'Of course.'

'When you consciously break our agreement, I have to react, you must understand that. You're printing details

184

of evidence we've found about the boy in today's paper, making it completely worthless in any future trial. It's entirely possible that we'll never solve this crime, thanks to you.'

'Well,' Schyman said, 'that has to be something of an exaggeration. Aren't you supposed to be remanding someone this afternoon for this particular crime?'

'That's not the point. The fact that she's in custody is no thanks to the media. As a result, I've decided to follow your lead and re-evaluate our shared activities, which will naturally have consequences not only for us but for you as well.'

'And?'

'The series of articles that Patrik Nilsson is planning, about the south of Spain, with the working title "Costa Cocaine", is, as you are no doubt aware, the result of close collaboration between the Stockholm Police, the Justice Department and the *Evening Post*. I'm afraid that we're going to have to disregard any agreements reached on this matter and look for another newspaper.'

Schyman sat bolt upright. 'Now hold on a minute,' he said. 'That's our series of articles. It's grown out of our angle and our research.'

'I'm sorry, but I'm not the one who decided to break our agreement.'

'No, but—' Schyman said.

'And I'm going to have a few conversations with some of the officers whom I know usually supply you with the more informal details concerning our investigations. That's all over now. We've got other papers we can talk to. Good afternoon, sir.'

God, what a pretentious bastard!

Schyman put down the receiver and leaned back in his chair, holding the paper up in front of him. It wasn't that bad, was it? He looked through the article again, with a more critical eye. Patrik had written about the find in the marsh the previous evening. 'HEROES' was the headline across pages six and seven. The picture desk had bought the rights to a photograph from the *Katrineholm Courier* in which the missing boy's grandfather and some other men were standing gloomily at the scene. The subtitle picked up the speculation of the front page: *Have They Found Alexander's Grave?*

At least they had managed to squeeze in a question mark at the end.

The article said that the old men had braved the terrible weather and carried on the search when everyone else had given up. They had known Alexander's clothes and favourite teddy bear immediately. Now the search was focusing on that particular area of marshland; the whole of the Södermanland police force was involved and the army was going to be called in.

The description of the marsh was rather Gothic and dramatic, all about stagnant water and swarms of mosquitoes.

Surely that wasn't worth getting too excited about.

He lowered the paper to his lap where it crumpled untidily.

Why draw a connection between a series of future articles and a possible case of overstepping the mark? Did the press officer have a hidden agenda?

He glanced through the glass wall into the newsroom. A few latecomers were on their way to the union meeting.

Once upon a time he had been active in the union. Seriously militant, if he remembered rightly. Hadn't he actually been union representative on one of the local radio stations up north? In those days, before the commercial stations, journalists would spend years out in the bush. In the eighties, employment regulation had been incredibly strict: eleven months probation, then you were out on your ear. People used to end up stuck in the middle of nowhere, with no chance of ever getting to Stockholm and the national television channels. No permanent positions had come up since TV2 launched in 1968, providing work for an entire generation of agitators.

Those were the days. All appointments lasted a life-time, and everyone knew who the Chancellor of Justice was. And no reporter was ever in the lap of the police.

Well, that was dubious even then, he thought, as he watched Berit Hamrin making her way to the meeting. If Berit was going, maybe they were going to discuss something important. What could it be?

Of course. They were going to choose a new union representative. He'd almost forgotten.

He got up, grabbed the newspaper, and went to sit opposite Spike. 'Not going to the union meeting?' he asked, putting his feet on the desk.

'I've been expelled,' the head of news said. 'I forgot to pay my sub.'

'That's a bit mean of them,' Schyman said.

'Sixteen years in a row,' Spike said. 'I have to say I don't blame them.'

'What have we got on the boy for tomorrow?' Schyman asked, pointing at that day's front cover.

'We're trying to find a new picture of the kid, ideally wearing the pyjamas and hugging the teddy.'

'How's the search going?'

'No luck so far. His relatives just snap at us and put the phone down.'

Schyman opened the paper again, looking at the

picture of the marsh. Voices from the union meeting bounced between the desks towards him. They had got as far as approving the agenda.

He slumped deeper into his chair and tried to close his ears. 'How did we find out what they discovered in the marsh?' he asked.

'How do you mean?'

'Who leaked?'

'Hell, no one. The old boys talked to the *Katrineholm Courier* last night. That's where we got it. *KC* were running it on their website just after midnight.'

'So we can thank the local press, new technology and the uselessness of the competition in that order,' Schyman said. 'When things like this come up, I want to be involved in the discussion. I've just had a conversation with the police press officer, and he wasn't particularly happy.'

Spike looked up at the ceiling. 'He's a verbose bastard.'

Schyman turned the page. The union meeting was accepting the accounts. 'He's tearing up our agreement on Patrik's series about "Costa Cocaine". Either he really was as angry as he sounded, or he needed a reason to get us off the story.'

'I always thought that was weird,' Spike said. 'I mean, why should we send people all over Europe just to write about how fucking great the Swedish police are?'

Over at the day-shift's table the committee was being granted the authority to act on behalf of the members. It had two proposals for a new chair. They couldn't decide so both names were being put to the membership. The first nomination was the political reporter, Sjölander, and the second was the newsroom secretary, Eva-Britt Qvist.

Really? Schyman thought, pricking his ears. I wonder

188

why Sjölander is suddenly taking an interest in the union. The political reporter, a former head of crime reporting and former American correspondent, had none of the characteristics usually associated with union representatives. Sjölander was smart, ambitious and highly regarded – unlike most union reps after a short while. The ones who made the union into a career were usually whiny, untalented and work-shy.

Eva-Britt Qvist, on the other hand, more than met the criteria usually associated with local union reps. Schyman had managed to get her out of his hair by making her responsible for the office budget and attendance. She was at the top of the list of people he wanted to get rid of. It was hardly surprising she'd put herself forward, he thought. As union representative, she'd finally have a bit of power and influence.

'Lindholm's wife is being remanded this afternoon,' Spike said. 'If we're lucky, we can get something from that.'

'I doubt it,' Schyman said. 'The prosecutor will batten down the hatches, and refer to the confidentiality needed for the preliminary investigation.'

'Yes, and the killer's evidently completely mad,' the head of news said.

Tore from Reception was talking: 'There are plenty of us here who'd like to see a new sort of union rep. Someone who listens to us. This year it's time for the whole orchestra, not just a soloist. It's time we had a bit more influence.'

There was a murmur of agreement. A show of hands was asked for.

Why is Tore in the Journalists' Association? Schyman wondered. Didn't he used to work in graphics?

'I make that twenty-seven votes for Sjölander,' Tore

said. 'And twenty-eight for Eva-Britt Qvist. We have a new chair!'

Scattered applause.

Anders Schyman sighed. Now he would have to sit and discuss cutbacks with the person who used to open his post. 'Did Patrik go down to Södermanland last night?' he asked, nodding towards the article containing the evocative description of the marsh.

'No,' Spike said. 'Why ever would you think that?'

'Stagnant water and swarms of mosquitoes,' Schyman said.

'Everyone knows what a marsh is like. Have you seen this?' Spike pointed at the screen. 'The Foreign Ministry are hinting that Viktor Gabrielsson is about to be released.'

Viktor Gabrielsson? Who the hell was he, again?

'Really?' Schyman said. 'How come?'

'They're getting close to a "diplomatic solution". This is from the main news agency: "The Foreign Ministry in Stockholm has indicated that, after spending fifteen years in a New Jersey prison as an accessory to the murder of a police officer in Long Island, Viktor Gabrielsson could soon be extradited to Sweden."'

Ah, that one, the old police murder.

'I'll believe that when I see it,' Schyman said.

Spike clicked on and read the next message. 'The girl who won Big Brother is going to have an operation to remove her silicon tits,' he announced. 'She's going to bury them symbolically in a Plexiglas coffin, then auction them on the Internet. The money's going to kids in war-torn Rwanda.'

Anders Schyman stood up. 'Check with the staff at Alexander's nursery if we can go and look at the pictures on the walls,' he said. 'Nowadays they always have loads of photos of the kids that they pin up on notice-boards.'

The head of news looked up, eyebrows raised. 'Where the fuck do you think we got the pictures of the kid in today's paper?' he said.

Anders Schyman went back to his office and closed the door behind him. He was about to sit down when there was a knock.

Annika Bengtzon was standing outside. She pulled the door open before he had time to wave her in. Her hair was all over the place and she had the terrier-like expression on her face that never boded well.

'What?' he said wearily.

'I've found some really interesting stuff on David Lindholm. He was charged with beating people up twice because he was doing favours for the drugs Mafia. He beat up small-time gangsters who tried to con them out of money.'

Schyman made an effort to keep his expression neutral. 'He was charged? When?'

'Eighteen years ago. And twenty years ago.'

'You say "charged". Was he found guilty?'

'No, and that's really dodgy as well. He was let off both times.'

'And you want to write about this?'

'I think it paints a completely different picture of him.'

'And the information comes from . . . ?'

'The preliminary investigations, and I've also met one of the men who was beaten up. He says he's pleased David's dead.'

He had to cover his eyes with his hands to summon some strength. 'So you want me to publish a story saying that a murdered hero was actually a thug working for the drugs Mafia, and we're basing this on the fact

191

that he was found *not* guilty of charges of using excessive force? Twenty years ago?'

She bit her lip. 'You're twisting everything.'

'Slandering the dead,' he said. 'That's a serious offence. Editors-in-chief have gone to prison for that.'

'Yes, but—'

'I've already been hauled over the coals for our editorial decisions once today. I don't want to hear any more about this. Go and find yourself somewhere to live.'

'Yeah, yeah.' Annika Bengtzon left the room.

He sat down in his chair and propped his head in his hands.

It can't just be my imagination. This job has got a hell of a lot messier over the past few years.

The remand proceedings were announced in one of the high-security courtrooms and Nina stood up quickly, before everyone else. She still felt uncomfortable in her uniform, after all these years, and knew she should have got over it by now, but this situation was particularly exposed and unusual.

There were a lot of journalists in the hall outside the courtroom, reporters from press and radio, and at least two television crews. She could see them studying her, wondering what she was doing there.

Hyenas! Here to get their mouthful of flesh.

She shook away the thought and headed towards the courtroom.

Detective Inspector Q slid up alongside her and held the door open. 'Go and sit right at the front,' he said quietly.

She looked at him in bemusement.

'We're going to be on our own on the public benches,' he said.

She did as she had been told. The judge's seat was right in front of her, the prosecutor to the left and the defence to the right. Nina had been in this room many times before, a witness in a lot of remand proceedings.

But nothing like this one.

She glanced over at the door behind the defence bench. It led to a waiting room, which was linked directly to Kronoberg Prison via the Walk of Sighs. That way they could bring people held in custody straight into the high-security courtroom without having to steer them through the crowds outside.

You're sitting behind there now. Do you understand what's happening?

The room filled quickly – reporters with recording equipment, court artists with large pads. They rustled and jostled and chatted, their muttering sounding like a waterfall.

Nina leaned towards Detective Inspector Q. 'Which public defence counsel has been assigned to her?' she whispered.

'Mats Lennström.'

Who?

'Who's he? What's his track record?'

Before Q had time to answer, the door behind the judge's platform opened and the chief judge and chief clerk took their places. A second later a dark-haired man in a suit came in from the waiting room, followed by a prison guard, who led Julia to her seat.

Nina leaned forward instinctively. *God, what did she look like?* Her hair was messy and unwashed, her prison uniform creased, as if she'd slept in it. Nina's throat constricted. 'Why didn't she get a different lawyer?' she said. 'Can he really handle a case like this?'

Q gestured to her to keep quiet.

Prosecutor Angela Nilsson came in, sat down and adjusted her skirt beneath her thighs. She had changed her clothes: this outfit was blue-grey.

The presiding judge banged his gavel on the desk and complete silence fell.

Nina stared at Julia. She was seeing her face from an angle, and her eyes seemed shiny and empty. There was something innocent about her messy hair and the out-size collar of the prison shirt.

How thin you look. You're probably not eating. I bet you think the food's disgusting.

The judge cleared his throat and started to explain the formalities, remand proceedings and the parties summoned. Nina watched Julia.

'This isn't working,' she whispered to Q.

'If you can't be quiet you'll have to leave,' he hissed back, and she closed her mouth.

Angela Nilsson began: 'Mr Chairman, I propose that the court remand Julia Lindholm in custody on suspicion of having committed murder in Bondegatan in Stockholm on the third of June,' she said, in a monotone. 'In justification of this action, I note that the tariff for this crime is longer than two years' imprisonment. I also refer to the two motivations for holding the suspect on remand, as documented in my proposal: the danger of collusion, and the danger of the suspect reoffending. I also propose that the court impose certain restrictions upon Julia Lindholm.'

Nina held her breath and waited for Julia's reaction. Nothing.

The presiding judge turned to the lawyer, Mats Lennström. 'Mr Lennström, please go ahead and present the position of the accused.'

'Thank you. We object to the prosecutor's proposal

of remand. There are no identifiable reasons to suspect . . .' He lost his train of thought and leafed through his papers.

Nina groaned inwardly.

'What is the position of the accused towards the matter of guilt?' the judge asked.

The lawyer hesitated. 'Mr Chairman, I would prefer that this matter be dealt with in a closed session,' he said, glancing towards the public benches.

The presiding judge turned towards the prosecutor. Angela Nilsson shuffled slightly in her seat and glared at Lennström. 'Considering the confidential nature of the preliminary investigation, the prosecution would also prefer a closed session.'

The judge turned to the public benches. 'Then I must ask members of the public and representatives of the media to leave the courtroom,' he said, and banged his gavel on the desk.

The next moment the room was filled with hubbub, and Nina kept her eyes firmly on Julia.

She didn't seem to notice that people were moving about.

When the doors closed, the silence was almost tangible.

'So, about the question of guilt,' the judge said.

The lawyer put his expensive ballpoint pen down on his documents and looked right at him. 'The fact is that my client is too ill to offer any opinion on the question of guilt. It is simply not possible to conduct a conversation with her.'

'What do you mean?'

'I was appointed to this case on Saturday. Since then I have tried to communicate with my client, but I don't think she understands who I am. I have reason to believe that my client is in need of acute psychiatric care.'

The judge leafed through his papers. 'I thought she had already received treatment,' he said. 'At Södermalm Hospital, just after she was apprehended?'

'My client has a long history of psychiatric problems,' the lawyer said. 'She has been on sick leave from her position with the police for almost two years on grounds of stress. She spent some time in a psychiatric ward for depression. I have serious reason to believe that this treatment must be recommenced immediately.'

'What has led you to that conclusion?'

Lennström clicked his pen. 'My client refers repeatedly to another woman who was present in the apartment on the night in question,' he said. 'She calls this other woman "the evil one" or "the wicked one", but she can't name her.'

The presiding judge stared at Julia. 'So you believe that she . . . might have more than one . . . ?'

'It is incompatible with the criminal justice system's responsibility to provide care to allow an unwell individual to be remanded in custody, even in a medical facility.'

The judge turned to Angela Nilsson. 'Does the prosecution share the opinion of the defence?'

The woman sighed theatrically. 'This notion of hearing voices is starting to become far too popular.'

'What do you mean?' the judge said, raising his eyebrows.

'Julia Lindholm has chosen not to co-operate with the investigation. I wouldn't like to speculate upon her reasons.'

'I see,' the judge said. 'On what grounds does the prosecution base its request that the accused be remanded in custody?'

Angela Nilsson sorted through her papers and

composed herself before she started to speak. 'David Lindholm was found dead in his home at three thirty-nine a.m. on Thursday, the third of June. The preliminary post-mortem report indicates that he was shot in the head, which was the direct cause of death. After that the body was shot once more, in the torso.'

'Could any other woman have been present when the fatal shot was fired?' the judge asked.

Angela Nilsson turned a page and the silence echoed. 'The suspect was apprehended at the scene of the crime. A gun, type Sig Sauer 225, was found at the scene, and a preliminary forensic investigation has been able to prove that this gun bears the fingerprints of the accused. The pistol is registered as being the accused's service revolver. Whether or not it is also *de facto* the murder weapon is currently being investigated by the National Forensics Laboratory, but the calibre matches the bullets found during the post-mortem and there are two bullets missing from the clip.'

There was dead silence in the courtroom. The clerk was taking notes. A fan was whirring somewhere.

'Then we have the situation regarding the suspect's son,' Angela Nilsson went on after a short pause. 'The boy, Alexander Lindholm, who is four years old, hasn't been seen since his father was murdered, and is currently still missing.'

Nina sat forward. Julia had raised her head when the prosecutor mentioned Alexander's name, and now she was looking round the sealed room. She looked at the lawyer sitting next to her as if she didn't recognize him, and stood up. He put a hand on her shoulder and persuaded her to sit down again.

'As things stand, I don't want to specify any particular suspicions surrounding the boy's disappearance,'

Prosecutor Nilsson continued. 'There is still a chance that there is a straightforward explanation for his disappearance, but if Alexander Lindholm is not found alive and well in the very near future, I will apply to have the preliminary investigation expanded to cover the murder or kidnapping of Alexander Lindholm . . .'

Every time the boy's name was mentioned Julia looked around the courtroom. Eventually she twisted on her chair in such a way that she caught sight of Nina sitting in the public benches.

No, Julia, not now!

The thought didn't get through. Julia stood up and took a hesitant step towards Nina. Her eyes were wide open and innocent, as they had been when she hadn't dared to jump from a haystack, and she was standing with her feet slightly turned in, as she did when she was scared or needed to pee urgently.

Pull yourself together, Julia. I can't help you now.

'Will the accused please sit down during the proceedings,' the judge said.

Julia took an unsteady step towards the public benches. 'Alexander?' she said. 'Where's Alexander? *No!*' She hit the lawyer's arm when he tried to get her to sit down again.

Nina clenched her hands helplessly. Julia was only making things worse for herself by not co-operating. All she had to do was tell the court what her life had been like. No one had anything to gain from her protecting David, least of all herself.

Nina looked up again. Two prison guards who had been standing by the door each took hold of one of Julia's arms and bent her forward.

She struggled. She was whimpering as she tried to get

free. The guards sat her on her chair, and she slumped to one side.

You should have reported him. You should have listened to me. I would have stood by you. They would have had to believe you.

If only he'd hit me. A couple of serious bruises, at least, ideally a few broken ribs as well.

What he's doing to you is worse. It comes under a different category. He can't lock you in like this. Unlawful imprisonment, coercion . . .

Suddenly Julia toppled off her chair.

She fell to the floor with a dull thud and lay on her side with her legs pulled up. Nina was on her feet at once.

One of the guards grabbed Julia's arm to pull her up but she didn't respond. His colleague came over, took her other arm, and raised his baton to strike.

Sit up, Julia, get up!

There was complete silence in the courtroom. Everyone had frozen where they were. The only movement came from Julia's legs and feet, which had started twitching spasmodically and uncontrollably. Suddenly the guards let go of her arms and stood up, backing away from her.

Julia lay on the floor with her head back and her body jerking violently. Nina gasped. *Oh, God, what are they doing to you?*

'Medics to the courtroom,' the judge said, into a microphone that was evidently part of an intercom system. He sounded unsettled.

Nina took an involuntary step towards Julia, but Q grabbed her wrist. 'Sit down,' he hissed.

The judge raised his voice. 'Can we have a doctor or a medic to the courtroom?'

Nina sat where she was, completely paralysed, as a medic ran in clutching a bag. He bent over Julia's jerking body and spoke into a crackling radio. 'We've got a tonic-clonic seizure,' he said, holding the radio to his mouth with one hand as he examined Julia with the other. 'I repeat, we have a primary generalized tonic-clonic seizure. I need back-up and an ambulance immediately. I repeat, *immediately*!'

'Take her out through the side door,' the judge said. He was now standing up behind his desk, horrified by the scene in front of him. 'Hurry up!'

Another two medics appeared, carrying a stretcher. They picked Julia up and Nina could see that she was stiff as a board, rigid, stuck in an unnatural pose with one arm and one leg sticking straight out.

Then, as she was being lifted on to the stretcher, the spasm seemed to ease because her body relaxed, but Nina wasn't sure she'd got that right: the medics rushed out with the stretcher.

There was complete silence in the courtroom once the doors had slammed. The guards were staring at the door through which Julia had disappeared. Prosecutor Angela Nilsson was sitting on the edge of her chair, frowning suspiciously at the place where Julia had been lying. Mats Lennström was standing with his back to the wall.

The judge sat down and struck his gavel. 'Well,' he said, rather shakily, 'if we could bring the proceedings to a conclusion . . . Angela?'

The prosecutor simply shook her head.

'Defence?'

Mats Lennström hurried to sit down again. 'Well,' he said, adjusting his hair, 'in conclusion I would like to point out that my client has in no way acknowledged liability for the accusations made by the prosecution. But if the prosecution's proposal were to be accepted, I petition the court to order an immediate paragraph-seven investigation of my client. As well as immediate treatment, her mental state at the time of the crime needs to be examined at once.'

'The court will adjourn,' the judge said, hitting the desk with his gavel again. He vanished into his office to calm down and have a cup of coffee before announcing his decision.

'I'm going,' Q said. 'I've got an interview to carry out.' He stood up and made for the exit.

Nina sat where she was, unable to move. Her heart was thudding and she was sweating. She hadn't known that Julia suffered from epilepsy.

She hadn't known that Julia had resigned.

I didn't know that Julia was so ill.

I don't know the first thing about her! I don't know her!

Maybe her Julia didn't exist, the Julia who never put up a fight, who always expected someone else to sort out anything unpleasant. Maybe she was gone or had never existed. Her Julia could never have shot David. Her Julia could never have harmed her child, *but what if this was a different Julia, a destructive one?*

Nina forced herself to take some deep breaths.

I believe in the system. I know that there is such a thing as justice. This is its very heart.

From that moment she knew exactly what was going to happen.

Once the judge had composed himself and had a second cup of coffee, the doors of the courtroom would be opened again, the media would be allowed in, Julia would be remanded in custody on suspicion of murder, and the case would have to go to court by 21 June at the latest.

There was no question that the preliminary investigation would be completed within a fortnight, which meant that Julia would be remanded in custody again, and again, and again, until the prosecutor had such a watertight case that she would never be let out.

A different Julia, not hers any more.

She couldn't stay in the courtroom another minute, not a single second longer. She stood up and hurried to the exit.

15

Annika was sitting on a sagging sofa outside Detective Inspector Q's office on the third floor of Police Headquarters. She leaned her head back and closed her eyes. For a day that had started so appallingly, things hadn't turned out too badly after all.

The children would be able to start back at their old nursery later that week. The manager had seemed genuinely pleased about it, presumably because they would boost the nursery's income. She had entered Kalle at the Eira School, a bit further away on Kungsholmen, to start in the autumn. Thomas could shoot her if he didn't agree with that. She had also found a flat. As long as you had money, there were flats to rent even in the centre of the city, albeit on business contracts and for absurd sums of money. She had taken a three-room apartment on Västerlånggatan, in the heart of Gamla Stan, for 20,000 kronor per month, on an unlimited contract. A ridiculous amount of money, of course, but she still had some savings. Once everything was settled with the insurance company, she'd buy the sort of flat she wanted . . .

That *she* wanted.

She took a deep breath and listened to how it felt.

Alone, without him.

She clenched her jaw to hold back the tears.

My children. Not going to be looked after by someone like you. I'm going to apply for sole custody of them. Not one second longer. I'm going to get them.

She tried to breathe calmly.

She had taken as much maternity leave as she could.

She always stayed at home when they were ill.

She had never neglected them, had always delivered them to the nursery clean and in one piece.

He can't take the children. He's got no case. He'd have to prove that I'm highly unsuitable, otherwise I win.

The detective was walking down the corridor with a mug of coffee in his hand. 'Do you want some?'

Annika shook her head. 'I have to get home to the kids,' she said. 'So I want to get this over with quickly.'

Q unlocked his room and sat down behind the desk. Annika followed him in and took the familiar visitor's chair.

'So, she's been remanded in custody now,' Annika said. 'I suppose she'll be convicted quick as anything. Unlike David. The cases against him were dropped, after all.'

Q fumbled with a tape-recorder to the left of the computer, said, 'One two, one two,' into a microphone and rewound to make sure it sounded okay.

'I met the man David almost beat to death, but there's no need for you to worry. His halo is still firmly in place. No one wants to know what David was really like.'

Q leaned towards her. 'This is about the fire in the house on Vinterviksvägen,' he said. 'Just answer my questions, okay?'

Annika nodded.

He switched the machine on and ran through the usual stuff about the interviewee's name, the time and location, then asked the first question.

'Can you tell me what happened on the night of Thursday, the third of June, this year?'

Annika bit her lip. 'Can you switch that off for a moment?' she said.

Q lowered his head demonstratively for several seconds, then pressed the pause button. 'What?' he said.

'Is it actually suitable that you're conducting this interview with me?'

'Why wouldn't it be?' Q said.

'Won't it be invalid? Because of our special relationship?'

He leaned back and raised his eyebrows. 'Speak for yourself,' he said. 'I've had special relationships with other reporters, but not with you. Tell me what happened that night.' He turned the machine on again.

She closed her eyes for several seconds, trying to locate the memories she had filed away. 'I was on the upstairs landing,' she said. 'It was dark. I'd brushed my teeth, even though there was no toothpaste. I was on my way into the bedroom . . .'

'Was your husband at home?'

She shook her head. 'No. We'd had a big row earlier that evening. He'd left. Both the children wanted to sleep with me, and I agreed.'

'So the children . . . ?'

'Were in the double-bed in our room.'

'What time was it?'

She sighed and thought for a moment. 'I emailed you a draft of an article,' she said. 'It must have been half an hour after that, forty-five minutes, maybe.'

He rolled over to his computer and opened his email

205

folder. 'It arrived at two forty-three,' he said. 'So you were standing on the upstairs landing of your house at a quarter past, half past three in the morning, and then what happened?'

She licked her lips. 'There was a crash from downstairs,' she said. 'Like a window being broken. I went down the stairs, four or five, before I realized what had happened.'

'And what had happened?'

'Someone had smashed the window. The big picture window next to the front door. There was glass everywhere. I ran down the rest of the stairs, but I couldn't see anyone outside.'

'How did you react?'

'At first I was just surprised. Then angry. I wasn't scared until there was another crash from Ellen's room.'

'Were you barefoot?'

Annika looked up at him in surprise. 'Yes,' she said, 'or, rather, I think I was wearing socks.'

'Did you cut yourself on the glass?'

She saw what he was getting at and felt the blood rush to her face. 'No,' she said, 'but I'm not lying.'

'Then what happened?'

'The window in Ellen's room smashed as well. I ran back upstairs. The door was open, and I could see the glass was broken. Something came flying through the window. It was dark and rectangular and had a burning tail.'

Q was chewing a biro. 'What do you think it was?'

Annika gulped. 'I realized when it hit the floor and smashed. I just managed to get the door closed before the room burst into flames.'

'So the window was already smashed? It didn't get broken by the firebomb?'

'I hadn't thought of that,' she said, 'but, yes, that's what happened. The glass was already smashed.'

'And this was the room at the north-east corner of the house?'

Annika paused. 'Yes,' she said, 'that's right. Closest to the junction.'

'And then?'

She screwed her eyes shut. 'Kalle's room,' she said. 'A brick came through the window, breaking the glass, and landed on the bed. The bottle came a few seconds later. It hit the wall above the bed and shattered instantly.'

'What happened when the bottle broke?'

Annika could see the flames in front of her, the way the fire had followed the petrol fumes, the curtains and bookshelf catching.

'Everything was alight,' she said. 'There was a smell of petrol and everything was burning.'

'And Kalle's room, that's the one facing south-east?'

'That's right.'

'Then what did you do?'

She shook her head. 'I backed away,' she said, 'because the heat was so intense. I thought of the children and went into the bedroom.'

'Did you close the door to Kalle's room?'

Annika stared at Q, wide-eyed. 'I don't think I did, actually,' she said.

'But you closed Ellen's bedroom door?'

She scratched her head. 'I think so.'

'Why not Kalle's?'

'I don't know. It was so hot. I wanted to get to the children.'

'And what did you do when you reached them?'

'I woke them up and lowered them to the terrace using the bottom sheet.'

'Both at the same time?'

'No, Kalle first. Then Ellen.'

'And what about you?'

'I jumped.'

'You jumped.'

'And landed on the terrace table. That's when I saw him.'

'Who?' Q said.

'Wilhelm Hopkins, our neighbour. He was standing there, hiding in the bushes. I'm absolutely convinced he started the fire.'

Q looked at her so intently that Annika started to feel her skin itching. 'Are we done, then?' she asked.

'What were you doing up so late at night?'

'I've already told you. I'd been working, then I sent my article to you and the newsroom.'

'Yes, at two forty-three. What were you doing between then and half past three?'

Her throat tightened. 'Mostly sitting and crying,' she said in a quiet voice. 'We'd had an argument, my husband and I, and I . . . well, I wished we hadn't. I was feeling sorry for myself.'

'Because your husband had left you?'

Annika smiled weakly. 'Yes, more or less.'

'Any thoughts of revenge?'

'What for?'

'For the fact that he'd left you. Because you were on your own.'

'No,' she said, 'not at all.'

The detective sighed and picked up some sheets of paper from his desk. 'Do you know what this is?'

She shook her head.

'A judgement from the district court in Eskilstuna,' he said. 'Nine years ago you were found guilty of manslaughter and given a probationary sentence.'

She was sitting absolutely still, her brain racing. *Where's this going? What next?*

'There's one very interesting witness statement in this report,' Q said. 'The police officer who was first on the scene after your boyfriend died: do you know what he said you said? Your motive for hitting him so hard that he fell into the blast furnace?'

All of a sudden she was back there again, in the summer heat, in the abandoned foundry in Hälleforsnäs, the dust whirling through the air and Whiskas's dead body in her arms. '"He shouldn't have attacked my cat. He really shouldn't have done anything to Whiskas. Do you understand?"' Q read out.

'Could I have some water?' Annika said.

'You acknowledged revenge as your motive on that occasion when you killed someone,' he said. 'Now you claim that you had no thoughts of revenge this time?'

'There's quite a difference between having your cat killed and being left by your husband, isn't there?' Annika said.

Q studied her for several long seconds. 'Considerably more people commit murder for the second reason,' he said.

Annika felt the room lurch. *What's he saying? What's he doing?*

'It was Hopkins,' Annika said. 'Hopkins set fire to the house.'

'Hopkins called the fire brigade,' Q said.

'He must have been feeling guilty.'

Silence descended.

'What?' Annika said eventually. 'What is it?'

'Because we have no witnesses and no forensic evidence, there are no obvious grounds for suspicion and therefore I have no reason to hold you. You're free to go.'

Annika sat there staring at him. 'Free to go?' she said. 'Why wouldn't I be free to go? What would have happened to my children if I wasn't free to go?'

Q seemed genuinely troubled. 'There is an ongoing preliminary investigation into arson and possibly also attempted murder, but the prosecutor hasn't yet made a decision about that. These are crimes that can carry a life sentence. Someone started that fire, and you were there. Do you understand what I'm saying?'

Annika almost burst out laughing. 'Are you mad? Am I a suspect? Am I the only suspect? Are you telling me that I'm officially suspected of committing these crimes? *Is that what you're saying?*'

'Not officially, not at the moment. But the fire was started by someone who had a reason to start it. You're at the top of the list of informal suspects.'

Annika glanced out of the window. It had started to rain again.

I'm going to apply for sole custody. I'm going to get them. My children. Not going to be looked after by someone like you. Not one second longer.

'Nothing will happen until the investigating officers have received all the forensic results,' Q went on. 'That could take a while, I'm afraid. Then, when we know more, there'll be three alternatives: either you will be charged or cleared of all charges. Or the case will be dropped through lack of evidence. In this third instance there would still be concerns about you, but not enough to send you for trial.'

'I didn't do it,' Annika said. 'It wasn't me.'

'Do you know?' Q said, getting up. 'Almost everyone says that.'

Part 2
NOVEMBER

JULIA LINDHOLM CHARGED WITH DOUBLE MURDER

Prosecutor seeks life sentence

Updated 15 November, 09.54.

The case of the murder of Police Superintendent David Lindholm is approaching its conclusion.

Yesterday Lindholm's wife Julia was charged with two counts of murder and aggravated kidnapping at Stockholm City Court.

According to Prosecutor Angela Nilsson, Julia Lindholm shot and killed her husband on the morning of 3 June this year. During the days immediately before that, she also kidnapped, murdered and hid the body of their son, Alexander, four.

The findings of the criminal psychiatrist are partially confidential, but the published sections indicate that Julia Lindholm suffers from a psychiatric disorder. This is not severe enough, however, to suggest that she should be sentenced to a secure hospital.

'Considering the brutality of the crime and the vulnerability of the victims, the only suitable sentence is life imprisonment,' Angela Nilsson has told eveningpost.se.

The investigation has been protracted as a result of the psychiatric examination, as well as the amount of work required from the National Forensics Laboratory.

One source indicated that the investigating officers have been waiting for Julia Lindholm to confess where she hid Alexander's remains.

'These days it is possible to try someone for murder even

if no body has been found,' says professor of criminology Hampus Lagerbäck to eveningpost.se. 'The Thomas Quick case proved that.'

Julia Lindholm's counsel, lawyer Mats Lennström, questioned the decision to go to trial.

'As far as the murder of Alexander is concerned, there are no witnesses, no explanation as to what happened, no forensic evidence. I will be asking for that charge to be dropped.'

The court case is due to start next Monday, 22 November, at 10.00 in the high-security courtroom of Stockholm City Courthouse.

Monday, 15 November

16

The rain had turned into biting snow, the first of the winter. The flakes dissolved the moment they hit the tarmac, gathering in grey-brown pools.

Nina pulled her zip up to her chin and stuffed her hands into the pockets of her jacket.

There'll be a lot of road accidents today if this keeps up.

She looked at her watch without taking her hand out of her pocket. Her shift wasn't due to start until four o'clock.

Plenty of time.

Her teeth were chattering. *It's only the cold, nothing else.*

Bergsgatan ran uphill all the way from Scheelegatan to Kronoberg Park. The entrance to Police Headquarters lay about halfway up the hill: she shouldn't have been out of breath already.

The wind's against me, and I'm probably a bit tense as well.

She hadn't spoken to Julia since the awful meeting in her cell. After she had been officially remanded in custody the restrictions had been watertight, but through Holger she had learned that Julia had spent almost the

217

entire time either in psychiatric care or in the prison's hospital wing. Not a single visit had been authorized, not for her parents or anyone else.

'Are they trying to make an example of her?' Holger had asked.

'I don't know,' she had replied. 'Maybe.'

But now the restrictions had been lifted because the charges had been laid, the court case was imminent, and the preliminary investigation had been made public. Only the pre-sentence psychiatric evaluation was still confidential, but Nina had seen that, thanks to Holger.

'I'm here to see Julia Lindholm,' she said in Reception, to the same guard as before. He pursed his lips and disappeared into the back office, leaving her to sweat.

A female guard, a different one this time, led her through the remote-controlled lifts and shiny corridors to an ordinary visiting room on the sixth floor, right next to the women's section. There were no windows, just a table, two chairs and a tinfoil ashtray.

'If you wait here, we'll be back shortly with the prisoner,' the guard said, closing the door.

Nina sat down on one of the chairs. The room was cold and felt damp. It smelt of smoke.

Only cigarette smoke, nothing else.

Grey-white walls loomed towards her. A low-energy lamp spread a weak, flickering light from the ceiling. She knitted her fingers in her lap.

Julia has been here for five and a half months. Surely I can handle four minutes.

The paragraph-seven investigation into Julia's mental health had proved that she was in a very bad state after the murder. It took an extensive criminal psychiatric investigation to come up with a diagnosis.

The examination had been conducted during August by the National Board of Forensic Medicine in Stockholm.

I wonder how Holger got hold of it. Probably through the lawyer . . .

The door opened, and the light from a window further down the corridor turned the figure in the doorway into a faceless shadow.

Nina stood up.

Julia came into the room, her eyes moist and her hair in a ponytail. She looked older, yet simultaneously younger. No make-up, angular shoulders. 'Nina,' she said in surprise. 'What are you doing here?'

Nina looked at the prison officer, who had stopped in the doorway. 'Thanks very much. I'll ring when we've finished.'

The woman closed and locked the door.

'Julia,' Nina said, going over and hugging her friend. 'It's good to see you.'

Julia kept her arms by her sides. 'Why are you here?'

'The preliminary investigation,' Nina said, taking a step back. 'It's been made public so now I can visit you. How are you?'

Julia turned round, went to the wall by the table and felt the rough surface with her fingertips. 'This is solid concrete,' she said. 'Every room in the prison is a separate concrete module, making each one its own fireproof cell.' She went on to the next wall, letting her finger trace a crack in the surface. 'This building's been here since 1975, but there's been a prison in Stockholm since 1252. It must have been founded by Birger Jarl, I suppose.'

She glanced at Nina, then concentrated on the wall again.

'The whole of the Kronoberg block covers 161,000

square metres of space. The latest extension was finished in 2005.' She turned to Nina. 'When this is all over, I'm thinking of applying to the College of Architecture. I'm unlikely to go back to being a police officer, after all.' She smiled fleetingly.

Nina caught her gaze.

Yes, she's in there. The lights are on and she's at home.

She smiled back, relieved. 'Maybe that's just as well,' she said. 'Doing something different.'

'But you're still there?' Julia sat down beside the table, picking up the tinfoil ashtray and inspecting its underside.

'Yes,' Nina said. 'My shift starts this afternoon, handover at four. There'll be a lot of single-vehicle RTAs if the weather doesn't change.'

'Pettersson in charge?'

'Pelle Sisulu,' Nina said. 'How are you feeling?'

Julia shrugged. 'It'll be so good to get out. The flat's still there, Dad's been taking care of the rent . . .'

Nina felt a sense of unease creeping back. 'So you think you'll be found not guilty?'

Julia put down the ashtray. 'Of course I do,' she said. 'If there's one thing we learned at Police Academy, it's that the criminal justice system works. I understand that they've had to keep me locked up while the investigation was being carried out and, to be honest, I think it's probably just as well, since she hasn't been caught. Otherwise she'll just come back and shoot me too.'

Nina felt her heart sink. 'You think they'll let you go home after the trial?'

Julia blinked her big blue eyes. 'Where else would I go?'

Nina pulled her chair closer to the table, leaned forward and took one of Julia's hands in hers. 'Julia,'

220

she said, 'has your lawyer been to see you? Has he been through the preliminary investigation with you?'

Julia shook her head, eyes wide.

What a useless defence counsel! It's a dereliction of duty for him not to have informed her about the charges.

'The investigation showed that you were suffering from a dissociative identity disorder,' Nina said. 'Do you know what that is?'

Julia was staring at her uncomprehendingly.

'It's also called multiple personality disorder. It's a psychiatric condition where a person has two or more separate personalities.'

'Schizophrenia?' Julia said.

'A split personality,' Nina said. 'It's a form of psychotic condition, in which several different personalities can act independently of each other. It can occur when the mind is trying to deal with a trauma. If necessary, a different personality takes over.'

'That's not what happened,' Julia said. 'It wasn't me. It was the other woman, the evil one.'

Nina squeezed Julia's hand. 'It's okay,' she said. 'I understand.'

'No!' she said, pulling her hand away. 'You don't understand at all. She was there, and she took Alexander away with her.'

'Where do you think she took him?'

'How could I possibly know that? If I knew that, I would have gone and got him!'

Nina forced herself to sound calm. 'The blood on the hall floor,' she said. 'DNA tests have proved that it was Alexander's.'

Julia stood up and stared at her. 'You don't believe me?' she said. 'You think I hurt Alexander? That *I* was the one who fired those shots?'

221

Nina stood up too.

'I don't think you should count on being released,' she said. 'The evidence is pretty solid. You were there, you were mentally unstable, your service pistol was used as the murder weapon, with your fingerprints on it . . .'

Julia turned away and rang the bell to be let out of the visiting room. 'If I'm so mentally unstable,' she said, 'they'll sentence me to psychiatric care and I'll be out in a year.'

'I don't think you can count on that either,' Nina said. 'The criminal psychiatric investigation suggests that you committed the crime under a temporary episode of mental confusion, but that you can still be sentenced to prison.'

Julia gazed at her, her eyes so blue and radiant in the flickering light that Nina felt ashamed.

'I'll come and see you again,' she said. 'I'm not going to distance myself from you, no matter what you've done.'

The door opened and Julia walked off down the corridor without looking back.

The preliminary investigation was something of an anticlimax.

Annika, Berit Hamrin and Patrik Nilsson were sitting at the crime desk, each reading a copy of the report, getting more and more frustrated. The newsroom was quiet at this time of the afternoon: people had finally learned that live broadcasts were going on all the time and had stopped shouting across the room at each other as they used to. All the television sets had the sound turned down and you could listen to the radio only through headphones.

'How are we going to divide this up, then?' Berit asked.

'I can take Q,' Patrik said quickly.

Annika hadn't spoken to the detective since July. In the back of her mind there was always a fear that he would call, or that there'd be a knock at the door and someone would say: 'You are under formal suspicion . . .' She had no idea how the investigation into the fire was going, and she didn't want to know until it was either dropped or she was cleared.

'Go ahead and call. I've got no problem with that,' Annika said, trying to maintain a neutral expression.

'Why would you have a problem with me talking to Q?' Patrik wondered.

'It's a good idea for you to talk to the police,' Berit said. 'I can nose around the National Board of Forensic Medicine and see if I can find out anything about the psychiatric examination.'

'I can talk to the defence lawyer and try to get an interview,' Annika said.

Patrik snorted. 'Good luck with that,' he said, and Annika started to get angry.

'Then we've got the victim,' Berit said. 'Admittedly, we wrote a lot about David Lindholm back in the summer, but it's probably time to update things.'

'I can do that,' Patrik said.

Annika put her pen down.

'Can I interrupt for a moment?' All three looked up. Eva-Britt Qvist was looking at them expectantly.

'Our saviour from the newspaper dragon,' Patrik said. 'What can we do for you today?'

'There's a general meeting tomorrow at two o'clock, at the day reporters' desk. Everyone has to be there. *It's about all our futures.*' She swept on through the newsroom.

'What are we going to do with the trial?' Berit said,

223

taking off her glasses and looking at her colleagues.

'I've got the children,' Annika said quickly. She had no desire to sit through days of judicial formalities that wouldn't give them anything new.

'I can take the expert analysis,' Patrik said.

'I'm sure you can,' Berit said, 'but wasn't Sjölander going to organize that? What do you say about news updates for the website?'

Patrik grunted something to the effect that political editors ought to stick to politics.

'If you take the summary of the news for the print edition, I can do the background and fact-boxes,' Annika said to Berit.

'Are you lot having a coffee morning or what?' Spike said, dropping a printout on Berit's desk.

'What's that?' Patrik said, snatching it.

'The cop-killer's free,' Spike said. 'Viktor Gabrielsson's on a plane on his way back to Arlanda. The Foreign Ministry finally managed to get him out. I never thought they would.'

'Bloody hell,' Patrik said, standing up, cheeks ablaze. 'Do we know when he's due to land?'

The small-time Swedish gangster Viktor Gabrielsson had been an intermittently recurring story for the past ten years, sentenced on dubious evidence for being an accessory to the murder of a police officer outside New York. He had served eighteen of his fifty-year sentence, but had always fought for the right to serve his sentence in Sweden.

'Goodness, what a lot of cop-killers we're going to have in tomorrow's paper,' Annika said. 'How on earth are we going to stop them getting mixed up?'

'There's a hell of a difference,' Patrik said. 'One case was in the US, the other in Sweden.'

'The plane took off from Boston five hours ago,' Spike said.

'Okay, we'll get going now,' Patrik said.

'What about the coverage of David Lindholm, then?' Annika asked.

'You can deal with that, can't you?' Patrik said, pulling on his coat as he made hand gestures towards the picture desk across the newsroom.

Everything was quiet around them when Patrik had gone. Berit and Annika looked at each other.

'Don't be too hard on him,' Berit eventually said. 'He's just young and enthusiastic.'

'Really?' Annika said. 'He's a year older than me.'

Berit laughed. 'Well, maybe he just seems more childish,' she said. 'Do you want to take over the stuff on David?'

Annika smiled wryly. 'To be honest, I think he's more interesting than Viktor Gabrielsson, but I've already tried to get his murky past into the paper and hit a brick wall. Do you think Julia Lindholm might be innocent?'

Berit looked at her over her glasses. 'Not the tiniest chance.'

Annika picked up her bag and headed off to the day-shift's desk. She unpacked her secondhand laptop and logged into the network, waiting for it to load while looking out across the newsroom.

Eva-Britt Qvist had installed herself in Anders Schyman's glass-walled office, and was talking and gesticulating; she did that most of the time these days. Schyman was leaning back in his chair, looking tired and harassed, which was what he did most of the time these days.

After the summer holidays the paper's management had announced that there would have to be serious cutbacks across the business, but mainly on the editorial side, which had caused several days of panic among the journalists. The editor-in-chief, oddly enough, had done nothing to calm people's nerves. He had allowed the union and the gossips to run on until the whole newsroom was in chaos. Eva-Britt Qvist had burst into tears in one union meeting that she was chairing, not because she was under threat, of course – as union representative she was the only one whose position was utterly safe – but because she was *thinking about the collective*.

Eventually Spike had had enough and roared that if people didn't get a grip and come up with a few headlines, they might as well shut down the whole fucking paper straight away instead of doing it the slow way with a series of cutbacks. The reporters, editors, photographers and web managers had made their way back to their desks and got to work again.

'A fuck of a lot of fuss just because some of us get to take things easy in the future,' Spike had said, putting his feet up on his desk as he took a bite of a super-sized pizza.

'You've given up the diet?' Annika had asked, only to receive a greasy middle finger in reply.

Once the atmosphere in the newsroom had stabilized, it was simultaneously more nervous and more focused. People were more alert, which Annika had nothing against.

Less chat and more work.

She was utterly immune to communal social events, like *boules* tournaments, after-work drinks and birthday celebrations. Now all that sort of nonsense seemed to have ground to a halt.

Excellent! Just let me get on with my job.

For the first time in several years, she had also had the chance to work full-time throughout the autumn, at least during the weeks when Thomas had the children. She had focused on a series of articles about the gradual dismantling of social services provided by local councils, as well as an overview of discrimination cases in the Swedish Labour Court.

'You should be fucking grateful for the chaos here in the newsroom,' Spike had said, on the day she had turned up with her article about the nine cases in which the Labour Court had decreed that it was okay for women to be paid less than men in the same job because they were worth less to employers.

'Believe me,' Annika said, 'I am.'

Without the paralysis that the others were displaying, she would never have got a piece like that into the paper, but when the alternative was empty pages, even articles with a feminist angle could squeeze in.

No, Annika had nothing against things being stirred up a bit.

If they sacked her, they sacked her, but Annika didn't think that was very likely. She had been employed on the paper for almost ten years and ought to survive if they decided to rationalize in accordance with employment legislation. This law about employment protection, so cherished by the unions, was based upon the premise of last in, first out.

If Schyman was allowed to choose personally whom to get rid of, she'd be okay too. If that wasn't the case, she would have been history long ago.

But on the other hand, a group of young hotshots, with Patrik Nilsson in the vanguard, had suddenly understood they were in the danger zone and had therefore shifted into *indispensable* mode. Their ruthless ambition wasn't making them indispensable, though: it was making them unbearable.

The only drawback of the cuts.

She sighed and logged into the phone book. She was looking for Julia's legal representative, the lawyer Mats Lennström, from the Kvarnstenen practice. The number was engaged eight times in a row (every reporter in the country must have had the same brilliant idea as she had to interview him), but then she got through to a secretary who told her that he was in court and wasn't expected in the office until the following morning.

So much for that story.

She spun on her chair, irritated that Patrik would be proved right.

Instead she went into the newspaper's archive and pulled out the articles that had been written about David Lindholm around the time of his death.

There, once again, were all the heroic deeds, the eulogies from Christer Bure and Hampus Lagerbäck at the Police Academy. She tried calling them and left messages saying she was trying to get in touch.

Then she looked through the amazing contributions the policeman had made to society. The hostage crisis in Malmö, solving the raid on the security van . . .

But that was it.

That can't be all? Where are the rest of the heroic deeds?

She repeated the search, broadening the terms of enquiry: david lindholm achievement* criminal* *search*. Loads of hits, but no new heroic deeds. But she did find an old article about police officers working undercover. David Lindholm was mentioned at the end of the piece as an example of an officer who had extensive contacts in the underworld, who had acted as a handler to people wanting to change sides, and had been a link between different worlds.

She pushed the computer away from her, deep in thought.

Timmo Koivisto had claimed that David Lindholm had worked for the drugs Mafia. Could that really have been true? Was there any other explanation as to why he had been attacked?

How well did David Lindholm manage to maintain the balance between right and wrong? And what did the criminal world think of his double-dealing?

She checked the archive again to see what had happened to the hostage-taker in Malmö.

After several false starts she found a piece in *Sydsvenska Dagbladet,* saying that the Appeal Court had upheld the verdict of the City Court. The man had been sentenced to life imprisonment for attempted murder, aggravated kidnapping, aggravated extortion and threatening behaviour.

Life? Wow! I wonder if he was such good friends with David Lindholm after that?

She called Malmö City Court and asked them to send her a copy of the verdict.

Then she searched for information about the American who had spilled the beans about the raid in Botkyrka, but found nothing.

She rested her chin on her hand and stared at the screen.

How come the information about the American had ever got out? If someone in the criminal underworld talked, you didn't usually plaster it all over the media.

This is bloody weird.

Why had David Lindholm revealed that he had received information about the raid on the security van from that particular prisoner? Was it even true? And if it was, had it really been David who had made it public?

And what had happened to the American afterwards?

She didn't even know what his name was.

She went into the website of the National Correctional Organization and found the phone number of Tidaholm Prison. She got through to a receptionist, asked to speak to the press officer, and was put through to the main office.

'Our press officer has finished for the day,' she was told.

'Oh, that's a shame,' Annika said. 'That'll probably mean we get it wrong in tomorrow's paper again.'

'Er, what?'

'That American who was serving a life sentence with you, the man who was friendly with David Lindholm, you know the one. We're running an article about him tomorrow and I just felt I ought to check with you that our facts are correct, because they seem pretty weird to me.'

'But he's not here now,' the man said.

'The press officer?'

'No, the American.'

Annika waited a couple of seconds, letting the information sink in. 'There! I knew it. The journalist who wrote the article got it wrong. He wrote that the man was still in Tidaholm with you.'

'No chance. He was transferred straight after the accident.'

Accident?

'Of course!' Annika said. 'And naturally he never came back?'

'I'm not so sure about "friendly" either,' the man

230

said. 'David Lindholm was his trustee. There's quite a difference.'

'Trustee,' Annika said, noting that down. 'Right.'

'What's this article about?' the man asked, beginning to sound suspicious.

'It's part of a series about life sentences,' Annika said, 'but I think I'm going to have to put it on hold because the facts need to be checked properly. Where's the American now?'

She closed her eyes and held her breath.

'You'll have to call our press officer tomorrow,' the man said, and hung up.

Oh, well, better than nothing!

Something happened to the American and he was transferred.

I wonder how happy he feels about it all now?

David Lindholm needed to be investigated, as closely as possible. Every little stone he left behind him had to be turned over.

She looked at the time. She had to get something to eat first.

She pulled on her jacket and went out.

17

Thomas was sitting at his desk on the fourth floor of the government building at Rosenbad, looking down on to Fredsgatan. It was snowing, and the flakes were being blown at the window, where they slid jerkily towards the sill. He could see people hurrying along the pavements, hunched with upturned collars.

The view really wasn't anything special.

He sighed and looked at the time, then checked again that the memo and outline were in the folder where they should be. Evaluating the cost implications of abolishing life sentencing had been more complicated than he had imagined. Not that the calculations themselves were particularly difficult, but the political aspects of the inquiry . . .

The intercom buzzed, making him jump. 'Thomas, where the hell are you? I'm sitting here waiting like some old maid.'

What do you think I'm doing, then?

He straightened and pressed the button to reply to his boss. 'I thought you were going to let me know when you were free.'

'Free? I'm never free. Come over now.'

Thomas stood up, pulled the hem of his jacket down

and made sure the top button of his shirt was done up. With the folder in his hand, he headed out into the corridor and off towards Per Cramne's room.

'So, tell me what's bothering you most, then,' the assistant under-secretary said, gesturing towards a chair as he rolled up the sleeves of his white shirt.

'It's turned out to be slightly problematic,' Thomas said, sitting down. 'I don't know that it's possible to abolish life sentences under the remit we've been given.'

'Of course it is,' Cramne said, walking round the room and stretching his arms. 'Nothing lasts a lifetime any more. Why should prison sentences?'

Thomas put the folder on the desk in front of him.

This isn't going to be easy.

'I'm thinking specifically about the frame of the inquiry,' he said, crossing one leg over the other.

Cramne stopped with his back to the room, looking out over Riddarfjärden. 'I mean, we can forget marriage,' he said. 'If that lasts a lifetime, I've lived three lives – so far, I should add . . .'

He doesn't want to listen.

'Are you thinking of getting married again?' Thomas asked, moving the folder slightly.

Cramne sighed, turned and sat down. 'Employment is another thing we can take off the lifetime list. No one has the same job from cradle to grave any more. Nowadays people don't just switch employer, they switch career several times during their working lives.'

Thomas felt in his pocket for a pen.

'We also swap our friends along the way,' Cramne said. 'We can choose not to have anything to do with our siblings—'

'Children,' Thomas interrupted, looking up, pen at the ready.

'What?'

'They're for life,' Thomas said. 'You can't escape being a parent.'

Cramne snatched at the memorandum. 'Shall we stop wasting taxpayers' money and do some work?'

Thomas coughed. 'The directives,' he said, picking up the document. 'They clearly specify that the cost of the criminal justice system mustn't increase if life sentences are abolished. But my calculations indicate that the costs will rocket if this is pushed through.'

'Be more specific.'

'You know the background, of course. The longest fixed term we currently have is ten years. Prisoners sentenced to life get an average of twenty years and six months, in terms of the actual sentence. Because they get out after serving two-thirds of the sentence, that means they're out in fourteen years, more or less. If we abolish life sentences, the new maximum term for murder would be something between twenty-one and twenty-five years, probably closer to the latter, meaning that there'd be a difference of up to fifteen years between the highest penalty and the next. That doesn't make sense, and it suggests that all sentences should be adjusted upwards. Also, the current option of imposing tougher sentences would be exploited more often.'

'That's just speculation on your part,' Cramne said.

Thomas took a deep breath. 'Not at all,' he said. 'I've discussed this with three professors of criminal justice, five researchers at the Council for Crime Prevention, and with the political group, of course.'

'And what do they say?'

'Within three years, every sentencing tariff would have increased so that we had a plethora of crimes attracting sentences of twelve, thirteen years . . . Experience in

234

other countries shows that tariffs rise across the board when life sentences are abolished in favour of lengthy statutory penalties. The next time we come to sentence a multiple rapist, he'd get eighteen years.'

'And?' the section head said. 'You're a civil servant. What you're doing now is making political judgements, and you're not supposed to do that.'

The man's voice was as silky as ever, but his words held an edge.

'These aren't political judgements,' Thomas said. 'They're realistic. My task was to evaluate the cost implications of a specific legislative change, and that's exactly what I've done. If we abolish life sentences, all other sentences will increase, and it will happen within three years, which would mean a thirty per cent increase in the cost of the prison system, according to the most cautious estimates.'

Cramne stood up, walked round his desk and went to the closed door. Thomas looked at him in surprise, noting that his face seemed slightly swollen, his eyes a little red.

Is he drinking too much?

'It's like this,' Cramne said, sitting on his desk close to Thomas. 'Criminals have been shown a hell of a lot of consideration throughout the time this minister has been in office. The sentencing tariffs need to be adjusted upwards – the whole criminal justice system demands it – but the politicians are putting the brakes on. The minister even wants to abolish certain crimes.'

'Such as?'

Per Cramne stood up again and went back to his chair. 'Treason,' he said, catching the blank look on Thomas's face. 'Throwing pies at the king, although perhaps that's a bad example.' He sat down with a sigh. 'Sentencing

235

tariffs are the only thing this government has left to deal with. They've thrashed their way through all the other big issues, including the whole wretched question of bugging, but they've always shied away from this. How much more bloody obvious do I have to be?' He leaned over the desk and laid his hairy hands on Thomas's folder. 'The directive about this not costing any more money is a restriction imposed by them. You have to find a way of getting round that. We have to make sure that this gets through. We have to be able to lock criminals up, and there has to be an end to all this kid-gloves treatment.'

Thomas stared at his boss.

He wants me to falsify the calculations in a parliamentary inquiry so that he can push through a policy that has no democratic basis.

With his eyes firmly fixed on the other man's, he nodded slowly. 'Okay,' he said. 'I understand what you mean. Thank you for making it so clear.'

Per Cramne's face cracked into a broad smile. 'Excellent,' he said. 'I look forward to seeing your new cost evaluations. Consider them cost proposals!'

Thomas gathered his papers, stood up, opened the door and floated out into the corridor without quite touching the floor.

Two other reporters were tapping away at their computers when Annika returned to the day-shift's desk. One had left a mug of coffee on her folded laptop.

'Excuse me,' Annika said, pointing at it, 'but I need to do some work.'

The reporter, a girl called Ronja, of all the ridiculous fashionable names, moved her mug so that it was no longer on top of Annika's computer, but half a centimetre away from it.

The other, Emil Oscarsson, was one of the guys who had found an extra gear in order to cling on to his job. He glanced up, then returned to his screen.

Annika knocked the mug so that the contents spilled over Ronja's notes. 'Whoops,' she said, switching on her laptop.

'What the hell are you doing?' the girl said, jumping up as the coffee dripped on to her trousers.

Annika logged into the national database and pretended not to have heard her.

'Why did you spill my coffee?'

Annika looked up at her in surprise. 'Well, go and mop yourself up, for heaven's sake,' she said.

The girl was on the verge of tears.

If you fuck with me, I'll fuck you right back.

'You're crazy,' Ronja said, as she made for the Ladies.

Emil was hammering away at his computer, pretending he hadn't noticed.

She went into the national ID database and typed in 'David Lindholm, male', the postcode for Bondegatan, and there he was.

Personal information: THE PERSON IN QUESTION IS DECEASED.

But the Swedish state didn't let go of its citizens just because they had died. Here were all of David Lindholm's personal details: his ID number, full name (Lindholm, David Ze'ev Samuel), his registered address on Bondegatan, the date he was registered, county, local council, parish, and then the information: *deceased*, 3 June that year.

He must have been Jewish. Ze'ev isn't a common Swedish name. Named after Ze'ev Jabotinsky, the Jewish activist?

She clicked to get his personal report. When the image

237

appeared on the screen, David's ID number was already included in the menu.

This isn't a game any more.

She clicked *select all* and, two seconds later, was rewarded with all the information available about David: financial records including repayment defaults, debts, tax information, details of any bankruptcies, official roles in registered companies, self-employment records, the registration number of his own company, any restrictions, and what vehicles he owned.

'You really ought to pay for my jeans to be dry-cleaned,' Ronja said, gathering her things in a pretty little briefcase.

The cutbacks start to be implemented in December. She'll be history in a few weeks' time.

Annika smiled at her. 'I usually put mine in the washing-machine. But perhaps you haven't got one?'

'Well, at least I haven't set fire to it,' the girl said, and marched out of the newsroom.

Annika glanced at Emil. His face hadn't moved a muscle.

She stared at the screen in front of her and had to hold on to the desk to stop herself falling through the floor.

At least I haven't set fire to it.

That was no coincidence, and Ronja was hardly Einstein. If she knew, then everyone on the paper was aware of the police's hypothesis.

Is that what they all think? Is that what they're saying? That I set fire to my own house? Tried to kill my own children?

She stared at the computer screen for another long minute before she pulled herself together and scrolled down to read further.

There!

David Lindholm had had ambitions as a private busi-
nessman.

He had been on the boards of four different companies, two of which had been de-listed; a third was
about to be declared bankrupt.

She printed out the information and pondered what
to do next.

It would probably make sense to get to the bottom of
all this, dealing with issues as they came up. She fetched
a cup of coffee from the machine, walked back via the
printer and picked up the list, then went back to her
laptop.

The first business on the list was a trading company
that had been deregistered fifteen years ago, Fly High
Equipment HB, and David was listed as a board
member. She hadn't known they kept a record of such
old information. Now she was getting somewhere.

She went into the database of registered companies
and clicked through to the page identifying the nature
of the business. 'Trading in parachute equipment and
accessories and conducting associated activities,' it said.

So, flying high was a literal description of what they
did. David Lindholm must have been an active para-
chutist in his youth – why else would he own a company
selling the equipment?

She clicked to see who the board members were, and
who had been its registered signatories. The computer
thought for a moment, and from the corner of her eye
she saw Emil packing up his laptop and getting ready to
leave.

'See you tomorrow,' he said, and she nodded to him.

David had been a registered signatory of Fly High
Equipment with two other men, Algot Heinrich Heimer
and Christer Erik Bure.

Bure, again. They must have been really good friends.

She went back to the national database and ran a couple of complementary searches.

Christer Bure lived on Södermalm, on Åsögatan.

She checked his details as well. No debts, no bankruptcies, no links to any companies except Fly High Equipment.

She looked up the second man.

Aha!

Algot Heinrich Heimer was dead.

She checked the date: 9 February last year.

Young, only forty-five, registered in Norrköping.

She bit her lip.

Forty-five-year-old men don't die just like that. Maybe he had help.

She opened another window, went into the archive of articles and looked up Algot Heimer.

No results.

She tried 'dead *or* murder', 9 and 10 February last year.

Site found, *wait . . .*

Bingo!

A forty-five-year-old man had been shot dead in a car park outside a shopping centre in Norrköping during the evening of 9 February.

Could that have been Algot Heinrich Heimer? How high could the odds be?

She quickly opened the home page of the Office of National Statistics, and saw from the population statistics that approximately 91,000 people had died last year. Something like 250 per day, and how many of them would have been forty-five-year-old men living in Norrköping?

Not many.

'Is anyone sitting here?'

One of the evening reporters, a girl, had stopped by the chair where Emil had been sitting. What was her name? Pippi, maybe?

Annika shook her head and the girl sighed. 'Why can't people tidy up after themselves?' she said, sweeping Emil's empty crisps packet, plastic cup and crumpled notes into the wastepaper bin. 'How do they expect anyone to work if they have to—'

'Sorry,' Annika said, 'but I'm trying to work.'

The girl fell silent.

Annika called the Norrköping Police and asked to speak to the press officer responsible for the crime unit. She was put through to a mobile phone and ended up talking to a woman who was picking her child up from nursery.

'Algot Heinrich Heimer?' she said. 'No, we never arrested anyone for that murder. It's still an open case.'

So it really was him!

'What happened?' Annika asked, as she heard a small child crying in the background.

'He was shot in the back of the head as he was walking across a poorly lit car park carrying a crate of beer. The murder weapon probably had a silencer. No one heard or saw anything.'

'No tyre tracks?' Annika wondered.

The child in the background sounded out of control.

'Yes,' the woman said, sounding exhausted. 'About one and a half thousand. It's a big car park.'

Annika thanked her and hung up.

She printed out Heimer's personal details and the article about the death in the car park. She leaned back in her chair, finished her coffee and looked at the time. Five to five. Thomas would be picking up Kalle from his after-school club now, then going to get Ellen from the nursery on Scheelegatan. She felt a burning sensation in her chest, the searing pain of jealousy and feeling not quite good enough.

I'll never get away from him as long as I live.

The girl unpacked her laptop from a big rucksack, then unfolded a napkin and put an apple and a banana on it. Then she took out a china mug and a Thermos flask, and poured what smelt like stewed herbal tea.

Annika went back to the national database and looked up the next company in David Lindholm's records, a limited company that had gone bankrupt: Pettersson Catering & Arrangement AB, listed as providing restaurant and catering services, importing and exporting foodstuffs, hiring restaurant and serving staff, trading in horses, confidential documents and associated activities.

Trading in horses?

Yes, that's what it said.

The details of board members and registered signatories contained a long list of names, ten in total. David Ze'ev Samuel Lindholm was a deputy member, two from the bottom.

Annika checked through them one by one. Apart from David, they were all still alive and lived somewhere in the Mälar Valley, not far from Stockholm. The chairman of the board and managing director of the bankrupt company had been Bertil Oskar Holmberg, registered as living in Nacka, just outside Stockholm. She did a search for his personal details.

Bloody hell!

The man was linked to fifteen different businesses, some de-listed, some bankrupt, and some still active. Among the latter were a solarium, a consultancy firm, a travel agency and a property company. He had eight notices for bad payment, and owed the enforcement office a total of 509,439 kronor.

Is someone like that actually allowed to run a company?

Apparently so: no restrictions were listed.

The young reporter was now typing very slowly and deliberately on her computer on the other side of the desk. Annika concentrated on ignoring her. She printed out all the information about Holmberg and looked through the names of the board members in the other companies. None rang any bells.

Why so many? And why this business in particular? Why was David a deputy board member? There had to be a reason: that he stood to profit by it, or was doing someone else a favour by being there . . .

Her mobile rang and she dived into her bag. She just managed to answer before voicemail took the call.

It was Thomas. 'Where are Ellen's winter clothes? How the hell am I supposed to look after the children if you don't let me have their things?'

Annika clenched her teeth to stop herself screaming. Monday was when they swapped the children. One parent had Kalle and Ellen for the rest of the week, dropping them off and picking them up from nursery and after-school club, then had the weekend to wind down with them. They would leave them at nursery and school on Monday morning, and the other would pick them up in the afternoon. That way they didn't have to see each other.

'I didn't send any winter clothes,' Annika said, 'because Ellen doesn't have any. They went up in the fire. You'll have to go and get her some new ones, and a pair of decent winter shoes.'

'*I*'ll have to? You're the one who gets the child allow-ance!'

Annika shut her eyes and propped her head on her hand.

Dear God, give me strength!

'You're the one who says he wants sole custody of the children, so you can show a bit of bloody initiative for once.' She ended the call with her pulse hammering in her ears.

God I hate him!

Thomas was pursuing a case for sole custody of Kalle and Ellen through the courts. He opposed any form of adequate access for her, but had agreed to supervised visits every other weekend.

That's only so he can have a free babysitter while he goes to the pub with his girlfriend.

Thomas was claiming that Annika's violent and criminal past made her entirely unsuitable to have custody, and that the suspicion that she had set fire to the home they shared meant that she was a direct threat to the children.

The initial custody hearing had taken place in July, on one of the hottest days of the year, and had been a truly unpleasant experience. Thomas had been aggressive and arrogant and had boasted about his job in the Justice Ministry to the point at which even his barrister had looked embarrassed. Annika's lawyer, a woman called Sandra Norén, had laid a hand on her arm and flashed her a quick smile.

She had explained that Annika had acted in self-defence on the occasion many years ago when her former boyfriend had died. As far as the allegation of arson was concerned, it verged on slander. Annika had rescued the children from the flames; Thomas

Samuelsson had already left the family to spend the night with his lover.

Annika had taken all her maternity leave, and nine times out of ten she was the one who stayed at home and looked after the children when they weren't well. Apart from two weeks during the football World Cup, when Thomas had conveniently taken some leave.

The judge had taken the interim decision that they should share custody, and Annika and Thomas had avoided each other ever since.

She put her phone into her bag and was settling back to work when her eyes met those of the late-shift reporter opposite. She was openly curious. She had evidently heard the brief conversation.

'If there's anything you feel like talking about, just say,' she said, her eyes sparkling.

'Thanks, but no thanks,' Annika said.

The next company that David Lindholm had been involved in was called Advice Investment Management AB.

So many empty phrases all in a row. Advice *and* investment *and* management.

'The company will provide financial advice, business development and associated activities, but nothing that could legally be deemed banking or credit-related,' she read.

David had been a deputy board member in this business as well. There were two full members living on the outskirts of Stockholm: Lena Yvonne Nordin from Huddinge, and Niklas Ernesto Zarco Martinez from Skärholmen.

She checked out Nordin and found that she was linked to two other companies, both de-registered: a cleaning company in Skärholmen and another investment business.

She had run the cleaning company with Martinez, and the investment business with Arne Filip Göran Andersson.

She sighed and looked at the time. Martinez didn't appear to be linked to any other companies . . .

Frustrated, she pushed the computer away.

Maybe she should have something else to eat. Life always seemed a bit easier then.

She pulled out her wallet to see if she had any meal tokens left. Yes.

'Do you fancy hanging in the canteen together?' the young reporter asked.

Hanging?

Annika put the tokens back. 'I think I'll just get something quick from the machine,' she said, heading over towards the sandwiches. She chose one with cheese, ham and a tired slice of tomato.

The last company on David Lindholm's list was called B Holmberg Property in Nacka AB. The business was still going, and managed property, conducted legal transactions and other associated activities.

Oh, well.

This is pretty boring. Viktor Gabrielsson would probably have been much more fun.

She swallowed a sigh and went through the details of the last company. Again, David Lindholm was listed as a deputy board member. The managing director and registered signatory was Bertil Oskar Holmberg from Nacka.

I know that name . . .

Yes. The guy who had run the bankrupt catering firm that had done all those other odd things. She clicked, went to the printer, waited impatiently, then gathered the papers into a neat bundle.

So, what am I going to do with all this?

Check out the dead man in the car park, look into the man with all the different companies, maybe write something about David's complex personality . . .

She consulted her watch – it was almost time for the early-evening television news.

It'll just be a load of stuff about Gabrielsson.

She thought about getting a mug of coffee but decided against it: she'd never sleep. When her mobile rang, she jumped.

Number withheld.

She put the earpiece in.

'The receptionist told me you were trying to reach me. What's this about?'

A man: she didn't recognize his voice.

'Who am I talking to?' Annika asked.

'You don't know who you tried to call? My name's Christer Bure. I'm a detective inspector on Södermalm.'

Arrogant, she wrote on her notepad. 'Thanks for calling back. I'm a reporter on the *Evening Post*, and I—'

'Yes, I know what number I called.'

She decided to ignore his rudeness. 'I'm writing an article about David Lindholm, and I understand that you were a good friend of his.'

'That's correct.'

'I also understand you were in business together a long time ago. Could you tell me something about that?'

The man at the other end cleared his throat authoritatively. 'There's not much to say. We were into sky-diving, and bought and sold equipment involved in it – rigs, parachutes, helmets, jumpsuits and so on, weight belts, cutters, straps and other spares. Altimeters and height alarms, of course . . .'

Sky-diving?

'You must have been fairly committed parachutists,' Annika said politely.

'It was David who got me interested. He was obsessed, jumping whenever he had any time off. If it hadn't been for that one bad landing in Skellefteå, he'd never have stopped.'

'Bad landing?'

'The Swedish Cup. He was jumping freestyle and landed all wrong, fracturing his seventh vertebra. He was lucky not to end up in a wheelchair. That was the end of his jumping career.'

'How did he take it?'

'How the hell do you think?'

Bitter because of a parachute accident? Annika wrote.

'David was very interested in a lot of other things too, of course,' she said. 'He was a probation worker, and a custodian.'

'Yes,' Bure said. 'He wanted to make a contribution besides just catching crooks. There aren't many who can maintain that balance.'

This might be a way in.

'So this was important to him?' she asked lightly.

'Of course – otherwise he wouldn't have done it.'

'And he carried on with this probationary work right up to the end?' She held her breath.

'Of course,' Bure said firmly. 'The last time he met Filip Andersson was just a few days before he died.'

'Right, Filip Andersson,' Annika said, searching her memory frantically. *Filip Andersson, Filip Andersson . . . ?*

'David volunteered as a trustee as soon as the legislation was passed. He was probably the only person who believed that Andersson was innocent. That was so typical of him, going in and supporting someone who was so despised.'

248

Ah, that was it: Filip Andersson, the financier who was found guilty of the axe murders on Sankt Paulsgatan. *So David was his trustee?* Trustees were contact-people for prisoners serving life sentences, a sort of aristocracy within the probation system.

'Did he have any other cases towards the end, do you know?'

'Why?'

'Well, he was the trustee for that American in Tidaholm, the one who had that accident . . .'

'That bastard,' Bure said. 'David gave up on him as soon as he ended up in Kumla. There was no reasoning with him after that.'

Annika was making notes.

So the American's in Kumla. Thank you very much.

'There's one other thing I've been wondering,' she said. 'You and David ran your business with a man called Algot Heinrich Heimer . . .'

'Yes,' Christer Bure said, sounding thoughtful now.

'Do you know anything about the circumstances surrounding his death?'

There was silence on the line for a few seconds.

'He's dead?' Bure said. 'I didn't know. How sad. Was it recent?'

He's lying.

'In that case, I'm very sorry,' Annika said. 'I didn't mean to break the news like that. He was shot, on 9 February last year, in a car park in Norrköping . . .'

'I don't know anything about it.'

His tone was very abrupt, and Annika realized he was about to lose patience with her.

'I've read the reports into the allegations of excessive force that were made against David,' she said quickly. 'You know, that business with the two young men twenty years ago. I think you were there, weren't you?'

There was another silence on the line, Annika could hear it crackling. 'Hello?'

'What the hell is this? Where did you dig up that old crap?'

Annika squeezed the phone cable. 'What's your opinion of it?'

'They were just mud-slinging, nothing but slander from the gutter. David was cleared on all charges and the cases were dropped.'

He knows exactly what happened.

'Did you see any signs of anything like that ever again?'

'What? People talking shit? Every day.'

'Of David being violent.'

'Okay, this conversation is going in a direction I don't much care for. What exactly do you want?'

'I just think there are some odd circumstances—'

'Listen, if you're planning to write shit about David, I'm not interested in helping. Thank you, and goodbye.' He hung up.

She decided she did need that cup of coffee after all.

Then she sat down to write an article about David's background. She could mention that he'd had various positions in different companies and that he'd injured himself in a parachuting accident. That he'd been Filip Andersson's trustee and had met him just days before he died was fairly interesting. She could even mention that he'd been accused of excessive force and cleared, as long as she didn't go into any details.

It ended up more like a feature than a news article, rather ingratiating.

She'd added some of the information that Nina Hoffman had given her when they'd met back in the summer, about David spending long periods working abroad. She had promised to let Nina know if she was ever going to use the information.

She sighed and called her mobile.

The police officer answered immediately.

'Just so you know,' Annika said, 'I'm writing about David for tomorrow's paper. I'm mentioning the fact that he and Julia spent some time living abroad, in Estepona, for instance.'

'As long as you don't put in anything about his criminal contacts,' Nina said.

Annika was taken aback. 'What?' she said.

'You didn't hear that from me,' Nina said.

Annika put her hand to her forehead and thought so hard she could hear the cogs whirring. What did this mean?

'I'm planning to write about it for tomorrow,' she said. 'About Algot Heinrich Heimer, Filip Andersson and . . .'

There was silence on the line.

'Hello?' she said. 'Nina?'

'My colleague's just got back into the car. My shift ends at midnight. I can meet you tomorrow morning. I'll call you.' She hung up.

There's something here . . .

She packed up her things, closed the laptop and stuffed all her printouts into a plastic folder.

'Are you leaving?' the late-shift reporter said. 'Lucky you. I've got to be here all night. It's stopped snowing now so with a bit of luck we'll get a few decent days before it starts again . . .'

Annika smiled at her. 'See you tomorrow,' she said.

18

The flat was dark. Annika closed the front door behind her and went into the hall without switching the light on. She pulled off her boots and hung up her thick coat.

She stopped in the doorway to the main room, taking in the silence.

In their flat on Kungsholmen, all the sounds of Stockholm had seeped through the badly fitting windows and loose air vents, the vibrations passing through the stone walls and ventilation pipes, the buses' squealing brakes and the sirens of the emergency vehicles. But here it was quiet. The sounds of the modern city didn't reach far into the medieval heart.

She sighed and heard the sound bounce between the walls.

Still without turning on the lights she went on into Ellen's room. The day she had got the keys to the flat she had taken the children out to Ikea and let them choose their own furniture, cushions and duvet covers. Everything in Ellen's room was pink. Even the grey-black winter light was making the duvet cover and velvet cushions glow pale pink.

She ran her hand over the bed's headboard.

Emptiness, emptiness . . .

She went into her son's room. In the daylight everything was blue, but at night it looked pitch-black. She sank on to Kalle's bed. He had forgotten to take Chicken with him this morning, and she picked up the stuffed toy and hugged it, his new favourite, the same as the one that had been destroyed in the fire. This Chicken just smelt a bit different. She breathed in the clean, antiseptic scent of newness.

I ought to do the washing-up . . .

She looked through the doorway into the main room, feeling the heat from the radiators, listening to the whispers in the corners.

Alone . . .

With silence ringing in her ears, she lay down, clutching the stuffed chicken. There was still a hint of happiness somewhere, freedom waiting for her in these dark rooms.

Sleep drifted in, and she let herself go.

The sound of her mobile came from far away, shredding the peace and quiet. She sat bolt upright. Chicken slid on to the floor. Where had she left her phone?

She staggered through the main room and out into the hall.

Number withheld, damn it. It must be the paper.

She answered, and was met by a solid mass of noise, shouting, music and voices.

'Annika? Is that you?'

Speechless, she slid to the floor.

'It's me, Thomas.'

He was in the pub, somewhere really noisy.

'Hello,' she said into the darkness.

'I've reserved two snowsuits. For Ellen. At Åhléns. One dark blue, the other pink. Which one do you think we should get?' He was slurring, quite badly.

'Where are the children?' she asked.

'They're asleep. I'm having a beer with Arnold . . .'

'Who's with the children?'

'Sophia's at home, so you—'

'If you want to go out, I can look after the children,' she said.

Disco-music pounded in the background. A woman was laughing loudly.

'I don't want to fight with you,' he said.

You're calling me from the pub when you're drunk. Are you tired of her already?

'Me neither,' she said.

'What shall we do about the snowsuits?'

Why are you calling? What do you really want?

'What do you think?'

'You always say we have to think about this whole girly thing. And boys. Maybe pink isn't great. I thought . . .'

'Which does Ellen want?'

'The pink one.'

'Get that one, then.'

'You think?'

She fought back tears.

Don't call me like this. Never again.

'Let her decide. The colour isn't that important.'

'Okay. 'Bye, then.'

''Bye.'

Neither hung up. The music throbbed. The woman had stopped laughing.

'Annika?'

'Yes?'

'Do you mean it? Could you look after the kids if I go out in the evening?'

Hang up! Leave me in peace! You're tearing me apart.

'Sure.'

''Bye.'

''Bye.'

This time she clicked to end the call and put the phone into her bag, then pulled her knees up under her chin. Somewhere deep inside she felt strangely pleased.

Tuesday, 16 November

19

Nina Hoffman's flat was on Södermannagatan. The traffic noise from the main road echoed loudly along the walls of the side-street. Annika had to stifle the urge to put her hands over her ears. The building dated back to the 1920s, pale brown, a characteristically blank façade, with narrow barred windows. The flats were usually cramped and dark.

She stepped into the entrance hall. When the door closed behind her the sound of traffic miraculously disappeared. She studied the list of names: Nina lived on the second floor.

Annika went up the stairs, found the door that said *N. Hoffman*, and rang the bell.

The police officer had cut her hair. She was wearing the same grey hooded jacket that she'd had on the last time they'd met, that rainy Saturday in June when she had been so upset at the way Julia was being treated. 'Would you like some coffee?' she asked, and Annika nodded. She took off her shoes and coat in the hall.

It really was a rather dark flat, a single room with a small kitchen alcove facing the inner courtyard. But the room was fairly large, with a polished wooden floor and comfortable furniture. Nina must have had the coffee ready, because she came into the living area with a Thermos flask and two mugs, which she put on the dining table. Annika handed her a copy of that day's *Evening Post*. 'The piece about David is on page eleven,' she said.

Nina took the paper and sat down to read, while Annika poured coffee into both mugs. Nina folded the paper. 'That wasn't very smart,' she said.

Annika took a deep breath and shrugged. 'Okay,' she said. 'What's wrong with it?'

'I think you should keep away from that side of David's past. The reason he used to spend time abroad was because people were after him. They don't care to be reminded of it.'

'And who do you mean by "they"? Different criminal gangs?'

Nina stared into her coffee without touching it.

'People David helped put away?' Annika went on. 'Crooks he beat up, or their families and business associates?'

'I don't understand what this has got to do with anything,' Nina said, pushing the mug away. 'David's dead, and Julia's going to be found guilty of killing him.' She leaned forward. 'I'm telling you this as a favour. It's not all the way it looks. People have hidden agendas. You look at David Lindholm and see a corrupt police officer with a solid façade, but you know nothing about his background. His mum arrived in Sweden after the Nazis surrendered, the only survivor in her family. She was sixteen years old when she arrived, and she was already sick. She's been in a care home since David was a teenager. Don't be so quick to judge.'

Annika straightened. 'I'm not judging. On the contrary, I believe there's a chance that Julia's innocent.

260

There seem to be plenty of people out there who had a motive to kill David, and they haven't even been investigated . . .'

'What would you know about that?'

Annika drank some coffee, feeling foolish.

'You haven't a clue about what the police have looked at, have you?' Nina said. 'You don't even know what conclusions the clinical psychiatric report reached, do you?'

'No,' Annika said. 'But she can't have been that ill, if she can be sentenced to serve time in an ordinary prison . . .'

Nina stood up. 'It's called dissociative identity disorder, or multiple personalities.'

Annika felt the hairs on the back of her neck stand up.

'The diagnosis explains her suppression of events as a temporary mental disturbance in which she assumed the role of a different person, the other woman.' Nina looked out at the courtyard. 'I became a police officer because I wanted to help people,' she said. 'Sometimes I think Julia followed me because she didn't have anything better to do. She'd probably have preferred to do something else, become a social worker or a teacher, maybe an artist . . .'

She fell silent and Annika waited.

'I keep wondering if there was anything I could have done differently,' Nina went on. 'What I missed, why I wasn't good enough . . .'

'Could there have been another woman in the flat?'

Nina shook her head. 'Everything points to Julia. What I don't understand is why she's still not talking. Now she could explain what really happened between her and David. Not that it would change anything in the trial, but people would be a bit more understanding.'

Annika looked at her hands. 'My house burned down in the summer,' she said. 'I know the police are investigating whether I was responsible. They think I'm guilty, but they've got no evidence, because if they had I'd have been arrested, even though I know I didn't do it.'

She glanced up at Nina, who was watching her carefully.

'What if Julia really is innocent?' Annika said. 'What if there really was another woman? Can you imagine anything that could possibly be worse than that?'

'It's been investigated,' Nina said. 'There was no one else there.'

'Maybe,' Annika said, 'but *what if . . .*'

Nina walked over to the table, put both hands down on it and leaned forward. 'Don't confuse what happened to you with anyone else,' she said quietly and emphatically. 'You might be innocent, but that doesn't mean Julia is. Julia's been ill, but she's better now and will be sentenced to prison for a very long time. That's all there is to it.'

'But why did she do it?' Annika asked.

Nina sat down. 'Something happened towards the end,' she eventually said. 'Julia never said what it was, but she was extremely frightened and worried. She hung up whenever I rang, didn't want to meet. I was seriously concerned about her mental state, but I never imagined she'd . . . that she could . . .'

The words ebbed away. Nina took a sip of tepid coffee and pulled a face.

'Okay,' Annika said slowly. 'If I've got this right, this is what happened: David had enemies in criminal circles. He kept in touch with some of them by acting as a probation officer and trustee, and he was on the board of various companies . . .'

Nina's head snapped up.

'You didn't know that?' Annika said. 'He was involved in at least four businesses. Is it common for police officers to do that?'

Nina's eyes darted to her watch. 'I was thinking of going to the gym.'

'I've got a union meeting anyway,' Annika said. 'Just one more thing: did David ever talk about the axe murders on Sankt Paulsgatan?'

Nina was carrying the mugs to the kitchen alcove. 'Why do you ask?'

Annika scratched her head. 'He was a trustee for Filip Andersson, the financier who was found guilty of the murders. According to Christer Bure, he believed Andersson was innocent. Why would he think that?'

Nina came over to Annika and stopped very close to her. 'David really did love Julia and Alexander,' she said. 'He was a troubled man with a sick pattern of behaviour, but Julia and Alexander were the only people he really cared about.'

'Did he know anything about the axe murders that nobody else knew?' Annika asked.

Nina pulled on a duffel coat, hoisted a gym-bag on to her shoulder and headed towards the door.

The union meeting started in fifteen minutes. Annika was definitely going to be late. She walked along Folkungagatan, not inclined to hurry. The world was the colour of lead. She couldn't shake the vague sense of unreality that was enveloping her. People drifted past her, like unfathomable shadows, with such rigid expressions that she wondered if they were really alive or just pretending.

She'd woken up that morning and not known where

263

she was. The light had been falling on her bed in the main room, grey and heavy, making it difficult to breathe. She had lived there for five months, spending the whole summer on Västerlånggatan in Gamla Stan, with tourists dropping their ice-creams in the doorway and the busker's out-of-tune version of 'Streets Of London' outside the window.

She knew she should be used to it, but she understood the problem: time spread out around her, as much time as she liked, day, evening and night. The gap left by the children: so much responsibility that had vanished to be replaced by a flood of colourless *time*.

She had no idea what to do with it.

The weeks without the children had been a period of freefall, without any frame of reference, minutes and hours of shrieking emptiness. Even Berit was away.

Annika's mother had got in touch after her sister's thirtieth birthday to ask why she hadn't been there to celebrate, and Annika had said she'd been working and hadn't been able to get away. It was a lie, which her mother had seen through.

Anne Snapphane had sent a few emails, with confused and aggressive accusations, mainly repeating the things she had said the night the house had burned down: that she had given up her own life to support Annika, that she hadn't allowed herself space to grow, that she had let Annika's shaky marriage ruin her own relationship, that she had realized she always backed down and therefore had to grab what she could now and live the best life she could . . .

Annika hadn't bothered to reply, knowing she would only fuel the flames.

The solution was work.

Every day without the children, in this new reality, she

had worked from when she got up until the moment she collapsed into bed. It hadn't resulted in many articles. And now Thomas was calling her in the middle of the night from bars.

She looked at the time. Eva-Britt Qvist's big meeting had started, the meeting about *their shared future*. She stopped on the pavement, shutting her eyes against the greyness. People carried on streaming past her, bumping into her and muttering apologies for treading on her toes.

One point of stillness, something to cling to. That was all she needed. A shape and a colour in the emptiness.

20

There was a great mass of people around the day-shift desk. Annika could see Eva-Britt Qvist's spiked hair sticking up in the centre of the crowd, and presumed that she must have stood on the table in an effort to conjure up some enthusiasm. 'This is about solidarity,' she said, in a voice that was on the brink of cracking.

Annika put her bag on Spike's desk. 'Have they been at it for long?' she asked quietly.

'A fucking eternity,' the head of news said, without looking up from his morning paper. The *Norrbotten Courier*, she noted.

'We have to stand up for each other!' Eva-Britt Qvist cried. 'This isn't the time for soloists, but for the whole orchestra!'

Scattered applause.

'Don't they use that metaphor every time?' Annika said, opening a bottle of mineral water that happened to be sitting on the desk.

Spike groaned and turned a page.

'If we accept management's demands to abandon the list dictated by employment regulations, our employers will be able to fire people as they choose. We can't let

266

management have their way! We have to stick together here!'

'What exactly does the paper want?' Annika asked, taking a swig from the bottle.

'People to shut up and do some work,' Spike said, pushing the newspaper into the recycling bin.

'After all the hard work we've put into this paper! After all the times we've shown how dedicated we are, time after time after time! Through reorganizations and online launches and cutbacks, we've put up with all of that and struggled on, recognizing our responsibility to our readers . . .'

An appreciative murmur ran through the crowd.

'We have to show that we stand united in our struggle against management and their blinkered focus on profits. We have to come up with powerful counter-proposals. We in the union are today proposing a united, collective and aggressive strategy to show the bosses that we're serious. We're going to sign ourselves off sick!'

Annika choked on a mouthful of mineral water.

Sign ourselves off sick?

She stared at Eva-Britt Qvist, who had raised her arms towards the ceiling as if she were expecting thunderous applause. 'Sign ourselves off sick?' she said. 'Is she mad?'

She put the water down on Spike's desk.

'We'll show them what happens when none of us comes to work. We'll make them see the consequences of failing to listen to their colleagues . . .'

'For heaven's sake,' Annika said, 'she's away with the fairies now.'

A young girl in a suit, Ronja, shushed her.

'What?' Annika said. 'Do you think it's okay for everyone to go off sick at the same time?'

Ronja turned her back and folded her arms.

'No, seriously, tell me,' Annika said. 'Do you think it's okay to exploit the social welfare system to take revenge on our employers?'

There was now complete silence around them, as Annika's last words filtered through the group.

Eva-Britt Qvist had lost her thread. Her eyes rested on Annika, and she pointed a trembling finger at her. 'Do you have something to say?' she asked.

Everyone turned towards Annika, whose heartbeat quickened. 'Signing yourself off sick isn't an aggressive strategy,' she said. 'Exploiting the social welfare system like that is actually against the law. False certification.'

Two red marks had blossomed on Eva-Britt's cheeks. 'Solidarity!' she cried. 'Do you know what that is?'

Annika shuffled uncomfortably, feeling her colleagues' stares burn into her. 'Well,' she said, 'what about our solidarity with anyone who's really sick if we use their money just to cause trouble for Anders Schyman?'

'Solidarity is when you unite in a collective,' Eva-Britt Qvist bellowed. 'It's when you look towards something bigger than yourself – but that's something you've never done!'

Suddenly Annika was utterly incensed. She took a couple of steps forward and her throat tightened.

For fuck's sake, don't start crying.

'Okay,' Emil the temp said beside her, 'surely we can debate the subject? This is a meeting, after all.'

'Everyone has to work together,' Eva-Britt Qvist shrieked. 'We've agreed on that!'

Bloody hell! Annika thought. A temp with a bit of go in him! 'Who's agreed what?' Annika said, to Eva-Britt Qvist. 'You and who else? What about us, your fellow members?'

'Annika's got a point,' she heard someone say behind her.

'This is a collective action!' Eva-Britt Qvist cried. 'We have to stick together to get our demands through.'

'What – firing people according to the "last in, first out" list?' Annika said. 'How is that fair?'

'Exactly!' Patrik Nilsson called.

People were shuffling about now, considerably more animated than they had been just moments earlier.

'We have to stick together!' Eva-Britt Qvist croaked.

'So that you keep your job,' someone on the far side shouted. 'What about us, then?'

'Yes, exactly, what about us?'

Annika took a few steps back, walked round Ronja and picked up her bag from the newsdesk. There was now so much noise that she couldn't hear what Eva-Britt Qvist was saying. It would be a while before she could sit and work at the day shift's desk again.

Anders Schyman watched Annika Bengtzon fish a lunch coupon from her wallet and disappear in the direction of the canteen. He was sitting in an empty radio studio watching the union meeting through the open door.

Eva-Britt Qvist was an even bigger disaster as union representative than he had imagined, and that was saying something.

She's not worth fighting for.

He remembered the huge fuss when one of the papers in Småland had tried to get rid of an intransigent union boss a few years back. The man had made himself utterly impossible in his workplace. He'd opposed everything, refused to work repeatedly on the grounds that the tasks he was given were beneath him, claimed he was busy with investigative reporting when he was actually surfing the net for porn, and when he realized he was on the point of being sacked, he'd got himself elected as union boss. The paper's management had still tried to get rid of him, with the result that the Swedish trade-union movement had lined up behind that one incompetent reporter. It ended with him being appointed an ombudsman at the headquarters of the Journalists' Association on Vasagatan in the centre of Stockholm. The whole of media-Sweden had celebrated: what a victory!

That the man left three months later, after his probationary period, was something that nobody had seen fit to report, apart from the Newspaper Publishers' Association. Today he was driving a taxi in Sundbyberg.

Playing to the gallery. That's how it works. Let them have their headlines.

Now they had had their big meeting. Now the masses were riled.

He stretched his legs.

The meeting had been interesting. It had revealed a couple of rebels he hadn't noticed before. He had taken it for granted that Annika Bengtzon would oppose Eva-Britt Qvist's imbecilic ideas, partly because she couldn't stand the former editorial secretary, and partly because she reacted instinctively against rule-breaking (unless she or someone close to her was breaking them in which case it was fine).

One advantage of having Eva-Britt Qvist in the post, from his point of view, was that she was a woman. She'd never have the same authority as a man. Her lack of success would be seen as her own personal failure, and the rest of the union committee wouldn't be tainted.

She'll be easy to rationalize away when this is over. No one's going to fight for her.

After a long series of local negotiations, he and Eva-

Britt Qvist had agreed a framework for the cutbacks. According to the agreement, members of the paper's editorial management were excluded from consideration under most aspects of employment legislation, and would not be included in any lists relating to the cutbacks. Schyman had claimed that anything else would be unreasonable, and she had soon backed down.

Maybe she was counting on becoming part of that group herself.

No exceptions had been specified, and there was no attempt to define precisely what 'editorial management' meant, very little explanation at all, in fact.

That new lad, Emil, and Patrik, of course. The young lads on the online edition, and the girls in Entertainment. They would all have to go, according to the union's list.

He sat and looked at the group of newsroom staff gradually breaking up into smaller groups before disappearing, each person going back to his or her work. Then he got up and headed back to his office.

This is going to be the newspaper with the largest editorial management team in the world.

The day shift's desk was littered with coffee-cups, Coke cans and orange peel. Annika swept the rubbish into a large recycling bin and made an effort to block out the rest of the mess. She unpacked her laptop and logged in. She took out her notes from the previous evening, the jottings of phone calls she had made, the sheets of information she had dug out.

The only question was: could any of this ever be used?

There were all the people in the various companies, the forty-five-year-old who had been shot in the car park in Norrköping, the American serving a life sentence who had disappeared from Tidaholm after an accident . . .

She paused when she got to her notes from her call to the officer in Tidaholm Prison. He had said that David Lindholm had been the American lifer's *trustee. Which other prisoners did David Lindholm have official links with? How do you find out that sort of thing? Would it be in the public domain?*

She couldn't recall having thought about it before.

She went into the website of the National Correctional Organization, checked their contact details, picked up the phone and dialled the number in Norrköping. She was put through to a lawyer who dealt with freedom-of-information requests.

'This is covered by legislation guaranteeing confidentiality to those within the criminal justice system,' the lawyer said. 'It's a matter of individual concern, which means that such dealings aren't in the public domain.'

'Is it possible to apply to see them?' Annika wondered.

The lawyer hesitated. 'Yes, it's possible. If we were to receive a request, we'd deal with it in the usual way.'

'Where?'

'Here, at our national head office. We have access to all the information.'

'So you think it might be possible to find out if someone has been a trustee and, if so, who for?'

The lawyer was thinking out loud. 'Well, we can't give out any information that may harm an individual. But revealing whether or not someone is acting as a trustee could hardly be regarded as harmful. But it might be more sensitive if the person in question had served a prison sentence themselves and was now acting as a trustee. We'd have to judge each application on its own merits.'

'Great,' Annika said. 'I'd like to make an application. How long will it take to get the answer, and who will I get it from?'

'Decisions like that are usually dealt with by our clerical staff, so it shouldn't take long. You'll have an answer within a few days.'

I want an answer NOW!

Annika asked for the woman's email address, thanked her and hung up. Then she composed a request to find out for whom David Lindholm had been a trustee or probation contact, going back as far as it was possible to check.

She sighed and pushed the computer away.

Oh dear. I'm treading water.

Behind her she could hear Patrik Nilsson talking to Spike, sounding agitated – presumably something about the homeward-bound cop-killer. 'It's a fucking scandal,' he roared.

Spike muttered something.

'My source is rock-solid. The government gave the Yanks something in return for Gabrielsson. We have to find out what it was. Landing rights for the CIA at Bromma?'

Annika stood up. She didn't want to hear any more.

Please, dear proprietors, put us out of our misery and get rid of the people you're going to get rid of, then let us get on with our work in peace.

She went over to the coffee-machine and selected black coffee. She stood by one of the tables, thinking about Julia Lindholm's diagnosis. *Multiple personalities. Sounds like a bad film.* Practically every murderer these days claimed to suffer from some sort of psychological disorder. If they didn't hear voices, they were on anabolic steroids or blamed poor potty-training and broken toys

273

when they were little. Everyone should feel sorry for the unemployed because they didn't have jobs, sorry for people who had jobs because they suffered from stress, sorry for the young who'd never been given a chance, and sorry for the old who had never made the most of the chances they'd had.

Wife-killers always felt *really bad* because they hadn't been able to control their wives, not been allowed to fuck them whenever they felt like it and not been able to decide whom they talked to. All too often the courts actually showed a degree of understanding to the unfortunate wife-beaters, producing page after page to justify why they should be treated as leniently as possible. Often they managed to get the names of the victims wrong as well – Annika had uncovered several such instances. The murdered women were called Lundberg, Lundgren and Berglund more or less at random, while the poor murderer, who of course had beaten his wife to death in a nice, humane way, was sentenced to the shortest term permissible by law because he was so sad that she had ended their relationship. Ten years in some low-security institution with a herd of cows and nice lawns, and they were out after six and a half.

And now Julia was supposed to have a split personality. *How sorry should we feel for her?*

She tipped the rest of the coffee away and went back to her desk. Patrik Nilsson had left the newsdesk and was sitting at his place hammering away at his computer in the crime section, and she breathed a sigh of relief.

She did a Google search and found a site about dissociative personality disorders. She read that two different personalities could deny each other's existence or reject each other, while they each identified the same body as their own.

God, how weird! The things the human mind is capable of!

'The sufferer switches between different personalities depending on circumstances and neither can remember what the other has done. In some cases the gap between them isn't as pronounced and the sufferer can be aware of their different personalities but has a more complicated relationship with them.'

So Julia could be aware of this other woman? That could actually be possible?

She clicked to read more.

Truly split personalities were extremely rare, she discovered. In total, there were something like a thousand known cases worldwide. Multiple personality disorders shouldn't be confused with schizophrenia, which was often the case. 'One reason for the misunderstanding is that the word *schizophrenia* literally means "split senses". This, however, reflects changes in associations and logical reasoning. A schizophrenic person has only ONE personality, but his or her thoughts and actions can often appear extremely disorganized . . .'

She picked up a pen and chewed the end.

She ought to be able to write about this. All she needed was one other source who could confirm what Nina Hoffman had told her about the psychiatric report. Who would be able to spill the beans?

The lawyer! He hadn't seemed particularly blessed with intelligence.

She looked up his name and number again: Mats Lennström at the Kvarnstenen law firm.

'Mr Lennström is in court until late this afternoon,' the secretary chirruped.

She hung up and called the prosecutors' office, but Angela Nilsson wasn't available. She called the National

Board of Forensic Medicine, only to be told that they never commented on their reports.

Which left Q, and she didn't want to talk to him.

Damn! Why couldn't Lennström be in?

She leaned over the computer, thinking. Who else might give her some gossip? About Julia, and about David? Was there anyone who had no interest in protecting David Lindholm?

The people he betrayed. The ones he shopped. Those who'd got life because they'd trusted him.

Names, she thought. Find their names and work out where they're serving their time.

She wrote a list on a piece of paper.

The American to whom something had happened at Tidaholm: moved to Kumla, in the central province of Närke.

The father who had taken hostages at a nursery in Malmö: now in Kumla.

The axe murderer from Södermalm, the financier Filip Andersson: also in Kumla.

Maybe it would be worth taking a trip to Närke, to visit a few criminals? But what the hell was the American's name?

She had the name of the man from Malmö, Ahmed Muhammad Svensson. Yes, that really was his name. It was there in black and white in the court report she had been sent.

How the hell am I going to find the American?

She picked up her pen and started jotting things down. What did she actually know?

He was an American and he was serving a life sentence.

That ought to reduce the options enough to make him easy to identify. There were currently 164 people serving a life sentence, 159 of them men. And it was hardly likely that many were American citizens. Because he had been tried within the Swedish judicial system, he would be in the public records.

I need to identify the trial. What could he have been found guilty of?

It had to be either murder, kidnapping, arson, posing a serious danger to the public, aggravated sabotage of some kind, or aggravated dissemination of poison or an infectious substance . . .

She stopped at the third item on the list.

Arson.

She heard Q's cold voice echo in her chest.

The fire was started by someone who had a reason to start it. You're at the top of the list of informal suspects.

She took a short walk round the newsroom.

The other crimes that were punishable by life imprisonment would hardly apply to an American, not in Sweden during peacetime.

She put her pen down and checked them out on the Internet just to be certain: incitement to mutiny, insurrection, high treason, treachery in dealing with a foreign power, arbitrary conduct in dealings with a foreign power, aggravated espionage, aggravated insubordination, undermining morale, disregarding preparations for war, unauthorized surrender, dereliction of duty, betraying the country, unauthorized possession of chemical weapons, mines and nuclear material.

Unauthorized possession of mines? Good grief.

She sighed.

So, which court? There were dozens of them in Stockholm alone. Probably a hundred or so throughout the country. Where to start?

She looked up Stockholm City Court and its various subdivisions.

She stopped, her fingers hovering above the keyboard.

If you're given a life sentence, you appeal.

His case should have been heard in one of the Courts of Appeal.

There were only six of those: one each for the regions of Götaland and Svealand, Upper and Lower Norrland, Western Sweden and finally one for the southern provinces of Skåne and Blekinge.

She looked at the time: they usually took calls until four.

She started from the far south and worked her way up.

She was looking for a verdict in which an American had been sentenced to life, probably for murder.

On her sixth and final attempt, the Court of Appeal for Upper Norrland in Umeå, she was put through to a helpful young man in the archive.

'That sounds like Stevens,' he said. A minute or so later he sent her the case report against Michael Harold Stevens.

Annika leafed through to the summary of the verdict and let out a whistle.

An impressive catalogue of crimes.

The American had been found guilty of murder, grievous bodily harm, kidnapping, attempted extortion, posing a serious danger to the public, obstructing the course of justice, and breaches of firearms legislation.

Sounds like a hired thug who messed up badly.

She flicked through the document, all thirty-eight pages of it. In summary, Michael Harold Stevens had admitted that he had blown up a car in a quarry outside Skellefteå, which accounted for the charge of posing a serious danger to the public. A thirty-three-year-old man had been inside the vehicle and had died in the

278

explosion, hence the murder charge. He had forced a thirty-two-year-old man inside another car (kidnap), drove him to a hunting cabin outside Kåge, put a pistol in his mouth (breach of firearms legislation), and made two demands: that he withdrew a witness statement (obstructing the course of justice), and paid off a drugs debt (extortion).

The two victims had both had criminal records. They were in the same criminal gang.

Stevens had also admitted taking part in the planning of the armed raid on the security van in Botkyrka the previous year.

She sighed with annoyance, and let the document fall to her lap.

This has to be the right American, but where does David Lindholm fit into the picture? What has he got to do with any of this? Who can I call and ask?

She looked back at the first page of the report to see who had been appointed to defend Stevens: a lawyer named Mats Lennström from the Kvarnstenen law practice.

Mats Lennström? But he's Julia Lindholm's lawyer!

She picked up the phone and dialled the number for the Kvarnstenen law practice.

'You're in luck,' the secretary trilled. 'Mr Lennström has just walked through the door. We weren't sure if he'd make it back here today.'

Annika shifted restlessly on her chair as the woman transferred her call.

'Lennström,' he answered, and Annika got the impression that he wasn't even sure of that.

'I'm calling about three things,' she said, once she'd introduced herself. 'First, I'd like to interview Julia Lindholm. We've met before so she knows who I am.'

'A lot of people would like to interview my client,' he said heavily.

'Yes, of course,' Annika said, 'but I know that all restrictions have been lifted now and she can see whoever she wants, so perhaps you could pass on my request.'

He sighed.

'Then there's this business of dissociative identity disorder,' Annika said. 'The National Board of Forensic Medicine has decided that Julia can serve time in prison, even though she's evidently been acting as someone else, this other woman. What's your view on that?'

'Er,' the lawyer said, 'well, that's their expert opinion, so I don't really have any comment to make.'

Hurray! Confirmation! Now it was publishable!

'And I was also wondering what really happened to Michael Harold Stevens,' Annika said.

There was a moment's silence, then the lawyer cleared his throat. 'Why are you wondering about that?'

'David Lindholm was his trustee, of course, but Stevens had some sort of accident at Tidaholm and was transferred to Kumla, and after that Lindholm was no longer his trustee. I wondered what happened.'

'Have you read the report from the trial?'

'Yes.'

'Then you know that Mike confessed.'

'Yes.'

The lawyer paused – it sounded to Annika as though he was taking off his jacket. 'Well,' he said eventually, 'it must fall outside the statute of limitations now. The policeman's dead, and Mike's never going to pursue the case.'

Annika waited in silence.

'David Lindholm was in charge of questioning Mike,' Mats Lennström said. 'He confessed to everything he

280

was charged with, and quite a bit more besides. The armed raid in Botkyrka, for instance.' He fell silent.

'But?' Annika said.

'When the sentence was upheld by the Court of Appeal, Mike was taken to Kumla for evaluation – everyone sentenced to more than four years goes there first. Then he was sent to Tidaholm, and presumably that was when he grasped he'd been fooled.'

'Fooled?'

'Yes, I should have checked it all a bit more thoroughly. Mike and David Lindholm had come to an agreement under the terms of which he would have served a shorter sentence at the facility in Ljustadalen. But none of what David promised him was legally binding. I ought to have realized . . .'

Annika sat up straight in her chair. 'Do you mean to say that you didn't know if it was legally binding or not? And that you didn't check, if you weren't sure?'

'You trust the police, don't you?' he said. 'Especially such a renowned figure as David Lindholm.'

What an idiot! It's hardly surprising they picked him to defend Julia, if they wanted to get her put away.

'What sort of accident did he have?'

'He slipped in the shower and fell on something sharp.'

Annika had to suppress an audible snort of derision. 'Puncture wounds,' she said. 'Mike talked, and five men were locked up for the Botkyrka raid. They weren't exactly happy about it. They had friends in Tidaholm. They sharpened their toothbrushes or cutlery and attacked him in the shower.'

'That's all speculation on your part.'

'Tell me one thing,' Annika said. 'What did Stevens do in return? Did he get back at the Botkyrka gang, or David, maybe? Or his wife? Or his son?'

281

'If you'll excuse me, I've got a lot to do,' he said, and hung up.

Annika sat there, staring into thin air for a whole minute.

There was nothing remotely heroic about the way David Lindholm had solved the raid on the security van in Botkyrka. Quite the reverse. He had used his public reputation to gain a man's trust, then betrayed him.

What an arsehole!

She moved on to the second man on the list, Ahmed Muhammad Svensson. She pulled out the report of the trial in Malmö City Court: attempted murder, aggravated kidnap, aggravated extortion and threatening behaviour. Ahmed Muhammad Svensson had married a Swedish woman and taken her surname to make it easier to fit into Swedish society. It hadn't worked out very well. He hadn't been able to find a job and had become depressed, then begun to hit his wife and their four-year-old daughter. In the end Mrs Svensson asked for a divorce.

Then Ahmed Muhammad had got hold of his neighbour's hunting rifle and gone to their daughter's nursery. He had arrived in time for the afternoon break, when all the children were eating rosehip soup and almond biscuits. He had announced loudly and in tears that he was going to shoot the children, one by one, until his wife stopped the divorce proceedings and the Swedish government gave him a million kronor. And a new colour television.

God, how tragic.

The hostage drama had got out of hand at once.

One young man, a student at a nearby sixth-form college, had been doing work experience at the nursery and managed to get out through the balcony door to the car park at the back of the building. Ahmed Muhammad Svensson had fired three shots at him, hitting a parked car and a lamp-post, hence the charge of attempted murder.

The lad had naturally sounded the alarm and ten minutes later the whole nursery had been surrounded by police and emergency vehicles. At the trial the staff had described how Ahmed Muhammad Svensson had been terrified by the commotion and had sat hugging the rifle as if it were his only salvation. The local police had obviously tried to talk some sense into him, but he hadn't been willing to enter into any form of dialogue.

It had just so happened that the experienced negotiator David Lindholm was in Malmö for a seminar that day. Someone high up in the police was aware of this, and Lindholm was called to the scene as an expert. Lindholm had, entirely of his own volition, gone inside the building and talked to Svensson for about two hours. The children had come out in groups of five, accompanied by a member of staff. Svensson's daughter had been in the last group.

Finally the hostage-taker himself had emerged, arm in arm with Police Superintendent Lindholm.

In court David Lindholm had testified that Svensson had threatened to shoot the children, the staff and himself, and that he had believed he was likely to carry out his threat at any time. Svensson hadn't said much, just that he regretted what he had done and would never have been capable of harming children.

And he was given a life sentence. Poor bastard!

Because David Lindholm had betrayed someone, again.

I wonder what he did to the third, Filip Andersson?

She shivered slightly: those terrible axe murders. The paper had printed acres of coverage. She typed 'facts filip andersson' into the computer and waited.

And waited and waited.

What's this? Why's it going so slowly?

Then the screen flickered and a short list of articles appeared. 'Notes and facts filip andersson' she read on the first one. *This looks very odd . . .*

She studied the screen, and realized she'd typed the terms of the search into the wrong box. She hadn't searched the Internet or the newspaper's archive, but the hard-drive of the laptop.

So . . .

She clicked on the file and up popped an ordinary Word document.

'Is he innocent?' she read.

Facts pointing to FA: 1. He had evidently been at the scene of the murders. His fingerprints were on the door-handle, on the female victim's handbag, and in four different places inside the flat. 2. He must have been present when the murders were committed. He left his trousers to be dry-cleaned the following day, the police found the ticket in his wallet and managed to pick the trousers up just before they were cleaned. On one trouser-leg there were traces of blood whose DNA matched the female victim. 3. He had a motive. The three people in the flat had deceived him somehow, although in what way is unknown.

Yes, so far this all makes sense.

Facts against FA being the killer: 1. Why weren't there any traces of blood from the other victims on his trousers or other clothes? Chopping up the victims like that means you have to be in close contact with them. You can't just swing at them: you have to stand on the arm or leg to hold it down on something solid, in these cases usually the floor, but in one instance a table, and for that to work the victims have to be either drugged or otherwise rendered compliant, in this case with blows to the head. It seems extremely unlikely that the murderer could have avoided getting any blood on his body and clothes, considering the quantity of blood involved. 2. Where's the murder weapon? Is it really just an ordinary axe? Wouldn't some sort of broad-axe or mattock or chopping tool, like a meat cleaver, have been more effective? 3. Why didn't he throw his trousers away? The traces of blood that were found were microscopic. Might he not have known they were there? Why not? NB check tomorrow. 4. There were a lot of fingerprints in the flat, many of them unidentified. 5. Most importantly: there were traces of blood and DNA from another person at the scene of the murder, and these have never been identified either. An accomplice who was injured in the struggle?

She was staring open-mouthed at the laptop.

This wasn't a published article. It wasn't even publishable. It was a list of notes someone had made to help them keep track of the case, possibly because they were covering the trial or . . .

Sjölander! This was his old computer!

She clicked 'archive', then 'properties', and sure enough, Sjölander was listed as the author of the document. It had been written almost four years ago to the day, just before Filip Andersson's trial.

So Sjölander had had doubts about his guilt.

So had David, according to Bure. More than just doubts.

He was probably the only person who believed that Andersson was innocent . . .

Why? How could David have been so sure of Filip Andersson's innocence? What did that mean? And why was Filip Andersson so quiet? If he was innocent, why hadn't he co-operated with the police?

She opened up the website of the National Correctional Organization again, and checked visiting times at the huge prison in Kumla: Monday to Friday, from nine a.m. until three p.m., weekends from ten o'clock until two.

Brilliant! Open every day! That's what I call service!

She dialled the number of the main prison office and introduced herself. 'I'd like to visit one of your inmates, a Filip Andersson.' The officer transferred her to the acting prison governor and Annika repeated her request.

'That won't be possible,' the governor said.

'Really?' Annika said. 'Why not? I thought you were open for visits every day.'

'We are,' the governor said. 'Three hundred and sixty-five days a year, except leap years. Then we're open three hundred and sixty-six.'

'So why can't I come?'

'You'd be very welcome,' the governor said, sounding simultaneously amused and weary, 'but the same rules apply to the media as to everyone else. Inmates can apply for permission to receive a visit or phone call from a particular individual, with their full name, postal address and ID number. They must also specify their relationship to the visitor. Then we evaluate the visitor, performing a criminal background check, and the inmate is informed either that a visit permit has

286

been granted or denied, or that a visit can take place only under supervision. Inmates are then permitted to contact their visitor, who must then book a time with us.'

'Wow,' she said. 'There are three men I'd like to visit. Please could you ask them to apply for permits to see me?'

The governor was a master of patience. 'I'm afraid not,' he said. 'We don't act as go-betweens any more. You'll have to contact the inmates yourself by letter or fax.'

'I assume I can't email?' Annika said.

'You assume correctly,' the governor replied.

'But they're allowed to reply by fax or letter?'

'Not by fax, but they're allowed to write letters. But I should warn you that they often don't reply. Most of them don't want any contact at all with the media.'

'What a nuisance,' Annika said.

'What's the purpose of your visits?' the governor asked.

Annika hesitated. What did she have to lose by being honest? 'I'm writing an article about David Lindholm, the police officer who was murdered. Three of your inmates had some sort of relationship with him. How long does it take to get a visitor's permit, assuming they do want to talk to me?'

'About a week, ten days. But I have to tell you that you can only visit one of our inmates, unless you're a close relative.'

Annika closed her eyes and ran a hand through her hair. 'What?'

'If you have three brothers, you can visit them all, but you can't have permits to visit three different prisoners without there being an exceptionally good reason. You'll have to pick one.'

'You don't seem terribly keen on having the media visit your prisoners.'

'We're not, really,' the governor said. 'But we don't prohibit it. And if you do come, I must warn you that photography is forbidden.'

Annika straightened. 'Why?'

'Chapter one, paragraph nineteen of the Criminal Custody Act 2006:26. "Audio recording and photography are not permitted within the premises of the facility."'

She slumped in her chair. 'Okay,' she said. 'Should I use the fax number on your website?'

'That would be best,' the governor said.

She said goodbye and pushed the computer away from her, glancing at the time, then looking out across the newsroom, with its flickering screens, bowed heads and coffee-stained desks.

He'll have picked up the children by now.

They'll be on their way home.

21

The lift doors were the lovely old-fashioned sort, two folding gates that had to be pushed aside to reveal the polished brass interior to those who inhabited the property in Upper Östermalm. Thomas could still remember how well thought-out the period detail had seemed the first time he had taken the lift up, with his own keys, to his own flat, in his own building.

'Daddy, she's pushing me!'

He moved his briefcase from one hand to the other and couldn't help sighing. 'Listen, both of you,' he said, grabbing his son's collar to stop him hitting his sister. 'Will you please stop fighting? We're almost home now.'

Yes, this is my building. Well, it's hers, but . . .

He tugged open the outer gate.

A howl of pain echoed through the stairwell. He looked down in surprise to see Ellen's contorted face lifted towards him. Her fingers were trapped in the folded gate, her eyes overflowing and her cheeks bright red. He quickly shut the gate to free her, and she curled into a little ball at his feet, nursing the damaged fingers in her other hand.

'Oh, little one, what on earth were you doing? You

mustn't put your fingers there when Daddy's opening the door.'

Blood was dripping on to the marble floor, and at the sight of it her screams increased. 'Blood, Daddy!'

Thomas could feel himself going pale. He wasn't good with bodily fluids.

'There, there, let Daddy see. Do you want me to blow on it?'

He crouched beside his daughter, but she turned her back on him and pressed her hand to her new snowsuit. Damn! Now it'd be covered with blood. 'Darling, let Daddy see.'

'You hurt me!'

'I know, darling, and I'm sorry. I didn't mean to but I didn't see you had your hand there. I'm so sorry.'

He picked her up, careful not to get blood on his coat. She burrowed her head against his neck, wiping tears and snot on the collar of his suit jacket.

'It *huuurts*.'

'It's okay,' Thomas said, breaking into a sweat.

'She's always so clumsy,' Kalle said, staring wide-eyed at the blood that was already turning dark on the floor.

'Okay,' he said, 'into the lift now.'

He guided his son in with one hand, holding his daughter with the other, then grabbed for his briefcase and put it inside the lift, closed the gates, and let Kalle press the button for the sixth floor.

The loft apartment.

The penthouse, as Sophie described it on her website.

'It *huuurts*, Daddy.'

'There, there,' Thomas said, watching impatiently as the floors slid by, the chandelier on the third floor disappearing past his feet, the panelled walls of the fourth with their patrician portraits and double doors.

'What are we having for tea?' Kalle was always hungry these days.

'I'm not sure. Sophia was going to make something.'

The lift stopped at the top of the building with a little shudder.

'Now, keep your fingers out of the way,' he said unnecessarily loudly, before he opened the gates.

He couldn't be bothered to hunt through his briefcase for the keys to the flat so he rang the bell with his free hand as he hoisted Ellen with the other. 'Shush, shush,' he said, rocking her rather helplessly.

Nothing happened. Ellen's screams started to subside. He couldn't hear any sounds inside the flat. The little girl was starting to feel very heavy on his arm. Was Sophia not at home?

He rang the bell again.

The door flew open. Sophia was wearing an apron and had her sleeves rolled up. There was a tiny wrinkle between her eyebrows. 'Did you forget your keys?' she asked, then noticed that Ellen was crying.

Thomas pushed past her and knelt to put his daughter down on the hall floor. 'Okay, now you have to show Daddy your hurt fingers,' he said, taking the child's hand.

'Has there been an accident?'

He closed his eyes for a second and swallowed, let go of Ellen's hand, then stood up and smiled. 'Darling,' he said, kissing her cheek. 'Ellen got her fingers caught in the lift door and she's bleeding quite badly. I need to get her cleaned up.'

'You did it,' Kalle told him sullenly, glaring at Sophia.

'Take your snowsuit off and hang it up, then go and wash your hands,' Thomas said, shrugging off his own coat. It would have to be dry-cleaned before he could

291

wear it again. He glanced down at his jacket. Same thing.

He looked at Sophia. She didn't notice his silent plea and went back into the kitchen.

Annika always took care of the dry-cleaning.

The thought hit him out of nowhere and made him blink.

Yes, that was how it had been, ever since he'd lost the ticket for the old angora cardigan her grandmother had given her. Now he dropped his coat and jacket on the hall bench. 'Right, then,' he said, picking up the little girl again. 'Let's go and put a plaster on them.'

She had almost stopped crying now. He carried her into the bathroom and discovered a cut right under the cuticle on her right ring-finger. She'd probably lose the nail.

'It's blue,' Ellen said, staring in fascination at the end of her finger.

'Like blueberry pie,' Thomas said, and she giggled.

He sat down on the lid of the toilet and put his daughter on his lap, rocking her gently. 'I'm so sorry,' he whispered.

'Do you get sweets for squashed fingers?' She looked at him hopefully as she wiped her nose on her sleeve.

'Maybe,' he said. 'If we've got any.'

'You can get them in the shop. Foam cars are good.'

They went into the sitting room, hand in hand. Ellen was still trembling a little with shock.

She's so fragile. I have to take better care of her.

Kalle had left his snowsuit on the hall floor. Thomas swallowed his annoyance and bent to hang it up.

When he stood up, Sophia was watching him from the kitchen door. 'If you keep tidying up after him like that, he'll never learn,' she said.

He shrugged, smiled, then held out his arms. 'You're right,' he said, tilting his head to one side.

She smiled back. 'You can sit down at the table – dinner's ready.' She disappeared into the kitchen again. Thomas went to the dining-table in the studio and ducked instinctively in the large, open space of the room. The ceiling height in the hall and bathroom exaggerated the difference: the studio had to be seven or eight metres tall at its highest point. The oblong skylights and muddle of beams made you think of Tribeca or some other hip New York neighbourhood (not that he had ever been in an apartment in Tribeca, but Sophia had, and she had explained the similarity to him).

'Kalle,' he called over his shoulder. 'Dinner.'

He could hear the bleep of a PlayStation game from his son's room, which wasn't really much more than a cupboard, and sighed. He picked Ellen up and sat her on a cushion so she could reach her plate. Sophia had thought buying a higher chair unnecessary: 'She'll soon be taller.'

She came in with a bowl of mashed potato and a frying pan full of slices of fat sausage.

'Kalle!' Thomas called again, sitting down. 'Dinner's on the table!'

'I just need to die first.'

'No! Come here *now*!'

Sophia was looking down at the table: she didn't like it when he shouted.

There was a demonstrative sigh, then the noise of the game stopped and Kalle came out into the studio. 'I was about to beat my highest score *actually*.'

Thomas ruffled his hair. 'Well, you can have some sausage instead.'

'Yum!' he said, scrambling up on to the tall, leather-covered chrome chair. 'Are those onions? Yuk. Can I scrape them off?'

'Just try one,' Thomas said.

'Here we eat what we're served,' Sophia said. 'Some wine?'

She was smiling at Thomas. He smiled back. 'Thanks, I'd love some.'

All food tastes so much better with wine. Meatballs and pasta taste better. Sausage tastes better. Even instant mashed potato becomes edible. I've drunk far too little wine up to now.

They touched glasses.

'How was your day?' she asked, tasting her Rioja.

He took a sip and closed his eyes. *Divine.* 'Oh,' he said, putting his glass down. 'Cramne's ignoring me since I pointed out how impossible it was to follow the directives. He just thinks it's a good idea to raise the sentencing tariffs, and I don't really think I have much of an opinion on that, but the costs are bound to increase, which conflicts entirely with the directives we were given for the inquiry.'

He took another sip, and Sophia nodded understandingly.

'I'm glad you pointed that out,' she said. 'Now this socialist government will have to think again, thanks to you.'

He put his glass down and looked at his plate. He'd voted for this socialist government and thought they were doing a reasonable job. He knew Sophia didn't share his opinion, but she probably imagined that he shared hers.

Annika always voted left of centre.

He pushed the thought away. 'What about you?' he said. 'How has your day been?'

Just as Sophia opened her mouth to speak, Ellen started crying. 'It hurts again, Daddy,' she said, holding her plastered finger towards him. He saw that the plaster was too tight: the tip of her finger had swollen.

'Oh dear,' he said, blowing on her hand. 'We might have to give you a little pill so you can get to sleep with that naughty hand.'

'Or sweets,' Ellen said, wiping her tears.

'Maybe you're allowed sweets even if you haven't squashed your finger,' Kalle said.

'You have to eat up first,' Thomas said. 'Then you can have a look in my briefcase.'

'Hurray!' Kalle said, waving his knife and fork and splashing sausage fat on the wallpaper.

'Oh, no,' Thomas said. 'Look what you've done!'

Sophia got up to fetch a clean dishcloth and wiped the wall. There was already a stain.

'Now sit nicely at the table,' Thomas said, and Kalle shrank away from his gaze.

They ate in silence.

'Can I get down?' Kalle said, putting his knife and fork together.

'Wait for your sister,' Thomas said.

Kalle groaned. 'But she's so slow.'

'I've finished now,' the little girl said, pushing away her plate.

'Okay,' Thomas said, and breathed out quietly, relieved, as the children rushed out into the hall to find his briefcase.

He and Sophia touched glasses again.

'This is the life,' she said, looking into his eyes as they drank.

He didn't answer, just looked at her glossy blonde hair and bright eyes.

Sausage and powdered mash. This was the life?

'It's not hard to make the world sparkle for a party,' she went on, 'but we need to make the most of an ordinary Tuesday, like today. It's important to add a bit of sparkle to everyday life.'

She was right, of course.

So why does it make me feel so embarrassed? Why am I just thinking this is bollocks?

'Are you thinking about work?' she asked, putting a hand on his arm.

'I'm afraid so,' he said. 'The verdict in the first appeal for clemency is due in Örebro District Court tomorrow.'

She looked at him quizzically. 'Clemency?'

He opened his mouth to go on, then realized that she didn't understand the workings of the judicial system.

Of course not, why should she?

'Up to now, people serving life sentences have only been able to get their sentences limited by asking for clemency, but that system was never entirely legally sound. The government never gave any explanation for its decisions, and they couldn't be appealed against, but for a while now lifers have been able to turn to Örebro District Court as well, to get their appeal for clemency adjudicated. They're represented by a legal ombudsman and are given a judicial motivation for the decision. The first verdict's due tomorrow.'

He took a sip of wine.

'It wouldn't be a bad thing if the case was rejected,' he said. 'Obviously it wouldn't be good if the first signal was that it was much easier to pursue cases in Örebro than with the government.'

'But why Örebro?'

He smiled at her. 'Where are the largest prisons?'

'Which prisons?'

'Kumla and Hinseberg. The largest male and female prisons respectively. And where are they?'

She opened her eyes wide. 'In Örebro County?'

'Bingo!'

She laughed. 'Imagine,' she said, 'I never knew that. What a lot I'm learning now I'm with you!'

He looked towards the children, who were sitting by the door to the hall sharing out the sweets between them.

He had had the same discussion with Annika long before, when the location of the new clemency procedure was still under discussion. She had also questioned Örebro as a suitable site, and he had said the same thing then: 'Where are the largest prisons?'

'Bullshit!' had been Annika's response. 'By the time they come to apply for clemency they're no longer in Kumla or Hinseberg. They're out in some open prison in the middle of nowhere waiting to be rehabilitated. The only reason this is being linked to Örebro is that it's in the minister's constituency.'

He remembered how taken aback he had been because the idea hadn't occurred to him. 'You're making that up,' he had replied, and she had shrugged.

Now he looked at Sophia again. 'What about you, then?' he asked. 'How are you?'

'Such a funny thing happened today,' she said, but at that moment Kalle came racing towards him.

'Daddy, tell her off! She took the last sweet because she said she was the one who got hurt.'

He emptied his glass and stood up. 'If you fight about the sweets, I'll take them away,' he said, then turned back to Sophia. 'You stay there, I'll clear up later. I need to get her snowsuit into the wash – there's blood all over it.'

He headed off towards the hall, and from the corner of his eye, he saw Sophia refilling her glass.

Evening Post – Stockholm Edition
Thursday, 25 November

'It Has To Be Life'
Experts unanimous after police trial

By Berit Hamrin

Evening Post (Stockholm). Life imprisonment. Anything else would be unthinkable.

Prosecutor Angela Nilsson was absolutely certain when the trial of Julia Lindholm concluded at Stockholm City Court yesterday.

'I've seldom been involved with such a calculated and brutal crime.'

Prosecutor Nilsson didn't spare the accused during her final statement in the high-security courtroom yesterday afternoon. She called Julia Lindholm 'emotionally cold' and 'cunning', and demanded nothing less than life imprisonment.

'Killing your child, refusing to say where you hid the body and then pretending that you're a different person . . . There aren't actually any words to describe what I think of that,' the prosecutor said, among other things.

The three-day trial in Stockholm City Court has seen a lot of emotion and grief. The presiding judge has had to call for calm on several occasions. David Lindholm's colleagues have been seen sobbing openly in the public benches. Julia Lindholm's parents have attended all three days, and her mother broke down several times.

Julia Lindholm herself was extremely concise in her testimony. She answered in monosyllables and showed no emotion. She claims that there was another woman in the flat on the night of 3 June this year, and that it was this other woman who shot her husband and then took her son with her when she left.

According to the forensic examination of the crime scene, there is nothing to suggest that anyone else was in the home, which is one reason why a psychological evaluation determined that Julia Lindholm was suffering from a mental disorder at the time of the crime.

Julia Lindholm's lawyer, Mats Lennström, maintains that there are clear gaps in the prosecution's case.

'Most troubling is, of course, the fact that Alexander Lindholm's body has never been found. But there are also other assertions that I believe must be questioned. Julia has already said she had mislaid her service revolver. And there were no traces of gunpowder on her when she was arrested.'

The prosecutor dismissed the defence lawyer's objections in her final statement.

'You can't get away with murder simply because you've managed to make the body disappear. The fact that the defence claims that she had mislaid her service revolver and had had time to wash her hands before the police arrived on the scene does not count as extenuating circumstances, but rather the opposite.'

The verdict will be announced on 2 December. Until then, Julia Lindholm will remain in custody.

Hampus Lagerbäck, professor of criminology, who was a close friend of the victim, is in no doubt about what this means: 'Clearly, she's going to be found guilty. No one I've spoken to expects anything but a life sentence.'

Part 3
DECEMBER

Wednesday, 1 December

22

It was snowing. White ice-crystals lashed Annika's face as she made her way along Vasagatan. The streetlamps were blurred and yellow in the darkness, and when she peered across at the Central Station she couldn't see anything but swirling snow. She felt giddy and groggy, unused to being up so early. She was having trouble judging distances and kept stumbling.

Taking the train instead of driving had been a stroke of genius, not just because she was so tired. The traffic was solid, wheels were spinning at the lights and no one was getting anywhere. She checked the time: fifteen minutes to go.

Almost two weeks had passed since she'd faxed her letter to Filip Andersson in Kumla Prison.

The acting prison governor had been right. Neither Stevens, the American, nor the Arab, Svensson, had replied to her faxes, although she had written to them three times. But Filip Andersson, the axe murderer, had come back to her by return. He would be very happy to see a representative of the media, and if she could send him her personal details at once, he would arrange a visitor's permit. He also took the opportunity to send her a lot of information about his case. The envelope exuded the heavy stench of miscarriage of justice. He had news for her, he said, and it was important that she was well acquainted with the facts of his case.

With a degree of reluctance, she sent him her personal details. Of course there was nothing confidential in what she was sending: her address and ID number were matters of public record, but she had still felt uncomfortable faxing them to him.

What could he possibly do, though? Hide under her bed clutching an axe?

And that was hardly likely, seeing as she slept on a mattress on the floor.

In fact, out of the three of them, Filip Andersson had been the one she was least keen to meet. She persuaded herself that this was because he was least likely to dish the dirt on David Lindholm. On the other hand, Filip Andersson was probably the most likely of the three to be able to express himself articulately. According to the trial report, Svensson had spoken through an interpreter, which suggested that his Swedish wasn't good. Maybe he hadn't been able to read her fax, but she'd had no other way of contacting him so had had to give up.

There had been nothing about interpreters in the report of the Stevens trial, so she presumed that his Swedish must be reasonable, but her limited experience of hired thugs suggested that he was hardly likely to be particularly talkative.

Which left the axe murderer from Sankt Paulsgatan. She had booked a time at the visitors' section of Kumla Prison for eleven o'clock today, 1 December.

She had to admit that she had slept badly. Not just because she was going to be locked into a confined visiting room with a mass-murderer, or because the children were back with Thomas and his wretched ice-maiden, but because something was gnawing away at her, something she had missed, and she hadn't managed to work out what it was.

I'll have to try to wheedle it out of him, whatever it is.

She had been through the verdict in Filip Andersson's case carefully, and had checked Sjölander's old computer for any more files relating to it, but had found nothing else.

There were certainly weaknesses in the case, but she hadn't found any glaring errors. Filip Andersson had been at the scene of the murders; he had had both the opportunity and the motive. According to one witness, the three victims had tricked him out of a large sum of money, which was presumed to have provided the motive: revenge. It wasn't mentioned in the report of the trial, but Annika knew that theft rarely went unpunished in Filip Andersson's world. Not to respond might be seen as an invitation to further attempts, which was evidently why Andersson had decided to make an example of them.

A gossip blog for journalists had provided more details about the nature of the victims' deception, but Annika had no way of knowing how accurate that was. The blog claimed that the three had been involved in an elaborate money-laundering scheme largely based on the Spanish coast. Through a number of different property deals, mostly conducted through Gibraltar, they had managed to process the considerable profits of trafficking cocaine from Colombia via Morocco.

Annika had some difficulty in envisaging the staid Swedish financier as the business partner of a South American drug lord, but what did she know?

The three murder victims, who were all fairly low down the criminal food-chain, had put the money in their own pockets and believed that Andersson wouldn't notice. Which was why he had chopped off their hands: they should have kept their greedy fingers to themselves.

But there were undoubtedly some details of the case that struck Annika as very odd.

Most significantly, if Filip Andersson was so high up the food-chain, why would he do the dirty work himself, allowing his smart trousers to be splattered with blood? Had all the thugs-for-hire been on holiday at the same time? Or was he simply a sadist?

If he had the ability and ruthlessness to build up an advanced drug-smuggling syndicate, would he really have left his fingerprints on the handbag of one of the victims?

And why hadn't there been more blood on his trousers?

And why on earth use an axe?

The entrance to the Central Station emerged through the swirling snow in front of her and she went inside, stamping her feet. She had booked a first-class ticket so she could sit in peace and do some work on the journey. The train was due to leave at seven fifteen, and after a change at Hallsberg she would get to Kumla at nine thirty-two. She would return to Stockholm on the one twenty-eight, and was already looking forward to it.

The Central Station was literally black with people, even though it was still extremely early.

Why doesn't anyone ever wear bright red in winter? Or orange? Do nature, the climate and the Swedish need to fit in drain all the colour out of us?

She hadn't had time for breakfast, so she bought a yogurt drink and an apple from a kiosk.

The train rattled into the station just as she emerged on to the platform. She found her carriage, then her seat, took off her coat, settled into the seat and fell asleep immediately.

She woke with a start when the tannoy announced, 'Next stop Hallsberg, Hallsberg next stop.' Groggy with sleep, she struggled into her coat and tumbled out on to the platform seconds before the doors closed and the train headed further south.

She was on the point of getting into a taxi when she remembered that she wasn't in Kumla yet: she still had the six-minute trip on a local train.

I have to pull myself together. I have to be focused when I meet the axe murderer.

She shook herself to clear her head. She had to run to catch the train to Örebro. The flat countryside with its brown fields and grey farmhouses spread out around her as the train set off, and her eyes found nothing to focus on until she saw a strip of pine forest on the horizon, blurred by mist.

She was the only passenger to get off in Kumla.

It had stopped snowing. Dampness hung heavy and cold over the town. The train rumbled off, leaving an echoing silence behind it. She stood there listening to it for several seconds. Around her she saw a big ICA supermarket, a Pentecostal church, the Hotel Kumla. Hesitantly she set off towards the exit, her heels loud on the concrete platform.

She descended into a grey tunnel and emerged into a grey square, beside a Sibylla fast-food kiosk. Her stomach was rumbling – she had left the apple and the yogurt drink on the first train. She went over to the hatch and ordered a thin-bread roll with two sausages, prawn cocktail sauce and a bottle of water. She couldn't hear if the lad inside said twenty-three or seventy-three so she offered him a hundred to be on the safe side, and got back change from seventy-three.

For a thin-bread roll!

And the mineral water was obviously ordinary tap-water.

Hardly surprising that people turn to crime here.

She gobbled the roll, threw the napkin into the bin and headed across the cobbles towards the taxi-rank, feeling decidedly unwell. 'Viagatan, number four,' she said, as she got into a large Volvo.

The walls and barbed wire of the prison began almost in the centre of town. The taxi drove alongside an endless electrified fence that eventually ended at a large metal gate. 'Okay,' he said, 'I can't get any closer than this.'

The drive cost sixty kronor, less than the thin-bread roll.

She paid, and the taxi disappeared, leaving her alone in front of the huge entrance. A double layer of fencing stretched out on either side, first a chain-link fence with several layers of barbed wire at the top, then an electric fence at least five metres high. The wind was whistling through the wire.

She hoisted her bag on to her shoulder and went to the entry-phone.

'Annika Bengtzon. I'm here to see Filip Andersson.' Her voice sounded small and thin.

There was a whirring sound from the gate. She pulled it open cautiously and went in. She found herself on a tarmac drive leading to the next gate. The fencing continued on either side of her so that she was walking through a caged enclosure with the wind pulling at her hair and round her legs, one hundred or so long metres of bare no man's land before she reached a building with two doors.

'VISITS TO INMATES', it said on the left one, so that was hers.

She pressed another entry-phone.

The door was extremely heavy so she had to use both hands to open it. She stepped inside a long entrance hall, with a pushchair parked just inside the door. A young woman with a ponytail was standing there, tapping at her mobile phone with her back to Annika, ignoring her. Three of the walls were covered with white metal lockers. The fourth had windows with closed blue curtains. Beneath the windows was a row of chairs. It looked like a dentist's waiting room.

She pressed a third entry-phone.

'Someone will be with you shortly,' a voice said curtly.

The girl with the ponytail put her mobile into her bag and left the building without looking at Annika.

She stood in the middle of the floor for a while, then leaned over and peeked behind the curtains. Thick metal bars, of course, white. She let the curtain fall.

She went to a notice-board next to the phone and read about opening hours and the renovation of overnight rooms.

'Take off your outdoor clothes and leave them in a locker.'

She straightened up and stared around her. The voice had come from a loudspeaker. She looked up at the surveillance camera in the top-left corner of the room and felt the blood rush to her face. Of course they'd be watching her.

She quickly took off her coat and scarf and stuffed them into locker number ten, as far from the camera as possible.

'You can come in now,' the voice said.

The lock clicked. She opened the door to the visitors'

section and found herself at a security check. A metal detector to the left, then an X-ray machine and conveyor-belt for bags on the right. Two uniformed guards, one male, one female, were watching her through a glass screen.

'You can put your bag on the belt and go through the detector.'

She did as she was told, her pulse beating fast. She managed to set the alarm off as she walked through the machine. 'Take off your shoes and put them on the belt.'

She obeyed. The noise stopped.

Then she was allowed to step behind the glass screen and go up to the desk.

'ID, please,' the man said, and she handed him her press pass.

'Would you mind opening your bag, please?' the woman said.

Once again, Annika did as she was told.

'There's a knife in your bag,' the female guard said, pulling out a penknife with the slogan *The* Evening Post – *sharp and to the point*. 'You can't take that in. Or that pen.'

'But what am I supposed to write with?' Annika said, hearing that she sounded almost desperate.

'You can borrow one from us,' the guard said, handing her a yellow Bic. 'You'll have to leave your mobile as well,' he added.

'You know what?' Annika said. 'I'll leave my bag in the locker and just take my notepad and pen in with me. Your pen.'

The guards nodded. She took the penknife and phone and went into the waiting room, opened her locker and put her bag inside, then went back through the door to the visitors' section and skirted round the metal detector without going through it. She smiled uncertainly and felt oddly eager to be pleasant. 'Do the prisoners get many visitors?' she asked.

'We have five thousand visitors a year, but they're fairly evenly spread out. Forty per cent of inmates never get visitors.'

'Goodness. Am I the first visitor to see Filip Andersson?'

'No, not at all,' the female guard said. 'His sister comes at least once a month.'

'And David Lindholm? As I understand it, he was here a few days before he died.'

'We see trustees and probation contacts here quite a lot,' the woman said.

The male guard had stuck Annika's press pass on to a notice-board with a big metal clip. He put a document on the counter in front of him and pointed at a list of regulations without taking his eyes off her. 'You may be asked to take off your clothes and be searched by two female officers,' he said, 'and you have the right to refuse. But if you do, you won't be allowed in. You could also be checked for drugs by a dog from the drugs squad. Again, you have the right to refuse. Same thing there, you won't be allowed in. You can't take any food in, and smoking isn't allowed anywhere. You have to sign to say that you agree to being locked inside the visiting room with the inmate.'

Annika nodded and swallowed. It was suddenly very quiet. She signed with the yellow Bic to acknowledge that she accepted the conditions.

'We provide fruit and coffee, and if visitors have children they can have juice. Would you like anything?' the female guard said, as she led the way down a corridor

313

with numbered doors. She gestured towards a table of refreshments.

The thought of anyone bringing children into these surroundings sent a cold shiver down Annika's spine. She declined the offer with a shake of the head.

'Here's room number five. I'll just check it's okay. You'll have to tidy up after yourselves.' The guard opened the door and went into the small room ahead of Annika. 'There's a toilet and shower here,' she said, pointing. 'This is the Stentofon, if you want the central guards' office. And next to it is the alarm. Oh, some-one's left some toys out . . .' She bent down and picked up a pink stuffed animal and a plastic spinning top from the floor. 'One of the inmates had his little son to see him yesterday,' she said apologetically.

'That must be difficult,' Annika said lamely.

The guard smiled. 'We try to make the best of the situation. The children get balloons when they leave. Jimmy blows them up.'

'Jimmy?'

'The other guard.' She gestured towards a low cup-board. 'There are sheets and blankets in there. I'll put a call through for the inmate now.' She went to the door, leaving Annika standing paralysed next to the item of furniture that took up almost the entire floor area: a narrow bed with a foam-rubber mattress.

The door closed with a muffled clang, and the lock turned.

Holy fucking Christ, what have I let myself in for?

The walls were creeping towards her, making it hard to breathe.

How am I going to handle this? I need a strategy!

There was one chair in the room, and she made up her mind to take it under occupation. There was absolutely no chance that she was going to end up on the bed next to the axe murderer.

She put her notepad and pen on top of the cupboard, deciding to use it as a desk. She glanced round the walls. There was one picture, a black and white image of some dock-workers labouring on a quayside, in a brownish-red frame. It was a poster for an exhibition of Torsten Billman's work at the National Museum, 17 June–10 August 1986.

Behind her were two windows, and she peered out past the curtains. The same white metal bars as on the windows of the waiting room with the lockers.

I wonder how long I'll have to wait. The inmates may have to come a fair distance.

The minutes crept past. She looked at her watch four times in three minutes, then pulled her sleeve over it to stop herself. She glanced up at the Stentofon, and her gaze settled on the alarm next to it. She was sweating, even though the room was fairly cold.

There was a rattle from the lock, a clunk, and then the door swung open. 'Just let us know when you're done,' the guard said, then stepped aside to let the prisoner in.

She stood up to introduce herself and stared at the man who walked into the room.

Who the hell is this?

Pictures of the trial had shown a long-haired man, pretty muscular, with suntanned skin and a curl to his lip. This was an old man with cropped, greying hair and a serious beer-gut. He wore washed-out prison clothing and plastic slippers on his feet.

Was such a transformation possible in just four years?

He held out his hand. 'I hope they weren't too hard on you with all the security checks,' he said.

Annika had to stifle an impulse to curtsy.

This place does weird things to people.

'No worse than flying to Gothenburg,' she said.

'Us inmates come from the other direction, and go through the same thing,' he said, without letting go of her hand. 'I agree, it's not that bad, although we have to change our shoes. Apparently there's a risk that we might hollow out the soles of our trainers and fill them with drugs.'

Annika pulled her hand away.

'Mind you, it's worse when we leave here and go back to our sections. We have to strip off. Then go naked through the metal detector. They have to check that we haven't hidden any weapons up our backsides, of course.'

She sat down in the chair, leaving the bed for him. He sat down, and their knees almost collided. She pulled back.

'They check the metal detector every day,' Filip Andersson said. 'That might seem a bit extreme, but the fact is that it works. Kumla's a damn good prison, in the eyes of society. Hardly any drugs here. Very few escapes. None since the break-out that summer, and we don't kill each other very often either.'

Annika gulped so loudly that the sound echoed off the walls.

He's trying to shock me. Nothing to worry about.

'A life sentence,' she said. 'How does anyone deal with that?' It wasn't the question she had planned to start with, but it popped out anyway.

He looked at her in silence for a few seconds. There was something watery about his gaze.

Is he on happy pills?

'I've got some information for you,' he said. 'New information about the case. I've applied for a retrial in the Supreme Court.'

316

He said it as if he had just detonated the news story of the century. Annika looked at him and tried not to blink. What did he mean? How was she supposed to react? *Really? How exciting!* Or what? Every small-time criminal tried to get a retrial in the Supreme Court.

She fumbled in the silence of the room, trying to think of something polite to say to move things on. 'What sort of new information?' she asked, and he gestured for her to pick up her pen and notepad, which she did.

'Have you read the documents I sent you?'

She nodded – she had glanced through them. At least, the ones at the top.

Filip Andersson rested his elbows on his thighs and leaned forward. Annika moved back slightly.

'I was convicted even though I'm innocent,' he said, emphasising every word. 'The application for a retrial proves that.'

Had the application for a retrial been among the papers he had sent her? She didn't think so. 'In what way?' she said, drawing a small question-mark on her notepad.

'The mobile phone,' he said, nodding emphatically.

She looked at him, at his bulging stomach and pale arms. The earlier impression of him being muscular had probably been wrong, the result of very well-tailored suits. Maybe he used to dye his hair. She knew he was forty-seven, but he looked considerably older than that.

'What?' Annika said.

'The police never checked the call log! I wasn't in Sankt Paulsgatan when the murders were committed.'

'So where were you?' Annika said.

He opened his eyes wide, then narrowed them to thin slits. 'What the hell has that got to do with you?' he said, and Annika felt her pulse race again. She had to make an effort not to draw away from him.

'Nothing,' she said. 'It's got nothing to do with me.' Her voice sounded far too high.

Filip Andersson lifted a finger and pointed right at her face. 'You don't know shit!' he said, with a ferocity he couldn't quite live up to.

Suddenly Annika's heartbeat slowed. She looked into his damp eyes and found desperation and hopelessness, someone clutching at straws.

He's like a cornered dog barking, but he can't bite in here. There's no danger.

The man stood up quickly and went over to the door, two short steps, then turned and came back. He put his hands on the arms of the chair and leaned over her. He had bad breath. 'You're here to write about my application for a retrial,' he said. 'Not to ask a load of fucking questions!'

'You're wrong there,' she said, not bothered by the fact that she was talking right into his face. 'I'm the one who asked to visit you, so this is on my terms.'

He let go of the chair and straightened.

'If you calm down and listen, you'll find out what I want,' Annika said. 'If you carry on making demands, I'll leave.'

'Why should I listen to you?'

'I know a lot more than you think,' Annika said. 'I was there.'

'What?'

'I was there.'

He sat down on the bed with a little thud, his mouth half open. 'Where?'

'I was in the patrol car that was first to arrive on the scene in Sankt Paulsgatan that night. I didn't see much, but I noticed the smell.'

'You were there? What did you see?'

318

She didn't take her eyes off him.

'The blood. It was splattered all over the walls, and it was dripping down the stairs. Slowly. It was thick, bright red. The walls were yellow.'

'You didn't see anything else?'

She glanced up at the dock-workers, struggling under the weight of heavy sacks in Torsten Billman's picture. 'Her hair. It was dark. She was lying on the landing, moving her head. Julia Lindholm was first up the stairs, then Nina Hoffman, and then me. I was last, Julia first, but Nina took charge of the situation. She was the one who drew her gun.' She looked back at him.

Filip Andersson was staring at her. 'Did she say anything?'

'She shouted, "Police!" and then "There are guns aimed at you. Julia, get the door. Annika, get out of here." I turned and ran.'

He was shaking his head. 'Not the police. Olga.'

'Who?'

'The dark-haired woman.'

He means the victim.

Annika swallowed. 'I don't know,' she said. 'I don't think she said anything. She died before the ambulance arrived.'

The silence in the room had changed now: it was no longer uncertain, but heavy and suffocating.

'What do you know about Algot Heinrich Heimer?' she asked, and Filip Andersson started, just a little twitch around his mouth, but Annika saw it.

'Who?'

'He's dead, but that's hardly your fault. How did he know David?' Annika already knew this, at least in part. They had both been involved in the parachute-equipment business.

The financier looked at her with empty eyes.

'If you haven't got anything more to say to me, I'll go now,' Annika said.

'They were childhood friends,' the man said quietly. 'David was like a big brother to Henke.'

Henke?

'But things went badly for Henke?' Annika said.

'David really did try to help him, but it was no good.'

'Why was he shot?'

Filip Andersson shrugged. 'Maybe he did something stupid.'

'Or he was just a way for someone to get back at David. Mike Stevens is in here, do you know him?'

Another shrug.

'What about Bertil Oskar Holmberg, then? Who's he?'

'I don't know.'

'You're sure?'

'I didn't do it. I wasn't even there. I wasn't in Sankt Paulsgatan.'

Annika studied the man before her, trying to see his eyes.

The pupils are an opening into the brain. I should be able to see his thoughts.

'If you're telling the truth, that means someone else did it.'

He stared at her.

'If you're telling the truth,' Annika said, slightly louder now, 'that means you know who the real killer is, but you'd rather sit in here serving life than say what you know. And do you know why?'

His mouth was hanging open.

'Because at least you're alive in here. If you say what you know, you're dead. Aren't you? And why did you ask about Olga? Are you worried she had time to talk?'

He didn't answer. She stood up, and he followed her with his eyes.

'I can just about accept,' she said, facing the door, 'that you'd rather keep quiet about who really beat those people to death in order to save your own skin, but there's something else I just don't understand.' She turned round and looked at him. 'Why was David Lindholm the only person who thought you were innocent? Well? How come one of the most famous policemen in Sweden was the only one who believed you? Was it because he was so much better than all the other cops? Did he see something else in the investigation that the prosecutor, the defence and the court missed? No, that's not it, is it?'

She sat down on the low cupboard that held the sheets and blankets.

'The only reason David believed you was because he knew something that nobody else did. He believed you because he knew who really did it, or thought he knew. Is that right?'

Filip Andersson didn't move.

'I can understand you keeping your mouth shut,' Annika said. 'After all, you're where you are. But there's one thing I just can't understand. Why did David keep his mouth shut?' She stood up again. 'No one believes you,' she said, 'but David had every chance in the world to say what he knew. He would have been the hero of the hour yet again. There's only one reasonable explanation for the way he acted.'

The man was staring straight ahead at the curtains. He didn't answer.

'I've thought a lot about this over the past few weeks. David must have been terrified as well,' Annika said. 'Not of being killed, he doesn't seem to have been scared of death. No, he was scared of something else.' She went over to the chair and sat down again, leaning to one side to catch Filip Andersson's eye. 'What was important to David?' she asked. 'What meant so much to him that he would keep quiet about a mass-murderer? Was it money? Reputation? His career? Or girls? Sex? Drugs? Was he an addict?'

Filip Andersson fumbled with a handkerchief.

'What exactly were you and he involved in? What's the connection? He knew you before the murders. You were in touch long before then, weren't you? I have no idea whether or not you're guilty of carrying out those executions, but you're pretty damn crooked. How were you involved with a famous policeman? And why on earth did he risk his career by associating with you?'

Filip Andersson sighed deeply. 'You really haven't understood a single thing,' he said.

'So tell me!' Annika said. 'I'm all ears.'

He looked at her with great sadness. 'Are you really sure you want to know?' he said. 'Are you willing to pay the price of knowing?'

'Absolutely,' Annika said.

He shook his head and stood up slowly. He didn't look at her as he put one hand on her shoulder and called for the guards. 'Believe me,' he said, 'it isn't worth it. We're done now.'

This last sentence was directed at the Stentofon.

'Don't go,' Annika said. 'You haven't answered anything at all.'

The look on his face was almost tender. 'You're welcome to write about my application for a retrial,' he said. 'I think there's a real chance they'll consider it. I was in Bromma when the murders took place.'

Annika picked up her notepad and pen. 'Your mobile

phone was there. What's to say that you were the one using it?'

He stared at her but didn't have time to reply because the door opened and he left the room, his plastic slippers slapping on the floor.

What is it I'm not getting here? There's something else, something I should have asked him about. Shit!

23

She drifted towards the exit, through the hundred-metre-long metal enclosure. A gale was blowing, but otherwise it was completely quiet.

She stopped when she reached the outside gate. The fence stretched off into the distance on either side of her, and suddenly she felt so giddy that she had to grab hold of the gate. She pressed the intercom, time after time in quick succession, like a child.

'Can you let me out, please?' she cried. The lock clicked and the gate swung open and she was standing outside the metal fence. The air was instantly colder and clearer. 'Thanks,' she said, to the mute surveillance camera above her.

She let the steel door click shut behind her, then walked and walked along the edge of the enclosed site until finally she was back in town again. She turned left into a road called Stenevägen, which went on and on, with different schools on either side, then wooden houses, brick houses and even a few prefabs. Eventually she could see the railway line ahead of her. She stopped and shook her sleeve to uncover her watch.

An hour and twenty minutes before her train.

She looked towards the station. She'd had quite enough

of Sibylla's fast-food kiosk. To her right lay something called Svea's Café. She took a deep breath and went in. She settled down at a window table with coffee, biscuits and the local newspaper.

A woman on a bike had been knocked down and slightly injured at the junction of Fredsgatan and Skolgatan in Örebro just before one o'clock the previous day.

Another woman was demanding seven thousand kronor in damages because someone had spat on her in a pub.

A Social Democratic Youth Group in Pålsboda had been awarded a council grant of ten thousand kronor to build a music room.

She closed her eyes and could see the stairwell on Sankt Paulsgatan before her.

She pushed the biscuits away from her and went to get a glass of water instead. She sat down at the table again and looked out at the fast-food kiosk.

Are you really sure you want to know? Are you willing to pay the price of knowing? Believe me, it isn't worth it.

She rested her forehead on the palms of her hands. He had actually confirmed what she had said. It wouldn't hold up in a court of law, but he had more or less confirmed the scenario she had outlined.

David Lindholm had been involved in some sort of shady dealing with Filip Andersson, although exactly what remained unclear. But they had known each other for a long time and were somehow mixed up in the axe murders on Sankt Paulsgatan, both of them.

Now David had been murdered as well. And Filip Andersson had chosen to spend the rest of his life in prison rather than be killed too.

It couldn't just be coincidence. It had to fit together somehow.

The three victims on Södermalm had been beaten to death with an axe.

David had been shot.

No similarities there.

Apart from the excessive cruelty. The symbolic castration.

She gasped.

Thou shalt not steal. Off with their hands. Thou shalt not commit adultery. Off with his cock.

If Filip Andersson is innocent, then the real killer is still out there somewhere.

Bloody hell! It could be the same person!

The next conclusion crashed into her head.

Which means that Julia didn't do it! So maybe Alexander's still alive!

She pulled out her mobile and called Kronoberg Prison in Stockholm. There was no point in trying to go through Julia's useless lawyer. The restrictions placed on Julia Lindholm had been lifted, so there was no legal reason why she couldn't visit her.

'My name is Annika Bengtzon. I'm a reporter from the *Evening Post*,' she told the officer. 'I spent a night in a patrol car with Julia Lindholm four and a half years ago. We were both pregnant at the time. I believe she's innocent and I'd like to interview her. Could you pass on my request, please?' She left her mobile and home phone numbers.

Then she got up and ran over to the station, even though the train wasn't due for half an hour.

She changed trains in Hallsberg, as she had on the journey down. She forced herself to think calmly, trying

326

to structure her ideas and evaluate them objectively.

Am I really on to something, or am I just chasing shadows?

According to her first-class ticket, she was in carriage one, seat ten. Only when she had made her way through all the carriages did she realize that there was no first-class compartment anywhere in the entire train. All the seats looked exactly the same, squashed together like sardines, without so much as a folding table on the seat in front.

Typical of Swedish railways. Taking your money but not coming up with the goods.

The only seat that happened to be occupied in carriage one was number ten. A large man had settled down, spreading his briefcase and thick coat over her seat. She sat down in an empty one. The train moved off with a jolt. Just thirty seconds later they had left the town behind them. She stared out at the landscape rushing past, naked woodland with blackened branches, barns, an abandoned car, a yard full of firewood, red cottages, ploughed fields. The Swedish drawing-pin factory, stone-walled farms, and endless forests of fir trees.

She took out her mobile, thinking carefully as she formulated the text message. Didn't want to promise too much. *Have met Filip Andersson. Food for thought. Think Julia may be innocent. Can we meet?*

She leaned back in her seat with a sigh.

She caught a glimpse of some brownish-grey water in Kilsmo, and three deer ran across a patch of felled woodland. She stared after them, trying to see them through the undergrowth and scrub, but they were already gone, the moment had passed and she was overwhelmed by the familiar landscape, the Södermanland she had grown up in, with its stubbornness and watchful isolation.

The train slowed as it went through Vingåker and she opened her eyes: a football pitch, a car park, a block of flats with brown and white panelling. She blinked and then they were gone. A bird of prey in a tree, more water – could that be Kolsnaren?

Where will my children have their firm foundations? Where will they find security? In which smells? In which rooms? In what space, in which music?

A scrapyard, a residential suburb: they were approaching Katrineholm.

Time is all that anyone has. Like youth, and life, it seems obvious as long as you have it. Then it's just gone.

It was getting dark and she could see her own reflection in the window: she looked tired and thin. Not beautifully emaciated like Hollywood stars, but bony and hard.

The train stopped, near the Savings Bank and McDonald's and all the buildings round the square, so painfully familiar and out of reach. She had belonged there, but she had chosen to leave. These would never again be her streets, and they would never be her children's.

She turned her head away to shut out all the people flooding into the carriage.

Think Julia may be innocent.

Nina read the text again before deciding what to reply. *Think may be.*

Irritated, she clicked to get rid of the message.

She had taken two weeks' holiday, and was going back on the night shift at ten o'clock that evening. First she had spent three days supporting Holger and

Viola through the trial, then a week with them at their farm outside Valla. She had walked the fields with Julia's father and watched television serials on the sofa with Julia's mother, and all the while the space in the rooms and stables had been dominated by a total and overwhelming emptiness.

They've only got me now.

She sank back on her bed, looking round her cramped one-room flat.

Holger and Viola had decided to stay in Söderman-land and not drive up to Stockholm to watch the sentence pronounced. She had said they could stay at hers if they liked, just as they had done during the trial, but they had declined. They'd thought they'd just be in the way, even though she had assured them that wasn't the case, but they didn't really want to leave the farm, although they no longer had any livestock to look after.

People were talking behind their backs. Nina had seen that with her own eyes. The way people turned away demonstratively in the local supermarket. They had both got older and more frail over the past six months. Viola's hair was completely white now, and Holger had developed a limp.

The sentence was due to be pronounced at one thirty tomorrow.

The trial had been stiff and conventional, the same as usual. For Holger and Viola, the formalities had been a drawn-out nightmare. Surreptitious questions from both of them when they thought the other couldn't hear.

What does it mean, Nina, what the prosecutor said? You know about this sort of thing. Is it bad for Julia? Will she go to prison? How long for? Oh . . . Where will she be, then? Örebro? Well, that's not too far. We'll be

329

able to visit. She'll be let out for Christmas, won't she? No? Maybe later on, in a few years' time?

And now that journalist had popped up again, with her *Think may be.*

She pressed the keys hard as she replied. *Don't agree. Julia guilty. She's done her parents a lot of harm. What do you want?*

It sounded unpleasant, but she didn't care.

She sent it quickly before she had time to change her mind.

She went to the kitchen for some water, and the reply reached her mobile with a bleep before she had time to put the glass down.

Have been to Kumla & met Filip Andersson. Interesting. Cd be worth discussing. I'll be at Sthlm C in 5 mins.

Discussing?

Filip Andersson. Think may be.

That could mean anything at all. It didn't impose any obligation on her.

She grabbed the phone. *At home. Come over.*

She gathered together some bills from the dining-table and put them on the bookcase, straightened the bed-clothes and put some coffee on. Then she sat down on one of the dining chairs, waiting for the water to stop gurgling through the machine.

She had just set out mugs, milk and sugar when the doorbell rang.

The journalist looked a mess, as usual. She marched into the flat with her great big bag and thick coat and the words poured out of her. 'There's a pattern I didn't see before, and I probably wouldn't have believed it if Filip Andersson hadn't reacted the way he did. He claims he's innocent, and there are certainly a number of questions surrounding the evidence that convicted him. Either he's a very good actor, or he really is scared and browbeaten.'

'Please, take a seat,' Nina said, pulling out a chair for her, using the voice she usually reserved for difficult drunks and cocky boys on mopeds. 'How do you take your coffee?'

'Black,' Annika said, perching on the edge of the chair as she fished a little notepad out of her bag. 'I've written down a few things that I can't make sense of.'

Nina poured the coffee, glancing at her from the corner of her eye. There was something slightly manic about her, something a bit too intense. She was like a terrier whose jaws had locked shut, unable to let go.

She could never have been a police officer. She's not diplomatic enough.

'The sentence is due tomorrow,' Nina said, sitting down opposite her. 'It's a bit late to be presenting evidence that could change things.'

'This isn't evidence, exactly. It's more circumstantial assumptions.'

Nina sighed to herself: *circumstantial assumptions.* 'I see,' she said. 'And what do they tell us?'

Annika hesitated. 'It's a bit of a long shot,' she said. 'The fact is that it's so awful I don't quite believe it myself. It's too cruel, too calculated, but if you were violent and ruthless enough, it's just about possible.'

Nina couldn't think of anything to say, so waited in silence.

Annika Bengtzon bit her thumbnail as she read her notes. 'There's a link between the murders on Sankt Paulsgatan and David's murder,' she said. 'Has that ever occurred to you?'

Nina waited silently for her to go on.

'All the victims were hit on the head first, the ones

331

in Sankt Paulsgatan with an axe, David with a bullet through the forehead. Then the bodies were mutilated. Thou shalt not steal, off with your hands. Thou shalt not commit adultery, off with your cock. Both cases show very strong symbolic gestures.'

Nina's eyes widened in disbelief. 'Do you know what?' she said. 'There are more than four years between these crimes, and apart from the fact that they both took place on Södermalm, there's no connection between them at all.'

'There are several connections,' Annika said. 'You and Julia were present at both crime scenes, for instance.'

'Pure coincidence,' Nina said.

'Maybe,' Annika said. 'But the most important connection is David himself. He knew Filip Andersson – they'd had dealings in the past. According to the gossip in the blogosphere, Filip Andersson had some sort of business on the coast of Spain, and didn't you say that David and Julia lived down there for a while? Six months, outside Málaga?'

Nina shifted irritably on her chair. 'That was to get away from some gang in Stockholm. It was nothing to do with Filip Andersson.'

Annika leaned over the table. 'Are you sure? There couldn't have been another reason? Was he infiltrating Andersson's gang? Or working for him?'

Nina didn't answer.

'How long is it since David and Julia were in Spain? You said Julia looked like a ghost.'

'She'd just got pregnant and was throwing up all the time,' Nina said.

'So it was just before the murders on Sankt Paulsgatan,' Annika noted. 'Julia was in her fourth month that night we spent together.'

Nina shook her head. 'There's nothing to suggest that David ever had any dealings with Filip Andersson. Nothing at all.'

'David became his trustee when he was given his life sentence and, according to Christer Bure, David was the only person who thought Andersson was innocent. They must have known each other before that, and David knew something about the murders that no one else did.'

Nina couldn't hide a deep sigh. 'Sorry to be so blunt,' she said, 'but you sound like an over-enthusiastic private detective.'

'There are other common factors,' Annika went on. 'There are the murders, the symbolism, and the desire to catch the wrong killer.'

Nina stood up. 'Now, hang on a minute,' she said.

'Sit down,' Annika said, and the look in her eyes was suddenly pitch-black. Nina did as she was told. 'If you manage to carry off the challenge of first killing several people, then getting someone else convicted of the crime, you'd have to be astonishingly cunning and calculating. There's only one thing that I can't get to fit.'

'What?' Nina said.

'Julia's service revolver. David was shot with her gun.'

Nina could feel herself going pale. A new sort of silence had settled around her and she could feel her hands getting clammy. 'What do you mean?' she said, and her voice sounded odd.

'That's the missing link. I can get everything else to fit, but I can't find an explanation for the murder weapon.'

'Julia's gun went missing a year ago,' Nina said. 'It was when she was at her worst and it was all very embarrassing. She couldn't remember what she'd done with it. That's nothing new. It came out during the trial.'

Now it was Annika's turn to go pale. 'What are you saying?'

Nina rubbed her hands together in an attempt to warm them. 'We always have to lock our weapons in at the station when we finish a shift, but Julia sometimes kept hers at home. David had permission and they had a special gun-cabinet in the bedroom.'

'So she used to keep it in more than one place?'

'That's right. And if a police officer is going to be off-duty for more than thirty days, they have to hand their service weapon in to the weapons store. When it became clear that Julia was going to be off sick for a long time, she was asked to hand in her pistol, and that was when she realized it was missing.'

'Missing?'

'It wasn't in the gun-cabinet at home in Bondegatan. She went to the station and checked if she had left it there, but she hadn't. She was beside herself, of course, couldn't work out where it had gone.'

'So what happened?'

'She reported the gun missing. She didn't want to say it had been stolen, she just couldn't work out where it had gone. An internal inquiry was set up to find out if she was guilty of breaking the law, or of dereliction of duty, or possibly just misconduct, seeing as she had evidently managed to lose her Sig Sauer . . .'

'Why haven't I heard any of this before?'

'You can't have been paying attention. The defence mentioned it during the trial, but nothing much was made of it. I can only assume that it wasn't in Julia's interests to reinforce the image of her as a confused and irresponsible person.'

'So what happened in the inquiry into the disappearance of the weapon?'

'It hadn't reached any conclusion before the murder, but everything pointed to misconduct, which wouldn't have had any consequences. The lenient findings were mostly for David's sake, of course. When the gun reappeared the inquiry was dropped, seeing as she had evidently found the weapon or had had it in her possession all along . . .'

'But she hadn't,' Annika Bengtzon said. 'Someone started planning this murder a very long time ago, and Julia was being set up to take the blame right from the start.'

'That can't be true,' Nina said. 'It sounds like a conspiracy theory in the same class as the Roswell landing.'

But Annika was no longer listening to her. Her gaze had turned inwards and she seemed to be talking out loud to herself rather than to Nina. 'If Julia is actually innocent, then Alexander really was kidnapped. Which suggests that the true perpetrator is capable of almost anything. Chopping the hands off people who are still alive with an axe, for instance.'

She looked at Nina again. 'Could David have been gay, or bisexual?'

'I doubt it,' Nina said. 'What's that got to do with anything?'

'The murderer must have had a personal relationship with David. Otherwise he or she would never have blown his cock off.' Annika nodded to herself. 'There really was another woman in the flat. Someone who had access to the keys, or could make copies of them, to the front door and the gun-cabinet. It must have been one of his lovers, and she must have been desperate to get revenge for something. She must have known about Björkbacken because she hid Alexander's things in the marsh there. Talk about the ultimate revenge: shooting

335

the man, getting his wife locked up for the murder, and stealing their child.'

Nina was sitting as if she'd been turned to stone, unable to think any more. 'The sentence is due tomorrow,' she said.

'It can be appealed,' Annika said. 'Can you help me get in touch with Julia somehow, or at least arrange for me to talk to her? Or maybe write a letter? I've called the lawyer a hundred times and left messages at the prison. Can't you help me?'

Nina stood up. 'I'm working tonight, and I've got a lot to do.'

24

There was a cold, bitter wind as Annika stepped out of the front door. She thought about taking the Underground, but decided to walk. She needed to burn off the disappointment of failure.

I begged her, like a child. She must think I'm completely mad.

If Nina won't see the connections, no one will.

She pulled on her gloves and started walking towards Slussen, forcing herself to leave the conspiracy theories on the pavement of Södermannagatan.

But everything could have fitted, especially as Julia's service pistol had been missing for some time.

Annika shook herself. She had to pull herself together and get a bit of perspective. It wasn't up to her to free Julia Lindholm. Even if she was innocent.

Am I going mad?

She struggled up Östgötagatan, forcing her legs to move faster in the cold. Her eyes were watering, mainly because of the wind.

Does anyone know when they're on the brink of going mad?

What if she started finding secret codes in the morning papers, like the Nobel Prize-winner in the film *A Beautiful Mind*? The one who wrote masses of incomprehensible gobbledegook on scraps of paper and thought he was the cleverest man in the world.

She quickened her pace as she reached Mosebacke Square, skirting round the South Theatre and stopping to look at the view of Stockholm harbour. This was one of her favourite places on the entire planet. If she could live anywhere she liked, she'd buy a flat on Fjällgatan or somewhere up near Ersta Hospital. The view was incredible, all the water and light, with the medieval buildings along Skeppsbron to the left, Skeppsholmen with its museums straight ahead, Djurgården and the amusement park to the right, and Waldemarsudde jutting out into the water in the distance. One of the Vaxholm boats was heading towards the quayside, its lights twinkling in the water. People had been living here for a thousand years, even before Birger Jarl had decided to build the capital of Sweden on these islands at the opening of Lake Mälaren.

If I can only get hold of the insurance payout. If I'm cleared of all suspicion of arson. Then I shall live here.

She turned away and hurried home to look up the main online estate agent and find out if there were any flats for sale with a view of the harbour.

She had just crossed the big junction at Slussen and turned into Västerlånggatan when she felt that she was being watched. The cobblestones of the medieval streets were wet and slippery, and she slid as she glanced back over her shoulder. She stopped and listened, slightly out of breath.

The street curved to the right ahead of her, deserted. The wind had torn an old poster down, whirling it around her feet. The shops were all shut but the bars were open, and through the steamed-up windows she could discern people eating, drinking and laughing. Nothing. No steps, no voices.

Am I getting paranoid as well?

She hoisted her bag on to her shoulder and started walking.

There it was again, the sound of footsteps. She stopped again and spun round.

No one.

She was breathing fast.

Pull yourself together, for God's sake!

She had gone past the Seven Eleven and was just passing the arched opening of Yxsmedsgränd when someone stepped out of the shadows and grabbed her arm. He was wearing a balaclava. His eyes were bright. She went to scream but a second person came up behind her and put a gloved hand over her nose and mouth. The scream ended in a stifled whimper. She opened her mouth, felt a finger slip between her teeth and bit down as hard as she could. There was a muffled curse in her ear, then he hit her over the head. As she fell she was dragged into the alley. It was completely dark in there. She was pulled into a doorway. The wind was howling but her body felt strangely hot. The two men, they had to be men, pushed her up against the wall. She caught a glimpse of a knife in the gloom.

'Don't poke your nose into things that don't concern you,' one said.

It was a whisper, not a real voice.

'What things?' she said quietly, staring at the knife. It was pointed at her left eye.

'Leave David in peace. It's over. No more poking about.'

She was panting now, panic closing in. She couldn't reply.

'Got it?'

Give me some air! I can't breathe!

'Do you think she's got it?' one voice whispered to the other.

'No, I think we're going to have to make it a bit clearer.'

She felt them grab her left hand and pull her glove off. The knife vanished from in front of her eye. At last she got some air.

'If anyone asks how you cut yourself, you did it cooking,' the voice whispered, then the glove covered her mouth again, and she felt a fierce pain through her hand and up her arm into her chest. Her head was thudding with the shock and her knees gave way.

'Stop asking questions about David. And not a word about us. Next time we'll cut your children instead.'

They let go of her and she sank on to the cobbles as warm blood pumped out of her wounded index finger.

At A&E she said she'd cut herself in the kitchen.

A stressed doctor sewed her together with eight stitches, and told her to be more careful in future. 'What were you chopping?'

How could doctors be so young? Younger than the temps at the paper.

'Chopping?'

'Was it chicken? Some other meat? The wound might be infected.'

She closed her eyes. 'Onions,' she said.

'If you're unlucky, you could have lasting damage. Some of the ligaments were cut.'

He sounded unhappy, as if she were wasting his time with her carelessness.

'Sorry,' she said.

'Make an appointment to see the district nurse in your health centre, and change the dressing every day. She'll make sure you haven't got an infection, and will take the stitches out in a week or so.'

'Thank you,' Annika said.

She didn't mention the bump throbbing on the back of her head, and took a taxi that was waiting outside the entrance. She told him to drive to number 30 Väster-långgatan, then leaned back in the seat.

'Is it okay if I drop you off at Kåkbrinken?' the taxi-driver asked.

Then I'll have to walk past Yxsmedsgränd.

'No,' she said. 'I want you to drop me off at my door.'

'I can't. There's no traffic allowed up there.'

'I don't care.'

He dropped her at the top of Kåkbrinken and she slammed the door so hard the window shook.

She was left standing on Västerlånggatan, her heart hammering in her chest, staring at the archway that covered the entrance to Yxsmedsgränd. Her left hand was throbbing and stinging, and she could smell the man's glove, taste the leather.

They're not here now. Whoever they were, they're not still here. Pull yourself together!

She put one foot in front of the other and slowly walked down the street, staring hard at the opening of the alley.

The shadows were deeper there, sucking up all the oxygen and making her gasp for breath. She hugged the plate-glass window of Flodin's on the other side of the street and made her way past, beyond the alley and towards her building without once letting Yxsmedsgränd out of her sight.

'Annika,' someone said, putting a hand on her shoulder.

341

She screamed and spun round, her right arm raised ready to strike.

'Goodness, whatever's the matter?'

Annika stared at the person who had stepped out of the doorway of number 30 Västerlånggatan. Tall, blonde, not exactly thin, with a shocked and reproachful expression on her face. 'Anne!' she gasped. 'What the hell are you doing here?'

Anne Snapphane smiled nervously. 'I'd like to talk to you. It's important.'

Annika closed her eyes and felt anger and impotence flooding through her, everything she had kept dammed up from previous snubs and insults. 'You know what?' she said. 'I don't give a damn about what's important to you. Frankly, I couldn't care less.'

'I understand that, Annika,' Anne said, 'and that's what I'd like to talk to you about.'

'Go away,' Annika said, feeling in her jacket pocket for her keys.

'If you just give me a chance to explain—'

Something snapped inside Annika's head and she spun round and pushed Anne away with her uninjured hand. 'Go to Hell,' she shouted. 'I hope you die, you egocentric little parasite.'

Somehow she managed to get the door open and pulled it shut behind her, then ran up the stairs without turning the lights on. She stopped outside her front door and listened for any sounds from below, but everything was silence and dusty shadows.

She unlocked the flat and went into the living room without turning on the lights, as had become her habit. She stood still on the wooden floor and waited as the cares of the day gradually subsided and died. There was something comforting about the darkness and silence. The darkness didn't scare her, it never had. On the contrary, it hid her and gave her the space to explore new paths.

The telephone rang, shredding the silence.

She went to her mattress, which she had left unmade that morning, and hesitated over whether or not to answer, then picked up the receiver.

It was Thomas. 'Sorry to call so late, but things are a bit of a mess.'

Sober this time, calling from home.

She sat down by the window and looked up at the dark sky between the buildings. 'In what way?'

'Ellen's not well, so I'll have to work at home tomorrow, which isn't really a problem but we're supposed to be going out tomorrow evening. It's Sophia's mother's birthday and we've got tickets to the opera. I can't leave the children alone and the babysitter has just called to say that she isn't well either, and you did say . . . Well, I was wondering if you could maybe look after the children tomorrow night . . .' He said all this without taking a breath.

He means well. He sounds desperate.

'How is Ellen?'

'She's been sick and she's got a temperature, but she's always like that when she gets ill, isn't she?'

'Have you spoken to a doctor?'

'It's nothing serious, but I don't want to move her. I was wondering if you could maybe come here.'

Come . . . where?

'Here, to Grev Turegatan. That way she won't have to leave her room.'

Her room? Her room is here. With a pink duvet!

'Perhaps they could come here,' Annika said.

'Well, this is my week, and she's got a temperature . . .'

Sophia Fucking Bitch Grenborg is starting to get tired

*of the kids. She wants me to take more responsibility to
let Thomas off the hook.*

'Okay,' she said quietly. 'I'll come. What time?'

He told her the address and she hung up, with a feeling of failure in her chest.

*I want you to be drunk with longing when you call.
Drunk! From the pub!*

She suddenly felt that she was going to be sick. She was just about to get up and go into the bathroom and stick her fingers down her throat when the phone rang again.

'Shut up, for God's sake!' Annika threw it across the floor. The receiver flew off and bounced as far as the wire would reach. She covered her eyes, fighting to stop herself panicking.

'Hello? Hello?'

A voice from the phone: it sounded like a woman's.

*If it's Anne, I'm going to Artillerigatan to strangle
her.*

She shuffled over to the phone, holding her hand to her chest, and picked up the receiver. 'Hello?' she said quietly.

'Hello?' a high female voice said. 'Is that Annika Bengtzon?'

'Yes,' Annika whispered.

'This is Julia Lindholm. They told me you called, that you wanted to visit.'

Annika stood up, trying to breathe properly. 'Hello,' she managed. 'Yes, that's right.'

'I had a boy,' Julia said. 'What about you?'

Annika closed her eyes. 'A girl. Her name's Ellen.'

'Does she live with you?'

She stared into the shadows dominating the flat. 'Sometimes,' she said. 'We're . . . getting divorced.'

'That's a shame.'

'Yes, well . . .' She cleared her throat and tried to pull herself together. 'I still work for the *Evening Post*. I know your sentence is being pronounced tomorrow, but no matter what happens, I don't believe you did it. I'd like to talk to you about that.'

Silence on the line.

'What makes you think I'm innocent?'

'Long story. I'd be happy to tell you, if you'd like to hear it.'

'You can come early tomorrow morning, if you like. I'm allowed visitors from eight o'clock.'

'I'll be there,' Annika said.

Thursday, 2 December

25

Anne Snapphane walked down Västerlånggatan and stopped outside number thirty. She looked up at the building and saw lights on in some of the windows on the second floor. Maybe Annika was in those illuminated rooms because she lived somewhere in this building.

She's bound to be up: she's always been a morning person.

She had walked past here all autumn, every day since she'd started renting space in the office shared by freelance journalists in Tyska Brinken. She had looked up at the building and stopped at its entrance almost every day, wondering if she should go up and knock on her door. She really did miss Annika. Every time she ground to a halt with an article or couldn't get hold of someone she wanted to interview, she had to stop herself phoning her friend. Annika could always find anybody in a flash. Anne had never been able to work out how she did it. And whenever life got messy and men let her down, she missed Annika particularly: she always had coffee and dark chocolate in the house, and usually a pair of new boots to cheer her up.

Her career as a lecturer had stagnated during the autumn: she hadn't had any new bookings and the agency had stopped getting in touch. Which was just as well. She needed time to herself to think things through. Her eagerness to be seen in the media and become a famous face was just superficial: she had made up her mind to try to find some inner values, the things that made her a good person. She wanted to live the very best life she could, and to do that she had to get to grips with the people who sapped her energy.

Annika was the person she really needed to talk to. She had actually tried to arrange a conversation since the summer, emailing and phoning, but never got any answer.

She shivered, not just because of the raw early morning.

Their encounter the previous evening had left her feeling wretched. She had been working late and was on her way home to Artillerigatan, and as usual she had stopped at number thirty and looked up at the building, thinking about important things. She had stood there for a minute or so, two minutes maybe, when she saw Annika coming towards her, all the while looking back over her shoulder.

It hadn't been a good meeting: Annika had been incredibly cruel, and Anne didn't want to have to put up with that sort of thing any more.

She took a deep breath, pulled out her mobile phone and dialled Annika's familiar number. The call went through, one ring, two, three, four, and then she was there. 'Hello, it's Anne. I'd like to talk to you.'

'What for?' She sounded very tired, but not newly woken.

'Yesterday was all wrong . . . Listen, I'm standing outside your door, can I come up?'

'What are you doing here?'

350

'I'm not stalking you, I share an office with a few other people in Tyska Brinken, you know, in that building I used to live in . . .'

'Really.' She was curt and dismissive.

'Can you spare me a few minutes?'

'I'm just on my way out.'

'At half past seven in the morning?'

She didn't reply.

'I'll wait down here. You can choose to go past me if you like.' Anne ended the call.

It really was dreadful weather, damp and penetratingly cold. She stamped her feet and rubbed her hands together. Darkness was still clinging heavily to the rooftops. The sound of the traffic on the Munkbro highway skirting Gamla stan stood no chance of finding its way through the cold and the stone buildings. The medieval streets were eerily silent and deserted.

God, I couldn't live here. I can't imagine how Annika puts up with it.

The lights in the stairwell came on. Thirty seconds later the door opened.

Annika stepped on to the pavement with her mobile in her hand. She was pale, and her hair was a mess. 'What do you want?' she said, without looking at Anne.

'I want to say I'm sorry,' Anne said. 'I've been behaving like an idiot, and I hope you can forgive me.'

Annika looked at her now, with her enormous eyes, so open and vulnerable and trusting.

She doesn't know how revealing they are.

Anne wanted to reach out a hand and touch her, but resisted. Annika wasn't good at physical contact. 'You've helped me in every way a person could,' Anne said, noting that she felt tense and nervous. 'You've helped me with work and contacts, you've given me money and childcare and friendship. You were always there and I took you for granted.' She stopped and took a deep breath.

'You were always there, and I muddled myself up with you. I thought I should have everything that you had. And when I didn't get everything that you had, I thought it wasn't fair.'

Annika was standing completely still, not saying anything, just looking down at the ground. Anne noticed that she had a few grey hairs.

'That was wrong, I see it now, but I didn't before.'

Annika looked along Västerlånggatan. 'I'm on my way to a meeting,' she said.

'I miss you,' Anne said. 'I'm very sorry if I've hurt you.'

Annika gave her a quick glance with those naked eyes. 'I have to go now,' she said.

Anne nodded.

Annika walked away, her mobile phone still in her hand, wearing a thick padded jacket, her skinny legs inside a pair of black cowboy-boots.

Communication wasn't Annika's strong point.

Oh, well, I'll just have to be the communicator. She can't be the best at everything, after all.

Annika walked quickly towards Kronoberg Prison.

Over the past six months, since the terrible night of the fire, she had blocked Anne Snapphane from her mind. She had turned her into a non-person, a stranger. She had started to forget about Anne, and the fact that she had suddenly turned up to say sorry had shaken things up.

I made myself into her curling assistant, someone who ran ahead sweeping the course to make it easier for her to glide along.

She stopped at a crossing and swallowed the feeling of injustice. She admitted to herself that she had only swept the course as she had wanted to, and had sent Anne in the direction she herself had thought best.

And their friendship had capsized. Anne had taken for granted that Annika would sort everything out for her, from money, clothes and a flat to lectures and new jobs. Annika in turn had assumed that Anne was an inferior loser who was incapable of doing anything for herself.

As if I wanted her to become dependent on me, so that I could feel important.

The lights went green and she hurried over the road.

Anne refused to be there for me when my life was falling apart. She sent me out on to the street with the children when Thomas left me and the house had burned down.

Her anger was still sharp and white-hot.

She arrived at Kronoberg Prison at a minute to eight, went into Reception, showed her ID, put her things into a locker and took the lift up with just her notepad and pen.

No metal-detector, no X-ray machine.

She was shut into a windowless room containing a table and four chairs. Annika stared at the walls.

Imagine, we're still locking people up like this for breaking rules imposed by someone else. It's utterly barbaric.

The door opened. The prison officer stood to one side and a petite blonde woman came in. She was wearing jeans, slippers and a grey top, and her hair was tied up in a ponytail. A few locks had escaped and were dancing round her face. She stopped inside the door and pulled at the sleeves of her top. 'Hello,' she said.

'Hello,' Annika said.

'You look just the way I remember you.'

'So do you.'

That isn't true. She's shrunk. Older and smaller. Unless the uniform made her seem bigger last time.

They shook hands and sat down at opposite sides of the table. Annika put her pen and notepad down. The weak low-energy lamp in the ceiling was casting deep shadows under Julia's eyes. Her top hung limply on her shoulders.

'So, you had a girl,' she said. 'Is she sleeping okay?'

Annika nodded. 'Always has done. My first, Kalle, used to scream every evening until he was six months old. I got so tired I thought I'd go mad.'

Julia relaxed. 'I know what you mean. Alexander didn't go through the night until he was two. Do you think it's easier with girls?'

Annika studied the woman's eyes behind the shadows. They were wide and so empty that a shiver went down her spine.

This isn't at all healthy.

'I think it's easier with a second child,' Annika said. 'You've had time to practise. And you know it's all going to pass, the colic and sleepless nights and all the bad stuff . . .'

Julia shook her head. 'I don't know if I'd ever dare have any more children,' she said. 'I felt so terrible after Alexander.'

'Maybe that wasn't just the result of the birth or him,' Annika said, 'but other things as well.'

Julia's eyes stopped at a point on the wall. She sat in silence for a long time. 'They think I killed him,' she eventually said.

'I know that's what they're saying,' Annika said, 'but I don't believe that.'

354

The shadows under Julia's eyes deepened as she pulled back against the wall. 'Nina says I'm going to prison. Do you think that too?'

Annika felt her throat go dry. 'The experts seem to think so,' she said, 'and if they're right, I believe a great injustice will have been done. I don't believe you did it. I think there was another woman in the flat, and I think she took Alexander.'

Julia was sitting completely still. 'Why do you think that?'

'I think there's a connection between David's murder and that terrible triple murder we stumbled upon the night I was with you in the patrol car. Do you remember Filip Andersson?'

Julia Lindholm leaned her head back and looked up at the ceiling. 'No one believes me,' she said. 'Not even Nina. They just keep asking what I did, not what the other woman did.' She turned her eyes towards Annika. 'You know Nina, don't you? I feel rather sorry for her. She's so alone. She lived with her mum in a little cottage outside Valla. She had brothers and sisters but they were much older. Her mum was a real hippie – she lived in some commune on the Canary Islands when Nina was little. She was nine when she started at Valla School, and she couldn't read or write. She used to stay with us on the farm most nights. Has she ever mentioned that?'

She leaned forward over the table. 'There's one guy at the station, a really great officer called Pelle Sisulu. He's been in love with Nina for years, but she refuses to take it seriously. She doesn't think she's worth loving. I wish I could help her . . .' She leaned back in the uncomfortable chair again and looked closely at Annika. 'I feel so sorry for people,' she said. 'David grew up without his dad – he only had a step-father who kept coming and going. When David was nineteen he disappeared and never got in touch again. I think that's why David went into the police.' She tilted her head to one side. 'Should I feel sorry for you, Annika?'

Annika took a deep breath. 'No, I don't think so.'

'So you've got someone who loves you?'

Yes, the children.

'Should I feel sorry for myself?' Julia asked.

Annika nodded.

'Is that why you believe me?'

'No,' Annika said. 'There are several connections between the murders, and I don't think the police have investigated them properly.'

'So you believe there was another woman?'

She nodded again.

'That's what I've been telling them all along!'

'I know. The question is: who is she, and where could she have taken Alexander? Do you have any ideas?'

Julia shook her head slowly.

'Do you remember Filip Andersson? The axe murderer?'

Julia shivered. Her gaze slid along the wall.

'I went to visit Filip Andersson in Kumla Prison a few days ago,' Annika said. 'I think he might be innocent too. Someone else might have committed those murders, and if that person got away then he, or she, could have murdered David as well . . .'

They sat in the visiting room without speaking for a long while. The ventilation hummed somewhere up in the ceiling. Julia was sitting completely still, staring into the wall.

'I know someone was there when I woke up.'

Annika sat in silence, the hairs on the back of her neck standing up. Julia was fiddling with a strand that had come loose from her ponytail, tucking it behind her ear.

'There was a bang,' she said in a shaky voice. 'I think it was the bang that woke me up. I didn't know what it was – I thought I might have been dreaming.'

She looked up at the ceiling. 'There was a funny smell. Something horrible, not the way our bedroom usually smells. A bit burned, maybe . . . Someone was moving about in the room. I think I said something.'

The sound of the ventilation seemed to get louder in the silence. Annika stared at the woman, unable to take her eyes from her mouth.

'Then there was another bang, and my ears popped, a sort of ringing, howling sound . . .'

The shot to the groin. Thou shalt not commit adultery.

Julia took a deep breath, which sounded rough and shaky. 'I've got a bit of a cold,' she said apologetically. 'I'm a bit bunged up. I suppose I got it from the guards, or prison officers, as we're supposed to call them.' Julia nodded to herself and wiped her nose on her sleeve. 'My heart was pounding right through my head, my body. I don't know how I can describe . . .' She brushed the hair from her face.

'Did you see someone?' Annika asked quietly. 'Did you see who fired the shot?'

'It was completely dark. David can't sleep if it isn't pitch-black. I don't know, I didn't see anyone.'

'Do you remember what you were thinking?'

Julia shook her head. They sat in silence for a while. Julia pulled a paper handkerchief from her jeans pocket and blew her nose, then crumpled the tissue into a little ball.

'Then what happened?' Annika asked.

'Alexander was crying. I could hear him, even though my ears had gone deaf. So I got up to go and see if he was all right.'

'Where was he?'

Julia looked up at her in surprise. 'In his room, of course. He'd been asleep. I mean, it was the middle of the night.'

'And then what happened?'

Julia seemed to shrink and her shoulders hunched. She seemed to be trying to make herself smaller. Locks of hair tumbled in front of her face.

'Alexander was standing in the hall. He was hugging Bamse. She was standing behind him, holding the knife. He said, "Mummy." She looked at me. I could feel her looking at me.'

'The other woman? The one who was in the flat? What did she look like?'

Julia's eyes flickered across the wall.

Annika had read her description of 'the other woman' in Berit's report of the trial. Medium-length hair, possibly short. Not fair, not dark. Medium height, normal size.

Julia looked down at the table. The psychiatrists had concluded that she was describing herself when she had told them about the murderer. The lawyer must have explained that to her. 'It wasn't me,' she said, scratching her wrists. Annika noticed that she had scabs on her arms from where she'd scratched herself before.

'What did she do with the knife?'

The scratching got more frenetic.

'She cut . . .'

'It's all right to tell me,' Annika said.

Julia's hands stopped. 'She . . . she cut his cheek and put her hand over his mouth . . . and she was wearing gloves . . .'

'She cut Alexander's face?'

Tears were welling in Julia's eyes.

'And I did nothing,' Julia said. 'She said, "I'll suffocate him. I'll smother him if you scream. It's so easy to kill little children." That's what she said . . . Oh, God . . . what have I done?'

And she started to cry.

Annika sat still on the other side of the table and watched. Then she reached for her bag to give Julia a tissue, but remembered she'd had to leave it in the locker down in Reception.

Julia let out a deep, sobbing sigh and wiped her face on her sleeves. 'I didn't help him. "If you follow me, I'll cut his throat," she said. He was crying. He said, "Mummy." That's when she cut his cheek and I tried to scream but nothing came out, and after that I don't know what happened . . .' She shuddered and was crying again. 'I couldn't help him. She cut his face with the knife and I didn't know what to do. I was so frightened he was going to die.'

The blood on the floor. Alexander's DNA.

'I think the woman knew David,' Annika said. 'Can you help me track her down?'

Julia felt for the used tissue and dried her eyes. 'She's lethal,' she said. 'David was terrified of her. "She's mad," he said. "Don't go anywhere near her."'

Annika got goose-bumps.

Is she talking about herself now?

'Who is she? Do you know her name?'

Julia shook her head again. 'She had an abortion,' she said. 'While I was expecting Alexander. David never admitted it, but I knew that was what had happened. I found a picture of the ultrasound. It would have been a girl. I should have left him then. I should have realized he was never going to stop seeing other women.'

'Was she the one who used to call?' Annika asked. 'The one who used to phone when Alexander was little, telling you to let go of him?'

Julia shrugged. 'Don't know. Maybe. He had more than one.'

'When did David say that about the woman being so dangerous?'

Julia looked up at her in surprise. 'What woman?'

'You said David talked about her, the dangerous woman. When did he do that? Was it when Alexander was small?'

'Oh,' Julia said, 'no, not at all. It wasn't that long ago.'

'Just before he died?'

Julia put a hand over her mouth. Her eyes filled with tears again. 'It was my fault,' she said. 'I did absolutely nothing because I was so scared she was going to hurt him even more. She was evil! The blood was running down his cheek – you should have seen how terrified he looked, and she put her hand over his nose and mouth so he couldn't scream, or even breathe. She had gloves on, and I was so scared . . .'

'But when did he say it?'

'When he was drunk. Alexander and I had been out to the cottage, cooking sausages outdoors, and we went to watch the May Day Eve bonfire in Hälleforsnäs, and when we got home he was so drunk. He wasn't angry, mostly just scared.'

'Earlier this year? Four weeks before he died, then?'
She nodded.

'You say David was scared? Did he say why?'
She shook her head.

'How could you tell? That he was scared?'

'He asked me to forgive him. Said he'd hurt me. That he hadn't meant to. That I should take care when I answered the phone, and not to answer the door if anyone knocked.'

Annika recalled Nina describing how distraught Julia had been during the last few weeks before the murder, how she'd shut herself away and not answered the phone. 'But he never said what her name was? Nothing about who she was?'

Another shake of the head.

Annika shifted on her chair. 'She has to be seriously disturbed,' she said. 'She's probably got criminal connections. If she did have an abortion and sent David a picture of the ultrasound, he must have been the father. Which means that she must have had some sort of contact with him over a long period, at least four and a half years. Right back to the time you spent living in Spain, at least. Had you ever seen her before?'

Julia merely shook her head again.

'Would you recognize her if you saw her again?'

Julia hesitated, then nodded.

'If I got hold of pictures of women David had dealings with for different reasons, would you look at them and see if you know any of them?'

Julia nodded again.

'One more thing,' Annika said. 'I'm a reporter on the *Evening Post*, as you know. Can I interview you and write about you for the paper?'

Julia was clearly bewildered. 'But what would I say?'

'Well, you could start by telling me what it's been like for you here in prison.'

26

Anders Schyman welcomed the chairman of the newspaper's board into his little office with a flamboyant gesture. 'Can I offer you anything?' he said, taking Herman Wennergren's coat and laying it ceremoniously across his desk. 'A glass of water? Some coffee from the machine?'

'Don't overdo it,' the chairman snapped, adjusting his cufflinks.

Schyman had been invited to lunch with Wennergren on the veranda of the Grand Hotel, but had declined out of consideration for the poor finances of the paper's proprietors. That hadn't gone down well, evidently. There was now an item on the agenda of the next committee meeting proposing that his own entertainment budget be cut, not that he gave a damn about that. It was the petty act of revenge that annoyed him.

'I have to say that this sounds deeply troubling,' the chairman said, sitting down on the rather flimsy visitor's chair. 'An editorial management team consisting of eighty-two people is completely unreasonable. How on earth can we afford it?'

Schyman sat down, and pulled his chair closer to the desk. He pulled a sheaf of calculations out from under the chairman's coat and handed them to his visitor. 'It's the simplest, cheapest and quickest way to make the necessary cuts,' he said. 'In accordance with locally negotiated wage agreements – you've got those in appendix four – no productivity bonus is paid to members of the editorial management team. It's included in their basic salary or recompensed in other ways. We chose to introduce a "responsibility bonus", and those payments are made only to people in active leadership roles.'

'Ahem.' Wennergren leafed through the documents. 'And this will solve the problem of the cutbacks?'

'We have to take into account the union's demand that we follow the "last in, first out" principle. Sixty-two posts are going, most of them on the editorial side. As you can see from the proposals, we're clearing out top management as well. The committee would remove the managing director of his position and transfer his responsibilities to me. I'm going to negotiate with the local union representative straight after this meeting. Which is why I wanted to run my alternative proposal past you before I set to work.'

'I see,' Wennergren said. 'Well, we can certainly manage without our current MD. So, what's this alternative proposal of yours?'

'If the union kicks up a fuss, I'll dismiss the entire editorial staff. They would all have to reapply for their jobs, and I'll reinstate those I want.'

The chairman frowned disapprovingly. 'We've tried that before, and there's always a catch.'

Schyman threw out his arms. 'You're the ones who want to impose the cuts. I'm just a facilitator. Will the company support my proposal, even if it means a certain amount of turbulence?'

Wennergren stood up and consulted his watch, a Rolex Oyster (which Schyman regarded as ridiculous). 'We would appreciate it if any turbulence could be kept to a minimum,' he said. 'Can I have my coat, please?'

Schyman smiled, aware that by having this meeting here and not on the veranda of the Grand Hotel, he had saved the company at least two thousand kronor, and himself at least three hours of his life. 'I'll do my best,' he said.

As soon as the chairman of the board had disappeared towards the lifts to go back to his chauffeur-driven Volvo, he asked the receptionist to call Eva-Britt Qvist.

She appeared outside his room a mere ten seconds later. 'What did Herman Wennergren want?' she asked, pulling the door shut behind her.

Yet another good reason for meeting him here.

The editor-in-chief adopted a deep frown. 'I wanted to make sure that the board and our owners were absolutely sure about the cutbacks and that they understand how serious this is. But they won't be moved. They really do want this to be carried out. They're not even sparing their own ranks – our new MD will lose his job. The whole committee is behind our preliminary proposal, but is also prepared to support our alternative plan.'

Eva-Britt Qvist nodded thoughtfully and sat down.

'We're pleased that the paper has accepted its responsibilities and is following our preferred list when it comes to redundancies.' He handed over a document containing a list of names. 'Based on our locally negotiated agreements, the list of posts to be lost looks like this,' he said.

Eva-Britt Qvist began reading.

I wonder how long it will be before she realizes.

He checked an urge to time her.

At least two minutes passed.

'But,' Eva-Britt Qvist said, 'this doesn't follow the last-in, first-out principle. Where's Emil Oscarsson, for instance? He was the last person to be taken on – surely he only arrived this summer.'

'Ah,' Schyman said, handing her another list. 'This is the new list of editorial management.'

Eva-Britt Qvist turned pale. She read for a long time in silence, going through the whole list several times. Then she lowered the document. 'So this is how you think you can get away with it,' she said. 'But, let me tell you, we won't agree to this.' She stood up.

'Sit down,' Schyman said.

'No,' she said, in a loud, clear voice. 'I'm going now.'

'In that case we have an even greater problem, you and I.' He stood up as well, a head taller than her.

She stopped, her hand on the door-handle.

'I have just been authorized by the chairman of the board to dismiss the entire editorial staff,' the editor-in-chief said. 'Then I will reinstate those I actually want, rather than those I am obliged to keep. Even if it means the closure of the paper, we're going to get this through. Because we don't have any alternative. Carrying on as we have done up to now simply means that we will reach the same disaster more slowly.'

'And if we protest?'

He looked at her hard.

Bet everything on one card.

'There'll be a lot of important work for you at this paper, Eva-Britt. Don't let something like this ruin your whole career.'

She gasped. 'That's a threat.'

'Not at all,' Schyman said, looking affronted. 'I'm just keen to keep you, even after the cuts. We need

365

experienced administrators, and we have to bear one thing in mind. Not even my position is secure.' He opened the door. 'Nothing lasts a lifetime.'

Annika Bengtzon was just walking past. 'You've heard?' she said. 'Mind you, it was entirely predictable, with that idiot defending her.'

'What?' Schyman said.

'She's the sixth woman ever to be given a life sentence in Sweden.'

'We won't accept this,' the union representative whispered, looking close to tears.

'We can probably come to an agreement,' he said quietly, and smiled amiably.

As she headed to her place at the day shift's desk, it occurred to Annika that Eva-Britt Qvist had looked terrible. She took out her laptop, notes and documents relating to David Lindholm. First she wrote up her interview with Julia, under the heading 'Accused Police Officer's Wife Speaks Out'. It didn't reveal much of what Julia had said. She left out everything about the other woman and what she had done. The article was more a description of the prison and Julia's time there, nothing remarkable, with no contentious allegations.

She went to the coffee machine to get herself a mug of tea. She took some headache pills and persuaded herself that the fact she was feeling unwell had nothing to do with the evening ahead, when she had agreed to look after the children in Sophia Grenborg's flat. She was doing it for their sake, Ellen and Kalle's, because they needed her and were missing her.

Once she had sent the article to the shared file store, she sat down to structure her real work.

Women who had had personal dealings with David.

Who had he been with? Where do people meet their bits on the side? At work? In their free time? In bars? Among mutual friends, with shared ambitions and business interests?

And how was she going to get hold of pictures, even if she managed to put together a list of names?

The passport register was no longer open to the public; neither was the register of driving licences. A lot of people were in pictures on the Internet, or in different image archives, but she needed definite identification of every one. Otherwise it would be a complete waste of time.

Well, she'd deal with that later.

The criteria were fairly clear. There shouldn't be too many alternatives.

Someone who had known David well. Who had had a sexual relationship with him. Who had had access to his home. Who was sufficiently criminal and ruthless to murder him, frame Julia and kidnap Alexander.

This is an attack on a whole family. She must have been planning it ever since the gun disappeared.

She shrugged off an image of Thomas, Sophia and the children.

The woman must have got hold of the keys to the flat in Bondegatan, stolen Julia's Sig Sauer from the gun-cabinet in David and Julia's bedroom, without fingering it and without smearing Julia's prints. It was no more complicated than that. She laid out the printouts she already had, pulled her notepad and pen from her bag, and decided to try to structure the search.

1. Women who had been on the same committees as David. Easy, but there would probably be a lot of names. And it wasn't a particularly likely list either, so she decided to wait with that one.

2. Women related to the men who were in prison, thanks to David: wives, mothers, daughters, sisters and, ideally, lovers as well. Harder to dig out the information, but not impossible, and more likely to produce something interesting. She'd make this one her first priority.
3. All the women David had worked with. There must be hundreds. The best way of checking them would be to find group photographs.
4. Women he'd acted as a probation contact for. Were there any?

She remembered that she hadn't heard anything from the National Correctional Organization after her freedom of information request to see the list of David's trustee activities, so she looked through her notepad and rang the lawyer's direct number. She picked up after four rings, then disappeared to look up Annika's request and returned a minute or so later. Annika heard the rustle of paper.

'I can confirm that David Lindholm was active as both a probation contact and as a trustee over many years,' the lawyer said. 'Sometimes he was a probation contact for, let's see, up to three people simultaneously, but while he was a trustee he had no other responsibilities.'

'Is it more demanding being a trustee?'

'Yes, you could probably say that. Providing support to someone serving a life sentence is tough.'

'Can you tell me anything about who the inmates were?' Annika said, then held her breath.

'I can't identify them. We're bound by confidentiality legislation within the prison service, and have to protect individual privacy. We've come to the conclusion that this isn't public information and therefore can't be handed out.'

'Okay,' Annika said. 'Could you answer just one question: was any of them a woman?'

The lawyer leafed through the documents. 'Well, I don't know . . .'

'Could you check? I don't know how this works. Could a man be a probation contact for a woman?'

'I don't think there's anything prohibiting it, or the reverse, of course.'

'You don't have to tell me who she is, just if there was anyone . . .'

More paper shuffling.

'No,' the lawyer said. 'No women, only men.'

'Thanks,' Annika said, and hung up.

Okay. She could get rid of point four.

She got going with the second group on the list. She went into the national ID database and typed in Stevens, Michael Harold. It was a nuisance not being able to use her left index finger when she typed.

Stevens was registered at an address in Sundsvall. Annika kept the address and surname but changed the gender of her search. Bingo! There were two women at the same address with the same surname, Linda Helena and Sarah Linda Hillary. The former was thirty-three years old, the latter eight.

Wife and daughter. The wife will do nicely.

She printed out the details, then looked up Ahmed Muhammad Svensson from Malmö. She found an old record, and tracked back until she had his daughter Fatima and his ex-wife, Doris Magdalena.

I'll have her as well.

Filip Andersson, full name Arne Filip Göran, wasn't married, and never had been. It didn't look like he had

369

any children either. Because he had such a common surname, it was impossible to track down his mother through the database.

She stretched her neck. Her headache was starting to ease. The pills must be kicking in.

I'll try Googling him instead.

He was listed in Wikipedia under the category 'Swedish criminals', but there was nothing about a wife or fiancée. The search-terms 'filip andersson wife' brought up loads of results, but nothing to suggest that he was married.

She sighed. Thin pickings so far.

She tried the national police website instead to see if she could find any group photographs of the staff at different police stations, but all she found were a few portraits of grey-haired gentlemen with titles like national head of police and general director, as well as a few blonde-haired women, senior directors and the head of National Crime.

Shit. This isn't going well at all.

She pulled out the printouts of David Lindholm's business activities and decided to list the names and ID numbers of any women who had been involved in his old companies.

The first file she looked at was the one about Fly High Equipment, the parachuting company David had run with two other men, Christer Bure and the prematurely deceased Algot Heinrich Heimer, also known as Henke.

She decided to check out any women in Henke's life, and now things started to move.

Algot Heinrich Heimer had left a wife, Clara Susanna, and three daughters, who were now twenty-three, twenty-one and nineteen. Their names were Malin Elisabeth, Lisa Katarina and Claudia Linn. It was likely that David had known these women. He could well have had sex with them, or at least one of them. Annika made a note to try to find pictures of all four.

The next company she checked was Pettersson Catering & Arrangements AB, the one with a large number of board members, which dealt with catering as well as horses. She made a note of the four women on the board. She also looked up Bertil Oskar Holmberg's wife, Victoria Charlotta, eighteen years younger than her husband.

This could be something . . .

She glanced at the remaining printouts: Advice Investment Management Behzad Karami and B. Holmberg Property in Nacka AB. She looked at her watch: she needed enough time to get home and do some washing before heading to Grev Turegatan.

Oh, what difference does it make what clothes I'm wearing? Anyway, they won't have time to dry properly . . .

She concentrated on the people behind Advice Investment Management AB: Lena Yvonne Nordin in Huddinge, and Niklas Ernesto Zarco Martinez in Skärholmen. She added Lena Yvonne to the list, and checked her other professional dealings, the cleaning firm in Skärholmen that she ran with Martinez, and the investment company with Arne Filip Göran Andersson . . .

The room around her went totally silent. The light from the windows turned a corrosive white, and she opened her mouth to say something but nothing came out.

Arne Filip Göran Andersson.

The axe murderer from Sankt Paulsgatan.

She gasped.

It couldn't be anyone else.

371

I knew it! I KNEW I'd seen his full name somewhere before and it was in these printouts. This is what I've been looking for . . .

Hands trembling, she hunted through the printouts she had just got from the national database. Yes, the financier Filip Andersson was also named Arne and Göran.

Annika glanced back at the woman who connected them. Lena Yvonne Nordin. She sorted the documents in front of her, trying to see the links. Lena Yvonne had run two investment companies, one with Niklas Martinez, and the second with Filip Andersson.

This is the link! Here's the evidence that David and Filip Andersson had dealings with each other! A woman called Lena Yvonne Nordin.

Annika made a note of her name and ID number, then took out her mobile phone and called Nina Hoffman.

'I've found something!' she said, standing up, unable to conceal the excitement in her voice. 'Damn it, I think I'm on to something. You know I said there was something I couldn't quite work out? I know what it was now! You know the axe murderer, Filip Andersson . . . Nina . . . ?'

She stopped and listened to the silence on the phone.

'Nina? What is it? Has something happened? Are you crying?'

'Life,' Nina said, taking a deep breath. 'I knew she'd get a custodial sentence, but *life*! And for killing Alexander as well. This is just awful . . .'

Annika swallowed and sank back on to her chair. Her finger started to throb and ache. 'I know,' she said lamely. 'It's really . . .'

'Her lawyer, the useless idiot, says he's considering an appeal seeing as Alexander's body hasn't been found.

As if that makes any difference!' She was crying openly now, angrily and violently.

'What does Julia say?'

'Don't know. Holger's been told they've taken her back to the medical wing. She must have collapsed.'

Annika tried to think of something sympathetic to say, but failed.

'This is typical,' Nina went on. 'They gave her an inexperienced know-all to represent her, knowing full well that he'd fail. I've never seen such a show trial in my life, or such a sloppy murder investigation! Of course she was going to get life! Anything else was out of the question! Just because David Lindholm's dead, and someone had to pay, they made up their minds it was going to be Julia, and then they decided to sacrifice her child as well . . .'

'Nina,' Annika said. 'There's something you could do to help me. I've been looking through various archives and I've found something I'd like to look into.'

'What?' Nina said.

'I've found a connection. There's a woman who links David Lindholm with Filip Andersson.'

'What sort of connection?'

'Two investment companies. They were both owned by a Lena Yvonne Nordin. She ran one with David Lindholm and the other with Filip Andersson. Does that name mean anything to you? Lena Yvonne Nordin?'

Nina Hoffman fell silent, breathing shallowly down the phone. Then she blew her nose. 'No.'

'There are others as well, other women . . . I've got a list of names and ID numbers. Would you be able to find photos of them from the National Police Registry?'

'What for?'

'I think the woman in the flat might be one of them. I can't get into passport records any more, so . . .'

She could hear Nina Hoffman breathing. 'Why do you want pictures of them?'

'Julia thinks she'd recognize the woman who took Alexander.'

The police officer groaned. 'So you're thinking of showing them to Julia?'

'Of course.'

'I can't do it,' she said. 'I can't help you.'

'Of course you can!' Annika said. 'It's just a matter of putting in a request for them!'

'I don't want to get involved.'

'Don't give me that!' Annika said, more harshly than she'd intended. 'I'll send the list to the station straight away.'

'No!' Nina said. 'Absolutely not. My colleagues mustn't know.'

'A letter, then? Do you want me to send it to your home address or the station?'

'Well, I'm working tonight so if you want to post it . . .'

'I'll get it couriered over at once.' Annika hung up and looked at her watch. It was high time she went home.

She packed up her laptop and put the list into an envelope, then called Reception to arrange for a courier.

27

The flat was a mess. Annika hadn't bothered making the bed since the children had gone to Thomas's. She dropped her bag on the hall floor and stood in the doorway, looking at the state of the living room.

She was living in an unconverted office space so there were no wardrobes, which meant that her clothes, bed-linen and towels were piled in heaps along one wall.

I have to sort my life out, and I have to start with my home.

She sighed, hung up her coat, then rolled up her sleeves.

There were only twelve names for Nina to match with pictures. Stevens's wife, Svensson's wife, Henke's wife and daughters. The four women on the board of the catering company, Bertil Oskar Holmberg's wife, and the woman from the investment companies.

Twelve.

She started picking up clothes frenetically from the living-room floor and stuffing them into a laundry basket. She was halfway through when the phone rang. 'Hello?' she said crossly into the receiver, dropping the dirty laundry on the floor.

'I'm trying to reach Thomas Samuelsson,' said a deep male voice, with a pronounced Stockholm accent.

'Are you, now?' Annika said, putting her uninjured hand on her hip. 'He's not on this number any more.'

'Do you know how I can get hold of him?'

'Do what everyone else does. Call him on his mobile.'

'I've tried, but it's switched off. Have you got his new home number?'

Annika took a deep breath and let rip. 'He's moved in with his mistress,' she said. 'You can try calling him there.'

'Oh, shit,' the man said. To Annika's annoyance, he sounded almost amused. 'So the mistress has a phone?'

'Who can I tell him called?' Annika said, hearing how unfriendly she sounded.

'My name's Jimmy Halenius, I'm calling from the department. Is that Annika?'

Annika straightened her back. Jimmy Halenius, the under-secretary of state. Thomas's boss, and the minister's right-hand man. 'Yes,' she said, 'it is.'

'Thanks for dinner, I should say, although it was a while ago now.'

They had met once, at the fateful dinner she and Thomas had held in the villa out in Djursholm a few days before it had burned down.

'A pleasure,' she said curtly.

Was that right? Is that what you said when someone thanked you for your hospitality? I should get hold of a book on etiquette.

'I've read Thomas's memo and I need to get hold of him at once. Can you give him a message?'

'Why?' she said. 'What's so urgent?'

The man fell silent. His tone had led her to expect something oily and sexist, *Nothing for you to worry your pretty little head about*, or something in that style, but he didn't say anything of the sort. 'I've left a message on his voicemail, but he hasn't called back,' he said, sounding rather at a loss.

Annika took a deep breath. 'He's working from home today. Ellen isn't well. I'll be seeing him this evening. I'm looking after the children so that he and Sophia can go to the opera.' Why was she telling Jimmy Halenius all this?

'Just ask him to call me,' he said.

'Because otherwise I'll read about it in tomorrow morning's papers?' she blurted out, and could have bitten her tongue out. *What the hell did I say that for?*

But the under-secretary of state just let out a little laugh. 'Something like that,' he said, and hung up.

Thomas had evidently said nothing about their divorce at work. Mind you, why would he?

She put the phone down and gathered up the rest of the dirty washing. The last thing on the pile was the cornflower-blue top Thomas had given her last Christmas, the only thing that had survived from her former life. She had been wearing it the night the house burned down. She was thinking of putting it on tonight, because it brought together the person she had been then and the person she had become. Besides, she knew Thomas liked her in it. It was a feminine cut, scooped at the front with a deep neckline, not her style at all, really, but she liked the colour.

She squashed it into the basket, fighting back tears. *Why do I care what he thinks?*

The colour of honey, heavy with stucco detailing, bay windows with leaded glass. This was one of the Grenborg family's rock-solid investments. Annika was

377

standing in the darkness on the other side of the street, looking up at the attic flat, the sharp light coming from the windows in the roof.

They're in there. In that white light.

She had been here before. A year ago, last November, the day after she had realized Thomas was having an affair, she had stood in this exact spot and looked up at the building. She felt a lurching sensation in her head, and had to grab hold of the wall behind her to stop herself falling. She struggled against dizziness and the urge to be sick before she was able to cross the street to the main door, dark brown and ornate.

She pressed the entry-phone – she hadn't been given the code.

She answered: Sophia Fucking Bitch Grenborg. 'Come in, come in. Sixth floor, at the top, the penthouse.'

The penthouse? Christ!

The entrance hall was yellow and black marble, the lower part of the walls clad in dark wood panelling, with smoke-coloured brass lamps. The carpet was dark blue, soft as down.

She took the stairs slowly and unsteadily.

The attic floor was much less interesting than the rest of the building, a white security door in the middle of a whitewashed brick wall. She remembered the nameplate, brushed steel, and there was a handwritten note beside it: *T. Samuelsson.*

She rang the bell.

Thank goodness it was Thomas who opened the door. She hadn't seen him since July. He'd cut his hair. His fringe was sticking straight up and looked a bit odd. It made him seem much older. His features were sharper than she remembered them. He was wearing a black suit and polished shoes.

I always polished his shoes. I wonder if he's started doing it for himself now.

'Aren't you allowed a first name?' she asked, pointing at the note.

'You're a bit late,' he said. 'We have to go straight away.' He was visibly nervous, turning away and reaching for a coat hanging from an ornate wrought-iron coat-rack.

Sophia F. B. Grenborg skipped out behind Thomas with her hand outstretched and an ingratiating smile glued to her face. She was wearing a bright yellow top, which, with her yellow hair, made her look like an Easter chick. Annika realized that the top was exactly the same design as her cornflower-blue one – *Thank God I didn't have time to wash it.*

'Mummy!'

The voice came from the living room, and was accompanied by quick footsteps. Kalle shoved Sophia Grenborg out of the way and threw his arms round Annika's legs. Ellen came skipping along behind him, clutching her new Poppy. Annika dropped her bag and coat on the floor and crouched down, taking both children in her arms, laughing and rocking them from side to side. It felt like she hadn't seen them for months, even though it had been only Monday when she had dropped them off at school and nursery. She kissed their hair and cheeks, hugged them, tickled them, and kissed Poppy too, just to be on the safe side.

Thomas cleared his throat. 'Well,' he said, 'we ought to be going . . .'

'How are you?' Annika asked, stroking her daughter's hair from her face and looking at her carefully. 'Have you been sick any more today?'

Ellen shook her head.

Annika looked up at Thomas. 'So she hasn't got a temperature?'

'Since about lunchtime,' he said. 'She can go to nursery tomorrow, so she ought to be in bed by eight. What have you done to your hand?'

Annika stood up with her daughter in her arms. 'Cut myself cooking. I need to do some work once the children are asleep. Is there a computer I can borrow?'

'Of course,' Thomas said, gesturing with one hand towards a large studio space that seemed to take up most of the flat.

Annika went past Sophia Grenborg without taking any notice of her.

'This is my office,' Thomas said, opening the door to a cramped little space beyond the kitchen. 'You can work in here. We won't be late, will we, Soph?'

Soph?

'Well,' *Soph* Grenborg said, pulling on her coat and a pair of nap-leather gloves, 'I think Mother wanted to have dinner afterwards. She may even have booked a table at Operakällaren.'

Mind you, he used to call me Anki . . .

'I'm not planning on going anywhere,' Annika said curtly, without looking at her, then took Kalle's hand and headed towards the sound of the children's favourite television programme. Thomas came after them and watched as they settled down on the black-leather sofa in front of the plasma screen. He stopped in the doorway. Annika sensed him looking at her and felt her pulse-rate increase.

He still looks lovely even with short hair.

'Thanks for doing this,' he said quietly.

She swallowed and kept her eyes on the screen.

'Thomas, are you coming?'

How can he put up with that voice?

He disappeared from the doorway and she heard keys and mobiles being dropped into pockets and bags, then the door closed and silence spread through the horrible penthouse suite.

The children went to bed at the same time and with the same amount of fuss as they did at hers. They washed and brushed their teeth, then sorted out their clothes and put the dirty ones into the laundry basket, chose a bedtime story and snuggled down under the covers. Ellen had had a sleep during the day and had trouble settling down. Annika lay beside her in the narrow little bed and sang to her quietly until she fell asleep. She stroked the little head and soft shoulders, closing her eyes and inhaling the smell of her daughter's hair, feeling it tickle her nose.

You're a little miracle.

She carefully disentangled herself from Ellen, then stood in the doorway looking at her. She was getting more and more like Thomas, with her blonde hair and blue eyes. She felt a tightness in her chest and went out into the flat. She shivered and wished she'd brought a cardigan.

It wasn't just that the temperature was low: there was a draught coming from somewhere and the pared-back furnishing emphasized the chill. Everything was white, apart from the black-leather seating, and the tables, which shimmered with glass and chrome.

The children had small rooms next to each other in the furthest corner of the large studio. There was just enough space for their beds and a small shelf with a few toys; the walls were bare and there were no rugs on the floor, no curtains and no extra blankets.

I'm just looking for faults. The children aren't suffering here. As long as Thomas cares about them, they'll be fine.

She had never thought she might divorce. Naïvely, she had assumed that love would be enough: if she loved him enough, everything would turn out all right, pretty much like a bedtime story.

I forgot to love him, and now it's too late.

She looked in on Kalle, tucking him in and picking up Chicken, who had fallen to the floor. Then she walked through the flat to the little space behind the kitchen, and sat down in front of Thomas's laptop. He hadn't changed his user ID or password, still using his first name for both. The connection was fast, as good as at the paper.

She went on to the national ID database and typed Lena Yvonne Nordin's details into the search page. She called herself Yvonne, she was forty-two, and her address was a post-office box in Skärholmen, on the outskirts of Stockholm. According to the list of old records, she had previously lived in Uppsala, and her marital status had been 'widow' for the past ten years. She tried searching for other people called Nordin, male and female, age unspecified, registered at the same post-office box to find out if she had any children.

No. At least, none called Nordin.

Annika couldn't see a printer in the office. She went out into the hall and fetched her notepad and pen from her bag and jotted down the details. She opened another window in her browser and checked to see if Yvonne Nordin had a landline or a mobile. She got forty-nine results for that name, from Boden in the far north to Simrishamn in the south, but nothing in either Skärholmen or Uppsala. Lena Yvonne Nordin brought up one result, in Uddevalla, but that woman was also named Mari, so it wasn't her.

She went into the register of property and searched for anything connected to Lena Yvonne Nordin's ID number.

Nothing.

Annika logged into the database of car registration numbers.

Nothing there either.

She chewed her lip.

She used to run more than one company . . .

She went into the register of companies and brought up the details of the three companies that Lena Yvonne Nordin had been linked to. The only one that was still active was Advice Management Investment AB, the company on whose board David Lindholm had sat. The other two had been deregistered. But there was a name there that she had seen before and not yet checked: Niklas Ernesto Zarco Martinez, also registered as living in Skärholmen.

She opened another window and looked up his details.

Deceased.

Annika blinked.

Niklas Ernesto Zarco Martinez, thirty-five, had died on Christmas Eve the previous year.

Lena Yvonne had a remarkable ability to spread death around her.

Feeling uneasy, she looked up Advice Investment Management AB's business activities. The company was based at the post-office box address in Skärholmen. Going back to the vehicle-registration site, she typed in the company's registered number and there it was. *Bloody hell!*

The company owned a Toyota Land Cruiser 100,

registration number TKG 298. The vehicle was a couple of years old, but was listed as being taxed, insured and roadworthy, which meant that it was in use and on the road somewhere in or not far from Sweden.

Yvonne, I've found your car.

Encouraged by this success, she went back to the property register and typed in the company number, waiting patiently as the laptop chewed through several million legal transactions.

I ought to be pleased he cares about the children. It's a terrible thing to accuse me of having set fire to the house, but can I really blame him? Everyone thinks I did it, after all. And he does look after the children . . .

The computer bleeped and Annika looked up at the screen.

One result.

Number 2:17 Lybacka, in the parish of Tysslinge, in Örebro Council district.

What?

Yvonne Nordin's company owned a property north of Örebro?

Annika's pulse started to race.

The transaction was dated exactly a year before, 2 December.

What does this mean?

2:17 Lybacka wasn't an ordinary address, but one of those hopeless property allocations that didn't tell her anything. How could she find out where 2:17 Lybacka was?

She went into the website of Örebro Council, to see if they had any maps, and found, to her surprise, that you could search for specific properties using their virtual satellite images.

I love the Internet! This is almost too easy!

She entered the property details in the search box. The map on the right flickered and a low-resolution satellite image popped up, apparently showing a patch of forest.

'2:17', it said, in the middle of the picture, and she zoomed out to see where on earth it was. A couple of clicks later, she could tell from the satellite picture that 2:17 Lybacka was a small house with an adjoining barn in the middle of the forest. Another couple of clicks took her to an ordinary map, showing roads and villages. Because she didn't have a printer she drew a sketch-map, then zoomed out a bit further to discover that the property lay north-west of Örebro, through Garphyttan and up in the forest.

So why did you buy that place a year ago, Yvonne? Does it play a part in your plan?

She went back to the Örebro Council website, looked up Tysslinge parish and the area known as Lybacka, and discovered there was a small national park there, and a few abandoned earthworks known as the Lybacka Pits. Nearby was a bog called Ängamossen, which was described as being 'covered with scattered, low-growing pines. The bog is surrounded by magical, ancient woodland . . .'

She clicked away from the natural description and went into the online telephone directory, but couldn't find a number for 2:17 Lybacka. In the end she fetched her mobile from the hall and rang Directory Enquiries instead, but that didn't work either.

She hesitated for a moment, then called Nina Hoffman and asked if she had got the photographs.

'I haven't had time,' Nina said.

'It'll be interesting to see if Julia recognizes any of them. I'm sitting here checking—'

'Sorry to interrupt, but I'm in the car. Can we meet outside Police Headquarters early tomorrow morning? Eight o'clock?'

Annika could hear the rasping voice of the police radio in the background. 'Sure,' she said.

They hung up, and Annika closed all the windows. Her eye was caught by the Outlook Express icon.

I've read Thomas's memo and I need to get hold of him at once. Can you give him a message?

Why? What's so urgent?

She started up the email program, clicked on 'sent messages' and looked through the list of recipients. The last one was sent to sophia.grenborg@sdcc.se, Swedish District and County Councils, presumably, and had the heading 'miss you darling'.

She gulped and carried on looking.

Almost at the bottom of the screen she saw it.

jimmy.halenius@justice.ministry.se, with the heading 'memo'.

She opened the email and clicked on the attachment without even blinking.

She shivered as she read it. Thomas was telling the under-secretary of state that the directives he had been given to work with in the inquiry were impossible to follow. It simply couldn't be done. If life sentences were abolished, the cost of the criminal justice system would increase so greatly that the long-term state budget would have to be renegotiated.

This is absolute dynamite!

That was followed by a careful analysis of the effects that time-limited sentences would have on the criminal justice budget. The reasoning seemed to be that a very long, fixed-term sentence instead of life would drive up all the other tariffs in the criminal code, which would result in the cost of the prison service rising by at least 25 per cent within three years.

She left the computer on and went out into the big room. She stopped and looked up at the ceiling; she felt as though she was in a church.

Penthouse flat! How pretentious could someone actually get?

She glanced at the time: the opera-goers should be back soon. She walked restlessly round the studio, past the dining-table and the seating area, and went back into the television room. The late news was due to start in a few minutes. She managed to get the digital box working and find the right channel just as the programme began.

Julia Lindholm's life sentence was the lead item. The news presenter managed to call Julia a 'double-murderer' and 'police-killer' in her short introduction to the piece.

First on was Prosecutor Angela Nilsson, marching quickly, her back ramrod straight; the cameras were wobbling about like the worst Danish Dogma film. She declared that the verdict was both expected and justified. She looked simultaneously pleased and stern. 'The court unanimously shared my opinion,' she said, 'so I think it was a deserved sentence.'

Anything else would be rather odd.

The crush inside the court building on Fleminggatan was chaotic. Journalists kept bumping into each other and Prosecutor Nilsson had to raise her hand against the camera lights to see where she was going. 'There are no words to describe the calculated cruelty that Julia Lindholm has shown the families of the victims,' she said, sweeping through a security door.

What families? She's the only one left, along with her parents. And Nina, I suppose.

Then her lawyer appeared on screen, the young Mats Lennström, his hair stiff with gel, and beads of sweat on his forehead. He seemed to be leaning so far forward that he actually bumped his nose on the camera, leaving a little smear on the lens.

'Well, it was obvious that the court was going to reach this verdict, seeing as my client was kept in custody while we waited for the sentence,' he said, his eyes flickering over the crowd of journalists. 'But I don't agree with the sentence imposed. In particular, I find it difficult to understand the court's reasoning with regard to the boy, er, Alexander. The problem is that we still don't know how he was killed.'

Annika shifted irritably on the sofa. *How do you know he's dead?*

'Will you be lodging an appeal?' one male reporter shouted.

'Well, I'm considering that, but I haven't had time to talk to my client yet, so I really can't comment . . .'

Mats Lennström stumbled further along the corridor and disappeared through another security door.

A third person appeared on the screen, Professor Lagerbäck, an expert in criminology of the more populist persuasion, and he briskly summarized the verdict against Julia Lindholm in four cliché-ridden sentences: 'It was obvious she was going to get life, nothing else was ever on the cards. She blasted the manhood off an iconic police officer, and then tried the old line about hearing voices. The only thing that I think has been astonishingly shoddy in the investigation of this case is that the police haven't managed to find the little boy's remains. I actually think that's a great scandal.'

Annika switched off the television, leaving a deafening silence.

Everyone's so sure. Why can't I let go of the idea that Alexander is still alive?

She checked the time: twenty past eleven.

Where on earth are they?

Annoyed, she stood up and went out into the hall to get her mobile. She sent Thomas a fairly neutral text message. *Do you know when you'll be back?*

A minute later she got a reply. *In an hour or so.*

She sighed. What on earth was she going to do until half past twelve?

She walked over to the rooms where the children were sleeping, then leaned over and kissed their necks. She went out into the kitchen to get something to eat from the fridge but changed her mind, she didn't want to touch any of Sophia F. B. Grenborg's food.

She ended up standing by the door to the bedroom, their bedroom. She stood there listening to noises from outside, from the stars up above, and out in the stairwell.

At least an hour before they get back. I'll make sure I leave everything as I find it.

Holding her breath, and without making a sound, she pushed the door open. One bedside lamp was on. The bed wasn't made. The bed-linen was black. There were dried white stains on the under-sheet. On the floor lay a pair of black panties with stains in the gusset. She looked towards the wardrobes. They filled an entire wall. She went over to the first and cautiously opened the door.

Suits. Thomas had bought new ones. She opened the door wide. These were more expensive than his old ones, which had gone up in the fire. Carefully she stroked the material, wool, cotton, silk.

He's always had good taste, although he looks best in jeans and a T-shirt.

389

She closed the door and opened the next. Soph's dresses. They were yellow and red and white and black and flowery, a few of them covered with sequins. The pressure in her chest increased. She closed the door and opened the next. Her underwear. Pants, suspender-belts and bras, all made of lace with hooks and pearls.

I don't have a single bra like this, I never have done. Does this sort of thing turn him on?

They were cream and red and deep purple and black, some with shoulder-straps, some without, some wired, others not.

She picked up a silky push-up bra, decorated with lace, and held it in front of her. It was far too small. She made to put it back, then stopped.

She'd never find out I took it. She might wonder where it'd gone, but she'd never know for sure.

She closed the wardrobe door with the bra in her hand, looking round the room. She hadn't touched anything else.

She went out quickly, closing the bedroom door behind her, then into the hall and stuffed the bra into the inside pocket of her bag.

At that moment a text message arrived. From Thomas. We're going to be a bit late.

She tossed the mobile away.

I don't want to be here any longer now! Fuck!

Tears welled in her eyes. The chalk-white walls leaned in on her and she ran into Kalle's room and knelt by his bed. 'Darling,' she said. 'I miss you so much . . .'

He opened his eyes and looked at her, bewildered. 'Mummy? Is it time to get up?'

She forced herself to smile. 'No, not yet, I'm just giving you a kiss. Go back to sleep.' She got up and left the room, stumbled through the studio space and stopped at a low cupboard against the far wall. Above it was a row of pictures in elegant frames, the sort they had in American television programmes. They showed Thomas and FB with their arms round each other on a yacht, Thomas and FB with their arms round each other in front of the Eiffel Tower in Paris, Thomas, FB and the children at his parents' place in the country, out in the archipelago . . .

All of a sudden she couldn't breathe. *The bastard!*

She started to cry.

His mum must be so pleased now I'm out of the picture. I bet she thinks Sophia Fucking Bitch Grenborg is a much better mother than me. How could he do this to me?

Self-pity hit her like a wave, with a force that knocked the breath out of her.

He's going to pay, the bastard!

She hurried back to Thomas's office behind the kitchen, sat down at the computer and wiped her tears with angry fingers. The computer was on standby but woke up at once when she touched the mouse.

She pulled up the email to the under-secretary of state again. If this memo leaked, the consequences for the whole inquiry would be immense. If the basic directives couldn't be followed, the entire proposal would collapse. The whole thing would have to be scrapped and they would have to start again from scratch, the government formulating the terms of reference for a new inquiry with new directives and new members.

Thomas would lose his job.

She stared at the memo, feeling her heart race. She looked at the time.

Half past twelve. They'd be back soon.

He'll be okay. After all, he's got little Soph.

How could she make sure no one knew where the email had come from?

She couldn't just forward it because Thomas's email address would be visible. And she couldn't send it from her own account, because everyone would be able to work out how she had got hold of it.

She would have to set up a fake address, anonymous and inconspicuous, but still credible enough for her colleagues on the paper to sit up and take notice of it.

She checked the time again, and went into hotmail. com.

Fingers trembling, she created an entirely new email account.

deep-throat-rosenbad@hotmail.com

It took all of three minutes.

Then she forwarded Thomas's email to the new address, waiting nervously until it appeared in the Hotmail inbox. She deleted all the details that identified the writer of the memo and where it had come from, then sent it off again, this time to the email address used by the *Evening Post* for members of the public to give them tipoffs.

It ought to pop into the inbox at the paper more or less straight away.

The reporter checking the email account would discover a new sender, Deep Throat Rosenbad, named after the confidential source used by Bob Woodward and Carl Bernstein when they had uncovered the Watergate Affair. They'd open the email and read her short message:

What I am sending you here is an internal and highly confidential memo from the Ministry of Justice. The

contents will have serious consequences for the future
programme of the government. Under-secretary of
State Halenius is aware of its contents.

No more than that. That was enough. All the key words
were there, the ones that got tabloid reporters going:
internal, confidential, government, Ministry of Justice,
serious consequences, under-secretary of state, aware . . .

Finally she deleted all the Hotmail files from Microsoft
Explorer's browsing history, went back into Outlook,
deleted the forwarded email from the list of sent mail,
and shut down the computer.

In the silence that followed she heard the lift machinery whirring into action out in the stairwell.

She switched off the light in the office and ran quietly
through the studio, landing on the black-leather sofa just
as the front door opened. She got up at once, went out
into the hall and did her best to look tired and uptight.

'How did you get on?' Thomas asked.

'Fine,' she said. Without looking at either of them, she
picked up her bag and coat and disappeared through the
door.

Friday, 3 December

28

Annika went into the Seven Eleven on Klarabergsgatan and bought a breakfast roll and both evening papers. Her hands were trembling slightly as she put the money on the counter, slightly uneasy about what the paper would have done with the confidential memo.

What if it leads to a government crisis?

What if they didn't understand what it meant and just ignored it?

She wasn't sure which would be worse.

She inspected the cover of the *Evening Post*. It was dominated by a photograph of a smiling Julia with a garland of flowers in her hair and the headline: *Life.* Then: *Exclusive – Police wife Julia Lindholm speaks out about the murder of her husband David, her son's disappearance and her future in prison.*

That didn't match what she'd written, but she didn't have the energy to get upset.

There was nothing about the memo on the front page.

She leafed through the paper, then noticed she was standing in the way of other customers and moved to the back of the shop, spreading the paper out on top of the ice-cream freezer. She took a large bite of the roll, getting mustard on her bandage. *Damn!*

Her interview with Julia Lindholm was on pages six and seven. Eight and nine carried analysis of the life sentence, but on page ten, *Ah, there it is*, she found the article about the Ministry of Justice's confidential memo.

Emil Oscarsson had written the piece. He had grasped the potential of the story and had called and woken the under-secretary of state and the minister's press secretary, as well as the leader of one of the opposition parties. The angle was that the inquiry was heading for disaster and the Ministry of Justice had been forced into emergency measures to stop the costs of the prison service careering out of control.

Annika swallowed hard.

What have I done?

She wondered if the main radio news broadcasts had picked it up and were running with it in their morning bulletins, but she had no radio so no way of knowing.

What are the consequences of this? For Thomas, and for the government?

Her mobile rang and she dropped the roll as she grabbed for her bag to dig it out.

It was Nina.

'Julia's still in the medical wing. She's not allowed any visitors.'

Fuck.

'Give me two minutes.'

She pushed the roll and both papers into the bin, then ran off towards Bergsgatan.

Nina Hoffman was in her police uniform. She looked as if she hadn't slept a wink.

'No, I haven't,' she said tersely. 'At half past four we found a man's body in a flat near Hornstull. Took a while.'

'Do the papers know about it?' Annika asked breathlessly.

'It looked like an overdose. I doubt they'd be interested. But we still have to investigate it, of course. What have you done to your finger?'

They were standing outside the entrance to Police Headquarters on Kungsholmen. Annika pulled her sleeve down over her left hand. 'I cut myself cooking,' she said, looking off towards Scheelegatan, feeling Nina's stern gaze on her.

'That's a pretty serious bandage,' the police officer said.

Annika looked at the ground, at the leaves stuck to the pavement, at her own shoes and Nina's heavy boots.

'Do we trust each other or not?' the police officer said, pulling her to one side to let a woman with a pram get past on the pavement.

'There were two of them,' Annika said, once the woman had gone. 'Two men. They pulled me into an alley when I was on my way home from yours the other evening, close to where I live in Gamla stan. They cut my finger, told me to say I'd hurt myself cooking. And if I told anyone about them, they'd cut . . . my children next time . . .'

She was having trouble breathing.

Nina took her hand and studied the bandage. 'What's this you've spilled on it?'

'Mustard. The strong sort.'

'I suppose you had to have stitches.'

'Eight. They cut a ligament. I bit one of them, and he hit me over the head to make me let go.'

'I told you – you have to be careful. You can't mess with these people.' Nina looked off down Bergsgatan.

399

'I think you should drop this,' she said. 'Think of your children.'

'Have you got the pictures?'

Nina hesitated, then nodded.

'Come on,' Annika said. 'The café over on Hantverkargatan will be open now.'

A few minutes later they were sitting at a cramped little table by the window.

Annika had some coffee, but Nina didn't want anything. She took off her cap and leaned her head against the wall. 'This is verging on professional misconduct,' she said flatly. 'I'm not supposed to go anywhere near this case.' She felt in her pocket and pulled out an envelope.

Annika opened it carefully and looked through the pictures. 'Which one's Yvonne Nordin?'

'Which one do you think?' Nina said dully.

Annika spread out the Polaroid pictures from the National Police Register on the little table in front of them, picking them up in turn and looking at them carefully. 'No,' she said. 'I can't guess.'

Nina turned one of the pictures over and pointed at the back, where the woman's name and ID number were written.

Yvonne Nordin had mousy blonde hair and unremarkable features, and looked to be in early middle age. She wore a serious expression, and was slightly overweight.

Annika picked up the photograph and inspected it. 'Do you think she's got money?'

Nina snorted. 'That's a completely speculative question.'

Annika was looking intently at the photograph. 'If she was responsible for the murders on Sankt

Paulsgatan, then she must also have been involved in Filip Andersson's shady affairs, which means she's got secret bank accounts hidden away on various tropical islands. I tried to look her up last night. She's registered at a covering address in Skärholmen, but I don't think she lives there.'

'Why not?' Nina asked.

'If she really did shoot David and kidnap Alexander, then there's a reason why. I think she's still got Alexander, and he mustn't be seen by anyone, not for a long while, anyway. Which rules out Skärholmen. But . . .' She pulled her notepad out of her bag and showed the police officer some uneven lines on one of the pages. '. . . she bought a small house in the middle of the forest exactly a year ago, north-west of Örebro. Just outside Garphyttan – here.' She pointed with her pen at a cross on the page.

Nina stifled a yawn.

'Julia mentioned that a couple of different women, unless they were the same one, got in touch with David and demanded that he leave her. One of them had had an abortion. Do you think that could be important?'

'Maybe I will have a cup of coffee after all,' Nina muttered, and Annika got up quickly and fetched her one.

'Do you think the abortion is important?' Annika repeated, as she put the cup down in front of the other woman.

'It can be a very traumatic experience,' Nina said, blowing on her drink. 'Some women never get over it.'

'Well,' Annika said, sitting down at the other side of the table, 'we shouldn't over-dramatize it. It doesn't necessarily have to be that traumatic. I had an abortion when Ellen was six months old, and I'm glad I did.'

Nina took a sip of coffee. 'You didn't see it as a problem at all?'

Annika stuffed her notepad back into her bag. 'Well, getting them to answer the phone was a nightmare. I spent ages ringing round trying to book an appointment anywhere in Stockholm, but all the clinics that could be bothered to pick up the phone couldn't fit me in for several weeks. In the end I gave up and had the abortion in Eskilstuna. I can still remember how relieved I felt when I got back to the car park afterwards. What is it? You look like you don't believe me.'

'Not everyone reacts like that. It can be a great sorrow, an act of betrayal . . .'

Annika shifted on her chair in irritation. 'That's what everyone's expected to say. It's like it's unacceptable to be glad you had an abortion, but I really was. I didn't want to have another child at that time.'

She could see Nina's disapproval. 'What? You think I'm a bad woman because I'm glad I had an abortion? Have I forfeited my right to be a mother?'

'No,' Nina said. 'But I really do have to go now.'

She got up, and Annika saw the woman behind the counter glance furtively in their direction. The police uniform had a way of making people feel guilty, even if they hadn't done anything wrong.

'I'll hold on to these pictures,' Annika said, putting them back in the envelope.

Nina stopped. She seemed to be hesitating. Then she leaned towards her and lowered her voice. 'Be careful,' she said. 'The people who cut you mean business.'

Then she put her cap back on and disappeared through the door, heading towards Scheelegatan.

Annika pulled out the pictures again and stared at them, one by one.

The women were dark and fair, young and old, some wearing a lot of make-up, others scruffy. She stopped at Yvonne Nordin, with her rather sad eyes and thin hair.

Are you a mass-murderer? How on earth am I going to show your picture to Julia?

She bit on her coffee spoon a couple of times, then took her pen and a sheet of paper out of her bag and wrote a short note to Kronoberg Prison: 'These pictures are to be given to Julia Lindholm. Best wishes, Annika Bengtzon.'

She got up and hurried towards Bergsgatan, where she handed the envelope in at the reception desk. Then she ran back to the bus stop outside number thirty-two Hantverkargatan, her old address, her home in Stockholm until the disaster at their new house. She refused even to look at the door and got on to the bus. The weather was uniformly grey and heavy. The sun had probably risen somewhere, but she wasn't sure it would ever again show its face here. The bus was full and she had to stand, swaying this way and that as the bus swung round corners. The air was fusty with damp clothes and bad breath. She got off at Gjörwellsgatan, breathing out deeply.

The newsroom was almost empty. Anders Schyman was sitting in his little glass room with his feet on the desk and that day's *Evening Post* open in front of him.

'Damn good piece about the cop-killer speaking out,' the editor-in-chief said, when she walked into the room without knocking. 'But have you seen the article on page ten? We've got hold of a confidential memo from the Ministry of Justice which proves that life sentences can't be abolished because it would be too expensive.'

'I saw that,' she said, sinking on to the visitor's chair. 'I'm working on something really big. Julia Lindholm says she's innocent – she's been saying that all along. There might be a way to prove it.'

'It came in as a tipoff last night,' Schyman said. 'From a "Deep Throat Rosenbad". What does that say to you?'

Annika ignored his question. 'I think she's telling the truth. I don't think she did it. Alexander's still alive.'

The editor-in-chief lowered the paper. 'I presume you have some sort of concrete evidence to back that up.'

She went over the triple murder in Sankt Paulsgatan four and a half years before, the way the victims had been hit over the head with an axe, then each had had one hand cut off, and how the financier Filip Andersson had been found guilty by both the City Court and the Court of Appeal, even though he had maintained he was innocent.

She outlined the parallels with David Lindholm's murder, first the shot to the head, then the mutilation of the body, and how Julia had claimed she didn't do it.

She explained about David's business interests, and how he had sat on the same board as a woman called Yvonne Nordin, who was also involved in a different company with Filip Andersson ('Do you see the connection?'), and that he had told Julia about a crazy woman who was stalking him and threatening to harm him, 'But we think she was the one who had an abortion . . .'

There was complete silence when she had finished.

Anders Schyman was looking at her sternly. 'The abortion?' he said.

'Yes, but I don't know how important that is.'

'What about Alexander's clothes and teddy bear? How did they end up in the marsh next to Julia's cottage, then?'

'She put them there.'

'Who? This Yvonne? And she was the one who had

404

the abortion? The one who's supposed to be holding Alexander, in other words?'

Annika pulled out the rough sketch-map from her bag and put it on the editor-in-chief's desk. He picked it up and studied it dubiously.

'There,' Annika said, pointing to the cross representing number 2:17 Lybacka in the parish of Tysslinge in Örebro County.

'And Filip Andersson is innocent, and Julia Lindholm is innocent?'

'Filip Andersson is doubtless guilty of an awful lot of things, but not the murders on Sankt Paulsgatan.'

'And Alexander isn't dead?'

'It was an attack on the whole family: kill the man, frame his wife and kidnap the child. He's alive.'

Anders Schyman put the sheet of paper down on his desk. 'Did they ever find out who set fire to your house?' he asked.

'What's that got to do with anything?' she asked.

The editor-in-chief looked genuinely concerned. 'How are you really, Annika?'

She flew into a rage. 'So that's your conclusion!' she said. 'That I'm trying to clear my own name by proxy!'

'Don't start harassing innocent people, Annika. Think before you do anything.'

She got up, knocking the map to the floor, and Schyman bent down to pick it up. 'Do you know what this reminds me of?' he said, handing it back to her.

She looked at the crooked lines and abbreviated road names. 'A Beautiful Mind,' she said quietly.

'A what?'

She swallowed hard.

'Do you need help?' he asked.

She shook herself in annoyance. 'I've been a bit

405

off-form, that's all,' she said, 'with the divorce and everything.'

'Yes,' he said, sitting on the desk and folding his arms. 'How's that going?'

'It'll be in court soon, this month,' she said. 'Then everything's over.'

'Everything?'

She brushed the hair from her face. 'No,' she said, 'not everything, of course, just the rough stuff. After that it'll get better.'

'Are you still living in that old office? When are you going to get a decent place?'

'When the police investigation's over and I can get hold of the insurance money.'

'And your husband?'

'He's living with his mistress.'

'If the divorce is almost legal, she's his partner, isn't she?'

She picked up her bag and put the map back in it.

'Is he still at the Ministry of Justice?'

'As far as I know.'

'What was he doing there? The inquiry into the abolition of life sentences, wasn't it?'

'Can I have a car for the day? I'll be back this evening.'

'What are you thinking of doing?'

'Meeting a source.'

Anders Schyman sighed. 'Okay,' he said, reaching for a requisition request. 'But I don't want you doing anything stupid.'

She left without looking back.

The car was an anonymous Volvo, an old model, dark blue and pretty dirty. She drove out of the garage and swung up on to the Essinge motorway.

There were two ways of getting to Örebro, north or south of Lake Mälaren. Without thinking, she headed south, towards Södertälje, then Strängnäs and Eskilstuna. She chose that way instinctively because she was used to it.

That's what we're like. We'd rather stick to what we know, even if it's no good, than change to something better but new.

There wasn't much traffic and the road was reasonably dry, so she could have driven faster if she'd wanted to. Once she'd got past Södertälje and turned off on to the E20, she set the cruise control for 135 kilometres an hour, just below the point at which she'd lose her licence if she was caught. Anne had taught her you could drive 'with VAT'. On roads with 30 and 50 k.p.h. limits you could drive 20 k.p.h. too fast, and in limits of 70, 90 and 110 k.p.h., the VAT increased to 30 k.p.h. Of course you were breaking the law if you drove with VAT, but it only cost you a fine. 'Look upon it as a congestion charge,' Anne had said.

She laughed as she thought about it. She'd missed Anne. She passed an articulated lorry from Estonia and the car flew along the road. The landscape drifted past without her really noticing it – she'd seen it all her life, grown up in it. The flat brown fields around Mariefred and Åkers styckebruk, the water of Sörfjärden shimmering dully to the right as she passed Härad, then the forests as she approached Eskilstuna.

She glanced at the digital clock on the dashboard: one minute to ten.

Ellen would be back at nursery now, and Kalle would be having his first break at school.

She turned on the radio to hear the news. The lead item brought her out in a sweat.

'The parliamentary inquiry into prison sentences and the abolition of life sentencing is being shut down because the directives were impossible to follow, the Ministry of Justice has announced in a press release this morning. This means that life sentences will remain part of the judicial system in Sweden for the foreseeable future. This has provoked harsh criticism from the opposition . . .'

No reference to the *Evening Post*, and no mention of what would happen to the people working on the project.

She turned the radio off and the silence that followed was deafening. The rumble of the wheels on the tarmac echoed through the car, forming new words in the voice of the newsreader. She leaned over and turned the radio on again, twiddling the dial towards the end of the FM frequency. Mix Megapol had a strong signal around Eskilstuna on 107.3, and she found herself in the middle of a relentless series of adverts that ended with a cheery jingle declaring that the station mixed today's hits with the best of yesterday's. She turned up the volume to block out all the voices and thoughts – Anders Schyman, Anne Snapphane, the newsreader, Nina Hoffman and Sophia Fucking Bitch Grenborg . . .

She turned off towards Kungsör to find fuel. It made sense to fill up. She indicated and turned off into a service station on Kungsgatan. She filled the tank with diesel and went in to pay. Then she went into the Ladies only to discover there was no toilet paper. With a groan she grabbed her bag to get out some tissues. As she rooted around in it her hand touched something soft and silky.

The lacy push-up bra from Sophia Grenborg's wardrobe.

She put the garment in the washbasin, washed her

hands, then sat down on the toilet seat again with it in her hands. The price tag was still attached. It had been bought in Paris: 169 euros.

She remembered the photograph of the Eiffel Tower, and the children on the veranda on the island in the archipelago, Gällnö. Her chest felt tight and she could feel her anger boiling inside her. She pulled the penknife from her bag. *The Evening Post – sharp and to the point.* She cut Sophia Grenborg's luxury bra to shreds, thin at first, then coarser and messier, until it was nothing but tattered fragments. She felt like crying but clenched her teeth, pulled out some more tissues, wetted them under the tap, wrapped them round the fragments of lace and flushed them away.

There. Gone for ever, and good fucking riddance.

She tried to feel pleased, put the penknife back into her bag and went out to the car. She headed off towards Arboga. She had to slow down as she ended up behind a recovery truck that was trundling along at sixty, almost driving her mad. Finally she overtook it and turned on to the E18 towards Örebro.

What am I going to do if she's there? What am I going to do if she's standing there with Alexander?

She wouldn't do anything at all, she decided. She'd just take a look, then leave and call the police if she had to.

Happy with her decision, she cruised through Örebro and eventually found the turning towards Garphyttan. The road became narrow and twisting again, in some places slippery with frost. The thermometer inside the car was hovering around zero and she drove very slowly.

When she got to Garphyttan she turned right at a Co-op supermarket, following the road past detached houses on the right and thick forest on the left. She passed a recreation ground, with a football pitch and a running track, and then she was out in the countryside again.

It started to snow, big, hesitant flakes that swirled in the air, unable to decide where to land. The forest was getting denser and darker. She turned on the radio for a bit of company but the only station she could get was P1, where a serious man was reading something literary about brown envelopes that were dissolving in damp and mould. She switched it off again.

I'll have to put up with silence. I've got to learn how to live with myself.

The landscape opened up and she drove past some farms in a village called Nytorp, then turned left and found herself on roads that reminded her of the forest tracks around Hälleforsnäs.

After a kilometre or so she reached a junction where she had the choice of going right or left. She pulled the map from her bag and peered at her directions. She had to turn right here, then left almost at once and follow the road until it stopped.

She tried to shrug off Anders Schyman's reaction when he had handed the piece of paper back to her.

She drove down the winding road for almost twenty minutes, passing a few cleared patches of woodland, without seeing a single person or a single house.

You like your peace and quiet, don't you, Yvonne?

Finally she reached a turning circle that she had seen on the satellite picture, pulled to a stop and let out a gasp.

A huge 4x4 was parked next to a barrier at the far end of the circle. She looked at the licence-plate: TKG 298.

That's her car, the Toyota Land Cruiser. She's here! I knew it!

Annika pulled up beside the SUV and turned the engine off, opened the car door and got out, her heart pounding. She went quickly to the Toyota and peered in through the windows. No child seats. No toys. No sweet papers on the floor as far as she could see.

In the back of the vehicle a piece of grey fabric had been pulled across to conceal whatever was in there. She'd had something similar in her SUV before it went up in flames.

She looked around, trying to get her bearings. Yvonne Nordin's cottage should be a few hundred metres north of there.

She must have heard the car approaching. There's no point in trying to creep up on her.

She zipped up her jacket, hoisted her bag on to her shoulder and dodged under the barrier.

The forest was thick and dark, pressing in on her from both sides of the path. Annika tried to think of it as unthreatening, noting that it was mainly fir trees with a few birches. The moss was as thick and untouched as the carpet in the entrance hall of Sophia Grenborg's apartment block. The tree-tops stretched up towards the steely grey sky. It had stopped snowing, but she could still smell snow in the air. In the hollows and behind rocks lay the remnants of earlier snowfall.

The frozen mud crunched under her boots, even though she was trying to tread softly.

A stream was burbling somewhere nearby and she peered through the trees but couldn't see any water. Did she dare leave the path? Would she ever find it again? She had a terrible sense of direction: she could never find anything without a map.

She decided to hang her bag on a branch beside the path as a marker. Then she stepped into the trees.

If Alexander is here, he'd love playing by the stream. He's probably built a dam where he can sail his boats.

A minute or so later she found the water. It was trickling between the rocks and little chunks of ice, a constant, harmonious burble unimpeded by any dams or toy boats. She suppressed a sense of disappointment. She followed the water both up and downstream for a bit, but there were no signs of human activity.

She found her way back to the gravel track, and a short while later she glimpsed a red façade through the trees. She slowed, finally coming to a halt behind a large fir tree. It was an old cottage, with windows on either side of the door and a double chimney. Smoke was coming out of one chimney and there were lights on in two of the windows, which had open, white-painted shutters. There was a large satellite dish on the roof. To the left of the house was an outbuilding, which she had taken to be a barn on the satellite image. Now she could see it was more like a storeroom. Perhaps it had been a hen-house or workshop once upon a time. The little forest track ran past the house and disappeared off to the right. It was completely silent around her. Even the wind and the trees were holding their breath.

Then she focused her attention and looked to see if there were any signs of a child's presence. A sandpit, a bike, a plastic spade, anything at all. She took a couple of steps out from behind the tree, and at that moment a woman emerged from the outhouse with a couple of large suitcases. She caught sight of Annika, stopped and put the suitcases down.

Annika's first instinct was to run.

She's going to chop me up. She'll hit me over the head and then cut off my hands.

'Hello!' the woman said cheerily. 'Are you lost?'

Annika gulped and stepped forward. 'I'm afraid I must be,' she said, walking up to the woman and holding out her hand. 'My name's Annika.'

'Yvonne Nordin,' the woman said, with a smile. She looked slightly surprised but not remotely worried. 'Can I help you at all?'

She was the woman from the passport photograph, no doubt about it. Average height, short, ash-blonde hair under a crocheted cap, warm and rather sad eyes.

'I'm trying to find the quarry,' Annika said. 'The Lybacka Pits – they're supposed to be somewhere round here, aren't they? Is this the right way?'

The woman laughed. 'You're not the first person to get that wrong,' she said. 'That little track is completely impossible to find. I've told the people in charge of the project that they have to improve their signage, but it's like everything else. If you want anything doing, you have to do it yourself.'

Annika couldn't help laughing. 'So I've driven too far?'

'About four hundred metres. There's a little red-painted post on the right, and the turning's immediately after that.'

'Thanks very much,' Annika said, glancing around, unwilling to leave just yet. 'You've got a nice place here,' she said.

Yvonne Nordin took a deep breath and closed her eyes in contentment. 'I think it's fantastic,' she said. 'I've only had it for a year, but I really love living here. When you're in my profession you can work pretty much anywhere these days. It's a great privilege.'

Annika saw the opening and grabbed it. 'How exciting,' she said. 'What do you do?'

'I'm a consultant,' she said. 'I run a company that

deals with investment and management. I have to spend a lot of time physically at the companies that employ me, like a sort of stand-in MD, but as soon as I get the chance I come out here to recharge my batteries.'

'Doesn't it get lonely?' The question slipped out before she could stop it, and it sounded far too sharp.

Yvonne Nordin looked at her in surprise, then nodded. 'Well,' she said, 'sometimes.' She smiled rather sadly. 'My partner died last year, on Christmas Eve, actually. I haven't got over it yet. The forest gives me some sort of solace. I don't think I could have got through the past year without this place.'

Annika felt shame rising in her chest, and couldn't think of anything else to say.

'I'd ask you in for coffee,' Yvonne said, 'but I was just about to set off.'

'Duty calls?' Annika managed, looking at the suitcases.

The woman chuckled. 'Isn't it silly that we always pack so much? All I really need are passports and tickets.'

Annika hoisted her bag on to her shoulder and fought to suppress the burning sense of guilt inside her. 'Have a good trip,' she said, 'and thanks for your help.'

'Don't mention it,' Yvonne Nordin said. 'Look in again some time.'

Annika went back along the gravel track, past the point where she had gone into the forest to find the stream, ducked under the barrier and reached the car.

It was incredibly cold now, and snow was falling again. She got into the Volvo, turned on the engine and the heater. She screwed her eyes shut and folded her arms over the steering-wheel.

How embarrassing.

She closed her eyes even tighter and the guilt rose into her throat, almost making her feel sick.

Thank God I didn't make even more of a fool of myself. Imagine, if I'd actually said anything . . .

She could hear Anders Schyman's words echoing in her head.

Don't start harassing innocent people, Annika. Think before you do anything.

She swallowed hard, shame throbbing inside her.

Sorry for being such a naïve fool. Sorry for stealing and wrecking and sabotaging things.

All of a sudden she started to cry, the tears stinging her cheeks.

Stop being so pathetic. You've got no reason to feel sorry for yourself.

She shook herself, wiped the tears on her sleeve and put the car into gear. She headed back along the winding track and, after a few hundred metres, passed the red post that Yvonne Nordin had mentioned.

I've got to get a grip on myself. I can't go on like this.

She drove on through the countryside. There was snow in the air and her stomach was rumbling. She hadn't eaten anything since the roll at a quarter to eight that morning.

She found a restaurant in Garphyttan and ordered the set lunch. It turned out to be a pizza and a soft drink.

Annika got a bottle of mineral water and sat down at one of the window tables.

There was a large factory opposite, Haldex Garphyttan AB, and she looked out at its car park.

So many cars. So many people who own those cars, washing them and getting them serviced, living their lives in Garphyttan without me having the faintest clue about it . . .

She was on the point of bursting into tears again, but pulled herself together.

I should follow Anne's example. I ought to ask for forgiveness.

Without thinking, she pulled out her mobile and saw that she had one missed call. Number withheld, so it was probably the paper.

She gathered her thoughts, then dialled a number she hadn't thought about for six months, a number she had dialled at least twice a day before then, but had since tried to erase from her memory.

'Hello, this is Anne Snapphane . . .'

'Hello,' Annika said. 'It's me.'

A short silence.

'Hello, Annika. It's good to hear from you.'

'Sorry,' Annika said. 'I've been behaving like an idiot too.'

Anne put the phone down and said, 'Can I call you back?' into another receiver, then was on the line again. 'You don't have to say you're sorry,' she said.

'I've got so many people I need to apologize to,' Annika said. 'I crash on like a steamroller without thinking about anyone but myself. Thomas is right. I shape my view of the world so that it fits me and my own criteria. And I completely ignore everything else.'

'You give a damn,' Anne said, 'and sometimes you go just a bit too far.'

Annika laughed, a small, joyless sound. 'That's probably the understatement of the day. I exploit people, I steal and I lie. I refuse to admit when I'm wrong.'

'Everyone gets things wrong,' Anne said. 'Everyone makes mistakes. You're not the only person on the planet who does that. And that's a good thing to try to remember.'

'I know,' Annika whispered, looking at the pizza oven. A flour-dusted cook with a beer-belly and bright red hair was sprinkling oregano over her Capricciosa.

'Where are you?'

She laughed again. 'In a pizzeria in Garphyttan. My lunch is on its way.'

'Where the hell is Garphyttan?'

'You don't want to know, and you don't want to know what it looks like.'

'Don't say any more. Textured wallpaper, flouncy, flowery curtains that are all shiny on one side.'

'Exactly.'

'What are you doing there?'

'Making a fool of myself, as usual. Could you bear to hear about it?'

'Of course.'

The pizza arrived in front of her, she mimed, 'Thank you,' to the red-haired cook, who evidently doubled as waiter.

'I behaved like a real cow towards Thomas. I've sabotaged his work and I went through the wardrobes in his new home, really mean.'

'Really mean,' Anne agreed. 'And really nasty.'

'And I've been poking about in the background of a murdered police officer, and I've been absolutely convinced that there's evidence, patterns that no one else has noticed. I've been assuming I was better and smarter than everyone else.'

'You do have a tendency to think the world is full of idiots,' Anne said. 'That's just part of who you are.'

Annika sighed and rolled the pizza into a long sausage, then picked up one end and took a bite. Fat ran out of the other end, making a little trickle that spread across the tablecloth. 'I know,' she said, with her mouth full.

'I've done so many stupid things. I've made a fool of myself in front of my boss, and a police officer called Nina, but I'll just have to live with that.'

Not to mention what I've done to Thomas.

'Schyman must have seen most of your bad sides before now,' Anne said.

'Now he thinks I'm starting to go mad as well, but that doesn't really matter. I'm just sullen and stubborn, and I always have to be proved right.'

'But at least you're starting to get a bit of self-awareness,' Anne said. 'That should make life easier for you.'

Annika swallowed the mouthful of pizza. 'I've been very unfair to you,' she said.

'Oh, well,' Anne said. 'I'll survive. I'm just happy you're prepared to get a grip on yourself and your life. Maybe you should go and talk to someone. What do you think?'

'Maybe,' Annika said quietly.

'It's probably not a good idea for you to see the same therapist as me, but I can ask if she could recommend someone.'

'Mm.'

There was silence on the line.

'Annika?'

'Yes?'

'Take care on the drive back to Stockholm, and get in touch when you're back. I've got Miranda next week – she's really missed Ellen and would love to see her.'

Tears welled in Annika's eyes again, this time tears of relief. 'Definitely,' she said.

'Well, let's speak soon.'

She stayed in the pizzeria for a while, drinking coffee that was surprisingly good and listening to a song on the jukebox in the corner, 'Losing My Religion' by REM.

Breathing started to feel a bit easier: it had been the right decision to swallow her pride.

She paid (the red-haired man worked on the till as well) and went out into the hesitant twilight. The air was clearer and colder, the skies were less cloudy and there was a stiff wind.

She got into the car and had just turned on to the road to Örebro when her mobile rang. It was on the passenger seat beside her and she glanced at the screen. Number withheld. Probably the paper again. She sighed and answered it.

'Annika? This is Q. Where are you?'

Suddenly the fear was back, big and black, sucking all the oxygen from the air.

'I'm driving. Has something happened with the investigation into the fire?'

'Julia Lindholm got the envelope with your pictures.'

Oh, no. Fucking hell.

'The prison staff called me after she'd spent an hour screaming.'

Annika slowed the car and pulled in at the verge.

'I'm really sorry, I didn't mean—'

'It's really bloody irritating to have you poking about in our investigation.'

She closed her eyes tightly and felt her cheeks colour. 'I'm really sorry if I've made a mess of things.'

'It says on the back of the picture that one of the women owns a cottage somewhere near Garphyttan. Is that your information?'

'Er, yes, she lives there. In a cottage not far from the Lybacka Pits. I was talking to her about an hour ago.'

'You were *talking* to her? Bloody hell. Where are you?'

Her voice was little more than a squeak when she

419

answered: 'In Garphyttan. And I'm really sorry I left those pictures. It was all a misunderstanding.'

'Julia says she recognizes Yvonne Nordin. She says it was Yvonne Nordin who was in their flat that night. That she was the one who took Alexander.'

'I'm so sorry I've made a mess of everything,' Annika said. 'I really am. It's all wrong. There's no child up at the cottage. Yvonne Nordin has nothing to do with this.'

'I intend to make up my own mind about that,' Q said. 'I've just sent a patrol from Örebro Police to bring her in for questioning.'

'Oh, no,' Annika said. 'But it isn't her. Everything she said was true.'

'What? What was true?'

'When she bought the house, and that her partner died. The company she runs, and the car she drives. She's a decent person.'

She could hear Q groan.

'Anyway, she probably isn't there,' Annika said. 'She was just about to leave. She said she was going away on a job.'

'Where? Did she say where?'

'Abroad, I assume, because she mentioned her passport. Has the patrol set off?'

'They'll be leaving any minute. Do me a favour and keep out of the way.'

'Sure,' Annika said. 'Of course. Absolutely.'

She was left sitting with the phone in her hand, wishing the ground would swallow her.

She'd made Julia think there was hope. Yvonne Nordin might end up missing her flight . . . God, she was such a loser.

She put her hand on the ignition key, then stopped.

Miss her flight? Tickets? Isn't it silly that we always pack so much. All I really need are passports and tickets.

She let go of the key.

Passports and tickets?

Why did Yvonne Nordin use the plural? And why did she need several suitcases if she was going away for work?

Because she wasn't going alone.

Because she was going to be taking a child with her.

She forced herself to get a grip on her thoughts.

I'm getting carried away again.

You couldn't keep a child locked up for six months. It wasn't possible to hide a four-year-old boy in a house in the woods without someone finding out about it.

Or was it?

In that case, he wouldn't have been out in the fresh air for six months. Hadn't been allowed to build dams in streams or dig in the mud with a spade. He hadn't been allowed to eat sweets in the car or pick films from the video-store . . .

The satellite dish! He's been watching Cartoon Network!

She looked at the time. A quarter past two. In an hour or so it would be completely dark.

But Julia had actually recognized her.

It would take her a couple of hours to drive back to Stockholm, although the car didn't have to be back until the following morning.

She paused with her hand on the key. *What if she gets away before the police arrive? I've got half an hour's head start on them.*

She started the engine, turned the car round and headed back towards the town. She drove through the

421

centre and past the football pitch, up through the forest and the cleared patches of woodland without meeting a single car.

Could there be any other roads? Of course there must be. Forest tracks, and you don't even need those with a vehicle like hers.

The Toyota Land Cruiser 100 was the sort of vehicle that American special forces used when they'd invaded Iraq – she'd seen them on the news footage. Thomas had commented on it once, that the US used Japanese cars when it really mattered.

Yvonne Nordin could drive straight through the forest all the way to Norway if she wanted.

She reached the red post showing the way to the Lybacka Pits, the flooded quarries where iron ore had been mined even in prehistoric times. She turned off and parked behind a fir tree, pulled on the handbrake and switched off the engine. She sat in silence in the car, listening to her breathing. There was quite a gale blowing now.

I don't have to go all the way. I can just take a look. The police should be here in thirty minutes at most.

She got out of the car and closed the door carefully.

Yvonne's house ought to be about a kilometre away through the forest. She hoped that the sound of the car engine hadn't made its way to the cottage.

She pulled out her bag and started to walk, having the sense to put her mobile on silent. Her footsteps crunched on the path, and she frowned and went in among the trees instead. The moss swallowed her steps with a soft, sucking sound.

It was getting dark very quickly, particularly down among the bases of the trees. She was forced to tread carefully.

Soon she caught sight of the turning circle ahead of her. The Land Cruiser was gone.

She bit her lip. *Shit!*

Then she noticed that the barrier was open.

Maybe she's driven up to the house to put her things in the car.

Annika jogged through the trees, found the little stream and decided to follow it through the forest towards the house. She was panting in the wind, partly from exertion but mostly from tension. She stumbled on a rock and fell first into the moss, picked herself up and hurried on.

The car was standing in front of the house, its headlights on and engine running. Yvonne Nordin was just coming out of the house with a suitcase in each hand. They looked heavy.

Annika pressed her light-coloured bag into the moss and crouched behind a narrow fir tree.

Yvonne Nordin walked to the side of the car and put the cases on the back seat, then closed the door and went into the house without shutting the front door.

Annika waited in the darkness and tried to control her breathing.

The woman came out again with another two cases. This time she went to the other side of the car and disappeared from view. The light inside the vehicle went on when the rear door on the passenger side opened, and Annika saw her put these bags on the back seat as well. Then she returned to the house, and this time she closed the front door.

Annika sat in the darkness staring at the car, at the house, at the door, at the shadows inside the windows whenever someone moved. It was damp and windy in the forest, making the trees and branches sway.

I've got to stop her leaving. Can I get any closer than this?

To the left lay the outhouse from which Yvonne Nordin had fetched the suitcases, and to the right, tyre tracks disappeared into the forest.

Halfway towards the house there was a well with a bucket and a traditional hand-pump, and from there it was just a few metres to the car.

She looked for shadows in the windows. No movement.

She took three deep breaths, grabbed her bag and ran in a crouch to the well.

How was she going to stop a Toyota Land Cruiser? She didn't know the first thing about cars.

She opened her bag and felt about through the mess inside. Was there anything she could use?

Her hand landed on the penknife she'd used to shred Sophia Fucking Bitch Grenborg's bra.

I've got to stop thinking of her like that. It's beneath me.

She took out the knife, hesitated for half a second, then rushed out and stuck it into the rear left-hand tyre. The rubber gave way and started to let out air with an audible hiss. She moved two steps to the right and pierced the other rear tyre as well. Then she ran back to the well in a crouch and had just crept behind it when the front door opened.

Yvonne Nordin stepped on to the porch, holding a little girl's hand. The child was wearing a pink dress, and had blonde curls that hung down over her shoulders. She dragged her, making her stumble on the steps, but she didn't protest and followed her obediently to the car.

Why isn't she wearing a coat? It's freezing out here.

Annika curled into a little ball as they approached the

vehicle, and held her breath when they passed the two side doors and stopped at the rear. She didn't dare poke her head out, but she heard the door open and Yvonne Nordin say: 'Get in.'

She stuck her head out far enough to see the child crawl into the car and lie down in the boot. Then Yvonne Nordin pulled the grey fabric over the compartment and shut the door.

Then the woman paused and looked around. Annika ducked behind the well and screwed her eyes shut.

As long as she doesn't discover the punctures! Don't look down!

Then she heard footsteps going away and peeped out cautiously.

The woman was on her way back into the house, presumably to turn out the lights and lock up.

Annika took a deep breath and ran to the car. She opened the rear door, folded back the cloth covering the boot and stared at the child lying there.

The child stared back with eyes that seemed utterly dead, and Annika realized at once that it wasn't a little girl. It was a boy, and he was pale and frightened. He had a vivid red scar along one side of his face. Annika gulped, felt in her jacket pocket and found a bag of sweets. 'Hello,' she said breathlessly. 'Would you like some sweets?'

The child's eyes flickered.

'I've got a whole bag,' she said. 'They're really good. Here!'

She put a bright green sweet in his mouth and the boy chewed and sat up.

'Come with me and you can have some more,' she said, holding out her arms to him.

And before she knew it the child was in her arms and

she put the grey cloth back in place. She closed the rear door and rushed towards the well, abandoning her bag to its fate, then raced towards the forest.

She crouched beside the little fir tree again as the lights inside the house went out and the front door opened. She put the boy in the moss, took off her coat and wrapped it round him.

'Here,' she said, giving him another sweet. 'There are different-coloured ones. I think the pink ones are best.'

The boy took the sweet in his hand and popped it into his mouth, then snuggled up to Annika with the coat wrapped tight around him.

Yvonne Nordin went to the car, put her handbag on the passenger seat, then walked round to the back of the vehicle.

Don't open it! Don't open it! Just go!

Annika tried to send thoughts to the woman through the darkness, but it didn't work. Yvonne Nordin opened the rear door, pulled the cloth aside and saw that the child was gone.

She moved incredibly fast.

She tore back to the house, opened the front door, turned the light on and disappeared inside.

Annika picked the boy up and rushed in the other direction, among the trees, the wind and the shadows. It was now completely dark. She couldn't see a thing and kept stumbling and almost falling. The treetops above her were whistling and singing, and the cold was biting.

Yvonne Nordin would have a gun, and quite possibly night-vision goggles.

I have to get away, as far away as possible, preferably towards the car.

She ran, the boy bouncing in her arms, following the

little stream down towards the turning-circle. The moss was soft and slippery, she stumbled and fell. *Is this the right direction? Am I going the right way?* She stood up again, clutching the boy to her, one arm round his body, the other round his fair head.

The first shot hit a tree-trunk a few metres to her right.

Don't panic, just don't panic. Run, run!

The second shot was closer, to the left.

It's a hunting rifle, or some other heavy-duty gun. Hard to aim properly.

The third shot whistled past close to her head.

She won't miss next time. I have to get out of sight.

She ducked down behind a stump, holding the boy close.

'I know you're here,' the woman screamed, through the darkness, the wind carrying her words. 'It's hopeless. Give yourself up and I'll let the child live.'

Where the hell are the police?

'Are there any more sweets?' The boy was looking up at her with shining eyes.

'Of course,' she said, pulling another out of her jacket pocket. Her hands were shaking so much she could hardly keep hold of it.

A fourth shot hit the stump in front of them, throwing shards of wood up into her face. She felt a splinter pierce her cheek and had to clench her teeth to stop a scream.

The boy started to cry. 'She's horrid,' he said. 'She's really horrid.'

'I know,' Annika whispered, and at that moment the forest was lit by headlights. A police car was heading slowly up the gravel track towards Yvonne Nordin's cottage. Another shot rang out and the windscreen of the police car exploded. Annika heard a yell of pain. The car stopped and reversed, leaving the forest as suddenly as it had arrived.

Come back! Don't leave us – she's shooting at us!

She sat completely still with the child beside her, utterly still, as a whole minute came and went. There was no movement, no sound. Another minute passed, then another.

Her legs were on the point of going to sleep because of the uncomfortable position she was sitting in and she tried to move her feet to bring back some feeling.

'Come on,' she whispered. 'I've got a car – we'll go to my car.'

The boy nodded and took a firm grasp round her neck.

She stood up carefully and looked towards the house. Then she heard a car engine start up, and far off in the trees she saw the headlights go on.

She can't drive and look through the rifle-sights at the same time.

Annika stood up straight and felt her coat slide to the ground. She ignored it and ran like the wind towards the road, the boy clasping her neck, towards the turning-circle, towards the police.

A headlamp was shining right in her face, blinding her, and she fell.

'There are guns aimed at you,' she heard a man say, from where she lay on the ground with the boy beside her. 'Are you armed?'

'No. But she's getting away, Yvonne Nordin – she's just got in her car . . .'

'Are you Annika Bengtzon?'

She nodded towards the light.

'Who's the girl?'

The light vanished, leaving her in complete darkness. 'He's not a girl. This is Alexander Lindholm.'

The wind was singing in the trees. The stars were visible in the gaps between the clouds and the moon was rising. Annika was sitting wrapped in a thick blanket behind the police car without a windscreen. Alexander had fallen asleep with his head on her chest. She leaned her head back and gazed up at the sky, then closed her eyes and listened to the song of the wind.

She could hear the police radios crackling and men muttering.

The ambulance would soon be here to pick up the police officer who had got splinters of glass in his face. The rapid-response unit and dog patrol were also on their way, and the police helicopter was coming from Stockholm with floodlights and heat-seeking cameras.

'And you're sure she won't get far in the car?' the police officer asked her.

'She might be able to change one tyre,' Annika said quietly, without opening her eyes, 'but not two. And you can't drive off-road on your wheel-rims for long.'

A comprehensive approach was being carefully planned: the suspect was evidently prepared to shoot at the police. Annika let herself be rocked by the sounds around her, as she sat with the child, feeling his warmth and regular breathing.

When the rapid-response unit arrived in their van they helped her up and put her into the back with the boy. They left the engine on to keep the inside of the vehicle warm. Annika tipped the rest of the sweets out on to the blanket.

'Do you think the pink ones are best too?' she asked, holding one up. For some reason she knew that each contained nine calories – Anne Snapphane must have told her.

Alexander shook his head. 'I like the green ones.'

They split the sweets by colour, green ones for him, pink ones for her, then shared out the white ones.

He had just fallen asleep when she heard over the police radio that they had located Yvonne Nordin fourteen hundred metres away from the cottage, trying to change a tyre. She had shot at the patrol, which had returned fire.

An ambulance was called to the scene, but there was no rush.

Yvonne Nordin had been hit during the exchange of fire and was believed to have died instantly.

ALEXANDER'S PRISON

Boy Held Captive for Six Months

By Patrik Nilsson and Emil Oscarsson

Evening Post (Garphyttan). Alexander Lindholm, four years old, was forced to spend six months living in a bare cellar two metres below ground.

Sometimes he was allowed up into the living room to watch television, but only if the shutters on the windows were closed.

'Alexander seemed to be relatively well,' says *Evening Post* reporter Annika Bengtzon, who met the boy shortly after his release.

The cottage lies deep in the forest, many kilometres from any main roads. A barrier stops traffic approaching the house.

This is where four-year-old Alexander Lindholm was found by Örebro Police yesterday evening.

'We think he's been kept hidden in this house since he was kidnapped from his home on Södermalm on 3 June,' a spokesman for Örebro Police said. 'Evidence inside the house supports this theory.'

Alexander was forced to live in a potato cellar that could only be reached via a hatch in the kitchen floor.

'We found what must have been his bed down there.'

Was there any lighting in the cellar?

'Yes, it had been furnished to look like a room, with

431

rag-rugs on the floor and a lamp in the ceiling. There were also some picture-books and comics.'

There was a television set in the living room of the cottage, and there is evidence to suggest that Alexander was occasionally allowed to watch children's programmes.

'We found crisp crumbs and a child's sticky fingerprints on the sofa,' the police spokesman said.

The police have not yet released any information about Alexander's kidnapper, the woman who is also believed to have murdered his father.

It is clear, however, that the woman planned the kidnapping carefully. Some of the items in the cellar were bought over a year ago, mainly in Gothenburg and Oslo.

Evening Post reporter Annika Bengtzon was on the scene when Alexander Lindholm was released.

'I don't want to comment on his physical or mental state, but he could certainly walk and talk.'

So he seemed to be relatively well?

'Yes.'

The miraculous discovery of Alexander's whereabouts raises many questions about the reliability of the Swedish judicial system.

'From a legal point of view, this is an extremely interesting dilemma,' says professor of criminology Hampus Lagerbäck. 'Here we have a case in which a person has been sentenced to life imprisonment for the murder of someone who is still alive. It will be interesting to see how the judicial authorities wriggle their way out of this mistake.'

Saturday, 4 December

29

Thomas tossed his dressing-gown on to a chair and crept back into bed beside Sophia. The sound of the cartoon was effectively shut out by the locked bedroom door. Saturday morning was still young and full of possibilities.

Sophia was asleep. She was lying on her side with one leg pulled up and her back to him. He moved closer to her and put his knee between her thighs. She was moving a little in her sleep. He nibbled her ear lobe. Slowly he slid his hand from her stomach towards her breasts. He was still fascinated by how small they were. He carefully squeezed one nipple and her body stiffened.

She turned to him. 'Hello,' she said, with a smile.

'Hello,' he whispered, kissing her neck. He let his fingers trace her spine, down to her buttocks, and pulled her to him.

She wriggled away and sat up. 'I need a pee . . .'

She pulled on her dressing-gown, unlocked the bedroom door and went out to the bathroom.

He lay down, staring up at the ceiling, feeling his erection subside. She was taking her time. He could never understand what on earth she did in there. Rather sullenly, he grabbed the duvet and wrapped it tightly around himself.

He'd almost nodded off again when she came back.

'Darling,' she said, touching his hair, 'shall we go to the museum today? I haven't seen Rauschenberg's *Combines* yet.'

He looked up at her and smiled, then took a firm grasp of her waist. 'Come and lie down,' he said thickly, tipping her into the bed. 'Now I've got you!'

She struggled free, annoyed. 'I've just done my hair,' she said, sitting up again, at arm's length from him. 'And I asked if you wanted to go to the Museum of Modern Art. You could at least answer.'

Disappointment turned to frustration and he thumped the pillow, pushing it up against the head of the bed. 'And all I wanted was a bit of affection,' he said.

'Affection,' she echoed. 'You wanted sex, admit it.'

'And what's wrong with that?'

She looked at him with her pale eyes. They were almost invisible when she wasn't wearing make-up. 'You can have affection without sex.'

'Yes, but I like sex.'

'So do I, but . . .'

'Even though you never come.' He'd said it without thinking.

She reacted as if she'd been slapped, jerking and going pale. 'What do you mean by that?'

He felt his mouth go dry. 'It's not a criticism,' he said.

'Yes, it is,' she said, sitting quite still.

'I just thought it might be more fun for you if you could have an orgasm as well. Maybe you could help yourself a bit. Or we could see if I . . .'

She got up without looking at him. 'It's not important to me. Don't tell me what I should feel. I'll take responsibility for my own sexuality, and you take responsibility for yours.'

He clenched his jaw. *Me and my big mouth.*

'I appreciate that it's been really tough on you,' she said. 'Losing your job must feel very unfair when you'd done your best . . .'

He threw back the duvet and reached for his dressing-gown. Saturday morning's possibilities had all drained away. 'I haven't lost my job,' he said. 'Where did you get that idea?'

She looked at him in surprise. 'But you said the inquiry had been suspended.'

'Yes,' he said, 'but my contract runs until October next year. I met Halenius yesterday afternoon. I'm going to be part of an inquiry into cross-border currency transactions.'

He studied her face. Was that a tiny hint of disappointment?

She took off her dressing-gown and got up to choose some clothes from her wardrobe. 'Do they know who leaked it to the press?' she asked, over her shoulder.

He let out a deep sigh. 'It was probably the press secretary. The bosses just seem happy the inquiry's been dropped. They never wanted to increase the sentencing tariffs, which would have been the inevitable conclusion.'

'So you're not out of favour, then?'

If he hadn't known better, he could have sworn she was disappointed now. 'I dare say I'll never work with Per Cramne again,' he said, 'but that's something I'm more than happy to live with.'

She turned back towards the wardrobe again. 'Have you seen my new bra? The French one, with the silk cups?'

He let out another sigh, silent and deep.

437

Annika stepped into Detective Inspector Q's office. Her finger ached: the wound had become infected and the district nurse had given her antibiotics. The splinter of wood in her cheek had been removed but had left a scab covered with a sizeable plaster.

She sat down and met his eyes. He was wearing a seriously washed-out shirt today, but it had probably been yellow once.

The policeman nodded towards her hand. 'What have you done to your finger?'

She looked at him coolly. 'Some thugs thought I was digging too deep.'

'Have you reported it?'

She shook her head.

'So who do you think did it?' Q asked.

'There are plenty to choose from. Yvonne Nordin's heavies, or Filip Andersson's, or possibly Christer Bure's . . .'

Detective Inspector Q sighed. 'What the hell were you doing, going back up to Lybacka?'

Annika's eyes narrowed. 'Is this a formal interview? Is that why I'm here? In that case I want you to stick to the rules. I want to see it in writing afterwards so I can give my consent.'

He sighed in irritation, then got up and walked round the desk to shut the door properly. He went and stood by the window with his back to her and his arms folded. 'You can't just go off and pay a visit to a suspected murderer entirely alone. Don't you get that?'

She looked at his back. 'I'm almost starting to think you care about me,' she said.

'I care about reporters on the evening papers,' he said. 'Or have done, at least some of them . . .' He

438

sounded oddly subdued, then turned and went back to his desk.

'Has Julia been released yet?' Annika asked.

'The hearing took place at two o'clock this morning,' he said, sitting down in his chair. 'She's at a care home for families now with Alexander. They'll be there for a while.'

'Will there be a new trial?'

'Yes. Both the prosecutor and her lawyer have put in an application to the Court of Appeal, and during those proceedings Julia will be formally declared innocent. Which will mean that the judicial side of things is all finished.'

'How is Alexander?'

'He's still got to have a proper medical examination, but evidently he's performing all the functions a four-year-old should. He walks and talks and knows how to use the toilet and so on. You probably know all that better than me . . .'

Annika nodded. She could feel the warmth of the little boy's body like cotton-wool in her chest. The long wait during the night had calmed her.

A woman from social services in Stockholm had picked him up from Örebro just after midnight, and the boy had cried and wanted to stay with Annika. She'd promised to visit him and bring more sweets.

'I wonder what happens to a small child when they're put through something like that,' Annika wondered to herself. 'Will he ever be normal?'

'There are a couple of things I want to ask you about,' Q said, 'but there's no real reason to regard this as a formal interview. Yvonne Nordin obviously won't be charged for David's murder or for kidnapping Alexander, so we can keep this informal. Did she shoot at you?'

Annika swallowed and nodded. 'Four shots. How did she die?'

'One of our marksmen hit her in the chest. There'll have to be an inquiry, but I can't imagine that he'll be reprimanded. The circumstances were difficult, it was dark, the middle of the forest, with all that implies in terms of visibility and complex judgements. And she did actually take aim and fire at the police, which of course she'd already done earlier.'

Annika looked out of the window. 'She'd got her bags packed. I wonder where she was going.'

'Mexico,' Q said. 'She had the tickets in the car, from Gardermoen, via Madrid. With a fake passport saying that Alexander was a little girl called Maja.'

'So she really was planning to drive through the forest to Norway?'

'That was certainly one option.'

Q clicked to open something on his computer. Annika picked at her bandage. 'Do you think we'll ever find out what really happened?' she said. 'With David, or the murders on Sankt Paulsgatan?'

'Seeing as Yvonne Nordin is dead, Filip Andersson has decided to talk,' Q said. 'His lawyer has already been in touch this morning to say that they're applying to have his case heard in the Supreme Court.'

'Do you think he's got any chance?'

'There were fingerprints in Sankt Paulsgatan that could never be identified before,' Q said. 'They were Yvonne's. But we have to find something else tying her to the murders. A weapon, for instance, or traces of the victims' DNA in her car, something like that. But the decisive factor will be whether or not Filip Andersson goes through with his decision to talk. He claims it was Yvonne who framed him, that she tipped off the police and left his trousers to be dry-cleaned.'

Annika looked at Q and tried to understand what he was saying. 'You don't waste any time,' she said. 'You've already spoken to Filip Andersson?'

'He knows far more than we ever realized. There are connections between these people that we never had any idea about before.'

'They ran a company together,' Annika said. 'Some investment company.'

'Yes,' Q said, 'but their relationship was considerably closer than that. Filip Andersson and Yvonne Nordin were brother and sister. Well, half-brother and half-sister, to be more precise.'

Annika blinked. 'You're kidding?'

'Why? Most people have brothers and sisters.'

'Yes, and I knew Filip Andersson had a sister, but not that it was Yvonne Nordin. She used to visit him in Kumla once a month.'

'You've got that wrong,' Q said. 'Yvonne Nordin, or Andersson as she was before she got married, didn't get on with her brother. You don't get someone put away for life unless you're seriously pissed off with them.'

'His sister visited him regularly. They told me so when I was there.'

'What do you mean, "there"? Have you been to Kumla as well?'

She squirmed on her chair, and tried to evade the question. 'Why was she so angry with him?'

'That's one of the things we're going to have to find out. But she certainly hasn't paid any visits to Kumla, I can assure you of that. I suppose he must have another sister. When were you there?'

'Earlier this week. But what about Yvonne's relationship with David Lindholm, then? Did they have an affair?'

'For several years. They ran the business together and were planning to get married as soon as they'd made enough money – or, at least, that's what Yvonne thought.'

'And she had an abortion that she never got over?'

'David promised her that they'd have another child as soon as he'd divorced Julia.'

Annika sat in silence for a few moments. 'How does Filip know that? If they didn't get on.'

Q didn't answer.

'Well?' Annika said. 'How do you know that Yvonne went crazy because she had an abortion?'

Q rocked back and forth on his chair a few times before replying. 'Our colleagues in Örebro found a number of things inside the house that pointed in that direction.'

'Like what? Baby clothes?'

'A room.'

'A *room*?'

'There was a sign saying "Maja's Room" on the door. All done out in pink, furniture, clothes, toys, all with the price tags still on. We haven't had time to go through everything yet, but there are letters and diary entries and little things she'd made for the dead child.'

'It wasn't a child,' Annika said. 'It was a foetus, incapable of life. Perhaps it wasn't the loss of the foetus that sent her mad but the betrayal of being dumped.' She shook her head at her own thoughts. 'But if you've already chopped three people's hands off, you were probably pretty mad anyway.'

'If it was actually her who did that,' Q said.

They sat in silence again. Annika could see the

442

woman in front of her, her nondescript features, her sad eyes.

'What did she say the first time you spoke to her, when you asked for directions?' Q asked.

Annika looked out of the window. It was snowing again.

'That she'd had the place for a year, that her partner died last Christmas, that she worked for her own company. It all fitted . . . She seemed so . . . normal. Pleasant, actually.'

'Niklas Ernesto Zarco Martinez wasn't her partner. He was a junkie who acted as the stooge in the company. He was lined up to take the rap when they went bankrupt and emptied the company of its assets. He got a syringe full of dodgy gear for Christmas last year.'

She bit her lip.

'So if Martinez was the stooge, what was David doing there?'

Q didn't answer.

'I can understand that he ran the company with Yvonne if they were having an affair, but why was he on the board of those other companies? Do you know?'

Q laced his fingers together and put his hands behind his head. 'The man's dead and it's not him we're investigating.'

'I think David Lindholm was extremely crooked, and those companies whose boards he was on, apart from the parachute business, were all fronts for money-laundering or some other criminal shit. He was probably on the board to keep an eye open, a sort of look-out.'

'Have you finished?' the detective asked.

Annika looked at the time. 'I ought to go up to the paper. I still haven't handed back the car I borrowed yesterday.'

443

'There's just one more thing,' Q said. 'We've had a response from England about a forensic sample we took from the fire and sent for analysis months ago, way back in the summer, actually. I think it might interest you.'

Annika stiffened, and suddenly it was hard to breathe.

'It was a brick that we found in the ruins of your house. Forensics worked out that it was used to smash the window before the firebombs were thrown in. The Brits have managed to find a fingerprint on it.'

Her pulse was racing, and her throat was dry as dust.

'And we've actually been able to identify it,' he said. 'It belonged to an old acquaintance. I assume you remember the Kitten?'

Annika swallowed and had to cough.

'Her? The hired killer from the Nobel banquet? But . . . why?'

'We're regarding the fire in your house as a closed case, from a police point of view. She started it.'

'But,' Annika said, 'I thought it was the neighbour. Hopkins.'

'I know that's what you thought, but you were wrong.'

'It must be a mistake. This doesn't fit her pattern. You said so yourself. The fire was a personal attack, a hate-crime. Why would she hate me?'

'Just drop it,' Q said. 'Accept that you were wrong. And you caught her, so how much more personal could it get?'

Annika stood up, walked over to the window and stopped to watch the falling snow. 'I know I get things wrong,' she said. 'Fairly often, in fact.'

Q sat in silence.

Annika turned back to him. 'But you're sure she was in Sweden that night?'

'Off the record,' he said.

'What?' Annika said. 'What is it?'

He gestured towards the visitor's chair. 'Sit down. We've managed to keep this quiet for six months. The number of people who know is seriously bloody limited.'

'It won't last,' Annika said. 'Everything gets out.'

He laughed. 'You are so fucking wrong!' he said. 'It's the exact opposite. Almost nothing gets out. So, off the record?'

She looked at her shoes and sat down again, then gave a quick nod.

'The Kitten was picked up at Arlanda early on the morning of the third of June this year,' Q said. 'She was planning to fly to Moscow on a fake Russian passport.'

Annika folded her arms. 'So? You arrest criminals every day, don't you?'

Q smiled. 'It's actually rather funny. She was very upset when we brought her in. Not because we'd caught her, but because her suicide pills didn't work.'

Annika raised her eyebrows. 'Yes, it's true,' Q said. 'She'd bought what she thought was cyanide, but it turned out to be Tylenol.'

'Tylenol?'

'A common American painkiller, with the same active ingredients as Alvedon and Panodil, which you can buy here in Sweden.'

'Ah,' Annika said. 'My favourites.'

'People have got Tylenol and cyanide mixed up before, but the other way round. Seven people died in Chicago in 1982 after taking what they thought were Tylenol pills. Turned out to be cyanide.'

'So what's so confidential about the Kitten biting into a painkiller? Why haven't we heard anything about this? She must have been remanded in custody, so she ought to have been charged by now.'

Q sat there silently. Annika's eyes opened wide.

'She hasn't been registered in any Swedish court. Not even her arrest. You've handed her over to the USA! Just like that!' She stood up again. 'You've sent her back to a country that still has the death penalty! That's a breach of the UN Convention, the same one you broke when you let the CIA pick people up from Bromma Airport . . .'

The detective superintendent raised a hand. 'Wrong again,' he said. 'Just sit down. The extradition was carried out at state level. She's from Massachusetts, and they don't have the death penalty there.'

'But the US as a whole does,' she said.

'Yes,' Q said, 'in thirty-eight states. But twelve don't, including Massachusetts. She'll get life imprisonment, that much is certain. And we're really talking about life, none of this eighteen years nonsense.'

'What's so controversial about that, then?'

'Just think about it!'

Annika shook her head.

It wasn't Hopkins! Imagine that I could be so wrong!

'So Hopkins called the fire brigade? He tried to rescue us instead of kill us?'

'We swapped her,' Q said.

She stared at him.

'We did a deal with the Americans and swapped her for someone else.'

She closed her eyes and remembered an animated conversation in the newsroom, hearing Patrik Nilsson's shrill voice inside her head: *The government gave the Yanks something in return. We have to find out what it was. Raids on people involved in online piracy? Landing rights for the CIA at Bromma?*

Something clicked inside. 'We swapped her for Viktor Gabrielsson!'

446

'Officially, she was arrested by the FBI. All the documentation shows that. We'll never be able to claim that she was in Sweden that night.'

'So you got the cop-killer home again. Do you think that was a good deal?'

'It wasn't my decision, but it meant I had to take charge of the investigation into the fire in your house.'

She was trying to understand. 'So you suspected her right from the start?'

'She was one on a very short list.'

'What does this mean for me?'

'Like I said, the fire is regarded as a closed case, from our point of view. Unfortunately the files will record it as having been dropped. Sorry.'

'What?' Annika said. 'So I'll never be properly cleared?'

He shook his head lightly and looked almost genuinely sad.

'But,' she said, 'what about the insurance money?'

'You can probably whistle for that.'

She had to laugh, if bitterly.

'You sold out my home, my children's home, just to get a bit of credit with the CIA and bring home a cop-killer.'

The detective tilted his head to one side. 'I'm not sure I'd put it quite like that.'

'So what do you propose I do?'

'You've got some money left in savings, haven't you?'

She sighed heavily and shut her eyes. 'Thomas and I split what was left over. My half wouldn't even get me a two-room flat on Södermalm.'

'You'll just have to get a mortgage, like everyone else. Or get a contract on a rented flat.'

She laughed again, a harsh laugh this time.

'A contract on a rented flat? And where would I find one of those these days?'

'The police union has a number of properties throughout the city. I can arrange for you to get a flat in one of them, if you like?'

She looked at him and felt disappointment rising like bile in her throat. 'Christ, this society really is crooked.'

'Isn't it?' he said, with a broad smile.

Annika went up to the newsroom and left the car-keys in a basket on the reception desk, grateful that no one was around to shout at her for keeping the car too long.

She felt oddly empty, relieved but sad at the same time.

The divorce would be finalized the following week, after the obligatory six months' breathing space. She would happily have postponed it, would have liked to discuss it calmly with Thomas, but the opportunity had never arisen; she'd never suggested it and neither had he. The fact was, they hadn't talked to each other properly on a single occasion since the evening when he'd left her and the house had burned down.

I got that wrong as well. I've messed up pretty much everything there is to mess up.

Although she had been right about Julia. She took a fresh newspaper from the stand and looked at the front page. ALEXANDER FOUND LAST NIGHT, it shouted. What followed was an absolute classic: *Grandmother in tears – 'It's a miracle!'*

The rest of the page was taken up with a picture of the little boy at nursery. (Spike had hit the roof when she'd refused to take a new picture of him with her phone and send it to him.)

She skimmed the text below the picture. It said that the mystery surrounding the disappearance of four-year-old Alexander Lindholm had finally been solved. The boy's grandmother, Viola Hensen, had given a statement: 'There are no words to describe how happy we are.'

Readers were referred to five double-page spreads, including the centrefold.

She leafed through the rest of the paper. Patrik Nilsson had written the articles about Yvonne Nordin's death and Alexander's captivity; Annika had provided him with the background information and was cited in several places. She was described as being present at the scene when the events took place, but she wasn't portrayed as an active participant. To her surprise, she was actually quite pleased about this, because at the back of her mind she was aware that she could easily have been wrong. Emil Oscarsson had written a summary of David's murder, Julia's trial and Alexander's abduction in an excellent piece. He was a real find.

She folded the paper and pushed it back into the stand. She felt exhausted. She went into the newsroom to discuss what she was going to write for the next day's paper with Spike and Schyman, and was surprised to see so many people there. Saturday morning was usually the quietest time of the week, but today the newsroom was close to packed.

'Are they all here because of Alexander?' Annika asked, putting her bag down on Berit's desk.

'Him and the redundancies,' Berit said, looking up over her glasses. 'The list was made public yesterday afternoon. Schyman's got round the employment regulations by promoting half the staff to management.'

'The old fox,' Annika said, sitting down on Patrik's chair. 'Including you and me?'

'We're not on either list. No need. We've been here

449

so long we wouldn't have gone on the last-in, first-out principle. So, I gather you've been off having an adventure.'

Annika put her feet up on Berit's desk. 'She was about to take off with the boy,' she said. 'She very nearly made it.'

'But you slashed the tyres of her car,' Berit said.

Annika stopped short and looked at her colleague intently.

'How do you know that? It wasn't in the paper.'

To her astonishment she saw Berit blush, which she never had before.

'Someone told me,' she said, then began hunting through some documents in one of her desk drawers.

'Who have you been talking to? Someone in the police?'

Berit cleared her throat and pulled out some sheets of paper. 'I spoke to Q.'

Annika raised her eyebrows in surprise. 'With Q? But I've only just come from a meeting with him . . .'

I care about reporters on the evening papers. Or have done, at least some of them . . .

Suddenly the penny dropped with such force that Annika gasped. 'It was Q!' she said. 'You had an affair with Q . . .'

'Why don't you say it a bit louder?' Berit said tightly.

'And there was me thinking he was gay!'

Berit took off her glasses. 'Does it matter?'

Annika stared at her colleague, at her grey-flecked hair and wrinkly neck. Tried to imagine her with the detective, the way they met up and flirted and kissed . . . 'Wow,' she said. 'He's actually quite good-looking.'

'And he's also very good in bed,' Berit said, putting her glasses on and going back to her computer.

'I've been made a member of management!' Patrik Nilsson said, holding up a copy of the lengthy list.

Annika dropped her feet to the floor and picked up her bag. 'Congratulations,' she said.

Patrik was beaming with pride but the young temp, Ronja, was on her way out of the newsroom with a box of her possessions. 'How did you get on, Ronja?' he asked.

'I don't care,' she said, head held high. 'I'm going freelance. I'll go to Darfur to cover the conflict there. Something really important.'

'Unlike the nonsense we deal with here?' Patrik said.

Ronja stopped and jutted her chin. 'There, it really is a matter of life or death.'

'Which it never is in Sweden?' Annika said.

Ronja turned on her heel and left them by the desk. Left them sitting on their fat backsides, lulled into the false assurance that their reality was more secure and better than hers.

Suddenly Annika felt ashamed, remembering how insecure and wretched she had felt as a temp.

'Tell me something,' Patrik said. 'Who tipped you off about Yvonne Nordin? Who told you they were about to arrest her?'

She looked at the young man, who was actually a year older than her, at his inquisitive eyes and smug smile and uninhibited self-confidence, and felt as if she was a thousand years old. 'I've got a source,' she said. 'A really good one.'

Then she went over to Spike to find out what he needed from her.

The afternoon had turned into evening before Annika had finished her article. It was a fairly vague account of Yvonne Nordin's background and motivation, without reference to any sources. She was aware that it was fairly thin, but didn't want to expose Nina, Julia, David or even Filip Andersson, so she stuck to the facts that could be verified: that Yvonne had run a business with David, that she had wanted their relationship to carry on and David to get a divorce, and that she might have been guilty of other violent crimes. That the police were investigating whether there was any connection to the triple murder on Sankt Paulsgatan, that Filip Andersson was applying to have his case heard in the Supreme Court (she actually did have references for this last fact, with a case number and everything).

She sent the article to the shared file store, shut down her computer, packed it away and put it in her bag. As she was walking past Schyman's room she saw him sitting behind his desk, rocking on his chair.

He looked grey and exhausted. This autumn had aged him.

I wonder how much longer he can carry on doing this? He must be close to sixty now.

She knocked and he started as if he had been immersed in his thoughts, then gestured to her to come in. She sat down opposite him.

'I daresay an apology is in order,' he said.

Annika shook her head. 'Not just now,' she said. 'I'm overdosing on them. How are you doing?'

The last question just came out, she didn't know where from.

He sighed deeply. 'These cuts almost made me give up,' he said. He sat in silence, looking out over the newsroom, his gaze roaming over the reporters and computers and radio studios and editors and online

452

staff. Outside the windows it was dark again, the short day replaced by a long, windy December night. 'I love this paper,' he said. 'I never thought I'd say that, but it's true. I know we get things wrong and sometimes we go too far and hang people out to dry in a terrible way, but we fulfil a function. Without us democracy would be more fragile. Without us society would be more dangerous, harsher.'

She nodded slowly. 'I want to believe that's true,' she said, 'but I'm not so sure.'

'You did a good job yesterday.'

'Not really,' she said. 'I didn't write anything. I refused to take a picture of Alexander.'

'I meant more generally.'

'It's a messy business,' Annika said. 'I don't think anyone really knows how it all fits together. Everyone involved had different motives and justifications for acting as they did. Maybe they're all guilty, just not of what they were accused or found guilty of . . .'

Anders Schyman sighed again. 'I think I'll go home now,' he said.

'Me too,' Annika said.

'Do you want a lift?'

She hesitated. 'Yes, please.'

They got up, the editor-in-chief turned out the lights but didn't bother to lock his room, and they walked through the newsroom and down into the garage to his car.

'Why did you think Julia Lindholm was innocent?' he asked, as they were driving down Norr Mälarstrand.

She decided to be honest. 'I think I identified with her. If she was innocent, then so was I.'

'Have you heard anything from the police? Have they reached any conclusions about the fire?'

She swallowed. 'No,' she said curtly, and looked out of the window.

He dropped her off at a bus stop on Munkbron. 'You really need to sort out a proper flat,' he said.

'I know,' she said, and closed the car door.

Epilogue

Friday, 24 December

Christmas Eve

The train pulled in, brakes shrieking, and stopped at the deserted platform. Snow was swirling around the engine and carriages, creeping in through gaps round the doors and between the joints, enveloping it all in a creaking sheath of ice.

She was the only person who got off.

With a groan the train rolled away, leaving her standing alone in the howling wind. She stood for a moment, looking at the ICA supermarket, the Pentecostal church and the hotel. Then she headed towards the exit with soft, silent footsteps. She passed through the icy tunnel, carried on past the taxi rank and Svea's Café, into Stenevägen.

The wind was hitting her full in the face and she pulled up her hood and tightened the drawstrings. Her rucksack felt heavy, even though it contained only a Christmas present and some sandwiches she had brought for the journey back. She walked slowly past the houses lining the road, holding up her hand against the wind so she could see in past the curtains and Christmas lights. Inside were warmth and friendship, crackling fires and Christmas trees sparkling and smelling of pine.

She hoped the people inside appreciated what they had.

The electric fence appeared in front of her and she turned left into Viagatan. Like so many times before she followed the endless barrier towards the gate and the car park, walking and walking and walking without ever seeming to get any closer.

She had icicles on her eyelashes by the time she eventually reached the entry-phone beside the main gate.

'I'm here to see Filip Andersson,' she said.

'Come through,' the female officer said.

The lock whirred. She pulled the heavy gate open, and walked quickly and determinedly up the tarmac path to the next gate. The snow had settled on the chain-link fence to her left, forming a rough wall of ice.

She reached the third checkpoint and pressed the button again. As usual, she had to use both hands to open the door to the visitors' section. She wiped off the snow and grit inside the door, folded her hood back and blinked to get rid of the ice around her eyes. Then she walked quickly to locker number one, where she left her coat and scarf. She opened the rucksack and took out the Christmas present, then locked the rucksack in as well. She pressed the fourth entry-phone and was let through to the security check. She put the Christmas present on the belt to go through the X-ray machine and walked through the metal-detector. It didn't bleep. It never did. She knew which shoes and belts she should avoid.

'Happy Christmas,' the female officer said, with a smile, as she put her police badge on the reception desk.

'Happy Christmas to you too.'

The officer hung the badge on the notice-board; evidently they were going to be in room number five.

'I've already written down your details so you just

need to sign,' the officer said, and she wrote in her neat, legible handwriting: *Nina Hoffman, relative.*

'I heard that the appeal is going well,' the officer added.

Nina smiled. 'We're hoping he'll be out before Easter.'

'Come on. I'll show you through. Filip's on his way.'

Nina picked up the Christmas present and followed the officer into the visitors' corridor, stopping to get an orange and a Thermos of coffee from the refreshment table.

'I couldn't help noticing it was a book,' the officer said, nodding towards the present.

'*La Reina del Sur,* by Arturo Pérez-Reverte. A thriller, about drug-smuggling on the Spanish coast.'

The officer looked impressed. 'Filip reads books in Spanish?'

Nina was no longer smiling. 'All three of us used to.'

Author's Acknowledgements

This is a novel. All characters are the work of the author's imagination, and all events depicted are fictional.

Nonetheless, I have taken great care to make sure those institutions and procedures that exist in the real world are correctly described in the novel. As a result, I have, as usual, conducted a great deal of research and taken up various people's time with a lot of often rather peculiar questions to find out how things work.

I wouldn't have been able to write this novel without their help. Their titles below refer to the positions they held at the time of my investigation.

Many thanks for your patience!

Matilda Johansson, a police constable in Stockholm, for research visits, the opportunity to investigate patrol car 1617, help with vocabulary and procedures and other details.

Thomas Bodström, chair of the Parliamentary Standing Committee on Justice, for information about the history and use of lifetime sentences, about directives and the establishment of government inquiries, and for proofreading and more.

Björn Engström, head of information at the Regional

Communication Centre, LKC, for details about police service revolvers and the consequences of their loss.

Håkan Franzén, responsible for the regulation of property damage insurance at Folksam in Stockholm, for information about the procedures involved in cases of suspected arson in insurance fraud.

Anna Rönnerfalk, psychiatric nurse, for help with the diagnosis and symptoms of patients suffering severe mental stress.

Peter Rönnerfalk, a director at Stockholm County Council, for details surrounding health service routines, including ambulance transport.

Ulrika Bergling, security advisor at the Kronoberg Prison in Stockholm, for allowing us to visit the exercise yard on the roof and for permission to take the photograph in the section for inmates kept in solitary confinement used on the cover of the Swedish edition of this book.

Kenneth Gustafsson, acting governor at Kumla Prison, and also Jimmy Sander and Hilde Lyngen, security officers at Kumla with responsibility for internal security, for a tour of the institution's visitors' wing and information about telephone and visiting procedures.

Eva Cedergren, legal advisor at the National Correctional Organization, for help with the application of freedom of information principles for probation officers and trustees within the criminal justice system.

Ulf Göranzon, press officer for the criminal police in Stockholm, and Karin Segerhammar, an administrator within the disciplinary offences committee of the National Police Board, for details about the rules governing freedom of information for cases dealt with by the committee.

Niclas Salomonsson, my agent, and his staff at Salomonsson Agency in Stockholm.

Emma Buckley, my British editor, and all the dedicated staff at Transworld Publishers.

And finally, and above all, Tove Alsterdal, who has been the first reader of everything I have written for the past twenty-eight years, for discussion, structural advice, outlines and character analysis and everything else that features in all my novels.

I have also had a great deal of help from Terése Klein's dissertation at the Legal Faculty of the University of Lund, 'Tidsbestämning av livstidsstraffet – En jämförelse av nådeinstitutet och lagen om omvandling av fängelse på livstid' (Determining the Length of a Lifetime Sentence – A comparison of instances of clemency and the law on the commuting of lifetime sentences).

I have availed myself of the author's prerogative and invented buildings, insurance companies and pizza parlours.

Any mistakes or errors which have crept in are entirely my own.

LAST WILL

LIZA MARKLUND

Knowing the truth can be deadly.

A frosty December night in Stockholm. Inside the City Hall, over a thousand guests attend the prestigious Nobel Prizewinners' dinner. With a lavish meal laid on to the backdrop of a full orchestra, this is one of the city's most glamorous events of the year. But things are different this year. Two shots are fired on the dance floor.

Crime reporter **Annika Bengtzon** is there, covering the event for the *Evening Post*. As the police realize she caught a glimpse of the suspect, she is far more interested in getting back to the newsroom.

But as more brutal murders follow, Annika finds herself in the middle of something far larger than she had anticipated. No longer just a reporter but also a vulnerable key witness, she begins to close up the gaps linking these crimes, just as the suspect starts closing the net in on Annika herself . . .

'Twists and turns you never see coming'
KARIN SLAUGHTER